Grave Misgivings

Phoenix

By C. E. Sundstrom

Prologue of Grave Misgivings *Phoenix*
First Published in Great Britain by Amazon.com via Create Space in 2014
Copyright © 2014 by C. E. Sundstrom
Grave Misgivings *Phoenix*
First Published in Great Britain by Amazon.com via Create Space in 2015
Copyright © 2015 by C. E. Sundstrom
Prologue from Grave Misgivings *Hope*
First Published in Great Britain by Amazon.com via Create Space in 2015
Copyright © 2015 by C. E. Sundstrom

ISBN 978-0-9924741-1-9

Printed and bound by Amazon.com via Create Space

Please follow on Twitter @ cesundstrom
Please like on Facebook @ http://www.facebook.com/cesundstrom
Website http://cesundstrom.com/

Cover Concept & Design by Lacey O'Connor.
www.laceyoconnor.com

For Joy

Thank you for your limitless love, support and patience.

Not as many weeds this time.
Will make an effort next weekend.
Promise.

My Cherished Proofreaders

Many thanks to everyone for their support, proof reading and honest appraisals.
My novels would be fiction without your help to bring them to life.

Michelle Daniel
Lisa Kyllo
Melanie Pearce
Christine Stonehouse
Len Sundstrom

Much Thanks

Much thanks to everyone who took a chance on a new author and bought a copy of
Grave Misgivings "Awakenings".

I hope you enjoyed the first installment in the series. I look forward to writing more stories for you in the future.

As an Indie Author my new career is just fantasy without:
- All your kind words, messages and encouragement.
- Your reviews on Goodreads and Amazon.
- Your likes on Facebook.
- Your follows on Twitter.
- Your recommendations to others.
- Your sharing of my posts.

I am forever in your debt for how each and every one of you has welcomed me and my small offering into the literary world.

Special thanks to all the Authors who have shared their tips and advice along the way.

Particular mention to fellow "author from Oz" Tracy M. Joyce for all her technical support and the odd kick in the behind.

Special mention also to a couple of new fans Craig McMurtry and Jayne Capovilla who have been prolific in their support, encouragement and promotion of Awakenings.

I am very lucky to have you as friends.

Sorry I can't thank everyone individually. I wish I could.

Have a great day.

C. E. Sundstrom.

Books by C. E. Sundstrom

Grave Misgivings Series

Awakenings
Phoenix
Hope (yet to be released)

"Hope is an illusion."

Julie Mahoney.

Prologue

Autumn 2001.

Tuesday Morning.

Salem, New Jersey.

A crisp bronze leaf drifts slowly to the ground. Its movements are uncertain, almost hesitant, as if it has a clear premonition of its fate and is desperately trying to prevent what is about to occur. Swaying, turning, pausing then continuing on its lonely journey. Finally it reaches its inevitable destiny, falling gently on top of the hundreds of similar leaves which cover the meandering curves of Oak Street on this fresh Tuesday morning. The leaf lies silent, without movement, seemingly resigned to the fact that there is no hope. Its journey has concluded. It is simply the natural cycle of life. Born, live, die. No living creature can expect to cheat death. No living creature ever does.

A sound reverberates, drifting in and out, as it is carried on the gentle breeze. At first it is indiscernible, an indistinct mish mash of voices. As the breeze grows steadily stronger, the sound becomes clearer. It is the joyful sounds of children playing, running, riding and getting up to limited mischief. This sound is the reason why properties in this particular suburb are so highly sought. Demand always far exceeds supply. This is a street where neighbors smile, wave and stop to chat; a rare thing in this day and age. Oak Street is a prime example of why people move to Salem, New Jersey. It is close enough to commute to offices in New York but safe, predictable and serene. It is America's best kept secret; a place where kids can grow and live safely and their parents can sleep, fully at ease, at night.

Joe Hawkins lives in one of the older buildings in Oak Street. Though he has spent several thousand dollars having the house re-clad in aluminum about six years ago, the basic structure of the building remains the same. It is nearing one hundred and fifty years old.

During the re-cladding, he insisted that the structure of his house remain completely untouched. In fact, he was so concerned about his precious house that he positioned his rocking chair on his front lawn every morning at seven o'clock precisely, waiting for the builders to arrive. He would sit there silently, glaring over the top of his newspaper, as the workers went about their business. In his own distinctive words, he was making, "Damn sure" no damage was done to his precious home during the re-cladding process.

Joe's one great love in life is the preservation of useful old things from by-gone eras. On a good day, he will joke that he aptly meets that description too. On most days he certainly feels like a relic from another time. He gains a sense of strength, of defiance, when he encounters old relics. It is like they have found some sort of magical way to endure the ravages of time and thus should be applauded and respected for their unintended longevity. He spends his free time scouring through markets, rummaging through yard sales and the like, searching for his next treasure to acquire and reclaim from the now disinterested world. It is a hobby that he finds very liberating, helping to keep his mind from dwelling on past problems for which he has lost the opportunity to remedy. Though resigned to the fact that he cannot change the past, his mind can't help but revisit and replay situations over and over again, situations which could have had more favorable outcomes if only he had been more diligent, more pro-active. At the end of the day, rehashing the past simply leaves Joe drained and hollow. Sadness overwhelms him as he relives each tragedy which has befallen his life. Collecting distracts his mind, grants him a little peace from a chaotic and spiteful world.

Joe has another strange quirk of which none of his acquaintances are particularly aware. However, over the years, he has made no attempt to hide it. He just doesn't talk about it. He is a very private individual. One who feels he will be wildly misunderstood by anyone he meets and converses with at length. For this reason, he keeps to himself. His determination to remain completely anti-social is the reason he has no friends to speak of. Life is easier that way, less complicated, less messy. However, his quirk remains undeniable.

When choosing a place to live, Joe searches for various characteristics. He likes quiet, peaceful and pleasant surroundings. He also prefers a reasonable climate, without the extremes in temperature. Overriding everything is one essential requirement, 'Joe's quirk'. For you see, Joe will only settle in a town with a name that appears to be compatible with his unique, warped view on life. The name of the place has to reflect who he is and what he is about, if it is to have any appeal to him. 'Salem' was just perfect, at least for his present stage in life. After all, where else would someone who regards themselves as little more than a warlock reside? By any definition, those few who know him well, regard him as some sort of warlock. He even has the obligatory black cat as a constant companion, though that is not through choice. It is more 'meant to be'; preordained by the greater universe. Oscar was never invited into his household, he just arrived one day, taking advantage of an open window and making himself comfortable on a sitting room chair. Joe never had the heart to turf him out. Oscar was just another stray, just the same as Joe. A kindred spirit.

His house is square. A simple yet sturdy and serviceable design; seven rooms, including a kitchen, sitting room, dining room, laundry and three bedrooms. Joe's bedroom overlooks the glorious view of colorful, century old street trees which were planted along the road by forward thinking town planners, now long deceased. The facade of the building is brilliant white. Window ledges are painted olive green as a stylish contrast. The shutters remain locked permanently open, no matter what the season or how cold the weather turns. Joe can't be bothered with such mundane tasks as opening and closing shutters. It would send him mad. That is, of course, considering that he might already be insane, by any thinking person's definition of that term.

Joe's house is not huge. Cozy and comfortable would be a more apt description. The two bedrooms upstairs are no longer used, other than for storage. If the truth be known, for several years now, they have been steadily filled to the brim with an eclectic collection of nick-knacks, papers, newspapers and notes scrawled on anything even remotely resembling a piece of paper. These rooms are kept locked at all times even though there appears to be no one desperately seeking admission. It is simply the case that Joe feels that the information housed in these rooms for future reference is too important and, most of all, private. Everything relates to the past in some way. Everything links him to the past. There are too many secrets here. Secrets Joe is determined to keep hidden.

Joe spends most of his time living in the lower half of the house. It certainly shows. Rubbish is strewn everywhere. Pizza boxes are mainly piled up in one corner of the sitting room in a vain attempt at tidiness. Clothes are strewn everywhere; over chairs, on the kitchen table, on the floor, even hanging awkwardly over a reading lamp which stands precariously on a stained, pine side table. There is no way of distinguishing which clothes are clean and which ones are due to be laundered. In fact, the scene leaves any unsuspecting visitor with the impression that most of the clothes are in desperate need to be washed.

Empty beer cans are scattered in a chaotic manner throughout all of the lower floor rooms. The black garbage bag, set aside for them in the kitchen, is empty save for three cans correctly stowed in a brief moment of house cleaning four months ago. Six month supplies of empty bottles of 'Jack' are partially visible from under disheveled cushions on the sofa. They also sit on the mantle in the sitting room and on several of the window sills. There is even a large collection which completely covers the top of the television. Recent newspapers are thrown onto a haphazard stack in the corner of the sitting room. It would be a gross understatement to say that any stranger who has the misfortune to enter into Joe's slum would quickly and correctly comment that 'it lacked a woman's touch'.

From amongst the sheets and blankets, thrown carelessly in a heap on the bed, something indiscernible begins to stir. After a brief struggle, a bleary eyed, grey balding head appears. Joe frowns as he slowly comes to terms with the pain undissipated from the night before. Scratching his scalp vigorously, he ruffles his long, sparse hair into a wiry mess. Moaning, still groggy as a result of the sedatives and alcohol consumed earlier, he rises awkwardly from amongst his refuge of blankets. Dangling his scrawny legs over the side of the bed, he takes a moment to gather some breath and elusive energy. He pauses, breathing deliberately, as he waits for his stomach to settle a little and the threat of a cataclysmic eruption to abate. Slowly reaching down, he pulls on some shoes; one a brown slipper, the other a fluffy purple moccasin. Joe is completely unconcerned with his appearance. When you live alone there is no one passing judgment on your fashion sense. Practicality is of greater importance. Both shoes are comfortable and available, that is all that matters.

Eventually Joe rises successfully with a loud 'creak' caused by straightening his arthritic legs. He busily rubs his half-closed eyes back to life with one hand while scratching his backside, through his baggy black and white polka dot shorts, with the other. Staggering through his self-created minefield of obstacles, he moves towards the sitting room as he searches desperately for his 'salvation'.

The bottle of pain killers is easy, still in his shorts pocket from the night before. Still containing a few more days respite. A source of liquid is harder to find. Tap water is out of the question. The mere suggestion of drinking that 'piss' would be enough to offend his sensibilities and incur the full force of his ill-tempered, unbridled wrath. Something strong which warms and clears the throat is what his heart desires. He tries several bottles of Jack Daniels, dispatching each losing candidate to a different spot on the floor with a casual, hate filled throw. Finally, he finds a bottle from behind a cushion on the couch. Holding it by the neck, he sways as he raises it above his head. Catching a narrow beam of light, seeping through a crack between the curtains, he illuminates its contents. He smiles as he discovers it still contains one more mouthful of precious elixir. Taking an inexact handful of tablets, followed by a Whiskey chaser, he completes his goal of trying to self-medicate some relief.

Joe's pain is constant and relentless. However, he is well aware it is not life threatening, not for him at least. It is an all too familiar pain which stabs viciously at his chest, causing him great discomfort. He has experienced this pain many times over the years though, in the past, it has been far less severe than its current inflammation. Joe is well aware of its cause, well aware that there is no doctor in the world who can cure what ails him. He has become an expert, untrained practitioner, who has become adept at self-treatment without doing self-harm. However, he is unsure of how to alleviate the pain this time. Though he won't admit it, this more ferocious pain scares him greatly. He is well aware the pain will pass, just not quite sure when. It has never lasted for weeks before; usually only minutes, maybe hours at most.

"So what are you planning to do, just ignore your pain? You know what it means, why don't you do something?" asks the familiar voice of the man seated in the only comfortable arm chair, located on the other side of the sitting room. The man is young, probably in his early twenties. He is dressed in a stylish leather jacket over a white T shirt. Grey trousers fail to hide his expertly polished leather shoes. His dark brown hair is slicked back with grease. His deep brown eyes glow with smugness. If, by chance, his eyes were filled with anger and self-loathing instead, their similarity would be unmistakable, they would be identical to Joe's.

Joe holds the bottle by the neck as he shakes his head, trying to ignore his brother. His vision remains cloudy; a major concern. Joe has developed, over the years, an ability to view situations clearly. To walk his way through what he can see in order to identify problems and try his best to alleviate any adverse situations. His inability to see the current situation with clarity prevents him from being able to promptly rectify his problems. He knows if he can't overcome his problems, then other people will suffer too. Many people will suffer. Many people will die. The painkillers and alcohol, though deadening the pain a little, are certainly not helping his situation at all.

"You can't ignore what is going on," Stanley implores as he stands lithely, brushing the creases out of his trousers. "You must act and act now!"

"Shut up!" Joe says as he stares into his brother's eyes. "What do you expect me to do? This is too big. This is just too damn big for me, for anyone."

Joe's brother returns the stare with pleading eyes. He wonders how Joe's sanity and strength are holding up. He has grave fears for his younger brother's mental state. After all, Joe has been through an awful lot since this all began. He has seen more tragedy than most during his lifetime. Stanley decides to change tack, "Hey, brother. Never forget. There is always hope. You must not......"

Joe fumes, all his emotions bubbling to the surface at once, "There is no damn hope! There is no such word. That emotion, that God damn sensation is lost to me. All that remains is pain, misery, death and ..... and ....."

"And what?," Stanley enquires partly through interest and partly to see if he can generate some measure of fight in this tired old man staggering awkwardly in front of him.

Joe looks at Stanley as rage courses through every cell of his body. Coolly he talks in a calm, clear, yet strangely manic voice. He leaves his brother with little doubt as to his state of sanity. His voice rises in intensity with each word uttered, "And with any luck there is another God damn bottle of this fine beverage to help deaden the pain. All I seek is a blissful stupor of ignorance so that I don't need to continue to listen to your pitiful drivel and meaningless piffle!"

Taking careful aim, Joe throws the empty bottle at his brother. His accuracy is exceptional considering his intoxicated state. The bottle somersaults and flies straight at his brother's head, causing a curious reaction. Instead of hitting him squarely, causing considerable injury, the bottle travels straight through him. Stanley's body changes, becoming a shower of sparkling dust particles. This metamorphosis occurs from head to toe until all the star dust falls steadily to the carpeted floor and disappears without a trace. Nothing is left of his brother. The bottle hits the back of the armchair and bounces harmlessly onto the floor. Laughter echoes through the room as Stanley continues to taunt his brother in Joe's empty, yet crowded, mind.

Joe turns away. His shoulders slump with a sensation of melancholy which slowly spreads through his body. The noise resonating in his ears is something he has never experienced before, something inhumane. It is a screeching, buzzing sound growing steadily in intensity. It is unrelenting as it builds to its ultimate crescendo.

Throughout the house, near every open window, Joe has placed dozens of different wind chimes in order to help dampen any imaginary sounds his mind might normally hear. There are ones with metal cylinders, another with glass butterflies. Several are ceramic. One is made from discarded cutlery. Joe's wind chimes are installed in such a way that they operate effectively, even in the absence of a gentle breeze. If there is no wind, he simply switches on strategically placed fans to activate the chimes. This process is normally extremely effective and fulfils Joe's yearning for a noise interrupted environment. The detailed steps he has implemented at least dampen the noises from which he seeks sanctuary. It is his way of making the most of the bad hand which life has dealt him.

Moving swiftly around the room, he switches on fan after fan until all ten are activated, creating a mini whirlpool of wind and a terrible racket. He stands with hands on hips, frustrated, head bowed, drained of meaningful ideas. This new sound is impossible to block out. It is a powerful, droning sound, filled with fear and horror. It is a sound that will not be denied, a sound which refuses to identify itself. It is a foreboding sound which Joe both respects and dreads greatly. It is the sound of an approaching 'shit storm', the likes of which the world has never seen.

Joe's epic staggering leads him back to the faded curtains drawn tight at his sitting room window. With a quick movement he opens the curtains, revealing a bright sunny autumn morning. He becomes aware of his mistake instantly as his eyes scream out in pain. He squints and moans loudly as he closes the fabric with a flourish. Suddenly, a little clarity appears in his mind. He begins to realize that some of the noises rattling through his tormented brain might be coming from his surroundings, rather than being figments of his furtive imagination. He focuses momentarily, trying to locate the source of the sound. Finally his brain deciphers the direction and cause of the unnecessary disturbance. There is someone pounding on his front door. He shakes his head as he wonders what more this day can bring.

Changing direction, he slowly shuffles towards the front door. Joe grabs at his eyes in obvious distress as he yells, "Okay, okay already. I'm coming for God's sake!"

The pounding continues unabated as Joe stumbles across the sitting room floor once more, lacking any sign of genuine coordination. Successfully negotiating the one step to the front door, he reaches for the handle. Looking down he sees Oscar sitting, staring at the door. Oscar turns and stares at Joe with his bloodshot eyes as a tuft of fur drops quietly from his mangy skin onto the floor.

"Don't you start," Joe says quietly to his only friend, the twelve year old scruffy, black cat. Lashing out in Oscar's direction, he flicks his slipper at the cat. Oscar quickly scurries away, out of sight, emitting a disgusted squeal. After all, he was only trying to help.

In an instant everything is gone. There is nothing; not a sound, a shape, an object or a smell. Joe is simply weightless, surrounded by a dark vacuous void. It is like he is floating in the center of a black hole. Only darkness, silence and Joe exist in this realm. Everything else, that ever was, has simply vanished. For a moment Joe is content. He is at peace. Drifting slowly in his private universe, he remains calm. He is not frightened in the slightest by the darkness that abounds. Instead he rejoices in its tranquility of emptiness. In his heart he prays that this is what death will be like, once his name is finally elevated in italics to the top of the Grim Reapers scroll of doom. An eternity of nothing would be heaven; no one wanting help, no one accusing him of inaction. No problems, no voices, just nothing, just heavenly peace.

Through the depthless black, Joe sees a small creature walking towards him. Instantly he recognizes his friend and loyal companion. Oscar walks slowly up to Joe, purring as he rubs affectionately against his leg. Joe nods resigned somewhat, "I know, I know old fella. I have to face what burdens me so. I know. It is not right to hide here. It's not right to lash out at you too when the problem is with me. I'm sorry for treating you wrong."

Joe sighs and belts the side of his head several times with the open palm of his hand. His action is primitive and painful though has been effective before in correcting the short circuit malfunction in his brain. Slowly his eyes become foggy then readjust as normality begins to re-appear like a billowing mirage in front of his eyes. Within a few seconds, everything has returned. He reclaims his world, reluctantly tolerating the normality returning in all its familiar glory. He glances around the room quickly, taking in his surroundings, satisfying himself that everything is right with his world. Ensuring that nothing has changed is important. His vulnerability is at its greatest when he has these episodes. Sometimes they last for seconds, sometimes for days. Thankfully this episode seems to be seconds or maybe minutes at most. Joe nods, satisfied nothing has changed, before continuing to move towards the door.

Hobbling on one clothed foot, he takes a step forward. Clenching his eyes shut in preparation for the light, Joe grasps the handle and yanks the door open as he yells, "What?"

A thin, blonde haired, well-groomed man in a smart, navy blue business suit is standing on the doorstep. He is carrying a clip board looking very officious and slightly startled. The man takes a step backwards as he regains his composure and assesses the situation before him. He was not expecting to be greeted by an aggressive, old, derelict of a man scratching his crotch in a pair of polka dot boxer shorts while wearing one fluffy purple moccasin. Straightening his suit, brushing back his already immaculately moussed hair, composure restored, he moves his arm forward in anticipation to shake Joe's hand. He says politely, "Good morning, Sir. I'm John Sparks, President of the West Salem residents group and I'd like to speak......"

Joe frowns, eyes locked firmly closed. He says angrily, "I couldn't give a damn who you are; I'm still not buying any raffle tickets or inedible cookies made in a Korean sweat shop three years ago by some peasant who doesn't even have clean water to wash their filthy hands with. That is why you are here aren't you? To be annoying, invading my privacy and the like? There is only one thing you can do for me today. You can go and piss off!"

With all the force he can muster, Joe tries to shut the front door.

John, places his shiny, size 11, business shoe in the doorway, preventing its closure. He draws a deep breath before stating his case succinctly, in a completely unambiguous manner for Joe, "Sir, you misunderstand the purpose of my visit. My conversation with you is of the utmost importance and cannot be left to another day. I implore you to at least allow me the opportunity to come inside and discuss the problem at hand, like mature gentlemen. I'm sure once we've discussed the issue thoroughly, we will be able to develop some form of resolution, to your satisfaction, that will satisfy all aggrieved parties in this instance."

With anger brewing from deep in his soul, Joe slowly opens his eyes and glares down at the insolent foot blocking his door. He pulls the door open once again, moving forward as he confronts his trespasser. He asks abrasively, "What the hell are you talking about? What problem? What's your problem?"

"This problem," John says as he takes a step backwards. He turns and motions with his arm in a wide arc. The area he highlights encompasses the entire region directly beyond the front step, out into the front yard and beyond.

For the first time, Joe looks around and surveys the situation outside the walls of his house. Blinking, he steps forward. Brushing John aside, gob smacked, he strives for a better look. Every muscle in his body begins to tense as he realizes the time has come. He gazes in disbelief at the sight in front of him. His brain tries to reason with the enormity of what his eyes are witnessing. However it is too bizarre, even for Joe. During his life he has seen many unusual events, which few would believe. The scale and nature of this event leaves Joe numb.

A breeze rustles Joe's wispy hair as a voice whispers in his ear, "Hope is......."

"Shut up!" Joe screams in anger towards his invisible tormentors.

"I'm sure we can fix the problem. Maybe if you stopped feeding them," John says, more as a token gesture than anything else. He can clearly see

Joe is not listening. Joe is wandering around, mouth gaping open, silent, in thoughtful contemplation. He knows the ramifications of this 'sign', though he refuses to admit to himself that there is a problem here. It is a problem too large for Joe to have any hope of fixing at this late stage, in his current state of mental and physical health. His body and soul are devoid of solutions.

On his lawn, his car, his fences, every branch of his oak tree, the road in front of his property and on all the adjourning properties they sit. All of them are behaving exactly the same way. There are too many to count. At a guess there must be thousands of pure, snow white doves cooing, all staring directly at Joe's house as if they are waiting for him, begging with their sorrowfully eyes to do something, anything that might help avert a catastrophe.

Residents have gathered together to look at this extraordinary, once in a life time event. They are climbing on the fences, standing on the lawn pointing, in the middle of the road taking photos. Some are smiling; some are more cautious and a little fearful. All in all, everyone is looking dumbfounded, wondering what has transpired to bring about this strange gathering of doves around a single house in a quiet non-descript street. The only person without unanswerable questions flooding through their mind is Joe. He knows exactly why they are here and what their large numbers mean.

"Oh my God, oh my God!' Joe begins to call out repeatedly. At first his words are nearly inaudible, drowned out by the incessant cooing of the birds and the dull murmur coming from the crowd. His words increase their intensity rapidly and, within a matter of seconds, Joe has the full attention of the assembled masses. It is at this moment that he turns sharply and starts to run in an awkward, slow, arthritic manner back towards the sanctity of his house. His body cannons into John's shoulder leaving him sprawled, bruised and shaken on the ground. Joe, inconsiderately, runs past him without offering an apology or a sideways glance. Grabbing the door handle, he slams the door shut behind him, bolting it firmly as he disappears from inquisitive eyes.

Everyone continues to stand around nervously, watching the masses of seemingly friendly doves gathered in front of them. Conflicting theories abound as to what they are waiting for. However, one thing is certain; they don't want to miss what happens next. Maybe, at the very least, someone will explain what is happening. Everyone feels it is more important to be watching this curious sight, first hand, rather than leaving for school or work. Something extraordinary is happening in their neighborhood today and they all want to be part of it.

Police and fire crews assemble. Though coordinated, they are unprepared to deal with this strange situation. They gather to one side in a huddle. Chatting, shaking their heads, while their faces remain emotionless as they try to assess the impossible situation in front of them. The camera crews, with their media vans, begin to arrive, setting up for their first live broadcasts of the 'Amazing Dove Incident'. Two reporters are preparing for a live cross as the whole scene changes unexpectedly for the worst.

One dove in the middle of the lawn suddenly spontaneously combusts in a ball of orange flames, causing an audible hush in the crowd. In a fraction of a second the unbelievable begins to occur. Several hundred of the doves die, raining down onto the lawn from out of the oak tree and along the line of the fence. Others catch fire, for no apparent reason, as they walk around or fly by. The fiery airborne doves begin to rain down like a barrage of flaming missiles, landing amongst the spectators, hitting some of their cars. Still more doves seem to disintegrate into balls of flame, disappearing in a cloud of dust and ash. About three quarters of the birds appear unaffected and continue to sit calmly amongst the chaos that abounds. They stare unflinching at Joe's house. It is as if they are waiting for his return, seeking his blessed gift of salvation. They wait in vain.

Children and adults alike begin to run in a frenzied, traumatized fashion. They desperately try to escape the carnage that is unfolding before their disbelieving eyes. Many are horrified, their brains in neutral, thoughts going blank. All they can think of is self-preservation. They clamber over each other as they run towards the perceived safety of their homes. Considering the apocalyptic nature of the drama unfolding before them, some fear their nearby homes are in jeopardy too. Some people run down the street trying to get as far away as possible from the danger at hand. Some just run, knowing instinctively they should run, yet not knowing when or where it is safe to stop.

The camera crews are nearly ready to start their coverage when the reporters pause. They hold onto their earpieces as they receive some form of message from a faceless person manning a control room some distance away. They appear distracted by the message, disregarding the incredible story unfolding right in front of them. They signal earnestly to the bewildered cameramen. Suddenly the crews begin to pack the equipment back into the vans at a brisk pace. The faces of the film crews are ashen, devoid of blood, as if they have all simultaneously seen a ghost. Their actions seem peculiar considering they have all independently made a collective decision to halt coverage of the biggest story of the century unfolding before their eyes. It is the most bizarre situation they would ever have the opportunity to cover, yet somehow, they are simply not interested.

Frantic announcements resound loud and clear over the emergency radios. There appears to be a larger story beginning to unfold; something which overshadows the bizarre events in front of the emergency services. The police and fire brigades all begin to pack up and leave. Visibly shaken, they clamber onto their vehicles. Flicking on lights, engaging sirens, they race to leave in a frenzied tangle of appliances. All are fearful. All are confused.

Though their minds refuse to acknowledge what is occurring, they all silently believe that it is something big. Something is happening at the World Trade Center in New York. The initial reports are saying there is some kind of major fire or bomb blast in one of the towers. Within minutes they are all hurrying as they hear the first frantic eye witness reports that a plane may have hit one of the towers. The story of the doves is overshadowed and lost from its rightful place as the lead story on every channel of the world's media. From this moment on there is only one story of significance, only one story that will be covered today and in the weeks to come. From this point on, nobody will remember the strange exploding doves.

Inside the house Joe is distraught. With tears running down his face he slumps into his old, comfortable armchair as he stares in disbelief at the scenes unfolding on the television in front of him. The pain in his chest is excruciating, though he knows all too well it is not life threatening. Death will not be a source of peaceful release from the misery that he endures. The screams are loud and long, inside his head. He shuts his eyes, though this doesn't help. He can still see them in pain, burning, moving around him in a disorientated manner, screaming for help, their arms outstretched, pleading. He says softly, repeatedly as the words catch in his throat as if they are barbed, "I couldn't...., they wouldn't listen....., I couldn't......"

Oscar walks slowly over to the foot of the chair. He looks up at the only human companion he has ever known. He surveys the pain visible in his tense facial muscles and the tears rolling steadily down Joe's face. Oscar stretches up to rub his head against his master's limp hand as a sign of respect and comfort in a time of grief. With a deft leap he lands on his master's lap, moving through a turn and a half before finally curling into a ball and settling. He purrs with vigor, trying to help in the best way he can, to alleviate some of the pain his friend is feeling. He has always been there for Joe in his hour of need.

Outside the house, calmness has descended. All the voyeurs have disappeared. The remaining live doves sit calmly next to the recently deceased. All the doves remain staring at Joe's house, cooing sweetly. They all seem to be waiting for something. There is nothing Joe can do for them now. It is all too late. Their pleading eyes continue to haunt him in the darkness behind his closed eyes.

From one of the Oak trees a single leaf is shed. Carried on the prevailing wind its movements are hesitant, almost uncertain, as if it has a clear premonition of its fate. Swaying, turning, pausing then continuing on its lonely journey, it moves towards Joe's front door. Gently it lands on the welcome mat. It lays silent, immobile, apparently resigned to its fate. It appears to realize that its life has finished. It seems to know there is no hope.

'Mysterious Ways'

An ancient and mysterious world.

Many peoples, all diverse.

Strange customs held strongly,

And the ability,

To naturally see a divine curse.

The modern world abhors them.

Cast scorn on their lot.

Though it shall not prevent them,

From predicting the future,

And declaring what's what.

Chapter 1

Sunday, February 26th, 2006.

After Midnight.

Crown Towers, Melbourne, Victoria.

So much has happened; I don't know where to begin!

I vaguely hear Peter say, "Its ok. I've got you," as I feel fingers playing absentmindedly with my hair. I lack the words to respond, a rare predicament for someone like me. I am never lost for words; NEVER. When I am planning or writing one of my novels the images and storylines flow freely, without obstacles of any description. Writer's block simply doesn't exist in my world. I have no patience for such trivial inconveniences. Tonight, or more accurately, this morning is somewhat different, however. I find myself distracted, stranded, left without the ability to participate in the real world at present. All I have at my disposal is the jumbled fragments of my mind. At this point in time they offer little in the way of comfort or assistance.

My mind is engaged in a desperate struggle as it tries to absorb what has occurred and consider its significant ramifications in regards to my future. There are just too many questions I need to find answers for. Too many complex riddles to solve. The most frustrating aspect of it all is that I lack an all knowing seer who I may seek guidance from. No great sage surrounded by hundreds of incense sticks sitting cross legged on a moss laden hilltop in the soft summer moonlight is waiting to provide me with worldly guidance. Sure Peter is my rock, providing the emotional support I so desperately crave. However, he stands in a darker place than I do when it comes to shedding light on my current "condition," for want of a better word. Who is going to answer all these questions going through my mind? Who is going to teach me how these visions, these dreams, these whatevers work?

Why me? Why am I seeing these visions? Is this condition temporary or permanent? Why does my chest hurt during these episodes? Where did that cat come from that saved me in the park? Am I the only one who has experienced these visions? Is there some reason why I see visions of particular people? Are these visions really glimpses of the future, a future which can still be molded in knowledgeable hands? Who is the little girl singing lullabies to me? Where is she? Why does she need my help? Searching deep within my soul, I fail to locate definitive answers to any of my questions. Each question just seems to produce more questions in a never ending, self-perpetuating cycle of confusion.

The one thing I hold onto is the truth, the absolute truth, that I am still Julie Mahoney. Nothing of significance has changed on that front. I am still a successful crime novelist. I remain committed in a rock solid, long term, loving relationship with my man Peter. Most of all I know my sanity remains intact, a little confused I'll grant you, though one hundred percent, bona-fide sane. Nothing in the last twelve days has changed any of that. I am still the same person that I always was. I just have visions of the future now.

I shake my head as I consider this notion.

This IS madness!

I can't believe it has only been twelve days since my strange story first began. I am almost certain that a lifetime has passed in that intervening space. So, so much has happened in that time. I guess it all began with that fateful accident, the car accident where I thought I had hit and killed a lady, a pedestrian distracted on her mobile phone. My senses were strangely heightened that evening; so much so that every detail remains fresh in my mind. I remember the storm building, hearing the rain pelting down on the roof of my car though failing to see any droplets. My nostrils began to burn with the stench of black acrid smoke though nothing was on fire. I saw a couple walking in the grassy paddock and recall just how out of place they seemed. Most of all I remember every last detail of the smartly dressed business woman and how she stepped absentmindedly out onto the road in front of my moving car. I see her eyes accusing me as her lifeless body slams into my windscreen before sliding slowly down the bonnet towards the unforgiving roadway below. I observe every sight, sound and smell with meticulous precision as they occur. In my mind I can still see it all take place like a jumbled, eclectic collection of movies all screening simultaneously. I wish I knew then what I know now. I had simply experienced a premonition of several future events mixed with the reality of the day. Ha! I guess it's not that "simple" after all when I describe my past experiences like that. It was at this point in my curious first vision that I blacked out. I don't remember anything from the time of the accident through to my reawakening in the hospital confines. I guess, looking back on it now, the blackout was due to my brain being overloaded with information that was unreal or, more importantly, ridiculously impossible to process rationally.

From that point in time my world began to spiral out of control at an alarming rate. The fact that my sanity was questioned by not only the attending physician but also my mother and sister whilst in hospital was truly frightening. The people I trusted most failed me in my hour of need. I was placed under medical supervision in the Psychiatric Ward of the South Morang Regional Hospital amongst highly deranged patients including the infamous child molester Chris Hagatie. I can still smell his foul breath and feel his saliva dripping down my face and chest as he hovers menacingly over me, restrained somewhat by his straitjacket. I shudder to think what would have happened in there if it wasn't for my new best friend, a stray black cat I named Serenity who managed to find a way into the secure ward and come to my defense when needed. After all, I could do little myself, drugged to the eyeballs, arms and legs restrained securely by straps to a hospital bed.

I am forever grateful for the deception Peter cleverly conceived and performed in order to procure my freedom. Waving a speeding infringement notice under the nose of the charge nurse, in a belligerent manner, pretending it was a court order requesting my immediate release was insanity which proved to be a stroke of genius. However, we weren't to know that my freedom required more than just a securely bolted door to be opened. I was not to know the visions were destined to follow me and haunt my waking hours. They were not about to grant me my liberty so readily. I am unchained though far from free.

The visions continued to follow me even though I remained naively unconcerned. I was blind to the premonition of Chris Hagatie murdering my doctor, Dr. Khan in cold blood. I saw his image standing there dressed in his white doctor's scrubs covered in blood and just assumed it was some sort of weird nightmare. I paid it no heed. I could have done more to save his life. I should have done more. I didn't.

When I returned home to Kinglake I missed yet another opportunity to save an innocent life. This time the victim was Emma, my new neighbor. She was about to perish as a result of a diabolical shooting at the hands of her volatile husband Malcolm. The confronting vision I experienced when I first met them failed to cause me to take drastic action. Seeing the ghostlike vision of Malcolm and Emma exiting their bodies and interacting in such a violent manner should have been sufficient to make me ensure that no harm ever came to Emma. Unfortunately It didn't.

I was there, I knew what the vision meant and I still failed to take any significant action to try to change the future that I saw would occur. My attempts were feeble, at best. That is simply unforgivable. I still feel nauseous just thinking about it. I guess these missed opportunities will haunt me for the rest of my days. In some respects I guess they are a fitting punishment for my incompetent inactions.

I need to remember. I must never forget.

Letting people fall into harm's way because of my inactions is something I am determined to avoid in the future. I now know I can change the future, I can make a difference in the lives of others who, through no fault of their own, find themselves in peril. I learned that when I met the business lady that I thought I had killed with my car. I was walking with Peter back from a night on the town when I realized that the lady standing beside me was the real life version of the ghost I had encountered in my waking dreams. Though stunned and confused by the fact that she was actually standing by my side, I still had the presence of mind to react, to reach out and drag her back to safety as the car running the red light ploughed through the intersection.

This "awakening," this realization that I could read these visions enough to somehow save a life that was in danger was an absolute revelation to me. On the wave of an adrenaline rush, armed with little more than sketchy information gleamed from yet another confused vision, I stumbled back out into the night, into the dimly lit Enterprise Park with the vague plan of trying to prevent a murder from taking place. With more than my share of good fortune, I survived my encounter with the badly scarred low-life stalking his prey and once more changed the future for the better, saving a pregnant prostitute and her unborn bub from certain death.

Overwhelmed, I staggered awkwardly back from this dalliance with the devil to my hotel room at the Crown Towers. My head was spinning. The images of what I had seen come to pass mixed with those which were yet to occur. They flooded through my brain as they blended seamlessly with a million unanswered questions as I stumbled back to my palatial hotel room.

As I reached the door I recall Peter greeting me. I remember him changing, morphing into the form of an unfamiliar woman, dressed in rags. I remember her smile as she holds out hers arms, displaying the baby held tight in bloody sheets. I remember her words clearly as she whispers to me, "Hope is a waking dream."

I don't remember much more than that as I unexpectedly utter a single, unexpected questioning word, "Mary?"

The last thing I remember is the lady smiling, glad that I have acknowledged her presence before she evaporated, becoming a waterfall of glistening stars which slowly disappeared into the plush carpet. I remember being overcome at this point, falling faint towards the desperate outstretched arms of my love, Peter.

In the midst of all this befuddlement, Peter was an absolute godsend. He carried me to the bed, helping me to change out of my soaking wet clothes. I cried tears of joy as I considered how I saved a mother to be and her unborn child. I cried tears of relief, allowing my anguish and fears to flow gradually away. I cried tears for the confusion, the questions that continue to torture my aching brain.

Peter undressed me, sliding beside me, under the bed sheets. He stayed close to me all night, rubbing my arm, whispering tender words. I am thankful that he stayed with me at this time, a time when I needed him more than ever. I listened closely to his words in silence as they steadily calmed and reassured me. I am comforted that I am not alone while I tackle this challenge thrust upon me. He is my rock and I know he will always be there for me.

So, that brings me to my present circumstance, slowly recuperating, lying next to my love. The memory of Peter's soothing whispers from earlier in the evening resonates loadly in my brain as I wake in the dead of night, "Its ok. I've got you."

Peter must be exhausted. He is finally asleep, arm across my waist. Gently I lift his arm and roll him onto his side of the bed. To my surprise he doesn't wake. He must have been up half the night watching over me.

Poor darling. How I must trouble you.

I decide the best course of action is to let him sleep.

A smile courses my lips as a mischievous thought enters my brain. I consider carefully how I can repay his love and kindness towards me. Biting gently onto my bottom lip I carefully lift the sheet high as I glance underneath. Checking that Peter is still quite asleep, I slowly reach down until my hand finds the mischief my mind so desperately seeks. I watch Peter for any sign of rousing, though he seems to remain perfectly asleep. I begin to work my magic. To my surprise it doesn't take much effort to produce the desired effect.

"Are you still asleep?" I softly whisper.

"Yeah, Sweetheart," comes his sweet reply as he smiles with his eyes locked closed.

"Good. Then you won't notice if I do this," I offer as I disappear under the sheets to give my man some extra special attention.

Soon sleep is temporarily abandoned. We make love so passionately and tenderly for near on an hour. I kiss him, holding him tightly with both hands around his neck. He responds to my advance, chewing my upper lip. As our passion grows, I sense his breathing becoming irregular. Holding each other tight as we move slowly, our bodies entwine. Our hands explore each other, massaging and caressing. Nothing is off limits. Exhilarated to the point of no return, though still reluctant to set each other free, I relax my guard and moan softly with delight. We are as one, not two. We could never be closer. We make love until we are spent, falling asleep in each other's arms once more. It is a wonderful conclusion to a harrowing night, a confirmation that our feelings for each other are strong. There can be no denial of that fact.

This is the reality I crave.

This is all I need.

I fall back to sleep, spent but happy.

'Sleight of Hand'

She shuffles the deck,
With poise and aplomb,
With speed and accuracy,
And a confidence, bar none.

You think you know,
The trick which is played,
Unaware the game is gone,
You've already missed, the sleight of hand.

Chapter 2

Sunday, February 26th, 2006.

7 A.M.

Crown Towers, Melbourne, Victoria.

We decide to leave for home early the next morning. Our holiday is well and truly over. We both long to be in familiar surrounds once more.

"I thought we might call into the Camberwell Market on the way home, just to stretch our legs a little," Peter suggests, reaching out and rubbing my leg affectionately. He draws me back to the real world, away from my pleasant reminiscence of last night. A little startled, I clamber to put my seat belt on.

"That would be good," I say, smiling at Peter, even though scouring the mountains of trash for bargains is the last thing I want to do at the moment. I really just want to go home. On second thoughts, I wonder if it is not such a bad idea, anyway. You never know, it might just give me an opportunity to clear my mind a little. Remove all these intolerable questions, leaving some room for answers to sneak stealthily into my brain.

"Great," Peter says, showing that he needs little encouragement. He starts the car and pulls out of the car park, away from the casino; away from the dramas that have dogged us here. The early morning sun streams through the windscreen, blinding for a moment as he pulls down the visor. Peter falls silent for a few seconds; I can tell he has something on his mind. He hesitates, his voice uncertain and quivering as he asks, "Do you want to keep talking about it?"

I turn and look at him with tired eyes as he glances my way several times nervously, trying to gauge what type of mood I am dwelling in. I know in his eyes, I can be a little unpredictable at times.

"Not really," I say hoping he will drop the subject.

"No, I just thought it might make things clearer for you."

I shake my head, knowing he is going to be like a dog with a bone until he gets his way, "You don't take no for an answer do you?"

He laughs, "Sorry Angel, I don't mean to be pushy. It's just that I thought it might help. Between the two of us, we might be able to work out what to do in order to, you know, cure you."

I frown, confused by Peter's uneducated diagnosis, "Peter, I don't know what these.... these visions are but I'm pretty damn certain they are not like the flu. You cannot get a tablet to pop from the chemist, have a good lie down and everything will return to normal. I can't see that happening, can you?"

"I guess not," Peter replies feebly.

"They seem to be more like a..... like a ..... like a gift. Yes, that's more like it, a gift, something that can be used to help people or change unfortunate events, manipulating them towards a more positive outcome. What I am experiencing is not a disease. There is no "cure" to alleviate its symptoms. They cannot perform an operation to remove these insights from my soul. "

"You don't know that for sure," Peter offers.

I nod, though I hate to admit that he may be right. There may be some sort of medication which helps to prevent the onset of these visions. That notion lends itself to a self-diagnosis that I am experiencing some sort of mental disorder. I hope with all my heart that this is not the case. I don't want these visions to be a symptom that proves there is something wrong with my brain or my being. Shaking the chill out of the length of my skin, I choose not to dwell on this idea as I continue, "I know, I know. This is all just guess work at this stage. I really need to talk to someone who knows what is happening and what this is all about."

Peter laughs again, more loudly this time, "And what, pray tell, is his or her name and address?"

I throw my hands in the air, laugh and nod in agreement, "Yeah, yeah. I take your point. I haven't quite worked that out yet, either."

Peter reaches for and grasps my hand, tenderly caressing the palm with a stray finger, "Look, Angel, you don't have to come up with all the answers straight away. Just try to relax and take things slowly. I hope the market will take your mind off things a little. That would be a good start, don't you think? At least we will be away from all the shit that has been going down."

I stare at the road ahead. I doubt the Camberwell Market will help to any extent though I can't see how it will hurt either. Anyway, Peter is trying his best and I should be appreciative. After all, that is all I can really hope for at this stage. I know one thing for certain. My experiences with these visions would be very difficult without someone else's aid and clarity of mind. I need a trusted confidante. I need someone whose love for me is beyond question. I need Peter by my side.

I look over at Peter as he drives onwards, oblivious to my attention. I search his gaunt features for any sign of what is actually going through his mind.

I wonder if you know what we are getting into?

*   *   *

Camberwell Rotary Market is already swarming with people when we arrive. The early bird bargain hunters have now been swamped by the Camberwellians sipping their Cappuccinos while idly looking for hidden treasure amongst the mountains of trash.

There are vinyl records through to the compact discs of today. Aroma therapy candles are well placed next to portable massage tables. Valuable antiques are scattered in amongst the voluminous modern decor items. There are the ugly, the beautiful, the scary and the bizarre. Until now, I had forgotten how marvelous a place this is to wander and reminisce about bygone eras for an hour or so. Peter is right. This is a welcome distraction for my troubled mind. A peaceful innocuous place filled with crowded solitude. It is the perfect place to escape from the world.

I begin to quietly examine an ugly lamp covered in a green fabric wondering if I can rejuvenate it into something glorious for my bed side table. Maybe recover it in red or pink. The addition of some sort of lace with gold trim might just be the touch it so desperately needs to reinvigorate its evaporated life.

I am so focused on the challenge of working out if the lamp is a bargain or a rip off at its $5.00 price tag that I fail to observe the movement behind me. I jump as a lady speaks softly into my ear.

"Can I help you?" her silky voice sooths.

Taken aback, I turn awkwardly in a half circle in order to address her, "Oh, I'm not sure......"

Standing there, looking at the lady before me, I suddenly realize she is not the seller of the lamp but rather another stall holder who has crossed the walkway in order to speak with me. She appears to be in her late forties with a slightly tanned complexion. She is wearing comfortable, flat sole black shoes and a ruffled green and purple striped, full length dress which rolls over her ample hips all the way down to ground level. The dress has small, metallic disks sewn into the fabric which act like muffled wind chimes as she moves.

Her ashen hair sparkles as it cascades from under her purple scarf. The color of her hair seems to be some sort of strange natural color rather than something she has dyed. Both her arms are laden with various bracelets; some with crystals, others with charms, symbols and words whose meanings are foreign to me. Her eyes are hidden beneath wide, dark sunglasses as she patiently waits for my reply. I feel a little uneasy. I am drawn to her eyes for some obscure reason. I wonder what she hides behind the tinting.

"Can I help you child? You seem troubled," she tries again, hands outstretched this time as she watches my face intently for a response. Her forced smile doesn't allay my intuitive concerns.

Placing the lamp back on the table I decline her offer of assistance, "I don't think so. I'm sorry. I don't believe in fortune telling."

The lady smiles, a smile of someone who is the keeper of many secrets, "I would have thought that was exactly what you believe in, particularly considering your recent experiences, Miss Julie Mahoney. Anyway, I am not really a fortune teller. I'm just an old lady who has seen many things, some of which are hard to explain to non-believers. What would I claim to know of the troubles which curse your soul?"

What? How do you know my name? Do you know what I'm going through? No, that's impossible.

Confused, I watch the lady turn and walk slowly across the way, disappearing back into a small tent set up on the edge of the car park. She doesn't turn to see if I am watching. Maybe she knows I am. Maybe she isn't a charlatan, as I first thought. Maybe she can sense there is something about me, something unusual. After all, how on earth could she possibly know my name?

I look around for Peter, though he is not to be found. He has wandered some distance farther down the aisle, lost, for the moment, in amongst the burgeoning crowd. I so keenly want him to come and speak to this lady. However, I feel time is precious. I am not about to let someone else enter the tent first. I can't waste time looking for Peter. All I can do is fill him in later. I have no choice but to act and act swiftly.

On entering the tent I see a smile light up the lady's face once more. She sits behind a small round table, seemingly waiting for my arrival. The interior of the tent is dimly lit by several candles that flicker harmlessly around the floor. There are no other decorations or props such as Tarot cards or a crystal ball. I must admit, this is not at all what I expected.

"Please be seated," she says calmly, beckoning to the empty chair directly opposite her.

I obey her request without saying a word. As I become seated, she reaches over and takes each of my hands separately in hers, facing my palms upwards. She tilts her head back as if she is calling upon some divine assistance from the spirit world as she begins to speak in a soft voice, "Mmm. The gift is strong in you, very strong indeed."

Excitedly I ask, "What is the nature of this gift?"

Tilting her head back to look me squarely in the eyes she taunts, "You have seen the properties of the gift yourself, though you remain blind to the possibilities."

"Possibilities? What possibilities?" I ask. I am intrigued by the riddles the lady offers with every word she speaks.

Vaguely she continues without expression of any emotion, "Some things must be revealed to you only when their time has come. We all learn much from experiencing what life has pre-ordained for us."

"You know precisely what I'm going through, what I'm experiencing. Yet you won't tell me what it is or what it is all about. Why?" I push a little more strongly. My frustration with the fortune teller's inability to provide straight answers grows by the second. She is a person of significance who I feel could aid me greatly, improving my understanding of what I am experiencing. I find her choice of words, so far, vague and unhelpful.

"Some things in this universe cannot be explained, they can only become apparent once you have lived them, felt them, endured them, enjoyed them or........."

"Or?" I ask nervously.

"Or survived them," she offers plainly.

It is so tedious to finally speak to someone who seems to know exactly what I am experiencing yet is unwilling to provide straight answers. Nonsensical riddles are not going to cut it with me. I need plain and simple answers. Something that is logical, making sense of it all would be wonderful. I guess I must remain patient and continue to try and extract the truth.

I try a different tact, appealing to her vanity, "You obviously have great powers yourself. Can't you help me to understand what my visions are all about?"

"You are greatly mistaken," she begins to explain as she releases my hands. She removes her glasses with the pretense of cleaning them. I can see clearly deep scarring around her eyes now which indicates she may have been burned by some sort of scalding liquid in the past. As she looks at me I can see her eyes glow iridescent red for the briefest of moments before she replaces her glasses once more. I dismiss this as simply a trick of the pale shimmering candlelight. She takes my hands again as I struggle to accept the fact she is horribly scarred. I am a little distracted wondering if she was born that way or if she suffered permanent scarring as a result of some sort of horrible accident. Maybe someone did that to her on purpose. The mere thought sends chills done my spine. As my mind focuses on this question, the fortune teller continues her reading, "My powers, as you call them, are extremely limited. I can sense some things, I can dream others. You are well aware that you see more than I. I know you have already seen premonitions which have changed the future. Some of what you have seen has already come to pass."

"How do you know that?" I call out in disbelief. I am beginning to find the knowledge of my circumstances that the fortune teller is relaying to me most intriguing. These details relate to things which she should have no knowledge of whatsoever. They are private details which only I know. Each detail she offers, adds credibility to her words. I wait with bated breath for something she knows, that I do not. I pray that she will share something crucial with me.

"I told you I am able to sense some things. That is all."

"Please, can you tell me all that you know about me," I plead quietly.

She releases my hands and pulls away from me, indicating that my reading is over, "I can tell you very little that you need to know."

I shake my head, feeling a little cheated. I feel in my heart that I can learn much from this stranger. I can't understand her obvious reluctance to share relevant information with me, "But you seem to know so much."

"I am merely the first step of a long and patient journey that you will undertake over many years to come," she confides. "It is a journey which only death can halt. It is a journey which you have already begun in your limited, awkward fashion."

"I don't know where I need to go," I state plainly, completely confused. This above anything else is the question I so desperately seek to clarify right now. How can I work this all out if I don't know where to go, what to do next? She needs to tell me this much at least.

"I can tell you only three things you need to know," she offers. She leans close to me, rubbing her thumb across her fingers in a motion indicating that a payment of some sort is both expected and required in order for our conversation to continue. "If, of course, you want to find out what is happening to you."

I am a little disappointed that she is stooping to extorting money from me in exchange for vital information. Though, I guess, that is how she makes a living. I fumble through my handbag and produce twenty dollars from my purse. This doesn't seem to spark her interest at all as she examines it with her fingers. With a sigh I produce a fifty dollar bill which she readily accepts along with the twenty already given. I say to her, "Of course I want to work out what is happening. That's why I'm here."

"Good," she smiles as she folds and tucks the money away in the top of her dress. "Very good. You must listen closely to my words as they are the truth and only truth will lead you towards enlightenment. Do you understand?"

I nod my acknowledgement.

"Good," she continues. "Firstly you should always trust your instincts. Your intuition is good, though sometimes you fail to accept the secrets it shares with you. You must believe in yourself. Your intuition will lead you down the path you must travel. This is your greatest weapon, one which you must carry with you at all times."

"Yes," I say a little uncertain as to what value this statement is to me. I always trust my gut instincts anyway. At least I think I do. That is how I became so successful as a writer. I am always willing to go down "the path less travelled" if I believe that is the right way to go.

"Secondly keep your mind open. There are many things in the universe that cannot be explained by a closed, rational mind. Sometimes you just have to believe, even though to do so could be interpreted by others as madness."

"And the last point?" I ask, worried that I am rapidly following a path leading straight to a dead end.

Was this worth seventy dollars? Peter is going to have a fit when he finds out I have casually thrown away all that cash!

"Yes, and lastly," she says slowly as she considers her words carefully. "Lastly you need to look deep within your heart. It is only from that secure, untainted location that you will discover the truth."

"What truth is that?" I ask completely perplexed. Her statement is merely a riddle. I imagine she wants me to find the answer I seek to a question I don't know by asking myself. Is that what she is trying to say or have I completely missed the point? That is just bullshit!

"You will discover the truth, the ultimate truth which will lead you onto your path of discovery," she confides, not really giving anything startling away.

"I don't know what you mean," I state honestly. I feel there is something I am missing, something obvious that I haven't thought of; something that is right before my eyes yet remains out of sight.

She sighs, a little bit frustrated with my lack of initiative, "Don't you feel it in your heart, my sweet thing? Don't you know that which can only be true?"

"Know what?" I ask, dumbfounded.

She removes her glasses once more in order to stare directly at me. This time there is no mistaking her glowing red eyes. They are not just a figment of my furtive imagination, they are luminous and real, "You are not the first in your line to have the gift. There have been others. You know the person who you need to seek. He can help you discover your past so that you may succeed in your future endeavors. You must go to him, the keeper of your line."

He?

I am stunned by this revelation. For some reason I thought my visions were simply my problem; something unique to me. It had never dawned on me that others in my family had experienced the same thing. The concept that the 'Gift' is hereditary I find unbelievable. Maybe it has skipped a generation or two, for I am unaware of anyone in my immediate family who has the same experiences as me. They have certainly kept it well hidden if they have.

I smile as I think of the perfect person to consult, the one person in the entire world eccentric enough to know every last detail about my ancestors and their lives. He definitely is 'the keeper of my line'. Though I have not seen him since I was a child, I remember him well. I remember that he was a bit of a loner. Even though he was probably fairly harmless, I did find him a little scary, from a child's perspective of course. However, I'm an adult now and I realize that, though a little strange, he is basically a good man with an obsessive hobby. Yes, I think it is well worth making a detour on our way home. Uncle Ken's house is roughly on the way home anyway. Well, close enough, in an easterly sort of way.

I look up, ready to thank the fortune teller for her help, however, she is gone. I can only assume she took advantage of my distraction and exited through the tent flap which now flutters loosely in the gentle breeze. Not one to stop and chat, I guess. She says what she has to then leaves it at that. I like her style. I guess there would be no point to life if all the questions were answered at once.

A most curious woman!

I stand and prepare to leave the tent. Suddenly I pause, audibly gasping as I watch in disbelief. The tent and all the furniture begins to fade. Within a few seconds everything becomes transparent before disappearing like a mirage. I am left awestruck, mouth gaping open once more in amongst the milling, noisy crowd. I stand completely frozen as my brain tries desperately to understand what just happened.

Did that really happen? I couldn't have imagined all that could I? Surely not! I'm not mad. I know I'm not.

"Miss, miss," I hear a young male call from behind me.

I turn, a little confused, still trying to fathom exactly what is going on. My brain struggles to construct a clear sentence. In the end I manage to mumble only fragments of words, "Wah…..what?"

"You dropped this, miss," says the beaming, chubby lad's face staring up at me as he waves some paper in my direction, held firmly in his right hand.

Eventually my eyes focus on the objects and I smile, nodding my gratitude as I take the seventy dollars from his hand. I smile as I watch him run back to his mother. His mother rubs his luscious mousy hair vigorously to his disdain. There is no hiding the pride for her son and his good deed which bubbles over in her sparkling blue eyes.

I look at the crowd surging around me. I see no trace of the fortune teller or her stall. I take a deep breath and smile. I say quietly to myself trying to block any uncertainty from my mind, "I know I am sane. This doesn't make sense at all, but I know I am sane."

I spy Peter in the distance and make my way slowly towards him once more. I shake my head as I laugh a little, "A most curious woman indeed."

'Guidance'

Expert advice sort,
From a strange direction.
A man who looks at the world,
With a different inflection.

The keeper of records,
The guardian of family ties.
The fountain of knowledge,
And the creator of lies.

Chapter 3

Sunday, February 26th, 2006.

Midday.

Melbourne, Victoria, Australia.

I have never known Peter to be so silent. I know he is trying to concentrate on the task of negotiating the correct combination of side roads, following a route which leads us roughly onwards, towards Uncle Ken's house in the leafy suburb of Kew. As he drives, he listens intently to each and every word about my unexpected encounter with the fortune teller. I assume he is trying to absorb all this new information and process it to his own, complete satisfaction. I know that's exactly what I'm trying to do. However, I can't help but think that his silence is a symptom of something else that troubles his mind. I know Peter well. Something is amiss.

After a while, he speaks apprehensively in a calm tone, "Angel......."

"Yes, Babe," I respond, eager to hear what is on his mind. Maybe I can help ease his concerns somewhat. I sure hope so. I can't afford to lose him now.

"Look, I don't know how to put this," he continues slowly.

I remain confused as to what is troubling him so. I know the meeting with the fortune teller has just added another layer of peculiarity to my story, to our lives. However, I fail to see how the tale of my recent encounter has resulted in a change to the status of our relationship. Oh, how I wish Peter would simply open up so that I can deal once and for all with that which is causing him obvious distress. With a note of urgency creeping into my voice I ask, "Peter, what is it?"

"It's not that important," he suggests, though I remain unconvinced by the underlining tone in his voice. "It's just I want to make something clear to you."

"Yes?" I ask fearing his pending response.

He stammers as he twists uncomfortably in his seat, "It....it.....it's just......you know......all I wanted to say was that I'm here for you and want to help. I guess, what I'm trying to say is that I would like to be present when you're talking with people about your visions. I mean I feel it would help me, to help you, if I can ask some questions too. I hope that makes some sense. Look, I guess it's not that important."

I suddenly feel ashamed that I didn't seek Peter's help last night when I went to Enterprise Park to prevent the stabbing of Elouise, the pregnant prostitute. I could have easily found him; he was probably in the closest bar trying to dampen his conflicting emotions. He wouldn't have taken much convincing. Peter would never let me walk headlong into danger on my own. Conversing with the fortune teller at Camberwell, I had effectively excluded him again. I can only imagine how this must hurt him. I have snubbed him twice when he needed to be involved. I am a proudly independent woman however I cannot afford to do that anymore. I have to keep reminding myself that it is not just me living through this drama, Peter is right here by my side. WE are living this nightmare. The visions affect us both. I need to let Peter in. I need him to understand my world. I need him to stay with me. I must not shut him out.

I lean over and kiss him on the cheek before grasping his free hand in mine, "It's important that you are involved with this too. I can't get through this without you. I'm not that strong. I'm sorry. I won't shut you out again. I promise."

"That's okay, Angel. Anyway, you're a lot stronger than you think. Taking on a hardened, lawless criminal wielding a knife in a dimly lit park takes a helluva lot of courage."

You're wrong Peter. It takes a hell of a lot of stupidity!

*　　　　　*　　　　　*

We arrive at Uncle Ken's, pulling slowly into the narrow, grey stone driveway. The sign on the hand carved, Maori totem letter box reads 'Ken H. Steping Residence'. The drive is steep and curves through a dense thicket of azaleas which still exhibit the odd flash of color here and there, even at this late stage of the season. It is a mere reminder of the glorious display they exhibited around a month ago.

"Okay," Peter says with a frown as I wonder what he is thinking. "So I gather by that little fella back there that your uncle is a tad peculiar."

I smile, "That is one of the terms you could use to describe him."

"What does the 'H.' stand for?" Peter whispers like it might be some sort of deep, dark secret which is only entrusted, in the strictest confidence, to a handful of close members of my family. I think at times Peter considers all my family to be a little strange. I guess he is right. I think that too from time to time. There is nothing sinister here, just a simple man, who keeps to himself and takes his chosen hobby to an extreme level.

"Well, you must promise not to tell Uncle Ken that you have knowledge of this," I whisper back, adding to the suspense, "For he hates his middle name with a vengeance. It's 'Horatio', if you must know. He thinks it sounds quite pompous."

Peter glances my way as he raises both his eyebrows for a second before breaking out into a hearty laugh. As he controls his inappropriate feeling he says, "Sorry. No, I'm truly sorry. I shouldn't poke fun at someone for their name. It's not his fault he was lumbered with that burden. I think he's right, you know. It is very pompous and old worldly, isn't it? However, there's one thing I don't get. If he hates his name so much, why does he keep the 'H.' on his letter box?"

"Well, that's Uncle Ken for you. He's a little different, as you have already gathered. Some might say he is a walking contradiction. He's always liked the initial in his name, says it gives his name prestige. You know, like an English lord, or someone of nobility. Anyway, that is who he is. He would be someone different if the "H" was missing. I hope that make sense?"

Peter glances at me strangely as he tries to comprehend and make some meaning from my words, "So he's a little bit cuckoo, is he?"

"Peter!" I exclaim, aghast at this presumption. "At worst I would say he is somewhat eccentric. I will have you know Uncle Ken happens to be one of the most decorated policemen currently serving in the Victorian Police Force."

"Really?" Peter says with his ample skepticism laid bare by the tone of his voice combined with his raised eyebrows. "So what happened to him? Did he have a nervous breakdown or something?"

"Nothing has happened to him," I say a little testy. "He has always been a little different, a little 'out there' if you like. However, that doesn't change the fact that he is highly resourceful and has been awarded two citations for bravery beyond the duty he has sworn to uphold. One of those awards was for saving a drowning boy, just off Sorrento. He took to the water in near cyclonic conditions, the like of which have not been seen again in the fifteen years hence. He found the boy unconscious in the pounding waves, rode the rip a mile across the shoreline keeping the lad's head above water. Finally, he dragged him back to the safety of the beach and the waiting life savers. He was utterly spent; spending the next fortnight in hospital recovering. However there was no way his conscience was going to let that boy drown. The second award was for single handedly stopping an armed robbery of a Commonwealth Bank in Smith Street, Collingwood. He managed to disarm and restrain two bandits, rescuing around twenty hostages without a single shot being fired."

"Wow! It sounds like he is some sort of living legend, an Aussie Bruce Willis."

I concur, "That he is. He is a living legend and then some."

Yet, as we park in front of his house, we are confronted by a living canvas, a portrait of a strange little man. He is standing in his garden, dressed simply in a brown terry toweling dressing gown and a pair of fluffy, pink, bunny slippers while hosing his Aspidistra. I can tell by the look on Peter's face that this is not quite what he is expecting. My uncle, on face value, doesn't fit the stereotype of a 'living legend'.

"G'day, Uncle Ken," I yell excitedly. Recognition spreads gleefully across his face. I run to him and fall immediately into a bear hug trap, my head pressed hard against his chest as he embraces me. After a few seconds he releases his grip.

"Well this is indeed a surprise, my Princess! It's been such a long time and look how you've grown. You're even more beautiful than you were as a child," Uncle Ken says as he discards the hose carelessly towards the nearest garden bed. I release my grip and stand back, rapt that he remembers me. I was always his little Princess. Ken moves towards Peter, casting a suspicious scowl as he looks him up and down and reluctantly offers his hand in conditional friendship. "Hi, I'm mad Uncle Ken. You may have heard some malicious rumors of my existence and the state of my sanity. Well, let me tell you, my dear lad, I am determined to prove to you that those rumors are a hundred percent true. My life is too bizarre to be the work of fiction."

Peter smiles and shakes his hand, unaware of Uncle Ken's habit of wringing the hand of anyone new he meets. I guess it is his way of asserting authority, right from the get go. Peter squeaks as he grimaces slightly, "I'm Peter, Julie's boyfriend."

"You're a lucky man, my son. You had better look after this one if you know what's good for you. She's the jewel of our rag tag family," Ken says, releasing his hold and winking at Peter.

"I will, sir," Peter says formally as he wriggles his fingers, trying to re-establish blood flow to his extremities.

"Good lad. Now my Princess, what brings you to my humble abode so early on this beautiful day? It must be years since you last came to visit. I can only assume you have some sort of pressing reason. Surely you did not drift accidentally into my fascinating realm," Ken states waving his arm around with a flourish in order to acknowledge the entire expanse of his little piece of the universe.

I decide to be straight to the point, "Well, I was hoping to gain some information on our family tree. I was wondering...."

"Well, wonder no longer my Princess," Uncle Ken says taking my hand and forcibly dragging me towards the house. "I always have time for anyone interested in family history. I could certainly do with the distraction. It's been one heck of a week. Some drunken teenagers ran a car into a ditch and then tried to claim that the car drove itself. They even discussed the car as if it were human, bestowing some sort of girl's name onto it. Old Mrs. Hennessey has been off her medication again, claiming to see vampires flying around at night. Then to top it all off we had reports of a rabid dog running amok throughout the streets of Kew. I ask you, have you ever heard of anything more preposterous? I mean if an author tried to write these fantasies as stories they would never get published; too fanciful for anyone to believe. Don't you agree?"

"What about the hose?" Peter asks from some distance behind us as he tries to catch up.

"The hose?" Uncle Ken asks, failing to comprehend the meaning of Peter's question.

Peter explains, "Yes, it's still running."

"Leave it, the garden needs a bit of water, anyway," Uncle Ken yells over his shoulder, not slowing his step in the slightest. Genealogy is his one great love and it is a rare occurrence that someone else is interested in his field of expertise. Uncle Ken is determined not to miss the opportunity. "Do try to keep up, my young man."

Peter employs a short sprint up the slope as he quickly narrows the gap between us before matching our pace as we march stridently towards the front door.

As we enter the house it becomes apparent very quickly, just how eccentric Uncle Ken really is. He has been a bachelor all his life; I doubt any woman would tolerate his blasé attitude. His life of solitude is clearly displayed through his choice of decor. The house has an unkempt manliness about it. Items seemingly discarded here and there without much thought or consideration. Lots of dust and a complicated method of filing which surely only a man could understand.

"Can I get you anything? I have an extensive range," Uncle Ken says as he flicks his slippers off to the side of the room. He scurries barefoot down the hallway to the kitchen, located somewhere out of sight in the near distance.

Peter turns toward me with a devilish grin as he whispers, "Vodka would be nice."

"We'd love a cuppa," I say as I poke Peter in the ribs while offering him a disapproving scowl.

Peter smiles and nods his approval, knowing full well that I will not accept any of his shenanigans here today, "Yeh, a cuppa would be just dandy."

"Splendid! I've got a particularly nice blend from the Tamil region which I only just imported from Sri Lanka last Tuesday," Ken says as he begins his preparations noisily, clunking cups and saucers as he goes about his business. A kettle whistles to the boil as he continues, "Yes, it costs about a hundred and fifteen dollars a kilo. Though, let me tell you, it's worth every bloody cent. The aroma, the taste of the tannins, mmmmm, mmmmm! It's simply quite superb."

Uncle Ken marches back into the living room holding a metal tray with three china cups of pre-poured tea, a small jug of milk and a tiny sugar bowl with a silver spoon. He motions us, with a tilt of his head, to take a seat. We sit on the sofa as he places the tray deftly on the coffee table before us.

"Milk anyone?" he asks, jug and first cup in hand.

"Yes thanks," Peter and I reply in unison.

"So tell me Uncle Ken," Peter asks as Ken pours milk into the first cup and, like a true gentleman, hands it to me. "Where did you get all this stuff from?"

I look around the living room in amazement. The room is completely cluttered with memorabilia and antiques from all over the world. Overlapping on the floor are oriental rugs with intricate hand woven designs. One in particular depicts some sort of story about life in a small village somewhere in China. On closer inspection each picture panel tells the story of honored family members over different eras, outlining the lives they have led. I come to the conclusion that these rugs must be a unique method some families have employed to maintain a history of their forebears and educating their descendants. They are, after all, a published family history of sorts and as such would appeal to avid, genealogical enthusiast such as Uncle Ken.

There are carvings which appear to be like Totem poles. Each of these has a unique design. Some are of animals such as eagles and the like. Others are carved with faces. Maybe they are the prominent people of the village, kings perhaps, or maybe they too represent a lineage or family tree. I feel this is more likely, considering Uncle Ken's obsession for genealogy in all its forms. Other carvings depict monsters with hideous, frightful expressions dominating their faces. Maybe these belong to family stories or myths that have been passed down from generation to generation. Maybe they aren't monsters but rather protectors of the family; warding off evil spirits which wander mischievously by. Maybe they represent tragedy which has engulfed the family at different times like famine, flood or unexpected death. I don't know. However, they are certainly eye catching.

"Well, my good man. All this 'stuff', as you so eloquently put it, is actually of significant historical value. Every single item is of particular importance to the field of genealogy. Some of the artefacts preserved here are highly sought after by various scholars and renowned museums around the world, particularly in England."

Peter remains awestruck, his eyes darting, his mind absorbing all the oddities on display around the room, "Yes, but where on earth did they all come from? This is too much for one man to have collected in his lifetime.

They don't look like the kind of items you would find in your average weekend garage sale."

Uncle Ken winks at me. I know he is fast warming to Peter. Peter's eyes openly reveal their fascination with Ken's magnificent collection. This room is a living representation of a 'Boy's Own Adventure', "No, they are not so easily acquired. In fact, I have made numerous trips throughout Europe and Asia over the years and have brought many items back to Australia during my travels. Looks can be deceiving. I was a regular Indiana Jones type character in my early days, scouring each of the corners of the world, searching for genealogical treasure."

Ha! Yeah, Indiana Jones wouldn't be caught dead in a pair of pink fluffy slippers.

"All this stuff," Peter sees the grimace on Uncle Ken's face. Instantly he realizes the error of his way, using careless words to describe the admiration he feels. Wisely, he retracts his words and offers more respect as he continues. "Sorry, all these artefacts couldn't have come simply from your travels. There are just far too many."

"You're quite right," Uncle Ken explains. "Many have come from the friends I liaise with around the globe. I dominate the cyberspace genealogy chat rooms and as such I am well known and respected in the global community. I make use of the local knowledge and contacts of others to aid purchases on my behalf. Other items I have sourced on E-Bay from unscrupulous dealers whose only interest in life is the never ending pursuit of the accumulation of wealth."

"Uncle Ken," I try in vain to grab his attention. He has a ready-made audience in Peter and is rapt to be talking to someone with gleaming eyes about all his marvelous possessions. However, I am well aware that once he starts to delve into his endless array of stories, we will be here for hours and I will still be none the wiser in regards to the information I so desperately seek.

"So tell me, Uncle Ken," Peter chuckles, knowing I am becoming a little frustrated. "What on earth did you get on E-Bay?"

Uncle Ken's eyes light up with delight as he walks swiftly, taking up position between two gargoyle statues sitting at the edge of the room. As he casually leans on the head of one, he gleefully chimes, "Well, these gargoyles I bought from an antiquities dealer in Canberra. They came with extensive certification, which I meticulously verified. This documentation proved essential to substantiate their authenticity. They appear to be the two missing gargoyles, attached to the House of Windsor, which were stolen around 1882. They are meant to protect the Windsor family and all their descendants from any bad luck which may threaten them. With all the dramas they have been through of late I'm sure they could do with them being returned to their rightful place atop Buckingham Palace. However, I am in no rush to return them to their rightful stately home."

"Wow!" is all Peter can say as he glances at me for confirmation that Uncle Ken isn't completely mad.

"Uncle Ken," I try again, hoping to catch him mid-spiel.

"Peter," Uncle Ken continues to ignore me. He is too intent on sharing his obsession with my besotted boyfriend. "Do you know what this device is used for?"

Peter leans forward and examines the strange little wooden box which Ken has thrust into his eager hands. His quizzical eye can see it is only about five inches square. Each side has an intricate carving of the same king sitting on his thrown. In each depiction the king is surrounded by slaves who are being punished, for some unexplained reason, with whips, spears and knives while their arms and legs remain chained. The drawings are quite blood thirsty and depict a merciless ruler who obviously had no qualms about using force to quell unrest or to encourage unswaying loyalty to his realm.

The box has a strange form of wooden corkscrew device which seems to enable a wooden block on the interior to be lowered into position. On the other side are two doors which fold outwards. Once the doors are folded back in they leave a circular hole in the center. There is a simple yet effective locking device which apparently is designed to ensure the box remains closed, when in use.

"It looks like it may crush grapes or be some sort of primitive nut cracker?" Peter guesses though I can tell he really doesn't have much of a clue.

Uncle Ken laughs, "Well, in some respects, I guess you are right. Some medieval courts of Europe, such as Slovenia, adopted the use of this device as a deterrent to undesirables. Every effort was made to discourage unwanted suitors from coming forward to seek the hand of the princess. The intentions of these suitors were often far from honorable. They were looking to undermine the ruling family through casual dalliances leading to scandalous rumors and innuendo. Sometimes the intentions of these suitors were more sinister in nature. Occasionally their two-faced plans would ultimately be to gain the trust of the King and take his daughter hostage for ransom. Sometimes the intent was to murder a daughter of the King in order to gain status or recognition from an enemy of the realm. This device is indeed a living reminder of a truly barbaric time in world history. As you can imagine, it was imperative that the purity and safety of the princess remained well guarded till the time of her arranged marriage. So, any poor misguided soul who turned up unannounced and without the correct lineage would be taken directly to the dungeon where a re-education process would take place. The suitors would soon realize the error of their ways with the help of this clever little device."

"How so?" Peter asks as he rolls the box over once more in his search for clues.

Uncle Ken's complexion becomes dark and brooding as he smiles in a devilish manner. He continues very slowly, making sure Peter hears and comprehends each and every word, "Well, my son. This device would then be placed over the chap's genitals, closing the doors and locking them inside the box. The lever would then be screwed down, steadily restricting the blood flow to this particular vital organ. The poor sod would then be chained to a post in the middle of the town square, naked save for the box protecting his modesty as a visual deterrent to other would be suitors. Of course after fourteen days or so, how shall I put this, things were prone to drop off. This ...."

"Uncle Ken," I say more loudly this time. Finally, I capture his attention as Peter hurriedly places the box on the coffee table before wiping his hands on his shirt.

"Yes?" Ken asks as he turns, halting his movement towards some strange looking spears in the corner which I know for certain would be the next topic of conversation. I don't need the benefit of premonitions to predict Uncle Ken's next move. He loves an audience and sees Peter as a fresh, untainted victim who he can subject to some of his well-worn stories.

"This is all very interesting but it doesn't relate to the urgent matter that brings us here," I say, glancing at Peter who pretends to zip close his lips. He knows I am not impressed by his antics sidetracking Uncle Ken. "It is a most urgent matter that I feel requires your expert knowledge of our family tree."

"Well, why didn't you just say so, Princess," Uncle Ken says as he drags an armchair closer to us and seats himself, a look of concentrated attention on his face. This is a side of Uncle Ken I don't remember seeing before. He has always been the hyperactive extrovert. I wonder how much effort it is taking for him to restrain his enthusiasm. "What seems to be the problem, Princess?"

I pause, wondering if Uncle Ken will consider me to be a complete idiot. I am heartened by the fact that he has been touched by many strange, amazing and mysterious things from this world, too much for one person in one lifetime. As I look deep into his eyes, I wonder what he will think of my fanciful story and whether or not he will consider me mad. Maybe he will be sympathetic. After all, I think he knows that most in the family consider him to be bonkers. He knows the pain that ridicule and scorn can bring.

"I guess the crux of the reason why I came here today is to ask you if anyone in our family tree has or is having the same experiences as me. I mean, I have been told that the things I am experiencing may have a genetic link to some of my relatives or ancestors. I am hoping you will know if that is the case. I don't know who else to ask. In fact, I am feeling a little lost."

"Right!" Uncle Ken says as he springs to his feet once more. "You have come to the right place."

His enthusiasm for the challenge is exhilarating to watch. He moves two African shields, laden with colorful motifs, so that he can open the door of a non-descript, large, brown cupboard located in the corner of the room. From my vantage point I can clearly see that the inside of the cupboard is crammed with photo albums, scrolls and exercise books, stored in a haphazard manner. Uncle Ken searches through a few of the scrolls until he finally finds the one he is looking for.

"This should help clarify the situation for you a little," he says as Peter moves the tray and tea set away. Uncle Ken rolls the chart out onto the coffee table before us so that its contents are facing me. The chart is so large that part of it rolls onto the floor. Crumpled edges and tarnished yellow paper reveal its age. I would guess that this chart was produced many years ago.

"This, my dear, is your very own family chart. It has both your parents' lineage back to at least the 1700's. Of course I have omitted the 'Brown' section which should flow back from your paternal great grandfather's side. All of this line has been researched thoroughly, though I have kept it confidential so that the more aristocratic members of our little clan don't send me solicitor's letters claiming liable, disputing our obvious connection to brothel keepers and sly grog sellers. Interesting stuff, as you would say, though not everyone's cup of tea. Sometimes family trees need to have secrets hidden so as not to cause distress to others. There are many historical instances where family trees have been fabricated by lies, particularly with the best intentions to protect the lives of others. The Jewish persecution by the Nazis in the Second World War is a prime example of this. The scholars of that time tried in vain to protect the innocent with falsified documents showing a completely non-Jewish lineage. Imagine the dilemma of having to hide the person you are, to forsake the practices and rituals you believe to be true and sacred in order to simply stay alive. Could you imagine that? I couldn't cope with it. I would be overwhelmed by a feeling that I have betrayed my people, my heritage, my God. Each day you would exist only as a shadow, a person with no reflection of who you truly are. No, I can only imagine what that would have been like. That time was simply horrendous. Anyway, I shouldn't let myself become distracted by such things when you have a burning question to be answered. If you tell me which particular branch you are interested in, I can retrieve further charts, some of which date back to around 1000 AD. I am hopeful we may find a link to whatever ails you."

I eagerly grasp the chart in both hands as I draw it nearer, seeking better light. I examine it closely. It is magnificent with its delicate calligraphy and vine like intertwining links between generations. I have heard the names before and can recall some of the stories that were whispered in my presence at family gatherings, when I was a young girl. For the life of me though, as I look at the chart in detail, I can't see any names which jog my memory. I can't remember any stories about ancestors who have experienced visions like I do. I can't remember anything odd that could equate to an individual having visions if it was scrutinized in the current light of day. No ghost stories or the like. To be perfectly frank though, I have not spent many minutes researching anything about my family history. I have taken my personal history for granted. I'm afraid, in general, that my ancestors are largely strangers to me.

I shake my head as I look at Uncle Ken, "This is an amazing chart but I don't really know which section I should be looking at. Most of these people are little more than names on a page. Their lives are completely unknown to me."

"Well, I know this is hard for you. However, I guess, if you can share with me what it is that the doctors think has been genetically passed on, I might be able to tell you which branch of the tree that trait comes from. There are several ailments such as cancer and diabetes which run rampant through various sections of the tree."

Uncle Ken smiles disarmingly at me, encouraging me to provide more detail. He is a smart man. He knows I have something important to tell him and he is using his best detective skills to try to pry this information from my shallow words while trying to appear too intrusive. I sigh, knowing that he will not give up until he has his way. At the risk of appearing an imbecile, I reluctantly continue, "Well, you see; I know this story sounds like madness."

"Please dear, continue," Uncle Ken says earnestly, excited that he may be about to hear something new related to the family tree.

I sigh; knowing that the only path leading to the answers I so desperately seek is paved with bricks of honesty. Determined to be brave and, more importantly, direct, I continue, "Well, you see. I've been experiencing some strange visions."

Uncle Ken slowly leans back in his chair, trying to absorb the full meaning of my words. By the expression on his face I can tell that he is taking me seriously and contemplating the meaning of my words, at least for now. Gesturing with a wave of his hand for more information he says, "Pray, continue."

I feel the ice is broken, with no obvious repercussions. This being said, I feel slightly more empowered to divulge more of the awful truth, "They appear to be visions of real people. I think they may be visions of the future, though I'm not a hundred percent sure if that is always the case. I know that sounds impossible however, if they are visions of the future, it would then be a reasonable assumption that the future can be changed. I think I can change the future. Does any of this make sense? I know I'm speaking like a lunatic though I hope, I so desperately hope that you know something about this. I hope that there is some connection to these visions in the history of our family. Please, you have to tell me. Do you know anything about this? Has anyone experienced stuff like this before?"

I watch as Uncle Ken sits thoughtfully in his chair for a few moments, unwilling to rush his response. I wonder what he is thinking. Is he strolling through the family trees in his mind looking for ancestors with similar traits or is he sifting through the stories and legends he has heard? Maybe he is considering how he can get this mad woman out of his house without causing a scene. As he absentmindedly scratches his chin, I find it impossible to gain any insight into thoughts coursing through his mind at all. Eventually he says softly, in an unusually restrained manner, "Yes, somehow it does make sense, just a little. I know this sounds far-fetched, yet there might just be some sort of bizarre genetic connection after all."

I am startled by his open and honest response. This was something I was not expecting. Suddenly it feels like a weight has been lifted. Somehow I feel comforted to know that I may not be the first to experience this strange affliction. My heart races with excitement as I lean forward, pointing to the chart, "Really, which line do you think?"

"That one there," Uncle Ken says pointing to an empty space where my great grandfather on my father's side should have been.

Confused I ask, "But there's no line there. It's just a dead end?"

Uncle Ken shakes his head as he continues, "No, not a dead end; just an omission."

I am astounded. I recall how Uncle Ken had pointed out that this line had been omitted because of some controversial history involving allegations of brothels and illegal alcohol. However, I fail to see how any of that could relate to my visions. I ask, mystified, "An omission, what does that mean?"

"Well you see, it's actually a deliberate omission. Some time ago I received some correspondence from a chap in America who is trying to track down descendants of a lady called Mary Murphy."

I fall silent as my skin turns cold.

"Mary!" I whisper under my breath. I consider the strange apparition who appeared to me last night upon my return to the hotel room, drained and exhausted, after my altercation with a knife wielding assailant in Enterprise Park. Her old world clothes, her strange accent and turn of phrase. Also I recall that eerie feeling that I somehow knew this woman, that in some way we had a connection. I remember calling out "Mary" before passing out into Peter's waiting arms. I shake my head, clearing my jumbled mind, as I focus on listening carefully to Ken's words.

"So is Julie a descendant of this Mary Murphy?" Peter asks, hoping he has latched onto the point of the matter. Seemingly he has forgotten that I called out her name. Maybe he didn't notice. After all, it made no sense. Only I could see her ghost.

"Well, that's just it," Uncle Ken sighs, obviously a little uncertain as to how he should explain his story to us. "Even with my wealth of knowledge of genealogy and all the world wide resources available, I am struggling to find a rock solid link between Mary Murphy and our family tree. It is for this reason that I have not included her line on our charts at this point in time."

I remain confused, "So, why did you suggest less than a minute ago that there might be a link between my visions and this uncertain lineage?"

Uncle Ken's eyes sparkle, "Well, that's why I refuse to throw out this information until I have proof positive evidence that it doesn't fit in. For the story of Mary Murphy is a most intriguing one. I would love there to be a link between her and our family. Could you just imagine how glorious that would be?"

"In what way is the story intriguing?" Peter asks, sensing, like me, that we are on the verge of something important, though still being kept completely in the dark.

"How should I put this? Mary Murphy supposedly possessed a curious gift. A sixth sense, if you like. Though a little fanciful, I grant you, the story goes that she experienced premonitions of the future," Uncle Ken says as he stares unflinchingly into my eyes, looking deep into my soul. I feel at ease as I look at the sparkle in his eyes. He smiles as he sees the look of disbelief on my face. "Just like you, if I am not mistaken."

"So she experienced the same thing as me?" I repeat as I contemplate what this might mean in the scheme of things.

"Well, Princess, I can't say that for certain, however, her story sounds a little like yours, with the limited knowledge I have about both of you."

I am eager to find out more, "Could you please share her story with me."

Uncle Ken pulls out a pipe from his dressing gown pocket and begins to fill it with tobacco, "You don't mind do you?"

We both shake our heads. We aren't going to be bothered by a little smoke. It is a small price to pay in exchange for vital information. Uncle Ken sits silently for a few seconds, considering his words carefully as he lights his pipe. Puffing away, he tries to ignite the tobacco. Eventually, he has a solid flame going as he continues, "Mary Murphy is said to have experienced her visions of the future way back in the late 1600's. Unfortunately, she felt she was duty bound to act on these visions. She had the best of intentions, seeking to help people she knew would be in serious trouble. However, in those times in America, people were very superstitious, fearful of anything they saw as the dark arts of black magic. Their ignorant closed minds were a constant danger to Mary and her family's welfare."

"You're not saying......?" I ask, feeling I know where this story is heading.

Uncle Ken nods, "Yes, that's right. She was placed on trial as a witch during the Salem Witch trials. The records for this time are very confusing, though. It is impossible to say whether or not she was convicted and hung. There is also no record of what happened to her two daughters, one of whom we supposedly descend from."

"Do you think I may have inherited this 'gift' from Mary Murphy?"

Uncle Ken says with the pipe stuck in the side of his mouth, "Well that's what this chap in America thinks. He is trying to track down people who descend from this lady and are having visions. At the time of his correspondence, I had never heard of anyone having visions or hallucinations so I just thought the guy was a crackpot. You come across crackpots regularly in genealogy. Some with family trees going right back to Adam."

"How did this bloke find you?" Peter asks. He is captivated by the story Ken is weaving for us.

"Via charts I placed on the internet. He could see the connection. I couldn't substantiate it though, so I have kept these charts separate to my main body of work. Maybe one day I can prove the connection."

I ask, perplexed, "So is there anyone else who is having these premonitions, someone else in the wider family? Someone I might know?"

Uncle Ken pauses before he shakes his head. His shoulders seem to suddenly tense as if his bones have turned magically into iron rods. An old black cat jumps lightly onto his lap and curls up rapidly as Uncle Ken pats him under the chin. He relaxes a little. As I listen to his words I sense he is not telling us something, "No one is admitting that; just you and this chap who may or may not be a distant cousin."

I am thrilled that there might be something going on here, rapt that these visions aren't just something going wrong with my mind. There are others out there. I am not alone. I know it in my heart. There must be a connection between Mary Murphy and me. In this world of insanity it is the only thing which makes any sense. I hold my breath as I ask the obvious question, "Do you know where in the U.S.A. he lives?"

"Yes and no," Uncle Ken says with a friendly grin plastered on his face. "I know exactly where he lives because he made contact with me again about a month ago. However, he is not in America anymore."

"Where does he live now?" I asked bewildered.

"If I recall rightly, he resides in a place just outside Bendigo; something with a catchy name. Not a name easily forgotten. Unfortunately, I can't for the life of me remember it, just at the moment. I'll get you his latest chart. That will have his address," Uncle Ken gently dislodges the cat as he stands, walks across the room and begins to rummage through the cupboard once more.

Peter asks, "Is it a place we may have heard of?"

With head down, Uncle Ken continues to search as he replies to Peter, "I doubt it, my lad. If my failing memory serves me correctly it's nearly equal distances from Adelaide, Sydney and Melbourne. Basically it is in the middle of nowhere. Far away from anything you could regard as modern civilization. I think that's what he likes about it. There are just a handful of locals who keep to themselves. It is an oasis with no prying eyes. It is a perfect location for someone with secrets to hide."

Why would he want to hide away from people? What questions is he afraid they will ask?

"Here it is. Oh no!" Uncle Ken exclaims as he looks at the envelope in his hand.

"What is it?" I ask as a sudden icy chill runs through my body from my shoulders, down through my veins, to the tips of my toes.

Uncle Ken turns to face me, the sadness obvious in his eyes. He holds the box in front of him so that I can see clearly the nature of the problem, "I'm sorry, Princess. I am so sorry that I can't help you any further. There doesn't appear to be an actual address. I guess that's his way of making sure the wrong people don't find him. Though we are living in more enlightened times than those of the Salem witch trials, people with outlandish views are still ridiculed and sometimes even persecuted for their strange beliefs."

I take the box from Uncle Ken's hand and examine the back in disbelief. The writing on the back reads simply:

Joe Hawkins

"What do we do now?" I ask, looking towards Peter for inspiration.

Peter shrugs his shoulders, "We'll work something out, Angel. We'll find him, somehow."

Joe lives in a small country town. Lots of bush and scrubland I suspect. No idea where beyond Bendigo it might be. Even if we find it, I'm sure there are plenty of spots known only to locals where someone can hide. How the hell do you find someone who doesn't want to be found?

"Here's the chart he sent at least," Uncle Ken declares as he holds aloft a massive volume of ragged pages. I feel the weight of the tome as he passes it to me. I place it gently on the coffee table. Opening it, I can see that it is made up of many interlocking charts. These charts list tens of thousands of people who all descend supposedly from the same common ancestor, Mary Murphy.

Flicking through the pages it appears very interesting, though hard to digest in just a few seconds. At a casual glance, I can't even see where it connects to us. "Can I borrow this for a bit?"

"Sure, take your time. I'm still not sure I believe it's true," Uncle Ken explains.

I nod my thanks as I sit there thumbing through this impressive work which obviously has taken years to research and document. It is impossible for a novice like me to know if it is accurate or not. However, I have an intuitive feeling spreading through my body. I smile as I remember the fortune teller imploring me to believe in my intuitions.

Maybe, maybe it is accurate. Maybe there is a link between me and this Mary Murphy.

Time will tell.

'Vengeance'

A murder committed,
A cruel death indeed,
By a devious witch,
Who paid no heed.

The tables are turned,
New plans are hatched,
Vengeance shall be swift,
As a pure life is dashed.

Chapter 4

March 15th 1692.

Salem, Massachusetts.

A blood stained knife spinning around with murderous intent, held by a small pretty hand in an otherwise pitch black room. A small patch of light is steadily growing from the center of the room. As this region of light grows larger and more intense Thomas is startled by Jane's lifeless body lying on a slowly spinning bed, floating effortlessly on nothingness. She looks at Thomas and outstretches a pleading hand silently before disappearing, submerged in an explosion of dark red blood. His heart races though he does not flinch. In fact he is unable to move a muscle let alone run from the gruesome scene playing out before his eyes.

An image far in the distance steadily comes to the forefront. At first it is hard to discern. Eventually its undeniable form is revealed. It is a hangman's noose, skillfully positioned around Mary's neck. She smiles at Thomas in a feeble gesture to reassure him that all is well. It fails to produce the desired effect. Suddenly Thomas and Mary are no longer alone. There is a crowd of strangers swarming around him, baying for blood, drowning out his futile protestations. He watches in horror as the masked hangman flicks the lever and Mary falls through a trap door. He tries to run to her. His feet remain glued to the earth before him. His muscles remain unresponsive. His path is blocked by the surging crowd. The more he fights, the further away the surging crowd takes him from his beloved Mary. He watches in horror as the image of Mary grows ever smaller. He watches her lifeless body sway at the end of a serviceable rope.

*   *   *

Thomas wakes with a start; heart pounding, body drenched in a cold sweat. With fear in his heart he glares straight ahead, eyes wide open. For a few moments he searches for salvation, an escape from the ghoulish images of the nightmares he has just dreamt. Slowly, as his eyes dart around the room in front of him, his panic eases. He comes to the realization that it is nothing more than a dream, a bad one at that. A subtle feeling of nausea begins to sweep through his body as his mind continues to wake. The dream has some basis in fact.

A headache reverberates in his skull, pounding out a regular and continuous beat. Thomas, groggy and sore, is well aware he is injured. He tries to reach up and touch the back of his head in order to assess the damage. He is certain his head must be cut. However, his attempt to self-assess his injuries is thwarted by the rope knots that bind his hands behind his back. As he struggles to free himself, the knots tighten, biting hard into his wrists, breaking the skin and drawing a little blood. His muscles relax as he reluctantly surrenders to his plight. He admits to himself that he is in a dire situation. It is particularly bad with what has happened and doubly so when he considers the uncertainty of the inevitable consequences that are yet to come. Thomas knows that his life and that of all of his family have been changed irrevocably in a matter of little more than a few minutes. One decision made in haste has resulted in everything he knows and loves to be lost. A tear rolls down his cheek as he thinks of his wife Mary.

"Don't worry thy self. We shall untie thee as soon as we take thy wife to town," Adam says. He sits on a chair opposite Thomas, backed against the far wall. He appears fairly calm though the tension is clearly visible in his stiff shoulders and posture. Too much tragedy has befallen his friends since Thomas and Mary first came unannounced to Jane and John's home. Adam is not about to lower his guard and grant Thomas any opportunity to add to the heartache. In Adam's arms lies the pitchfork. Resting gently, yet ready to be brought into action in an instant if it is warranted. Thomas bites his lip as he tries not to provoke his guard as Adam speaks once more, "We have no grudge with thee. Thou hath had naught to do with thy wife's bedevilment and foul deeds."

"Nay, she be not bedeviled, nor a witch. She be simply a soul who doth care, trying to save a helpless baby's life," Thomas pleads with his captor. He is under no false illusions. He knows Mary is in great danger and remains unconvinced that his safety is certain. He feels so pathetic that, at the time when Mary needs him most, he is unable to extradite himself from the ropes that bind him. His mind races as he searches for some way to escape.

Adam accepts not a word of this, "Nay, she be a witch and a murderess one at that. She shall be treated as such, tried fairly and justly before she be hung as all witches deserve to be. Thou will be blessed to be rid of her, as shall we all."

Thomas lowers his head as he considers Mary's torment and their years of struggle to remain hidden away from an overtly superstitious and mistrusting world. Mary's insistence that her visions are a calling has unnecessarily, in his eyes at least, increased the danger that surrounds all their lives. Her visions have brought them fair and square to this juncture; a day he has dreaded yet always feared would come to pass. Her insistence that she must save a precious unborn babe has cost the life of its tortured mother as well as shattering forever Thomas and Mary's precarious lives. A feeling of undirected hatred wells up from deep in his soul. His love for Mary remains unchanged. His anger is for his God in whom he placed so much faith to keep them all safe; a God which has seemingly forsaken them all in their desperate hour of need.

There is nothing Thomas can do. Slowly he raises his head again and looks around. Mary is lying on the floor, near the far wall, to the right of Adam. She lays prone, at an awkward angle, agony written all over her unconscious face. He can see her distinctive shot of grey in amongst her jet black hair, drifting down over her blood smeared face. He can see the deep cut across her cheek where blood continues to slowly flow from the wound caused by John's fist. Most of all he can see the undeniable beauty of the woman he still loves so much, even after all that has happened. The pain of not being able to reach her, to hold her, is unbearable. As his tattered mind struggles to form any sort of useful plan, tears well in his burning eyes. He remains frustrated that he is unable to help her in her time of greatest need. After all he has taken a solemn vow to always protect her from danger. As his mind dwells on this thought, the tears begin to spill forth from his eyes. With much sadness he lowers them again.

Outside the house John is overseeing the loading of Jane's body into the back of the tray hitched to two grey stallions. Seemingly he has regained his composure completely and is going about the process in a very matter of fact manner. John's mind remains focused on the process of loading his precious cargo. He attempts to block any thoughts of his beloved wife or her murder. It is the only way he can cope at this time. The horror of it all is too much to bear. One minute his wife is giving birth to their son, a truly joyous time. The next moment complete strangers arrive to extinguish all that has ever been important to him. His mind struggles to rationalize the situation as his hands shake violently. Several men are helping him, ensuring Jane is secure for the rough trip into town. Though it is an oft travelled road, the surface remains littered with pot holes and protruding rocks and boulders. The wooden wheels of the cart lack any suspension whatsoever.

Jane is wrapped from head to toe in a grey blanket bound with rope. Helen and John have taken great care that none of her skin is visible. They want to be as discreet as possible on their way into town. However, a sizeable blood stain is seeping through the blanket on one side. The shape of the package is also a problem. It clearly indicates a body is hidden within its fabric. They know full well that all their preparations will not fool anyone, not even the dullest of minds. Yet, they have to try and limit the chance of a commotion. John watches until Jane is safely loaded then he turns and walks back towards the house. He doesn't slow his step as he bends down and picks up a pail of water resting by the front door.

Striding into the house, he lifts the pail with his left arm, grasping the base with his right so he can tilt the bucket as he throws the cold water over Mary. Mary wakes with a start, her cotton dress drenched. She gasps for breath, shaken by the unexpected coldness of the water. She struggles for a second though soon realizes she is tightly bound. With venom burning from deep in her soul she stares up at John through her matted, unkempt hair.

"Good, thou still art alive. Thou can now be tried and hung as the witch thy art. Get to thy feet, evil beast!" John says dragging her crudely by the hair. Mary's face contorts in pain. She releases a muffled scream as she thrashes about, trying to free herself and thwart John's unwelcome advance. Thomas tries to protest though he is largely ignored. His captors remain unconcerned; they tied his knots, they know he is not in any position to help her until they choose to set him free. That is a choice Thomas fears they will be reluctant to make. His freedom only becomes a possibility once Mary is safely in the hands of the law in Salem. Thomas and Mary only have a fraction of a second to exchange sorrowful glances before Mary is pushed, stumbling, out the doorway of the house.

Adam walks towards Thomas who is straining for a better look at the view through the window. Placing a hand on his shoulder he encourages, "Don't worry. It shall all be over soon."

Thomas shakes his body vigorously, dislodging the hand from his shoulder. Comfort from the likes of Adam is the last thing in the world his heart desires. Thomas is silent as he watches the events unfolding outside with fear bulging in his heart. He begins to wonder if he will see Mary alive again. Maybe this is to be his final time.

Adam and Herbert climb up to the bench at the front of the wagon. John clambers into the tray next to his wife. Mary is standing on the ground, tied to the back of the tray with a long, sturdy rope, like a stray, rabid dog on a leash. She is as far away as practicable from both Jane and John. Herbert shakes the reigns, encouraging the horses to move forward. As the wagon begins to move something unexpected and extraordinary happens.

From out of the depths of the dense shrubbery at the edge of the track, a small black streak launches onto the back of one of the horses before leaping over Adam's shoulder as he ducks for cover. The startled horse rears and the wagon comes to a halt as Herbert struggles to regain control. John tries desperately to fend off the vile creature as it flies straight for his face. Jezebel succeeds in its goal of leaving scratch marks, gouged deep, into John's cheek. With a flurry of arms, John desperately fends the cat off, sending it tumbling towards the ground. Jezebel lands on her feet, taking a few proud steps before she comes to a halt, turning so she can watch John. She sighs deeply, trying to catch her breath. She savors her victory by sitting down and cleaning her fur like she is making preparations for the war that is to come. The cat is well aware that the battle to save her lifelong friend has only just begun. Jumping from the tray, John dispatches the cat back into the bush with a swift, running kick. Jezzie sails high into the air. Her paws flail vigorously as she tries to right herself in preparation for the inevitable fall. She lands awkwardly on a bush, scratched and bruised, pride dented somewhat. Regaining her composure quickly, Jezzie disappears into the undergrowth in order to clean her wounds and plan her next move. The cat remains hidden, yet is close enough to keep a watchful eye on proceedings. Jezebel knows in her heart that there is still hope that Mary can be freed, just not today.

John touches his cheek with his hand. He discovers his entire palm is covered in blood. He cusses under his breath. Pulling a kerchief out of his breast pocket he holds it to his face as he turns to face the wagon. He calls out to Adam as he points to Mary, "See that beast be the devil's familiar, come to help its evil master. Thou art a witch of the highest standing. There can be neither doubt nor uncertainty of the issue."

With this definitive statement concluded, he walks stridently towards an unsuspecting Mary. Coming from behind he delivers her a solid shove with his shoulder, sending her sprawling to the mud in the general direction of Salem. She regains her feet, filthy, glaring back at John just as the wagon begins to depart. The tension in the rope tightens rapidly and she is obliged to follow as it drags her along. John follows on foot, picking up a large stick. He flexes the stick, testing its tensile strength. He is believes that it will be perfect for encouraging Mary to continue walking later, when she begins to tire. He allows himself to grin at the prospect of dispensing some of his own justice as they process towards town. He knows whipping Mary will not bring his wife Jane back to life. However, it will provide John with much needed satisfaction that he is doing everything he can to defend her honor. As he walks he watches Mary closely, looking for the first stumble, waiting for justification to inflict some of his own punishment for her hideous crime.

And so Mary and John begin their long walk into town.

It rains for most of their journey. The road changes from patchy snow into a series of muddy puddles, seemingly increasing in depth as they walk onwards towards town. The mud sticks to the soles of Mary's shoes, weighing her down. Her feet are tired and blistered yet she does not take a break. She has felt the full force of the penalty for refusing to walk. Justice has been swift and bitter during their journey. John has made sure of that.

It takes nearly an hour for the procession to reach the outskirts of town. They begin to pass numerous homesteads which, collectively, make up the main township of Salem. Mary's back is torn and bruised from where John has belted her so many times in order to push her onwards. Her will to continue is waning yet somehow she finds the inner strength to continue on. She doesn't want John to see her weakening. Her resolve to prove her innocence and regain her freedom becomes stronger with every step.

As they reach the township, word spreads quickly that something is amiss. All the residents leave their houses and line the streets, scrambling for the best vantage points. They are horrified and dismayed at the scene that their eyes bear witness to. They know the package on the tray is a dead body; that has been confirmed by all the whispers and speculation exchanged along the road. Gossip and innuendo are the best ways to establish the nature of what is transpiring before their very eyes.

They wonder who has passed and what circumstances have occurred. They speculate as to how the death relates to the disheveled female prisoner bound and shuffling behind the wagon. As the procession passes each homestead the residents fall in behind, eager to see what is going to happen once they reach the town center. The high level of interest is understandable. There are no Theatres, no travelling carnivals which pass through town, no entertainment other than the drunken brawls just before closing time at the local saloon. For a quiet town like Salem, this is the only form of entertainment they have to savor.

When John and his crew finally reach the heart of town they are greeted by the mayor, Ewan McCormack. He has been alerted about the oncoming parade by one of the town's folk who has ridden at a gallop to raise the alarm. The mayor welcomes the warning wholeheartedly as it has provided him with sufficient time to conclude his business at 'Madame Bouvier's', a notorious house of ill repute, sprint home and adorn more regal attire. Standing on the town hall steps, he now looks resplendent in his mayoral robes, though a tad somber and a little afraid. He has heard the whispers to. In recent years there has been many witches come to light. This is different, however. None have been charged with murder before. The wagon comes to a halt at the mayor's feet. John gives Mary a solid shove with his boot to her backside, sending her face first into the mud.

"Thou be the image of evil most foul, the devil's loyal companion no less. Thy hath murdered my wife in order to deliver thy devil's spawn. The evidence be indisputable. Thee must pay for thy heinous crimes."

The gathering crowd watches as John moves over to the wagon and unties the rope around Jane's body. He unwraps her just enough to reveal her blood stained clothes and a pale, blood stained arm. The crowd gasps as one. Several women shield their children's eyes as they push them away from the horrific display.

John asks the crowd, "I ask thou, be there a one man or one woman who believes I doth not speaketh the truth? Let them speaketh now and declare me a prophet of falsehood."

The crowd stands silent in agreement. Their eyes, filled with fear and growing hatred, are steadily drawn towards Mary till all eyes are upon her.

Mary raises herself out of the mud and stands defiant, turning to stare at each and every person in the crowd individually. She dares not show the fear which overflows from her heart. Her goal is to let them see deep into her eyes, to look deep within her soul and gaze upon her innocence.

Mary knows the circumstantial evidence is bad. She must not only sway the judges, she must first sway the entire town. For if she fails to do so she knows she will hang till death comes to take her to a better place. The Elders are here for one purpose only. They are not here to ensure that justice is done. They are here to ensure the townsfolk feel happy and safe. Mary knows the occasional execution of a witch aids in the procurement of this harmony. Guilt or innocence is a trivial consideration.

In the bushes opposite the town hall, a pair of green eyes quietly watches everything as it unfolds. Mary spots Jezebel and is comforted. She is indeed a faithful companion. She cannot imagine how Jezzie could help her in her current predicament. At this point in time, that doesn't matter. Mary has always been safe while Jezebel has been by her side. At least Mary knows one thing for certain; she is not alone.

'Frailties of Mankind'

Words of Wisdom,

Frozen in time.

Simple yet confused,

Plentifully supplied.

If she scratches the surface,

Amazement she shall find.

She needs to delve deeper,

To discover the frailties of mankind.

Chapter 5

Sunday, February 26th, 2006.

Early Afternoon.

Heading towards Kinglake, Victoria, Australia.

The journey home to Kinglake is eerily quiet. Peter concentrates on the driving, staying completely silent for once in his life. I know he has a lot to say, though at this point in time, he has decided correctly that restraint is what is needed. This allows me to work my way through the massive chart, trying to decipher its long held secrets. I am oblivious to the landscape passing us by, totally captivated by the mysteries of the chart and the hidden skeletons of my family.

The chart, basically, is quite simple in its construction. Each person is connected to their parents and/or their children via a series of lines. Sometimes these lines just lead to a page number which, if followed, lead the reader to a location where the chart has sufficient room to expand to incorporate the next generation of descendants. Other pages outline succinctly the arrangement of the immediate family of that particular branch. The chart is written neatly in pen but occasionally little notes are penciled into the margins in grey lead. It is these tiny little amendments scrawled on the otherwise painstakingly crafted chart which intrigue me the most.

These notes are disturbing simply because of the language they use to describe the fate of the person shown at this location on the chart. Joe has used words such as 'suicide', 'murder' and 'accidental death' to explain how they have ultimately met their demise. All the extra notes involve incidents of tragedy, suspicion and, of course, death. I can only wonder if these notes refer to people who have experienced visions like me and have suffered as a consequence of being unwittingly discovered. The alarming fact is that Joe has written so many of these tiny notes on the chart. If these are indeed people he suspects experienced premonitions of the future, I am surprised there have been so many of us. I am also surprised there are no positive comments scrawled anywhere.

"We're here. Let's grab some lunch, I'm starving," Peter chimes, breaking my concentration.

I look up from the mountain of charts on my lap. Through bleary eyes I glance out through the windscreen at the familiar row of shops in front of us. I smile as I realize we are already back in the heart of Kinglake. We are finally home.

"Sure," I say as I bookmark and close the charts. I unbuckle my belt hurriedly, as my stomach growls its protestation in regards to my tardiness. Until now I was too preoccupied to notice I was ravenous.

Peter and I walk inside the Milk Bar cum Post Office, relieved to be surrounded by familiarity once more. The air seems so much sweeter here. I am looking forward to just lounging around, doing nothing, letting the madness of the last few weeks sink in slowly. My longing for normality will soon be quenched. I don't stay idle for too long.

"Hi Tony. How's it going?" Peter asks with genuine curiosity.

"No good Mr. Peter, no good at all. Very bad. Yes, very bad indeed," Tony says as a dark frown dominates his Asian features.

"What on earth's the matter?" I ask, bewildered by his obvious agitation. Tony is usually so cheerful and carefree. Such a sweet man who never fails to brighten my day with a second rate joke, that I have heard before, or a positive story he has heard on the news. In fact, I cannot recall any time when he has been upset by something. Sharing his problems with the world is not Tony's way.

"No good Miss Julie. You don't tell me, so how should I know? I can't know. I can't do much, no space. I can't do much at all. Big trouble, very big trouble indeed. She don't like it. No, she don't like it very much at all. Tony doesn't like it when she don't like it. No, no fun at all for Tony," he rants incoherently.

"Tony, Tony! Please take it easy. Calm down, man and tell us what the problem is. Maybe we can fix it?" Peter urges as he places a reassuring hand on Tony's shoulder.

"Mr. Peter, the trouble is here," Tony says excitedly as he points towards two large metal trunks lying behind the counter. The trunks take up most of the available space leaving only a narrow pathway through which Tony and his wife can shuffle through sideways. "No room for mail like this to be stored here. We need to be told and you didn't tell us."

"You mean someone posted these to us?" I ask as my brain begins to collate Tony's barrage of words into something that makes sense. I think I can see what the problem is.

"No Miss Julie. They are both posted to you, not Mr. Peter," corrects Tony, making sure the details of the matter at hand are correct. He has always been a stickler for details. "She not be happy, and Tony not happy if she not be happy. No good. Very bad indeed."

"Don't worry, mate," Peter tries to sooth as he moves behind the counter in order to get the first trunk out of the way. "We'll have these out of your way in a jiffy. Jeez, this one weighs a ton!"

Tony scurries to take the other end of the trunk. Between Peter and Tony they are able to drag the two trunks out to the car and, with much grunting, plonk them successfully in the boot. The car's suspension bounces under the burden of the excessive weight. The trunks are so large, it is impossible to close the boot. Peter ties the boot closed with a piece of bailing twine that he carries for such unexpected occasions as this. We do live in the country, after all.

Once they are both loaded, Tony's face begins to beam again. The weight on his shoulders has been lifted and he is back to his normal self, "She'll be very happy with Tony. Maybe Tony get very happy tonight too. Good, very good indeed."

"Too much information, mate," Peter says as he winks at me. "We'll catch ya later."

As we climb back into the car having forgotten our quest for food, Peter asks, "Do you have any idea what these trunks are all about?"

"Not the foggiest," I say wondering who might have sent them to me. The mystery that has become my life, takes another unexpected turn. I guess all I can do is hang on for the ride.

*   *   *

As we pull into our driveway, I catch a glimpse of Emma and Malcolm's house. I had only just met them when their premonition occurred. My mind recalls how the premonition terrified me to the core. I touched Emma's hand in my kitchen while she was enjoying a cup of tea. I was shocked to see the unnatural reaction this provoked. The ghost-like spirit of Emma disengaged itself and began pleading for mercy to the evil reflection of Malcolm her husband. I watched on helpless as the ghost Malcolm then abused and murdered his ghostly wife.

My actions in the days following this bizarre incident were both feeble and incompetent. I know my demeanor and words to the real Emma were received simply as madness, though I had to try. A tear forms in my eye now as I consider how I could have done more. I should have done more. I'm a little stronger now. Hopefully I won't make that mistake again.

Slowly I drift back to the real world, eyes fixed on the police tape that is still wrapped securely around the house; cordoning it off from the rest of the world. However, if the police tape were absent, there would be no evidence whatsoever from the exterior that a heinous crime has been committed here. It is simply a pleasant house nestled in the heart of a beautiful country town. From inside, it is a different story however. The large amount of blood on the floors and walls of the kitchen is testament to the evil which has been perpetrated there. As I look at the house, my mind plays a trick on me. I could swear that there is a woman peering out from behind one of the curtains; quite stupid really. My mind is still shaky. It will be a long time before I trust what I see.

I avert my gaze, feeling overwhelmed by a sensation that I failed to do enough. I let Emma down. There can be no denying that fact. Though how was I to know that the murder-suicide was going to actually happen and happen so soon? My mind is shrouded in fog. I find no answers as to how I might have been able to satisfactorily resolve this situation. I know the death of both Emma and Dr. Khan will haunt me for the rest of my life. I am certain of that. This is what inspires me to learn more, to understand these visions and what they are all about. I cannot carelessly stand idle and let someone else die.

Peter parks the car as close to the house as he can. It takes both of us to drag each of the trunks down the pathway, to the front porch, over the two steps and into the front hall. We don't bother to drag them any further, they are simply too heavy. I think it is only prudent to see what contents are stowed inside before I decide whether or not I will be unpacking them. The most likely situation is that they have been sent to the wrong person. If that is the case, then the trunks need to be as close as possible to the car so they can be returned to sender.

I stand upright, stretching my tight back muscles while catching my breath. There is nothing on the trunks to identify where they have come from, not even a clear postage mark on the plethora of stamps. The only writing on each of the trunks is the postal address to me, at this address.

I guess whatever happens, they won't be going back to the sender.

"Mystery number one is who these trunks are from? Were you expecting someone to send you something?"

I shake my head, "No, not really. No, I don't think that is something I can answer without opening them first. Anyway, mystery number two is where are the keys that open these locks?"

"I think I can help with that one," Peter laughs, "Have you forgotten?"

"What are you talking about?" I ask, not following his line of thought.

"You were sent a couple of strange keys before we left. Maybe......"

"Yes, of course. There was a note too," I call out as I rush into the kitchen. Searching through the junk in the fruit bowl on the bench, I quickly reclaim the mysterious envelope and its contents. "Here it is!"

I tip the opened envelope so that the contents fall neatly into the open palm of my hand.

Two old fashioned keys! They must be a match. They look to be of the same vintage.

"We need to read the note again too. It might make more sense now," Peter suggests.

"Of course," I say as I pull the note free and begin to read it once more. I smile as I read the words out loud. The first paragraph makes perfect sense now. However, the second and third paragraphs remain, very much, an unsolved mystery.

The note reads:

'Sorry for not sending these earlier, what was I thinking? Anyway I hope you enjoy the treasure, it should help to answer your questions.

P.S. If you want to meet me, just follow the signs.

At the Bendigo Safeway you will find an interesting ad for a Pet Rock on the notice board. I would highly recommend that you purchase this item as it will answer some of your questions.

Bye,

Joe.

"Do you think........?" Peter asks incompletely, after reading the note from over my shoulder.

I nod vigorously, "I do indeed. I think somehow these trunks must have been sent by the mysterious American, Joe Hawkins whom Uncle Ken was talking about. I believe they contain something important, something vital. I know it is all a bit weird, yet I feel the contents of these trunks are of the utmost importance in discovering what is happening to me."

"Well there's only one way to find out," Peter says determinedly, snatching the keys from out of my hand before moving towards the first trunk.

"Hey!" I protest feebly. I don't really care which of us opens the trunks, just as long as they are opened and hopefully have some of the answers I am seeking. However, my curiosity is aroused and I can't stand the thought of Peter playing one of his games with me, denying me access to something which I know is bound to help my cause. After all, Joe has no reason to know I exist let alone that I am experiencing visions. However, he does appear to know both these things and I suspect so much more. I believe the contents of the trunks will help quench my thirst for knowledge.

To my relief Peter turns the key in the first lock. It clicks loudly, heralding the forthcoming unveiling of the trunk's contents. He motions for me to stay back. I am confused by his gesticulations.

"But...." I protest.

Peter refuses to stand for my lip, "Look, we don't know this guy or what makes him tick. Uncle Ken says he is a crackpot. That family tree documents many people dying in dubious ways. I just want to be careful in case something dangerous is in here. Joe's motives for sending these trunks to you may not be honorable. Can you understand where I am coming from?"

Makes sense, dammit! I hate it when he is right. I am always the bull at the gate. Peter is always the calm and rational one. I guess together we make the perfect couple.

I stand back in an area of the hall which, I presume, is a safe distance away as Peter slowly opens the lid and peers inside. I can't see a thing from my vantage point. He opens the lid just enough so that he can see a little of the trunks contents. He looks confused as he reaches in and begins rummaging amongst the items inside.

"What is it Peter?" I ask, dying to see what the mystery contents are. "Can I come closer?"

"Well this might be the answer to all your questions. However......"

I struggle to contain my elation, though I remain a little cautious due to Peter's cryptic words, "What's the problem?"

"Well, it just might take you a little while to find the answers if the other trunk is anything like this."

Peter opens the lid fully as he stands back, providing me with a clear, unobstructed view. The trunk is completely full to the brim with hundreds of cassette tapes, videos, scrap books and journals.

"Oh my," I say, shocked at the size of the secret library exposed.

"Oh my, indeed," says Peter as he opens the second trunk to reveal it is similarly laden.

I look at the contents of both trunks, then back at the note. Pointing at the note I suggest, "Well, I guess I have no choice other than to go and buy that Pet Rock in Bendigo. I hope it will be a short cut to the truth. If not, this is going to take a while."

"I guess you're right," Peter smiles. "It may speed things up a little, though I have no idea how it is going to help. It's just a stupid kids toy after all."

I don't have a clue either. It just feels like the obvious next step. If not, I am in for the long haul wading through all this information Joe has so graciously provided me.

'Somewhere'

A journey seldom travelled,

To a place oft' missed,

To speak with a lost soul,

Pay attention young miss.

For his hair be grey and thin,

His mind feebly flawed,

His conversation fractured,

But his words say so much more.

Chapter 6

Monday, February 27th, 2006.
Early Morning.
Kinglake, Victoria, Australia.

Wrestling with my present, combined with visions of the future made sleep impossible last night. My plan was to go to bed early and get a good night's sleep in order to prepare for the long drive I have ahead of me this morning. Unfortunately, I can't rely on Peter's help for this one as he has work commitments he can't avoid. After all, we need an income coming in still, first and foremost.

My plan was on schedule at 8 P.M. last night when I showered quickly before slipping on my silk nightie and sliding beneath the covers. Peter had decided to sleep on the couch so that he could stay up late watching television without disturbing me when he finished. His 'B' grade horror films are of no interest to me. It was about 8.20 P.M. when everything started to go wrong.

I woke with the now familiar splitting pain in my chest. Armed with the knowledge that I wasn't suffering a life threatening heart attack, I tolerated the pain. I sat bolt upright, searching the room for anything out of the ordinary. My symptoms assured me that I was in the middle of a vision. I just needed to deduce what elements in my room were real and what weren't.

Senses all heightened and activated, I could readily smell the putrid smoke drifting through my bedroom. My head swings towards the window in response to a sound. My heart pounds as I think I hear a child weakly pleading for help. There is a sound like an animal rustling in the bush as a fine misty spray touches my face. Licking my lips I can tell it is pure, fresh water.

I hear a familiar thud as something lands on the floor before rolling to a halt by the wall. I don't look over to this spot. I know in my heart it must be a severed and bloodied finger, just like before. I don't need to see that again. A blood curdling scream roars through the room as the walls shudder. It dissipates as quickly as it begins. I recognize the mournful voice clearly; I have no doubts about this, whatsoever. It can only be one person. I am certain it has to be me, even though I remain silent.

Can I have premonitions about myself? Is the severed finger mine? Or is there something more sinister to befall my person in due course? What of the little girl? Who is she? How can I help her without any decent clues as to her identity or whereabouts?

I have no answers, just a bucket load of fears.

I sit, wide eyed for a few minutes, trying to watch carefully for the next clue. Finally, I realize the pain has disappeared and the visions have ceased. I shake my head; the visions make absolutely no sense to me. How can I possibly help if I don't have the foggiest idea what I am to help with? I just hope the trip to Bendigo will be more fruitful. At the very least it may allow me to access some assistance from the mysterious Joe Hawkins in regards to interpreting these strange visions.

It is now about 7.30 A.M., the day after the night before. I check my watch as I prepare to leave Kinglake. I have stirred for half the night, tossing and turning, trying to get that annoying vision out of my head. I am tired, though well prepared for my journey. Water bottle in holder, some grapes, a couple of apples and a sandwich packed for lunch. My plan is to reach Bendigo initially and discover the meaning behind the cryptic clue about a 'Pet Rock'. I have a nagging feeling that, considering how secretive and strange Joe appears to be, my journey might go well beyond Bendigo before I have an opportunity to meet him. There is no rational basis for this feeling, just an intuitive guess. I think Bendigo might be too populated for his liking, from what I have thus established. I suspect Joe likes to be left alone.

The sun at my back, shadows across the road flickering through the windscreen, I join the McIvor Highway at Kilmore. Initially I am heading towards Heathcote, then onto my ultimate goal; Bendigo. The landscape on the horizon is barren, dry and rocky with mangy looking sheep scattered here and there trying to scratch out some sustenance where there isn't much except dust.

Thinking ahead, I stowed a handful of cassette tapes from the first trunk as I exited the house this morning. It is going to be a long and lonely road trip. I hope they will aid my cause by increasing my knowledge base as I go. I desperately hope they explain precisely the nature of what I am experiencing and offer advice on how best to deal with it. I hope they will provide me with useful information on how to use the visions to help not only myself but others to overcome impending, dire consequences. At the very least the cassettes should provide some interest and company as I travel along the endless, isolated country roads which lead to Bendigo.

The first cassette reads:

Tape number one.

No better place to start.

Fumbling, one handed, I remove the cassette easily from its case and push it into the slot under my radio. It has been an eternity since I last played a cassette in the car, so long that I am unsure that the machine still works. I have a feeling the last cassette I tried to play, something by 'Goanna', was chewed up by the machine. If I remember right, it took me an hour to prize it loose. The tape was unsalvageable. I hope the fate of this cassette is a little brighter. It is too valuable a commodity to simply be damaged beyond repair by an old, poor quality, sound system. Unfortunately, the dodgy cassette player in my car is the only system I own which will play these old fashioned recordings.

I glance at the tape player as I drive along, trying to establish if there is a button I have to push in order to change it over from radio to cassettes. My fears for the cassette's safety grow as no recorded sound emanates from the system. I can hear the machine spinning its reels frantically, though still no sound is produced.

Please work. Don't chew up the tape. Please don't chew it up.

"Hello," screams the tape deck unexpectedly. I turn the volume down a little so that it is at a tolerable level. The gravely, adult voice continues, "These tapes were originally done on a large reel tape recorder. I have had them converted to cassettes for two reasons. One, I think it is vital that I provide an accurate account of what has occurred to me during my lifetime. It may be of benefit to others in a similar position. These recordings were my first real attempt to record my thoughts and detail exactly what was going on back then. The second reason is that they hopefully provide accurate information about what to expect on your journey. If you are listening to these tapes now I know you are experiencing the same sort of visions as me, otherwise I would not have sent you all this information."

I can't believe it, I should have guessed. Joe has visions too. That is why he is so interested in others with similar experiences. But how did he know I was having visions too? Has he seen this in his visions? Am I in his visions? No, perish the thought. Anyway, I am relieved I am not alone.

As if Joe is hearing my thoughts he answers promptly, "You may be wondering how I found you. Don't forget, I have visions too. I have had visions for a very long time now. I know how to use them in order to gain the information I need. Finding you was easy. I wish someone had sent me a record such as this, it may have helped. No, that is not right. It definitely would have helped. I wouldn't have made such a great hash of things as I have. History would see me in a completely different light."

The voice on the tape pauses for a second. You can hear his breathing on the tape as he adjusts something before continuing, "Anyway, I hope you have more luck with your visions than I had with mine. Oh, I must apologize for the sound quality. It wasn't that great on the originals either."

The tape falls silent once more. There is a click, like a machine being turned on or off. This is followed by static at a quieter level. I wait patiently for the tape to begin, wondering what it is that I am about to hear. Eventually I can hear a faint, though indistinct voice mumbling through the speakers. I turn the volume up slightly as I try to decipher what the boy is saying.

"Testing one, two, three. Testing one, two, three."

The young, uncertain voice stops speaking prior to the sound of two more clicks. Listening closely it sounds just like the recording machine has been turned off then back on for some reason. Finally words start to flow, "I ..... I wanted to record what is happening. Oh, by the way, I'm Joey Hawkins. I'm thirteen. I play junior baseball and I .... I ...... I have strange dreams."

Passing through Heathcote I can see Gaffney's Bakery and Cafe. This quaint little store has a prominent notice in the window indicating that they have won 'Best Country Bakery- Pie Section', for the last three years. I'm sure they have nice chocolate éclairs and cheese cakes too. My mouth salivates with the notion of it. However, my will power is strong. I have a long way to go and plenty of supplies of healthier food, if I need them.

I check my watch; 9 A.M. Taking a swig from my bottle of water I continue through the quiet town of Heathcote and beyond, passing the odd homestead and a few more scrubby trees identical to the ones that have lined my journey thus far.

The voice of young Joey continues to recount his story, ".......I'll keep these tapes secret, just for me. No one else would understand, anyway. How could they? My dreams are so strange. My story sounds insane. However, I know in my heart, if I think it sounds insane then it probably isn't. That's how it works doesn't it? I don't want to be locked up. I'm a good kid. I go to church every Sunday. I only skip the service every now and then to go rabbiting with the lads. I don't want to be shocked by high voltage. I've seen movies where they do that. I know I'm not mad......."

I shake my head and ponder this poor boy's predicament. The kid is trying to deal with something he has no credible information about. He can't talk to friends or relatives about it either for fear of being ostracized and condemned as insane. His only choice is to clarify his thoughts by recording them for posterity. His only confidante is his recording device, which he keeps hidden in a darkened bedroom so as not to be vilified by those who could not possibly understand. For God's sake the poor boy knows that no one will understand. As an adult these visions are a challenge and then some. As a child they would be nothing short of a nightmare. I am inspired just thinking about the fact that Joe has battled through his early teenage years and somehow found a way to survive to enjoy (probably not the right choice of words) a long, productive life.

"……. my dream the other night was simple. Though I swear, as God is my witness, that I was wide awake. It seemed so real, like it was happening before my very eyes, though I know that none of it was real. I saw the incident clearly. It looked like someone was hit by a car while trying to cross for school. I couldn't work out who it was or any details about the car. I guess it's not important; after all it's just a strange dream. Nothing to worry about…….."

The sign on the road reads 'Axedale' though as far as I can see it is an uneventful town at best. There are very few homesteads, lots of vacant paddocks and only a handful of scrubby trees. It is certainly nothing to write home about. In fact, I can see no reason why anyone would ever want to stop here, not even for a break. I continue to focus on the road ahead as the tape keeps playing.

"……. I had the same dream last night, third time this week. This was different to the other two. I could see the victim clearly for the first time. To my relief it was Gordon. Not that I want anything to happen to my brother, not at all. It's just that he is in Canada on a scholarship and will not be back in town for six months. That makes my dream complete and utter rubbish. It will never become real. I can now sleep a little easier at night…….."

I slow down to fifty miles per hour as I enter Junortoun. At least there seems to be a bit more life in this town. There are a couple of houses being built which indicates that new people have some interest in living here, though I know not why. I would not like to live out here even though the tranquility would aid my writing. Not long now for Bendigo, maybe only fifteen minutes. I can't wait to reach some sort of semblance of civilization once more.

"…….I have had the dream again, that is every night this week, so far. It is the same each time I have this dream. I feel a sharp stabbing pain in my chest which eases with time as the dreams fade. I don't know why. Anyway, I don't take any notice of the dream. I have heard that if dreams repeat themselves over several nights, they are likely to come true. I don't know if that is true or not. I read so many different things. I just don't know what I should believe anymore. However, I know my brother is in Canada and completely safe; he is nowhere near my school. The dreams are different each time, anyway. Sure the event, location and timing all seem similar. However, each time I see the event take place it is from a different angle. Surely that must break the rules; surely the dreams have no chance of becoming true……."

I enter Bendigo as I switch off the tape player. I always get confused here and today is no exception. I pass the prominent Dragon restaurant three times before I get my bearings. Finally, I find the Safeway supermarket mentioned in Joe's note and pull into its spacious car park.

It takes me just a few minutes to find the appropriate card on the message board, in amongst the hundreds of other notices on the long foyer wall. As I have suspected, Joe is not about to make it easy for me to find him. Holding the notice in my hand, I read it several times trying to decipher its meaning. It reads:

Pre-loved, rotating 'Pet Rock' for sale. Suitable for children. Preece Street, St. Arnaud.

I take the note with me and head swiftly back to the car. My intuition has proved correct. I knew without a shadow of a doubt that my journey wouldn't finish at Bendigo. I just wonder how far I will have to travel in order to find Old Joe. I pray I can successfully work out all the riddles he will leave. I'm positive there will be more. Playing his game is the only way I can follow the flimsy trail that leads to him.

My fear is that I have begun to follow a paper trail which may only lead to a dead end. After all, this could be Joe's peculiar way of trying to send an unwanted visitor on a wild goose chase. Somehow I don't think this is the case. If this was his plan all along, I don't think he would have gone to all the effort of making contact with me and sending me all those journals to wade through. My only real question at this point, is what does that damn riddle mean?

At least I have a street address.

*   *   *

"…….The dreams continue. I don't know how many times now; maybe thirty or more. Each time the pain in my chest occurs until the dream ends. The dreams have become very vivid. In the last one I could see the lines of pain across my brother's face as he lies dying in the gutter. I don't see any reason to let my brother or my parents know about my dreams. My brother is still safe in Canada. I just want them to think I am normal though I know there is something wrong with me. I know I am not mad. I am not sure anyone else would agree if they saw the world through my sad eyes……"

11.35 A.M.; an hour and forty five minutes since Bendigo. I pass the sign leading into St. Arnaud. Reaching for the tape player once again I switch it off. The tapes seem very repetitive and lack any useful detail at this early stage. Maybe they will reveal more as I delve further into them.

Driving slowly, I look around at my surroundings, watching for the only piece of definite information I have in my possession; a location,

Preece Street to be precise. I have no luck with my visual search. I sigh as I realize just how useful a country street directory would be at this present time. I decide to fuel up, as I see the Junction Roadhouse come sailing into view. My car has a little under half a tank left. I decide not to take a chance. There is such a large distance between the towns out here and who knows, I may still have a long journey to travel. That is, of course, if I can only locate where Preece Street is.

"Fill her up luv?" says the attendant walking over to greet me as he wipes his greasy hands on a tired old rag. He is dressed in full length blue overalls, skinny to the point of anorexia, looks about eighty years old and walks with a decided limp favoring the right side. He has a pleasant smile which reveals half the teeth are missing from his mouth. Despite his obvious signs of age and decay from living a hard life, it impresses me that he still has a spring in his step. It is so refreshing to get a bit of old fashioned personal service from a petrol station attendant. I don't mind a bit of courtesy every now and then.

"That would be great, unleaded thanks."

"Unleaded it is, Miss," he says as he inserts the hose into the tank, locking it on. He begins to squeegee my windshield as he asks casually, "Anything else I can do for ya today, Missy?"

"Well actually there is. You see I'm following a bit of a treasure hunt and my next clue should be at Preece Street. Would you happen to know where that might be?" I ask, hoping to speed up my search with a bit of local knowledge.

The attendant laughs as he disengages the hose from my car. His wizened features seem to unexpectedly experience great delight from my simple request, "That'll be forty three dollars for the fuel and fifty for the information."

I am completely flabbergasted at the audacity of this man, charging for a simple piece of information. It is not like he has to do anything taxing to meet my simple request. I'm sure he knows this town like the back of his cracked and gnarled hands. However, at this point in time, I know I need to find this road and find it quickly. I don't know how much more travelling is required and I don't want to use up all the available daylight. I have no idea how many more clues there will be and I can ill afford to be bogged down on this one. I reluctantly pull the ninety three dollars out of my purse.

The attendant laughs again as he takes forty three dollars, leaving the fifty in my hand, "I always say them city folk have no sense of humor at all, none at all. They wouldn't know a gag if it jumped up and bit 'em on the behind. Ha! Got ya good, Missy. If you turn around a little ya will find Preece Street is right across the road there, running next to the Rotary Park. Have ya self a nice day, Missy," he says as he turns and saunters back towards his office, shaking his head mumbling to himself in between snickers.

I look across the road in disbelief; Preece Street is clearly in view, just the other side of the Rotary Park. I wonder if that's the 'rotating' part of the riddle. Looking at the card again I see the words 'suitable for children' and smile.

A park with play equipment is suitable for children. I wonder if there is a rock.

Clambering back into the car, I rev the engine the short distance over to the park coming to a halt in a cloud of dust and loose stones. Instantly I can see a large rock in the distance with some sort of plaque imbedded in it, just near some of the play equipment. Walking over to it, the plaque seems to provide no information or clues at all.

A dead end! But wait....

I decide to check the large boulder more closely. I walk around to the back of the rock scouring every part of its surface with my eyes. It doesn't take long before I notice some graffiti written on the rough surface with some sort of permanent marker. I inspected the graffiti more closely. Taking a pen out of my back pocket, I jot the words onto the back of the card from the supermarket. The graffiti reads:

Stop and grab some chocolate cookies at the wizard of crays in Donald.

I sigh. This must be another clue from Joe. After all there is no conceivable reason why anyone else would write such a sentence on a rock in a park in the middle of nowhere.

More riddles. More travel. At least I am one step closer. How many more clues are there before I reach Joe?

I walk slowly back to the car, ready to continue my journey, wondering what Donald has in store for me.

Why can't he just leave a phone number or an email address like a normal person, for God's sake?

*   *   *

An hour later, it is with a feeling of great trepidation that I arrive on the outskirts of Donald. This feeling is, however, short lived as I notice something that catches my full attention instantly. I hit the brakes, coming to a complete stop in another cloud of dust, as I pass a series of silos near the rail line. Looking in my rear vision mirror I can see there is no traffic behind me. I throw the car into reverse and slowly move backwards until I can clearly read the weathered metal signs to my right.

I pull the card out of my pocket and read the clue again:

Stop and grab some chocolate cookies at the wizard of crays in Donald.

I smile as I unbuckle my seatbelt and alight from the car. Towering before me are two signs. One is for Kooka's Cookies; I'm sure they must have chocolate ones. Their reputation for quality biscuits has reached the big city. The second sign is the one I am more interested in. It isn't, as I anticipated, for 'the wizard of crays' but rather for something that still fits the bill; 'Oz Crays'. Reaching the other side of the road I scan the old battered sign for further clues. Down near the bottom of the sign I spy exactly what I am looking for; another piece of graffiti written on the metal in small print with some sort of permanent, black marker. I write the new message hurriedly, using some more of the dwindling space on the card. The graffiti reads simply:

Don't be two cowardly at Warracknabeal.

I smile to myself as I trudge off, back to the car, in order to continue my quest.

At least his clues tell me exactly which town I need to go to next. I must be thankful for small mercies.

*   *   *

Arriving in Warracknabeal, approximately an hour later, I decide to park and have some lunch. I park at the main intersection and survey the shallow landscape before me; just a few houses, a service station and a deserted road leading onwards and away from town. I stand outside my car, lunch laid out, picnic style, on the hood. Popping a grape into my mouth, I decide my first course of action is to phone Peter and let him know how I'm going. As I flick my phone open I wonder if he is starting to worry. After all, I have been gone for a while now.

No reception. That would be right!

I free the sandwich from its wrapper and devour it, enjoying the humble flavors within. The thought of chocolate cookies at Donald has sent my taste buds into frenzy. I have been strong. I have done the right thing. I made the correct decision to continue on my journey without a quick detour to the cookie place. Though now, an hour later, I could eat a cow, I am so hungry.

Sandwich gone, I glance around, looking at what the town has to offer.

Not much. I assume the 'cowardly' reference is another clue with a 'Wizard of Oz' slant. However, there are certainly no lions roaming the streets as far as I can see. Think. Where should I look? Where would a town like this have a lion?

The service station shows some promise. However, all the other clues have been hidden away from where people are congregating. I need a sign of some sort. After all, that is his chosen method for delivering his messages. Directly across the road from the service station, I focus my attention on a sign with numerous plaques attached to it. From where I am standing, I can only see the plain back of the sign. Munching on an apple, I carefully walk across the deserted road so that I can gain a better look at what is on the other side.

Facing the sign I begin to smile. I pull the card from my pocket and read the last clue aloud, "Don't be two cowardly at Warracknabeal. So your grammar is correct! There are two lions, at least, in this town."

To my relief there is a Lions Club sign amongst the plaques. On this sign is the image of two lion's heads. I quickly check out the back of the sign and, sure enough, another clue is found without outlaying any strenuous effort. This one asks:

Where would Dorothy and Toto go?

What an odd clue?

I know this clue has to relate to the 'Wizard of Oz' fixation that Joe seems to have, though I am not immediately clear as to what he wants me to do. Unlike the other clues, there is no town mentioned this time. Does he want me to travel back to Donald again? Surely not, that would be a complete waste of time. Why would Joe send me all the way out to Warracknabeal, a two hour return trip, if I was already in the right town an hour ago? The clue makes no sense at all. Donald can't be the right answer.

Think. Think damn it! Where would Dorothy and Toto go?

On the face of it, the question seems simple enough. However, the answer doesn't lead to a town. Not one that I know of anyway. Dorothy and Toto would go back to Kansas if they had their way, though that doesn't make much sense in the current circumstances. There is no town called 'Kansas' in Victoria. I doubt very much that there is a town of that name anywhere in Australia. If he is living in Kansas, America I can't see why he has chosen to drag me out to country Victoria. This can't be right either. Dorothy and Toto would go somewhere but where. Somewhere......somewhere.......somewhere.......

That's it!

I smile smugly as I look at the road sign outlining the towns ahead. It informs me bluntly that the town of Rainbow lies somewhere over the horizon in front of me.

Dorothy and Toto would surely go to Rainbow.

I finish off the last few bites of my apple as I walk briskly back across to the car. Throwing the core into the grass by the road, I climb behind the wheel and continue on my way.

How many more clues? I must be getting close.

       *   *   *

I watch the Willy Willy dance across the barren paddocks as I drive along the shimmering road at a steady pace. The homesteads, complete with large silos attached, are more frequent now, indicating I am nearing some sort of regional hub. This region appears to be supported largely on the back of wheat production and the like. I can see a town looming in the distance on the horizon, drawing nearer by the second.

Rainbow is a revelation. It appears like a mirage on the horizon. At first it seems to be a small, insignificant town. Though, as I draw nearer, I can clearly see it is much larger than first impressions would suggest. Hundreds of houses greet me as I head steadily towards the town center. I wonder what can sustain so many people, this far out, in the middle of nowhere. Maybe the wheat produces numerous off shoot industries such as rail transport and mechanical engineers. Maybe it is just another country town living on the edge; a farming town which is losing its youth to the better paid jobs of the cities. It looks like a farming town that might only be two bad droughts away from being a ghost town.

As I enter the main street, it strikes me as likely that there is another reason why the town of Rainbow survives; tourism. A giant rainbow arch dominates the street divide as it welcomes visitors to the town. Amazing murals of scenes representing the farming and rail history of the town are painted on some of the building walls. There appears to be a nice selection of cafes and gift shops scattered along the street. Enough of a sprinkling to encourage even the most weary of travelers to alight and stretch their legs, at least for a little while. Visitors will never find themselves parched thanks to the two pubs which both seem to be well patronized. A large sign proclaims that the annual 'Tractor Festival' will occur, as usual, in three weeks, no doubt causing the town to be overrun with tourists and their money. Overall, Rainbow exudes a first impression of being a nice, sleepy little country town where you can escape from the world for a while.

Maybe this is a place where someone like Joe could hide from the world, but where? Where would he hide?

I lock the car as I get out, wondering where I should start my search for the next clue. The last clue was so vague, after all. A car slows down and the driver beeps his horn. I turn and see the three occupants of the Ute wave their Akubra hats and smile as they pass by.

How friendly is that! *I wonder if all the locals do that to greet the tourists. My choice of clothes must make me look like a tourist.*

I move to the central park and the giant rainbow arch which welcomes people to the town. This incredible display must be a beacon to all tourists who pass through town. I wonder how many cheesy photos have been taken in front of this rainbow. I believe this is probably my best bet for finding the next clue for two reasons. Firstly, considering the last clue's vague reference to rainbows, this is the obvious spot in town. Secondly, all

the recent clues have led to signs with graffiti written on their reverse side.
I nod as I walk across the road.

The next clue must be here!

As I enter through the tiny gate which divides either side of the
immaculately trimmed box hedge, I consider I must be close. The arch
before me is about twelve foot high and highly colorful, depicting the
colors of the rainbow in all their majestic glory. I spot something obvious
that I didn't notice as I first drove in. It is a touch I should have expected
from a town that seemingly prides itself on being a friendly tourist Mecca.
At the bottom of one end of the rainbow rests a simple bucket, attached by
a hook to the base of the rainbow. The bucket is painted gold.

Ha! There's always a pot of gold at the end of the rainbow.

I walk briskly over to the bucket, my heart beating fast with anticipation
of the next clue. To my disappointment I find the bucket is empty, there are
no messages here. My eyes scan the front of the sign, then the back. Still
no messages. I stand, hands on hips trying to work out what should be my
next step. I bite my bottom lip, confused.

The clue should be here. Where else could it be?

"Can I help you," comes a craggy old voice from behind me. I turn,
startled that someone has crept up behind me while my attention has been
fully focused elsewhere. "Oh, sorry, I didn't mean to scare you miss, you
just look a little lost. I thought you may be in need of some assistance."

I regain my composure quickly and smile at the old man standing in
front of me. It is hard to gauge his exact age. He looks to be about eighty
or so, with his slightly hunched back, grey thinning hair and weathered
facial features. He seems so frail though I have a niggling inclination that
he is much younger than his image would attest; maybe sixty five or so. I
just can't shake my first impression that life has been hard on this man and

taken a heavier toll than the normal ravages of time. It is an odd judgment to make. I normally don't give any credence to meaningless first impressions such as this.

With the dilemma of having no more clues to aid my search for Joe, I feel there is no other choice other than to be direct. There is nothing wrong with my hearing. My ears pricked up immediately on hearing the undeniable American twang to the Old man's accent, as he spoke. I consider the notion that this weather beaten man before me is the bloke I'm looking for.

"Yes, I'm hoping you might be able to help me. I'm looking for an American chap who might live around here," I begin, watching his facial expressions for any tell-tale signs that will give his identity away. I don't expect, after all the hoops I have had to jump through, that Joe is just going to identify himself readily to a perfect stranger.

Emotionless he places both hands on his walking stick as he leans in for support. His body language shows no inkling of surprise, fear or tension. The old man maintains his composure impeccably as he calmly asks, "Really, and by what name does this mysterious man go by?"

I don't know whether or not he is toying with me, he is a hard one to read. I decide to play along with the game, if that is what this is, and just see where it leads, "Joe Hawkins. I need to talk to him about a matter most urgent."

"Well, well," he says as he stares at the ground in front of his worn leather boots while he considers his words carefully. "I don't think anyone's asked about that silly, old bastard in years; maybe never. I think you've wasted your time. Maybe you've been misinformed. I don't think that old fart is of any damn use to anyone, these days."

I am most surprised that the old man isn't Joe himself. I had convinced myself that it was too much of a co-incidence to find an American man of about the right age lurking around Rainbow, the town where the clues appear to have stalled. He certainly fits the image I had developed in my mind. However, I like the tone in his voice and the fact that, at the very least, he knows something about Joe. Maybe he is a friend, considering they are both originally from America. I have to pray he knows how to contact him. He is my only hope at this present time.

"Do you know Joe?" I ask excitedly.

"Of course, everyone knows that old fool. A bit of a loner, keeps to himself. A bit of a hermit you might say. What would a pleasant young thing like you want with a dried up old prune like that?"

I smile as I warm to the man's colorful take on the English language, "I can't tell you that. It's a personal matter between Joe and me. I hope you can understand where I am coming from. I don't mean to cause any offence."

He looks intently at me with a piercing gaze. For a brief moment, I am a little ill at ease with his scrutiny. I guess he is trying to unravel the mystery of the connection between Joe and me. Maybe he thinks I'm a long lost daughter, or granddaughter depending on how the case may be. Maybe his mind is trying to evaluate whether I am friend or foe. After all, Joe may have acquired the unwanted attention of many people wanting to do him wrong because of his visions over his long life's journey.

He pauses, waiting for me to continue. Finally he chooses to speak instead, "Well, fair enough then. A man should know not to pry into the business of a lady, particularly when it is personal. If you want Old Joe, I had better take you to him, hadn't I? Follow on little lady, follow on."

He begins to stagger towards the gate, hobbling heavy on his walking stick. Watching his legs bow in his corduroy trousers as he awkwardly shuffles, I offer, "My car's over here if we need to drive?"

He doesn't break his slow stride for a second as he beckons for me to follow, "You can do what you like, my girl, but his place is just behind this garage on the other side of the road here. Myself, I would prefer to walk on a beautiful day such as this."

The garage across the road is an old weatherboard building which appears derelict, completely boarded up. It is weather beaten, desperately in need of some tender renovation and a fresh coat of paint. The image it portrays is that of an abandoned building of little or no interest to anyone, anymore. My mind races with the thought that this would be the perfect place for a hermit to live in pursuit of his quest to be left alone. I catch up to the old man quickly and continue my questioning, "Have you known Joe very long?"

He peers over his thin, metal rimmed glasses as he gives me a sideways, disapproving glance. I sense he is uncomfortable with all my talk. Abruptly he says, "Too damn long. In fact it feels like I have known him a lifetime."

"So you're not friends?" I ask, undaunted by his reluctance to converse. I am not ashamed that I am a busy body, trying to gain as much information as I possibly can before I meet Joe. Any snippet of information I can pry free might be useful in making a good first impression. I have not come all this way to be turned away because Joe takes an instant dislike to me for some reason. That would be devastating.

"That miserable old git has no friends. I don't know what business you have with him though I'm sure you will be disappointed by his lack of hospitality. You won't get much help from him," he cusses as we walk down the side of the garage towards the back door.

"You never know, I might be able to charm him a little."

The old man pauses, turns to face me and looks me up and down as he make a quick mental assessment, "I doubt it. You have nothing he desires. Anyway, you stay here and I'll see if he's in. Joe, are you home, you old bastard?"

I am left standing patiently on the back porch as the old man wanders up the one step, opens the fly wire screen and strolls into the house. Looking at the back yard I can see a large motor bike, covered partially by a tarpaulin, which is swaying in the breeze. The surrounding area is littered by the odd smattering of bike parts, discarded carelessly here and there. Not a picturesque landscape by any means. The most striking aspect of the décor is the dozens of wind chimes hanging from the veranda. I am amazed at the depth and variety of chimes as they jangle away cheerfully.

Why would someone want so many wind chimes? Wouldn't all that racket eventually send you mad? Lucky he doesn't seem to have any neighbors.

I become distracted as I hear the footsteps of the old man coming back along the floor boards of the narrow corridor, seemingly on his own.

"Is he home?" I ask eagerly as I turn towards the back door.

The old man boots the wire door open as he marches out, "Yes he is." He moves sharply towards me, lifting a shot gun confidently in both hands and locking the cartridges into the firing mechanism, ready to take his first shot. The gun is pointed only a few inches away, directly at my head as he takes careful aim. It is impossible for him to miss at this close proximity. Certain death would follow if his shaky finger accidentally pulled the trigger. "And he wants some quick answers. What the Hell are you doing here? Why have you come to see me?"

'Heaven'

All manner of evil,
Dwell in this vile place,
The refuse of Salem,
Staring Mary in the face.

All is not as it seems,
For outside walks the devil,
Feeling righteous in his soul,
Though truly the most evil.

Chapter 7

March 16th 1692.

Salem, Massachusetts.

Mary stands silently, surrounded by all manner of odd characters. Beggars, thieves, rapists, maybe even murderers are mixed together and crammed into this tiny space. Altogether there are about fifteen men and women being held in the one cold, dark, dingy cell. For the most part they are spread out around the thick stone walls, thankfully, keeping to themselves. Mary is keeping a watchful eye on a lean, scrawny fellow who is pacing around the room in a most menacing manner. He watches her constantly through his one good eye, trying to hide his unnerving cheeky grin, a grin which is more distasteful because of its revelation of badly rotting teeth. Mary doesn't know what crime this chap has been arrested for, she only knows in her heart to be wary of him. Her intuition screams at her that there is much evil in this one, evil that is slowly devouring him from deep inside. She is glad her sister Sarah is not imprisoned in this cell. Maybe she has been lucky enough to be housed in one of the other cells with a better class of criminals. Mary knows that is a forlorn hope at best. All the criminals here are the discarded filth of the community.

Rubbing her hands where the now departed ropes have cut deep into her wrists, Mary surveys the scene around her. There is only one small bench for the entire cell. It is the property of the three largest and most unsavory looking men. The bald man sitting in the middle of the bench appears to be the power broker of the cell. He is flanked by his two lackeys. The lackeys appear to be devoted servants to the bald man, though a little slow in the mind. What the lackeys miss in brains they make up for more than adequately by their excessive brawn. Mary is well aware of what she has to do in order to survive in this cell. The bald man and his entourage are not to be reckoned with under any circumstances. They could, however, be the best of allies in this hostile place if she can somehow formulate a plan as to how get on side with them.

The entire cell is only ten paces wide. It is made of solid, cold bluestone. It has no flaws or imperfections. Thick metal bars go from floor to ceiling at the front of the cell. The door to the cell is locked shut by a heavy chain wrapped around several bars and sealed with a large padlock. There are two small windows at head height, leading to the outside world, located at the back of the cell. They have thick metal bars embedded deep into the rock. A breakout from this prison appears completely impossible. That is the way the town masons designed and built it. If the bars in the windows could be removed, the window space remains too small to allow the passage of an adult. Mary is petite yet still too large in stature to squeeze through the gap if the bars were removed. The stone wall is impregnable too. It is approximately a foot thick. All that leaves is the jailer's key. However, the key to the padlock is completely inaccessible to Mary and her cellmates. It remains safe, out of harm's way on a hook some twenty feet beyond the cell on the far wall, well out of reach. All in all, as Mary searches for some hope, there appears to be no logical means to escape.

The cell is wet underfoot. The original design did not include a toilet. The jailer doesn't see fit to provide a bucket. The smell of urine and feces is overbearing. Large, hairy brown rats wander about without fear, looking for crumbs or other scraps discarded by the prisoners. There is precious little reward for their search, yet search they do. They number around two dozen. Occasionally they fight one another releasing shrill shrieks of pain when bitten. Sometimes they walk across the feet of one of the women, startling them into agitation, much to the amusement of some of the men. Mary tries to block their presence from her mind. She doesn't care for mange ridden rats. She prefers to let her mind wander to a better place, to a time of love and happiness. Closing her eyes she travels away from the squalor to be with her beloved Thomas once more. She smiles as Violet and Rose play games in the tall, swaying grass as Jezebel watches over them, maintaining a discreet presence. She sighs as she considers these were indeed happier times. She prays silently that they will come again.

Footsteps resound through the cell announcing the arrival of a stranger. The sound resonates as they begin to walk down the stone stairs into the depths of the dank cellar where the prisoners are kept. Mary hears the steps moving ever closer. She is the only prisoner who reacts, the only one intrigued as to who might be coming to visit their living hell. A visitor to the cells is a rare occurrence. The other prisoners have been incarcerated here too long, they don't care. They know the sound of footsteps is not a prelude to hope walking in the door. Nobody is getting out of here alive. That is what they hold to be true. No fancy words spoken with a glib tongue could sway them to think otherwise. Mary, however, is not so jaded, not yet at least. She still believes there is a chance. She is determined to hold onto this glimmer of hope in her heart no matter what. Mary believes her story is not over until it is over. She has much to live for.

She turns and walks to the front of her cell, pressing her face hard up against the bars in order to gain a clear view of the base of the stairs. It only takes a few seconds for the owner of the footsteps to appear. First she sees the pair of heavy men's work boots, scuffed and weather beaten, then the corduroy trousers and white shirt clinging tight over his muscular torso. She catches her breath as she finally sees the man's face appearing out of the shadows, smiling. To her surprise it is John carrying a small cloth bag.

John walks calmly over to the guard and they exchange pleasantries in hushed, indistinct tones, partly with their backs to Mary. John reaches into his trouser pocket, pulling out something small, something indiscernible in the flickering candle light. John releases the tiny items slowly so that they gently fall, like shimmering snowflakes, into the outstretched palm of the guard's hand. As they fall, Mary sees the unmistakable glint of light reflecting off several coins. The guard smiles and gestures towards Mary's cell in an accommodating manner. John nods and turns, walking deliberately towards the cell, directly towards Mary. As he moves closer, Mary can see the three large claw marks across his face, infected and festering with green puss dribbling down his cheek. As John walks, he dabs at his wounds with a tarnished kerchief.

Jezebel hath fought valiantly!

Mary's mind rages with confusion. From her vantage point John appears to be happy, relaxed and completely at ease. This is not at all how she had imagined he would be at this time, particularly as he is standing here within striking distance of the woman who, in his eyes, murdered Jane, his wife in cold blood. She begins to wonder if he has come to his senses. Is that even possible for a man to change his emotional state so drastically in little more than a blink of an eye? Maybe he has realized she was only trying to help; to make good out of an inevitable catastrophic situation. Maybe he has come to help, to put an end to this madness. Come to set her free. This hopeful thought doesn't survive more than a few seconds as John arrives at the bars and begins to speak.

"Thou be thy devil's minion and I shall take great delight as I watch thee be banished to hell," John hisses with much venom. He continues to smile at Mary but she can see no mercy in his eyes. There is only hatred, devouring him from the inside, working its way through every pore to the surface. The evil that thrives in John's soul is the equal of any who dwell in the shadows of Mary's cell.

Mary is staggered, "Thou must be able to see. Thy wife and baby were both destined to die. I saved thy son! I would hath saved thy wife if it hath been God's will."

John spits in Mary's face and says, "Thou shall not speaketh of God's will. Thou murdered my wife and that be thy master's baby, not mine. Thou hath nothing to do with God. Thou art pure evil."

Mary cringes. Wiping saliva from her face she looks squarely at John. Earnestly she says, "Nay, thou art wrong. He be thy baby, thy own flesh and blood, thy son and heir."

John shakes his head, his faces darkens, "Nay, it be not true. It be thy devil's child and I shall hath naught to do with its raising."

Mary becomes scared as she begins to worry that the baby remains in danger. She fears John will do something foolish. She is worried he may have acted in a foolish manner already. She asks nervously, "What pray, is to be done for the innocent child?"

John looks upon her, his eyes glazing over, "He shall be raised by my sister, Helen Washington, as if he be her own. Helen and Henry be good Christian folk with means. They will bring him up in a manner fit for God. They shall keep him out of thy master's reach. I shall have naught to do with him. My sight shall never fall on him again. That spawn of Satan cost me a good wife."

John lifts the cloth bag and peels it back to reveal its contents. A wondrous aroma fills the air. All at once the prisoners rush to the front of the cell, pushing Mary roughly to the back in their eagerness to get to the bag's contents. They reach through the bars, begging for some of the loaf of bread revealed. The smell of freshly baked bread is overpowering to the starving prisoners, many of whom have not eaten in several days. The prospect of savoring this delectable treasure is a unbelievable dream come true to the unwashed mob.

John walks backwards as he slip the bread back into the bag. An evil grin spreads over his face as he gestures towards Mary, "Nay, thou can hath none of this 'til that unholy creature hath been dealt with in a manner that provides me justice and much satisfaction."

The mob turns slowly to face Mary. She clutches her crucifix seeking some sort of spiritual protection as she begins to walk backwards to the far corner of the cell. The mob walks slowly in unison, yet with sinister purpose, as they move steadily towards her. Hunger burns in their eyes. Some have not had a proper meal in weeks. The usual swill they receive consists of stale bread and half rotten vegetables that no one wants to buy from the farmers. Nothing is ever cooked. The smell of freshly baked bread sends them mad with desire. She watches them, cautiously stepping backwards until her back touches the cold stone wall. Mary has no choice. She decides to use the only weapon at her disposal, fear of the unknown.

Releasing her grip on the crucifix, Mary slowly begins to chant. Her voice is soft at first, yet steadily increasing in intensity. Her fellow inmates pause, watching her, though still yearning for the taste of bread. The aroma coming from the bag is intoxicating.

Mary pretends to be a witch, waving her arms as she chants, making eye contact at every opportunity. The villains step back as they become mesmerized by her antics. They all begin to fear she is casting some sort of horrible curse on them all in retaliation for their gluttonous thoughts. She intermittently spits and hisses at them for extra effect. The prisoners step back, fanning out around the walls. They become wary of the consequences of attacking Mary. However, they face her hungry, eager for the nourishment which is so close at hand, just beyond the bars. Even the bald man and his lackeys have moved to the edge of the cell, wary, watchful. Mary walks around the center of the cell defiantly, unhindered by the scoundrels around her. Silently she surveys the crowd, knowing she has fooled them into submission, at least for now.

The guard and John watch proceedings from outside the cell. John says categorically, "See, I now hath many witnesses. Thou all shall bear witness to the vileness of this creature. There be no doubt she be an abomination to mankind. There be no doubt that she be a witch of the grossest demeanor. Thou doth stoop to trickery at a moment's notice. Thou art a witch and shall die as one, hung until breathless."

John tosses the bread casually into the cell as he turns and walks away. Some of the prisoners see the bread flying through the air and rush to fight for any small piece they can acquire. However, it is Mary who pounces on the loaf first. The prisoners halt. Nobody wants to fight Mary for the bread. Mary stands upright holding the bread aloft like a trophy as everyone quickly grants her the luxury of some space once more. A plan begins to form in her head. She looks for and finds the bald man, still leaning against the wall. To his astonishment Mary tosses the bread to him. He acknowledges her gift with a wink and a smile. Mary smiles too, knowing that for the price of a loaf of bread, she has made an important friend. A friend who will hopefully keep her safe once darkness falls.

Turning back, she sees John striding towards the steps. Panic begins to flood through her as she sees an opportunity for freedom about to leave. She rushes to the front of the cell and screams, "Please sir, show me thy mercy."

John stops and turns slightly. With confusion on his face he asks, "Thou doth seeketh my forgiveness and mercy?"

Mary, sensing a glimmer of hope says, "Aye sir, I do. I be innocent, I saved thy son from a hideous demise. I allowed him to draw precious breath."

"Thou doth deserveth my mercy, it be purely Christian to be merciful," John says with sincerity as he nods to signal his agreement. John gives much thought each day to his Christian teachings and considers himself to be a righteous and loyal servant of the church. He knows that mercy is an important trait of his church that, no matter what, he must never choose to ignore.

Mary's face lightens. She begins to cautiously smile. Hopeful all is not lost.

John smiles and says as he turns and walks slowly away from the cell and up the stairs, "I be sure God will deal with thou in a benevolent manner once thou have been punished for your evil deeds on this earth. Maybe he shall show you his divine mercy if thou doth repent thy sins at heavens gate."

As John speaks, Mary's strength fades. She begins to cry and slumps in a heap on the cold, wet, unforgiving floor. The other prisoners ignore her; fearful it may be a sinister trick, by the powerful witch, to lure them into a trap. After a few moments she regains a little strength, stands and staggers towards the tiny window seeking some fresh air as she valiantly holds back her tears. She is pleasantly surprised to see a pair of green eyes staring back at her. She reaches through the narrow gap in the bars, gently patting Jezzie's black fur. The cat begins to purr as it lies on the window ledge outside the cell. Mary slowly begins to regain control over her emotions as she pats the cat and watches the bald man eating and distributing the bread to his closest colleagues. She thinks silently to herself how good it is to have some friends watching over her, keeping her safe, particularly when she is residing in such a dangerous place as this.

'Foreboding'

Birds fly north,
Against prevailing winds.

Dingo's howl relentless,
In the still of night.

Cats hiss and scatter,
Sheltering in shadows dark and deep.

For they all know things aren't right,
In this town as it sleeps.

Chapter 8

Monday, February 27th, 2006.

Afternoon.

Rainbow, Victoria, Australia.

Jesus!

I back away slightly, in shock at the audacious assault. However, this proves pointless as Joe follows my every step, stalking me with the gun pointed directly at my head. I halt as I realize I have nowhere left to go. As sweat beads on my brow, I am acutely aware of just how alone and vulnerable I am in this backyard. Foolishly, I know I have walked into a trap. A trap that I hope will not prove fatal.

I am such an idiot!

To my right, a deep guttural growl catches my attention. I glance towards the source of the sound while trying to keep a watchful eye on Joe. To my surprise, I see a very old, black cat stalking me slowly. It stands upright as it slowly paces towards me in a threatening yet somewhat awkward manner. Its arthritic bones won't allow it to slink down anymore. There are large bald patches on its back. Its remaining fur stands upright as a warning that I am trespassing on its turf. As the old beast growls its discontent, it reveals a mouth with only three greenish teeth left. As a fearsome predator, this cat has certainly seen better days.

My eyes dart left, seeking to find someone to help with my predicament. This is a hopeless cause. I am completely shielded from the road. As such I would require someone to walk down the side path, all the way to the backyard, in order to be seen. Save for the unlikely event that a postman arrives there will be no one to bear witness to the proceedings that are about to occur, not until it is too late for me, anyway. I realize now that I underestimated Joe. He has proved very cunning by drawing me into the sanctity of his lair. Why? Why would he drag me all the way to Rainbow simply to blast a hole in me. No, it just doesn't make sense. This is just a misunderstanding. However if I don't think my way through this soon, it will be a moot point.

Think for God's sake, think!

I consider my options rapidly, though I fear I have few. Grab the gun and risk it discharging. Call for help and be shot before anyone is alerted to my plight. My options are, at best, poor. I am just a quivering finger away from certain death. Though my predicament is dire, my resolve remains strong. I will not surrender hope while I am able to still draw precious breath.

"I asked you what the Hell you want with me? Did they send you? Did they?" Joe growls in a husky, yet determined voice. As I stare into his eyes I am a little confused. I had expected to see something different, something that fits his current demeanor; insanity perhaps or unbridled rage. Fear possibly, or confusion would be appropriate too. However, I am surprised that this is not the emotion I see in his eyes. All I see is pain and an old man crying out for help. As I stare into the twin barrels of the shotgun, I start to lose my fear of Joe. I begin to suspect he won't pull the trigger.

Please let me be right!

"You sent for me. Sorry, you invited me to come. Don't you remember?" I say fearing that Joe's mental stability is highly questionable. I watch his face as his eyes turn away slightly, blinking rapidly, like he is trying to consider the ramifications of my words. He appears to be dealing with numerous conflicting thoughts, all at once, trying to sort them into a cohesive notion which makes some sense. I wonder what is going through his mind now.

"I invited you?" he asks softly, the gun lowering slightly. Though he is struggling for comprehension, for a moment or two he seems to realize that I speak the truth. This, however, is lost again as his eyes focus sharply on me, questioning my very integrity. He corrects his hold on the gun as he continues. "Who are you exactly?"

My pulse racing, I answer promptly yet calmly, "I'm Julie, Julie Mahoney! You sent me two trunks of tapes and journals and the like. Please remember, please, you must."

Joe lowers his gun as he shakes his head in disbelief and says slowly, "Yes, yes. Of course, I remember. It's not like I'm getting senile or something. Julie Mahoney, yes I remember. You see the visions too, you poor thing."

I sigh, relieved that I seem to finally be getting through to this strange old man. To my relief the gun is held limp in his hand, innocuously pointing at the ground by his feet. I am comforted somewhat that the threat has eased, for the time being. However, I remain vigilant, far more cautious and watchful of his movements now that I know he is a little unstable.

My curiosity is sparked by his words. I have to ask, "How do you know I have visions?"

"Yes, yes, Julie Mahoney. What?" he says looking a little distracted, "Oh, yeah. I've seen you in my visions. I have a fairly clear idea on what you are starting to go through. Don't let my appearance fool you, I still have clarity of mind, sharp as a tack."

I am shocked and more than a little dubious of this statement. His faculties, in my humble opinion, appear to have deserted him long ago, "You see me in your visions? I haven't seen you in mine."

Joe stares into my eyes with a surety that contrasts drastically to his earlier confusion. He says simply, with the authority of a man who has lived a long and eventful life, "I've been having these visions for over seventy years. I still don't know why they occur or how they occur. However, I've certainly learned how to manipulate them to get what I want, little missy. I'm sure there are many things in your visions that you do not see. Don't worry, with a little encouragement, I will help you work it all out. Now tell me, do you take milk and sugar with your coffee?"

I am surprised by the rapid change of Joe's emotions. I am still trying to catch my breath, slow my pulse back to its normal resting rate. It is like I am dealing with multiple personalities. In the blink of an eye he changes from docile to aggressive, from vague to confident, then to charming and helpful. The changes are sharp and unpredictable. I wonder nervously, what will happen next?

I watch, cautiously trying to understand what this old man is all about. I can't figure him out. Not in the slightest. He seems to be many diametrically opposed emotions all at once. Good and bad wrapped up with a large bow in the one neat package. What is the truth and what is the skillfully crafted lie? I do not know. I remain uneasy though the immediate danger appears to have long passed.

Joe enters the house, holding the door open politely for his mate, the old black cat, as it slowly waddles inside, duly satisfied that I am no threat to either itself or its master. Common sense kicks in. I am apprehensive about following them into the house. I am somewhat reassured by the fact that he places his gun on the floor, just inside the wire door, out of reach for the moment. Conflicted by my emotions, I stop and think for a second. I want to run, though I know I will live to regret it if I take that option. However, I also feel an overpowering urge to discover more about the intricacies of my visions. Joe is the only man I am aware of who can teach me. With seventy years of experience he would have to be the world expert on these visions. I guess I am also curious to learn more about how the visions have affected his person, both mentally and physically. They have obviously created some 'issues'. Maybe I can use this information to ensure I don't end up like Joe. On first impression, he seems to be a complete train wreck. His mind is addled and his emotions are worn down to the nerve endings.

Hesitantly, I follow him into the house. I ignore the voices screaming out in my head. I can look after myself.

"Milk, no sugar," I call out as I try to act like nothing untoward has happened between us.

"Good, good. I'm sorry for all that kafuffle. You probably think I've lost the plot a little," Joe suggests as he turns off the boiling jug.

More like a lot!

"No. not really," I lie, trying my best to be friendly and at ease, knowing full well Joe remains my only 'tutor'. I sense he is a good man, though I still feel a little like I am swimming in a shark tank with a fresh rump steak tied to my back. I just can't shake this feeling.

I take a seat in his lounge room on an old, though very comfortable, brown, cushioned armchair. I can see old Joe fussing from my position. He is in the kitchen, pouring water from the jug into two completely different mugs; each with a serve of freshly ground coffee granules hidden in its confines. He looks for all the world like a doting grandfather attending to a favorite granddaughter who has unexpectedly come to visit.

As he staggers down the hallway, a mug in each hand, he continues, "No, it was wrong of me to react like that. I cannot apologize enough for my foolish behavior. However, you must understand the circumstances of my life. I have to be cautious when a stranger arrives in search of me. There are some people in this world who are looking for me because I have visions. I can assure you that they do not have my best interests at heart."

"Thanks," I say accepting the hot mug. I place it on the wooden coffee table before me as I let it cool somewhat. The aroma of coffee is already having a restorative effect on my being. "Is that why you moved all the way from America to Rainbow in Australia?"

Joe groans as he sits heavily in the armchair opposite me, a strange grin spreading over his face, "No, not really. The F.B.I. and others have shown an interest in my predictions for a long, long time. This is mainly because I have sought their help on occasion in order to try to successfully deal with some of the larger issues I have been forced to face. I would recommend you don't deal with any authorities. They are all the same across the world; they don't understand; they are all bastards! Anyway, as you have seen, I can protect myself quite well when push comes to shove."

I laugh a little, "Yes, I can see that. But why did you move to Rainbow then?"

"As I recall," Joe says as he scratches the stubble on his chin. "I moved here for five basic reasons. Hang on, it might have been six. No, no, it was definitely five. I'm sure of that, I think."

I look at Joe, waiting for him to continue. A pause settles over him as he seems to have lost his train of thought. Unfortunately, clarity of mind appears to be fleeting. I prompt, "You moved here because....?"

"Oh, yes. I moved here for five reasons, I am sure of it. The first reason is because I liked the name of the place, God damn it. I've always lived in places with catchy names. Living at the end of the Rainbow, so to speak, makes me smile. I hadn't smiled for such a long time before I moved here. All the play had evaporated out of 'life'. All that was left was serious, deadly serious. Blah! Enough of that self-indulgent drivel already, answer the question for God's sake. Ok, secondly, the town is isolated, not over crowded like the cities with all those God damn people everywhere. Thirdly, it's near Hopetoun and Hopevale. A man cannot live without a sense of hope close at hand. Fourthly, it's isolated out here, no crowds like them cities with all those God damn people. Finally it's.... it's...."

"It doesn't matter. I get the idea," I try to help him out of his memory loss.

"No, no I've got it. Yes, that's right. Rainbow is very isolated."

"Not all those God damn people out here," I suggest.

Joe looks surprised and pleased that I understand his reasons for moving to such an lonely place in the world. I am really just taking the Mickey. He doesn't seem to notice. A pleasant glint smiles in his eyes as I feel I might have, for the first time, been accepted as a friend. He eagerly agrees with my statement, "Yes, yes. Not all those God damn people. I couldn't have put it better myself. Less people around, fewer visions, less I have to deal with or try to ignore."

It is my turn to be surprised, "So you don't deal with all the visions? I mean you don't try to stop every calamity from occurring?"

Joe shakes his head, "No I'm getting too old to go gallivanting around all over the countryside, trying to fix other people's problems. I have enough of my own to worry about these days. The years have been unkind. Don't get me wrong, I'm a good, God fearing man and I like to help my fellow man as much as I can. However, I can only do so much. Though, since I've come to Australia, I've been able to access some help. God makes me pay a heavy price for the poor souls I refuse to help. I would rather not multiply his wrath."

Suddenly I have several new questions floating in my head. I need to learn how the visions work. However, I first want to know what he means by 'a heavy price is paid'. I ask softly, "You mean the pain in your chest when the vision appears?"

Joe smiles, somewhat comforted that he is finally talking to someone who can relate first hand to what he has had to endured for the majority of his life, "You get that too, do ya? No, I don't mean that. I mean I continue to see the people that have been lost through my inaction."

I am a little confused by this statement, "You mean their visions continue after the event?"

"Shhhhh," Joe says looking sharply to his side at nothing within a vacant room. Focusing back on me he continues, wiping a tear from his eye, "I will tell her if you let me! Please let me. Sorry for the interruption. Where was I? Oh, yeah, no, I mean the innocent victims remain with me. They talk to me, encourage me to act more often, hound me for doing nothin' and basically make my life a living hell."

"Oh," is all I can say. I am at a loss as I glance at the room around us. I wonder how many of the unsaved are haunting him in this room right now. After seventy years of visions, the number could be astronomical. I think of Emma and Dr. Khan and wonder if I will soon be paid a visit. I make a mental note to try to act on as many visions as I can, in the future, to prevent this from becoming a possibility. I cannot envisage the hell of having to live my life with such an unwelcome, unrelenting companionship.

"You'll see, my dear. It WILL happen to you too. Anyway, Steve helps me to do more than I have been able to and that is a good thing."

"Who's Steve?" I ask, surprised that he has confided in another person about his visions, particularly after the troubles he has faced in the past from non-believers.

I can see he is considering his words carefully as he pauses for a moment. Joe then smiles awkwardly as he says, "Steve's no saint. In fact he's has a fairly chequered history of making money through other people's misfortunes."

"Do you mean he's some sort of criminal?" I ask, wanting to get to the bottom of this unexpected development. I am beginning to feel like the gift of the premonitions is two sided, both dark and light. In order to do something good, I may have to overlook some things I would normally be uncomfortable with, for the better good, of course. I know I have visions to be resolved, that is quite clear, I also have a strong sense of what is right and wrong. However, curiously, I am wondering if this Steve can be of assistance in some way. Should I bite into the apple offered in the Eden garden? If Joe is working with this chap, maybe it is okay for me to work with him too. That is, of course, if I find he is not too dodgy.

"Well, sort of. He's still involved in that sort of activity yet, the thing is, he has changed into a Robin Hood type figure nowadays."

"What do you mean?" I ask, wondering what on earth he is talking about. In my book, a criminal is a criminal.

"Well, you see, he had a so called business arrangement go wrong about six years ago with one of Melbourne's leading underworld figures. Steve wound up left for dead with multiple stab wounds and his teeth in an awful mess as he lay in the gutter of Spencer Street. Unfortunately, Steve's predicament was not the worst part in this gangland war that played out on the streets of Melbourne."

"What else has he lived through?" I ask, flummoxed as to how this story might fit into our current situation.

Joe continues, "Well you see, this particular, well known, underworld figure has a motto. If you mess with him, he messes with you and your dearest."

Fearful of the answer, I ask cautiously, "So what happened?"

"Well, he kidnapped Steve's little four year old daughter, Melinda. The police found her in an abandoned warehouse, tied to the wall, some six weeks later. She had been brutally tortured then left to die a horrible, slow, painful death. It was a brutal murder of a complete innocent who was ignorant of, and untainted by, her father's unsavory activities. Steve was so beside himself that he couldn't face the prospect of identifying her body. He never did see his daughter one last time. Maybe that was a good thing; she was barely recognizable. Anyway, I met Steve while I was having vivid premonitions about his daughter's forthcoming abduction and death. Unfortunately, he didn't believe me that she was in grave danger."

"Though he did later?" I suggest.

Joe nods, "Yes, he learned the hard way to trust my intuition. This tragedy seemed to spark the metamorphosis into the man he is today. He made a difficult, life changing decision. He decided to try to help save as many innocent people from crime as possible. Since then he has used his vast array of contacts and resources to save innocents on a regular basis with, of course, the help of my visions."

"I find that hard to believe."

Joe smiles as he leans forward to emphasize his point, "That's why I wanted to get you up here. I can't drive anymore and I thought you could give me a lift."

"A lift where?" I ask, surprised.

"A lift to Melbourne of course, so I can introduce you to Steve. Once you've met him, you'll recognize he is a changed man. He is a decent guy, completely different to his reputation. Hopefully you can work with him to continue the work that I've started. That's my hope anyway. What do you say? Have you got anything better to do? Do we head off to Melbourne?"

I sit there silently trying to consider all my options under Joe's patient, watchful gaze. In the end I feel I have no choice. A drive back to Melbourne will certainly give me the opportunity to talk to Joe at length about his experiences with the visions. I feel this could be a cathartic experience for both of us. Who knows, this Steve might be better than the first impression I've garnered from Joe. Everyone deserves a second chance. He might be reformed, as Joe seems to suggest. If this is so, he might be in a position to help me tackle the visions more successfully and more safely than I have thus far. I think I need to take a chance.

"Why don't we," I say showing as much enthusiasm as I can muster. "However, can I use your toilet before we go? It was such a long drive to get here."

"Of course, my dear; second door on the right, straight down the hall."

"Oh," I say as I halt and turn slightly to face Joe, remembering one more thing.

"What is it, Sweetheart?"

"Would it be possible to make a quick phone call too? My mobile doesn't work up here and my boyfriend will be getting worried by now."

"Sure, the phone's over there," Joe says pointing into the kitchen. "Though you may have to excuse the dust, I have no cause to use it these days."

"Thanks. That'll give you a chance to pack a few clothes for the trip."

Joe laughs as he looks at me with a wry smile, "Already done, little missy. You forget I have premonitions. I have also seen us both in and around Melbourne so I must get down there somehow, mustn't I?"

"Yes, you must," I say a little startled as I walk towards the toilet door.

I have a lot to learn about how these premonitions work.

'Epic Journey'

An old man so wily,

His hair long and grey,

Trust him you must,

As you travel a long journey today.

His eyes dart about,

Fall for his charm, you may,

Mistrust him you must,

As you travel a long journey today.

Chapter 9

Monday, February 27th, 2006.

Afternoon.

Rainbow, Victoria, Australia.

I keep my conversation with Peter short and sweet; I simply provided him with a broad strokes overview of what has occurred thus far on my epic trip to the middle of nowhere. He is relieved to hear that I am fine and preparing to head back home tonight. I can tell by his voice, though, that he has been worried sick, probably more so since I have been out of phone range for the majority of the time.

Peter is surprised by the revelation that I am bringing Joe home with me, however he doesn't question my judgment. I am conscious that Joe is only a short distance away, sitting quietly in the lounge room. Though he seems old and frail, I am not about to take a chance that his hearing is less than perfect. He seemed very doddery when I first met him, yet he charged out of the house with the gun locked and loaded like a Stawell Gift runner. I don't know how much of his behavior is old age and how much is for show, to draw the unsuspecting into a false sense of security. His hearing and clarity of mind may be far better than his image would suggest.

I neglect to tell Peter about the 'shot gun to the head' incident. I can't think of the right words to explain it just at the moment. Anything I say will only alarm him unnecessarily. This tale will have to be discussed during a lengthy, private conversation with Peter, sometime later when Joe is not within earshot. Anyhow, I am now cautiously optimistic that Joe is possibly harmless. I know that lacks confidence, however, I have to take a chance that he will be friendly from now on. It is my only chance to get help with these visions. I must stay alert, keeping a close eye on him, just to make sure.

By the time we have another cup of coffee and I am formerly introduced to the 'God damn flea bag' named Oscar, it is about 3 P.M. I place a blanket on the back seat. Joe tenderly lifts his old mate into the car. To my surprise, Oscar curls up immediately, forgoing his usual preparation to sleep. We clamber into the car and set off on our journey.

"Did you get some chocolate cookies at Kooka's on the way through?" Joe asks, his voice tinged with excited anticipation. "I did ask you to get some, didn't I?"

Suddenly I feel ashamed. How could I know that they were actually important, not just part of the clues to unravel? I shake my head, "No, I didn't stop. I didn't know how far I had to travel so I tried to keep moving."

"Hell of a shame," Joe says, obviously disappointed. "You know their cookies are fairly special. They're the best in the state. I have found none better during my travels. Hell of a shame."

We begin our drive in the general direction back towards Melbourne. Joe is strangely silent, content to just watch the dry and dusty landscape pass him by. I begin to wonder why old Joe is so quiet. Maybe the cookies were more important to him than I had first thought. He did include a clear request for me to pick them up in his clues, after all. I decide to let the conversation rest for a bit. There will be plenty of time to chat over the coming hours and days. I adjust my rear vision mirror so that I can see Oscar. He is curled up, sound asleep, completely unfazed by the motion of the car. He looks like he has travelled much during his long life, all the way from America at least.

I notice Joe is settling in for the long drive ahead too. Even though it is broad daylight, he has his eyes shut and is snuggling into the corner between the seat and the door, trying to make himself comfortable. His face appears emotionless, as if he is drifting slowly off to sleep.

Lucky bugger! I could do with a break too after all the driving I've done today.

He lays motionless in this position for about half an hour. I assume he is asleep, it is hard to tell. Suddenly, without opening his eyes, he states, "I see you've started to listen to my cassettes."

"Yes, I've only just started. I haven't listened to much as yet. Just the first cassette so far," I speak without taking my eyes off the road. I have done a lot of driving today and need to concentrate hard on the road ahead. I am conscious that we still have an awful long way to go.

"Oh," Joe says, still with his eyes shut. "So you know about my brother's death."

I glance at Joe in disbelief, "No, no. I didn't realize it came to pass. I just knew you had a premonition about his death. I haven't reached that bit yet."

"You haven't got very far with the tapes then, have you?" Joe says, peering over his glasses in a critical manner. "Well, you'll get there eventually, I guess. They will be of great use to you, in the long run."

"So tell me, what happened to your brother. According to your tapes he was safe in Canada."

"He was indeed," Joe continues slowly, his voice beginning to waiver as he talks, "Until he was named Captain of their National baseball team. It was a great honor, particularly for one who was not Canadian born. He was so proud that he used the money he had saved from his allowance to fly back unexpectedly, to tell my parents and surprise me in person. We were all very close, back then."

I lean over, placing my hand on his knee in an attempt to try to comfort him. "Please, you don't need to continue if it brings up too many bad memories."

Joe looks at me as tears form in his eyes, "No, you seem very nice and you need to know these painful things which I know. You need to see the world through my eyes. You need to live inside my skin for a while. It may help you to avoid the agony that I have been forced to endured for a lifetime. I'll be right. I will. Anyway, I want to continue."

Joe takes a deep breath as he gathers himself, searching for the right words, "My brother, Stan, decided to fly back unexpectedly as you know. His first port of call was to my elementary school so that he could act like a real big shot, show off his new jacket and tell me and all my friends everything about his amazing adventures overseas and, of course, all about his selection and upcoming tour of America." Joe pauses before he continues, forcing barbed words out of his narrowing throat, "As he crossed the road that fateful day, all his hopes and dreams came to an abrupt halt. He was struck by a black Buick; a drunk, unlicensed driver behind the wheel. It was exactly the same as my vision, though this time played out at normal pace. I watched, helpless as it happened. One minute he was on the other side of the road, waving to me. The next,...... well you get the picture, anyway. It was a hard lesson, yet it taught me to never ignore my visions."

"Jesus, I can't even begin to contemplate how devastating that was for you. I'm so sorry," I say sympathetically. I can't imagine how I would have coped if my introduction to the visions had been as personal as Joe's first experience. I dread the thought. I try to push the thought from my mind though it is difficult to displace. I must be focused on the future rather than be mired in Joe's past. What's done is done. There is nothing I can do to help Joe appease the demons of his past.

Joe wipes his eyes on his sleeve, a little ill at ease with sharing his emotions with someone who is practically a complete stranger. He is a tough old man, his defenses created as a consequence of the hard life he has had to endure. I assume that all the males of his generation struggle with overt expressions of emotions. I can only imagine that Joe's unique circumstances, of living alone for so much of his life, has made it even more difficult for him to interact on a emotional level with others. Maybe I am the first person he has cried in front of. What a thought! As I glance at him now, I can see he is trying his best to be strong, "No, it's okay. It was a long time ago and Stan has forgiven me for not telling him about my dream. He says he would have ignored me anyhow. I was just his silly kid brother back then. What would I know about anything?"

I consider Joe's words carefully before I ask the question about the elephant in the room, "Do you mean you've seen and spoken to your brother during other premonitions, since his death?"

Joe nods, "This is what I was trying to explain before. Stanley is the first of my lost souls to join me on this strange journey. They haunt me, encouraging me to do the right thing and save lives from being needlessly destroyed. They never rest; they are always at me to do this, do that. They never do anything for me. A moment of serenity is all I seek. Is that too much to ask for? They don't have the decency to even offer me that."

"So you see more victims than just your brother Stanley?" I ask, listening carefully, trying to gain a clear picture of the world where he dwells.

"My dear, after seventy damn years or so of experiencing these visions, I have had visitations from many. I see, feel, smell, listen and have conversations with them. Hell, sometimes I even have full scale arguments with them. They do frustrate me so. It must add up to thousands of victims that I haven't been able to help by now. I did start to keep a record of them at one stage. Though, in the end, I couldn't see the point. It wasn't like they were ever going to let me forget them anyway, were they? It's so many now that sometimes I can't make out my brother, in amongst the swarming throng."

"Thousands, surely it can't be that many!" I say in disbelief. So far, luckily, I have not experienced anything like this even though I am aware a couple of people have died due to my inaction. I wonder if it is different for me. Maybe. Maybe that is just wishful thinking.

"I was in New Jersey during September 11," Joe says plainly as he avoids eye contact. "There was nothing I could do. I saw it all yet, in the end, it was all too overwhelming. It was too large. The authorities I tried to contact were too stupid. I was simply a mad man making a preposterous allegation that terrorists were going to use planes to destroy indestructible buildings. After all, there had been earlier attacks which had all ended in failure. After the event, the FBI changed their tune. They thought I was linked to the terrorist escapades somehow because my information, in hindsight, was very, very accurate. My words were too accurate to be lucky guesses, if you know what I mean. After all, I had named some of the victims and terrorists in order to try to gain their attention. I did this before the terrible events of September 11 took place. That's why I fled, with some difficulty, to Australia, to get away from those God damn bastards who don't listen. I wanted to get away from it all, reclaim my sanity if that is possible. Unfortunately the victims I couldn't save travelled with me to my new home. They have an undying enthusiasm to send me mad as punishment for my lethargy. They are my life long curse."

I am lost for words. I should have guessed that someone with Joe's history who has experienced visions for so many years would have had visions of major events, not just circumstances involving individuals. Eventually, I say some feeble words, "I'm sorry. I can't even fathom how that could affect someone. I'm so sorry."

"Don't be, little missy. You're a Sweetheart; a kind soul. Don't worry about an old worn out fool like me. I'm a simple man in a world far too complicated for the likes of me. Just take advantage of my mistakes and ensure you aren't damaged permanently, like I am. That is all I ask. Learn from my mistakes."

"You seem to be at peace with your lot in life now, just a little," I say, surprised at how he is still alive. I couldn't imagine living with the knowledge that I had failed to save so many innocent lives, murdered so callously. I admire Joe's strength. I wonder what inspires him to continue to be, to disregard stray thoughts in the wee small hours, thoughts which no doubt encourage him to end his own misery. There must be something which keeps him going, but what?

"I guess I am at peace. I haven't really thought about it till now," Joe muses, smiling at me in a slightly off putting manner. "What's done is done, I cannot undo it. Anyway, my time on this earth is nearing its end. I am pleased with what I have done. I don't dwell on what I have not."

"Don't say that. I'm sure you have a lot of years ahead of you," I try to reassure, even though I sense he is not in need of reassurance.

Joe shakes his head, "You forget, my little one, I've become very good at manipulating these visions in order to get the maximum amount of information. You see, I know when, where and what time I am due to die.

The only uncertainty is whether, at that time, I want to live or finally get some God damn peace and die. I know what I want. I want my last act to be considered worthy in the eyes of others. I want to be remembered by at least one person in the right light. That is not too much to ask for is it?"

"I'm sure you won't die. I'm sure you will fight on if you are forewarned. After all, if you know when and how you are to die, can't you take steps to avoid it?" I offer uncertainly.

Joe shrugs his shoulders, "Maybe, maybe not. Some things are not cut and dried like that, particularly when others are involved. Sometimes you need to be gallant. Anyway, my work is nearly done on this earth. I have no regrets. No, come to think about it, that is not quite right. I do have one. My only regret is that I never found someone special in my life. I never had the opportunity to start a family and enjoy the experience of watching my children grow up and have kids of their own. Anyway, that isn't to be. I am too old to dream of such foolish things now. By the way, have you seen your own death yet?"

I am taken aback by Joe's sudden change of topic. I have never considered the notion that I might be able to see my own death. Awkwardly, I answer, "No, no. I haven't even thought it was possible, till today."

Joe closes his eyes and snuggles back into the corner to sleep some more, "You will, little missy. You will."

Why do I get the feeling you're right.

*   *   *

Joe wakes just as we are arriving in Kilmore; it is just after 9 P.M. He has enjoyed a very restful sleep if his voracious snoring is anything to go by. His snoring hasn't been a bother to me. If anything, it has been a welcome companion, ensuring that I stayed awake during the long journey home.

"Head towards Federation Square," he says as he stretches out his creaking old bones.

"All the way into the heart of Melbourne, are you sure?" I ask, incredulous.

"Yes, that's where Steve is. I think he can help you with your visions; both now and in the future."

I am tired and eager to head home to be with Peter. I miss him so much and desperately need some sleep. To curl up next him in our own bed would be heaven at this stage. This side trip is going to add another two hours to our journey, maybe more. My body and mind scream out no, though somehow I feel I need to follow Joe's lead. After all, he knows more about the nature of these visions than I do. I need to trust his judgement, no matter how bizarre. Conflicted, I enquire, "Can't we see him tomorrow? Surely he doesn't want to be disturbed at this late hour of the day."

Joe shakes his head, "No, you don't understand. Steve's day has only just begun. He lives his life in the shadows and darkness. The early evening, through to the breaking dawn are his standard business hours. Anyway, the sooner you meet him, the sooner he may be able to help you with your premonitions."

"I guess you're right," I say reluctantly as I consider the horrific consequences of failing to help someone in my visions before their limited time expires. With my current visions, I have no idea when or where they will come to fruition. I have a nagging feeling, in the back of my mind, that Joe may have experienced visions which overlap with my own. This would explain why he has encountered me in his visions. I take the turn which leads to the highway, back towards Melbourne.

"So, little lady, are you going to enlighten me about your visions or are they a national secret?" Joe asks, studying my face in the intermittent flashes of other car's headlights.

"You mean my current ones?" I ask as Joe nods. "Well, let's see. I hear a child weakly asking for help. I think she is a very young girl though I'm not precisely sure of her age. She sings a lullaby sometimes."

"What sort of lullaby, do you recognize it?"

I nod, "Yes, it's 'Mary Had A Little Lamb'. Why, is that important?"

"I don't think that is something we can use at this stage but who knows, it may prove vital later. The main thing is that you are delving deep into your visions and remembering every last detail. Please continue. What else do you know about this girl?" Joe urges as he listens intently.

"What else?" I ask myself as I rack my brain to remember the detail. "Oh, yes. There's the sound of running water."

"Fresh or salty?" asks Joe. For a minute I am dumb struck. How does fresh water sound any different to salty? Finally, I follow what he means. I lick my lips as I remember the light spray touching the skin of my face; it is like a mist traveling slowly through the air.

"It tastes fresh," I say simply without contemplating its importance.

"Good," Joe proclaims, obviously happy with my progress. "You are using all your senses now. That will increase your perception. Initially I was only experiencing what I saw. I was ignoring what I heard, felt, touched, tasted and smelt."

My memory is jogged further by Joe's comments, "Oh, yeah. That reminds me. I smell putrid smoke. Like oil or chemicals burning on a large scale."

Joe becomes more somber, as he falls silent for a few seconds before continuing, "I have experienced that one too. It worries me greatly though I think that is a second vision creeping in. From what I have been able to deduce, that smoke is related to something very large that will occur maybe months or years from now. Sometimes the visions get tangled together."

"That makes things awkward doesn't it?" I ask rhetorically.

"Not really," he states plainly without explanation as he changes tack. "Have you seen any Roman numerals in your visions?"

Roman numerals?

I think for a second. My eyes widen as I recall my visions. I answer brightly, "Yes, yes I think I have. I think it was 'XII' and 'XIV'."

"Twelve and fourteen in Roman numerals, you must have missed thirteen I guess," Joe says smartly. "You know what that means don't you?"

I haven't the foggiest. Joe fills the silent void as he continues, "That means you completely missed the visions you experienced in relation to your first eleven innocents."

"That can't be right! I would have realized," I yell, a little distraught at this unexpected revelation. There is no way I could have missed eleven visions of misfortune.

"It is right, Sweetheart. Each event comes with a number. Sometimes you will have two or more numbers in the one vision. That will help you to determine which event will come first. You probably saw the visions clearly though dismissed them out of hand as either mere nightmares or as real events happening right before your eyes. You've got to remember that all your upbringing has taught you to only look at the real world. Those pretty emerald green eyes of yours are now fully open. You now know that world is completely false. There is so much more to see. All you have to do is take a look."

"I can't believe my eyes were blind to my visions for so long," I say emotionally, wondering who has suffered unnecessarily due to my ignorance. I struggle to maintain a good line as tears well in my eyes as a result of idle contemplation of this tragic thought.

"Was there anything else in your visions?" Joe asks as he dismisses my self-pity out of hand. I guess to him, my emotions are simply self-indulgent. I should be more focused on what lies ahead, not what I have missed.

"Well, I think I lose a finger somewhere along the way," I continue.

Joe is startled, "Good, it's good to have visions about yourself. That will help you to protect yourself against impending danger. When, where and how do you lose this finger?"

I smile, "How would I know that? I just saw the severed finger hit the floor and heard a scream that sounds like me. I didn't look too closely at anything. It actually made me a little queasy."

Joe is disappointed, "You need to be brave and look deep into these visions, no matter how horrific they appear. It is impossible to save others if you don't first protect yourself. You missed a big opportunity there."

"What opportunity?" I ask, thinking back to the blind boy, Frank and his statement that the dreams were opportunities.

"Well," Joe continues. "You can manipulate the visions to suit yourself. You can slow them down and stop the dreams from disappearing. This is particularly important if the vision relates to you being in danger."

I recall the incident with the vision in the mirror at the Crown Towers with some pride, "Yes, I know that. I slowed a vision down, prevented it from evaporating and even talked with one of the people in the vision. This enabled me to establish that a woman, a prostitute I mean, was to be stabbed in Enterprise Park, opposite the casino. I was able to use this information to prevent the crime before it was able to unfold."

"And you saved a life?" Joe asks with hope.

I smile, "Two, actually. The girl who was about to be brutally murdered was heavily pregnant."

"Good, good. But you can do so much more," Joe suggests with a cheeky grin.

"Like what?" I ask intrigued, realizing my gamble to bring Joe to Melbourne has so far been successful. I am learning so much.

Joe smiles, "Well, if you focus and concentrate hard enough I think you will discover you can freeze the vision and walk through it, just like you are taking a stroll through a museum. This allows you to examine items more closely and also look for extra clues around hidden corners. Things like watches, clocks, calendars, people holding receipts. In fact, anything which might have a time, date or place on it. This information can be vital in trying to deal with a problem."

I ponder this thought for a while. I will have to give it a try the next time I'm having a vision. The ability to gather information is all important. It gives me the opportunity to process exactly what the situation is and how best to deal with it. It also helps to protect myself from injury or death. From what I can see so far, these visions seem to be linked to events that are highly dangerous or involve aggressive people. The more knowledge I have, the longer I will live. Other people will live longer lives too, of that much I am certain.

"Anyway, Julie, I think we should be concentrating on this child. It seems like she has been or will be abducted and held against her will. In fact, I think by the way that she's been asking for help in your visions she may well have been abducted already."

"But I know very little. How can I help her if I know very little?" I ask, dismayed by the realization that the little girl may be in someone's clutches. I don't want to contemplate the vile and despicable torture she may be living through. With every minute that passes I grow more fearful that she may be in danger of losing her life.

"Can I use your phone?" Joe asks.

"Sure," I say as I hurriedly hand him my mobile.

Joe starts to punch in the number as he continues, "Well, the best thing you can do is remain calm and hope you get another vision. If you do, then make use of it and search constructively for clues. Once you get as good as me, you will be able to wander through a vision for an hour of more. Of course, that takes experience, skill, determination and a large swig of madness. I am yet to find out if you meet any or all of those criteria."

"Don't you worry," I say with grim determination. "I'll get plenty of information next time round."

Joe smiles as he speaks into the phone, "Yes, Steve. It's me, Joe. Yes. Yes. No, we're on our way to see you now. Is the usual spot okay? Great. What? Yes, I'm bringing a friend. She has visions too and is most interested to meet you. We'll see you in about an hour, I guess. Bye."

I glance at Joe, "Do you think this Steve can help us?"

Joe says soothingly, "Well, I wouldn't be cracking open the champagne and breaking out the fondue set just yet. However, Steve has an awful lot of contacts and he is very useful in obtaining information from people. He has come through for me many times in the past. I think you two will get on famously."

A chill runs down my spine. I am not quite sure why. I have grave misgivings about our planned rendezvous with Steve. I fear it will not be a fruitful meeting. Something is wrong. I can't quite place it, though I know something is wrong. It feels like a ghost has passed through me. Something about the unusual words Old Joe quoted. They have a familiarity which troubles me. Where have I heard it before? I frown as I concentrate, yet nothing comes to me. I will have to be patient. I will have to try and hope for the best.

Where the hell have I heard that saying about the Champagne and Fondue set? Who was it? Why is it important? Has Old Joe spoken to the same person? Surely not. Why is it important? Why is it important? Why?

'Impertinence'

Let the saint's,
Views be aired,
On what has come to pass.

Let the innocent,
Be tried guilty,
And punishment issued harsh.

Chapter 10

April 2nd 1692.

Salem, Massachusetts.

Just over two weeks has elapsed between Mary's arrest and her trial. Such a speedy response is unusual for the court of Salem. It usually takes months for a trial to take place. The cases scheduled to be heard have reached record levels in recent times with fear causing an explosion in the number of accusations regarding witchcraft. This plague of abnormal cases has added to the run of the mill cases involving robbery, drunkenness and assault. However, with many of the town's children becoming sick with fits, the community wants the Elders to take charge. The good people of Salem are demanding swift and vengeful justice in order to put an end to the scourge of witchcraft that now engulfs their town.

Mary's case has been brought forward due to the benevolence of the town Elders. They feel that they have no choice but for the trial to be heard earlier than normal due to the heinous nature of her crimes combined with the outcry from the townsfolk for justice to be done. It also provides them with the unique opportunity to execute both Mary (once she is convicted) and her sister Sarah (already convicted) at the same time. The good will created by two witch sisters being hung on the same day will certainly calm the community. It will also silence the numerous critics in town who say there needs to be faster trials and more frequent witch hangings. The hangings bring so much joy to the community.

Two burly guards escort Mary into the courtroom as the large crowd releases an audible gasp. The guards hold Mary firmly by her arms as they march her roughly to an area known as the dock. She sits high on a platform, silent, as if in a daze. Through bloodshot eyes she looks at all the hostile faces in front of her, searching for a familiar, friendlier one. The court is filled to overflowing with everyone dressed in their Sunday best clothes. All the benches are taken. There must be another fifty people standing around the side walls and at the back. Today is a landmark event. No one wants to miss a moment of what transpires. Eventually her eyes find Thomas, sitting three rows from the back. Mary hates the fact that she is still wearing the same dress as on that fateful day. She has not been granted a change of clothes. The blood smears have long dried, merging seamlessly with the filth from the cells. She has not bathed since she was incarcerated, her hair feels dirty and matted. She feels incredibly self-conscious in front of her worried and dotting husband. She wishes she could have a moment with a wet rag, a brush and a mirror though this is not to be. Oh, how she wishes Thomas could see her clean and dressed in her best clothes, particularly considering this could be the last time he sees her. It is not to be. Her eyes fall downcast.

Thomas is watching her, trying to discreetly catch her eye. He is wary of the people around him, wary of drawing attention to himself. Pale and sickly, he has lost a little weight. A smile tries to force its way onto his face through the corner of his mouth though fails to fight its way through the tense muscles. He hopes his presence helps to make Mary feel just a little more comfortable. Little does he know his presence is having the opposite effect. His appearance only serves to make her feel more uneasy as she squirms uncomfortably in her seat in the dock.

"All rise!" bellows one of the guards.

Everyone stands as the Elders enter the courtroom. Some women curtsy while some of the men bow as an added mark of respect for the nobles of the Salem community. The four Elders stroll into the room via a door at the back. They are the picture of implied aristocracy. Their silk white shirts, black jackets and trousers, stocking legs and shiny leather shoes are all essential requirements in creating an air of dignity as well as the illusion that the Elders are a superior class compared to those crammed into the gallery. Their clothes and refinement helps nurture respect, ensuring their decisions are never questioned.

The assembled crowd remains standing until they are told to be seated. Three of the Elders sit on chairs behind a cloth covered table on the main dais, leaving the fourth chair vacant. The table before them is empty save for the two jugs of water, four metal flasks, a feather quill pen in its holder, some parchment and a gavel and block. Ewan McCormack, the most senior of the Elders, steps forward as spokesperson for the group. He is a man of about seventy years of age. Even though he is getting on in years, Ewan still remains an imposing physical presence standing at about six foot two inches tall. His booming voice and his vocabulary of learned words make him perfect for his role of prosecutor.

"Today we cometh here to trial Mary Murphy, accused of witchcraft and murder most foul. Who accuseth her of these crimes?"

John rises to his feet nervously, trembling as he stands from his seat in the front pew, "I doth, sir."

Ewan raises a hand to his spectacles, bringing them forward, down his nose as he peers in John's immediate direction, "And who sir, art thou?"

John finds Ewan and the courtroom setting somewhat imposing. He fidgets a little as he replies, "I…..I be John Johnson, husband of the deceased."

Ewan continues as he glances at the notes scrawled on parchment in his hands, "Very good. The court recognizes and welcomes thy presence. Please accept our condolences on thy loss. Doth thou hath credible proof in relation to the accused and her crimes which thou shall provide this court?"

John says confidently as he pushes his shoulders back, "I doth sir. There be many who hath witnessed her witchery and murderous deeds."

"Good, thou may be seated," Ewan turns his attention to Mary as he strolls towards the dock. Mary is fearful, scared of the Elders and the life or death power they possess. "What say thee? Art thou guilty of these despicable charges?"

Mary shakes her head vigorously, "Nay, I be innocent."

A murmur rumbles through the crowd. Despising whispers in hushed tones circulate without restraint. The gallery needs no evidence. Through rumor and insinuation over the last two weeks, they have come to the conclusion that Mary is indeed guilty. There can be no doubt. They will not be swayed from this view, no matter what occurs in her trial. They are only present today in order to witness justice being done.

"Thou would do well to confess thy guilt if so and give praise to God."

Mary is dismayed. She doesn't want to lie to the Elders, nor cloud the facts of the matter at hand. Her hope is for understanding, though her heart lacks confidence with all the superstition that has replaced reason in the town. She says clearly, "Nay, I be innocent of these charges. I shall not lie."

"Doth thou believe no crime hath been committed?" Ewan asks as he glances around at the curious faces in the gallery.

Mary is unable to think of an accurate answer to this question, one which would explain her circumstances clearly. She knows that a woman died at her hand yet her conscience is clear. Mary feels Jane's life was lost no matter what transpired. She believes it was God's will for her to try to save Jane's baby. Struggling to voice the words, she says slowly, "I doth not deny what hath been done by my hand. I be innocent of partaking in witchcraft."

Ewan pounces on her response, moving rapidly across the floor, pounding his hand on the dock for theatrical effect. Standing over Mary in a threatening manner he continues to push, "So thou admit to the murder of Jane Johnson in cold blood with no reasonable provocation?"

Mary shakes her head and states quietly, "Nay, she died at my hand yet I did not murder her."

"But she died at thy hand?"

Mary nods, "That be true, though it be mercy, not murder. I hath seen that both would die if ...."

Thomas places his head in his hands knowing Mary is in trouble. He is well aware Ewan is clever and will leap on any of her mislaid words. Thomas can see how he is manipulating Mary in order that she will provide information making her appear that she is a witch. Thomas says a quiet prayer to God to give Mary the strength of both mind and soul to combat this fearsome attack on her character.

Ewan waves his arm towards the gallery as he speaks, "So thou doth declare before thy peers that thou hath visible appearances not natural nor common? Thou seeth death as it is to occur at some time forth?"

Mary takes a moment to collect her thoughts. Sweat beads are forming on her brow as she looks around at the nervous faces in front of her. She knows the hearts of the townsfolk have no mercy, just unbridled hatred for her and her despicable act of murder. Taking a deep breath she says, "Aye, but the visions be not from the devil."

The crowd gasps and mutters condemnation as the women begin to fan their faces vigorously as if the oxygen has suddenly been sucked completely from the room. Ewan raises his hand to silence the crowd. They respond immediately as he continues his examination, "What did thy vision foretell?"

Breathing deeply Mary chooses her words with much deliberation, fearful that no matter what she says, it will not help her cause, "I saw two coffins if I do naught to help. I also saw an important person being born at a later time; a descendant of this baby that lives. He is to be a great man, born only if this baby lives to see adulthood."

"What pact doth thou make with the devil in return for such visions?"

Mary is horrified at the mere suggestion of this unholy alliance. Looking squarely at Ewan she says defiantly, "I make no pact with the devil."

"But these visions are not natural. They be not holy. Do you suffer them voluntary?"

"Nay, I do not seek these visions. I am afflicted by them," Mary looks at the gallery as she says these feeble words. She reaches up and massages her tense neck. To her surprise several of the women in the gallery grab at their necks, screaming hysterically as if in pain. Mary studies these women with bewilderment.

Ewan points at the women. With venom he asks, "Doth thou not now inflict pain on the innocent thus?"

"I know naught of what causes their pain. It is not of my doing," Mary pleads knowing her words fall on deaf ears. She lowers her head, overcome by the burden of the false accusations coming thick and fast. When she moves, several of the women also lower their heads, seemingly in great distress. Mary wonders what they are doing. Are they trying to fake a witch induced ailment to prove her guilt? Or are they simply delusional, believing so much in the presence of witchcraft that they truly think she is casting a spell on them every time she moves? Mary shakes her head, fearful of the direction the trial is heading.

"Doth thou feel the need to continue to inflict pain, even after thou hath committed murder?"

Mary says sternly as she looks directly at Ewan again, "I doth not inflict their pain. I be innocent!"

Ewan takes a deep breath. Tired of this line of questioning he refers to his hand written notes. A mischievous smile spreads across his lips as he tries a different tack, "Doth thou see other likenesses other than man? Doth they frequent your waking hours."

Mary considers this question wondering what to say. She has always believed the truth will set her free, yet Ewan is clever, twisting her words for his own gain. Mary believes, at this stage, she has nothing to lose. Maybe the truth will prove her visions are not witchcraft. On the contrary she believes with all her heart that they are an act of God. She says quietly, apprehensive of how her words will be greeted, "I see birds."

Ewan raises an eyebrow, astonished by Mary's bold admission, "What sort of birds be they? Perhaps they be black crows bringing with them pestilence, suffering and death straight from the bowels of hell?"

Mary jumps to her feet. The women in the gallery do the same, screaming out in pain as if they are being stretched. Some appear to faint, "Nay, they be white doves. They be pure white doves sent by God from heaven, not hell!"

"Doth thou not thinketh these be illusions, trickery sent from hell to confuse the feeble of mind such as thy self?"

Mary returns to her seat, physically drained. Ewan's questions spin inside her head, making her feel dizzy. She chooses not to react to his insult as she says softly, "I do not. They appear when there be danger. They try to help. They be messengers from God."

"Did these apparitions appear before thou visited Jane Johnson on that fateful day?"

"They did."

Ewan looks at the gallery, directing his question more to the townsfolk than Mary. The townsfolk live to hear his next word wondering what he will ask. Ewan knows this and plays the crowd to perfection. He is nothing if not a showman. He would never disappoint an audience. Peering over his spectacles he asks his next question, "Doth thou befriend a cat?"

Mary knows where this line of questioning is heading. She doesn't care anymore. She remains true to herself, choosing to answer this question honestly, just like she has for all the others. She sighs, "I do."

"Is this thy beast?" Ewan asks as a guard brings in a Hessian bag with something squirming inside. Ewan opens the bag, reaches in and, to the accompanying gasps from the gallery, plucks Jezebel out of the bag by the scruff of her neck.

"Jezebel!" Mary screams.

Jezebel thrashes about, hissing and clawing aimlessly. Finally one of her claws reaches its target, leaving a long scratch mark down Ewan's arm. In shock, he releases his grip on the cat, letting it fall to the floor. The guards try to pounce though the cat is too swift, dodging and weaving its way to freedom through the open main door.

Ewan regains his composure as he holds his injured arm outwards for all in the gallery to see. A trickle of blood weaves its way through the maze of hairs on his arm before it drips onto the floor in front of his feet. In a loud imposing voice, drowning into submission the raucous gallery, he asks, "Is thy cat black like the familiar of witches?"

Defiantly Mary says, "Thou know it to be. Thou have been marked by its' claws. Yet still, I be no witch."

The gallery continues to make a raucous commotion. Conversations are loud and vigorous. Accusations and thoughts are spoken freely with venomous tongues. Ewan holds up his hand to silence the crowd. Finally decorum returns to the courtroom. He turns to face the other three Elders and asks simply, "Be there any more questions unasked?"

The three Elders shake their heads silently in unison. Ewan walks around the back of the table and stands behind his empty seat. He asks his fellow Elders succinctly, "What doth thou say in regards the charges of murder and witchcraft brought forth against Mary Murphy on this day?"

The three Elders stand. One by one they speak their judgment then sit back in their velvet covered chairs.

"Guilty."

"Guilty."

"Guilty."

Ewan nods as he says, "Guilty. It be unanimous. Let thou hang at the earliest convenience along with thy sister in the town center for all to witness. May God have mercy on your souls."

Ewan belts the block with his gavel, signifying the end of the trial. With a flourish he signs the decree to execute Mary. The gallery erupts in a chorus of approval, jumping to their feet as one. Only Thomas remains seated, head in hands, crying uncontrollably at the injustice he has just witnessed. Hopelessness fills his body making him feel ill in the stomach.

The guards drag Mary out of the docks. Defiant to the end, she maintains her poise. The guards refuse to relinquish their hold. A tomato, thrown by someone hidden in the gallery, splatters into her shoulder. She desperately searches for Thomas. She is unable to find him in amongst the surging crowd. She is still seeking him as they push her violently through the doorway which leads back to the cells.

Forlorn, she wonders if she will be granted the opportunity to see him again in this lifetime.

'God's Sanctuary'

The devil's minions,
Dance with glee.
Hidden in the shadows,
Behind God's sanctuary.

They desecrate his ground,
Feast on his apathy,
Devouring poor innocent unfortunates,
Who wander there foolishly.

Chapter 11

Monday, February 27th, 2006.

Night.

Melbourne, Victoria, Australia.

Stay calm Julie, stay calm!

I remain apprehensive as the three of us walk from the car park, down Flinders Street, towards Federation Square. Joe insisted that Oscar must come too. He is an astonishing cat, trailing Joe like a dog, as we nervously move towards our final destination.

To my delight, Melbourne seems to be a hive of activity tonight, particularly at this end of town. There is quite a crowd at Federation square, moving around, going to and from the restaurants. A sizeable group is standing, watching short films on the big screen as part of some type of festival. All these people give me comfort that there is plenty of help, just a scream away if necessary.

"Where exactly are we going?" I ask, trying to stay alert, planning a hasty retreat in my mind just in case things go drastically wrong. Tonight I need several plans in order to stay safe. The fortune teller told me to trust my intuition. I think something feels wrong. I must have faith in what I sense. I must remain on guard.

"He's waiting for us just behind St. Paul's Cathedral here. It's not far now."

St Paul's Cathedral is the finest Anglican Church in Melbourne. It is a huge landmark and major tourist attraction. In fact, it is just about the holiest of Melbourne's holy places. It is situated in a very prominent spot,

at the corner of Flinders and Spencer Streets, the spiritual heart of
Melbourne, if you excuse the pun, a location many thousands of people
visit daily. It surprises me that this is the venue for our rendezvous with
one of Melbourne's criminal identities. I guess if he is truly reformed then
this venue seems quite appropriate. If not, then I guess it would be the last
place the police would choose to look for him. Either way, now that I think
about it, this venue is perfect for our meeting.

We turn into the laneway next to the Cathedral, walking towards a
darkened set of wide stairs. The Cathedral itself consists of two floors of
large arched windows with three massive steeples prominent at its apex.
Each of the brick steeples has four smaller steeples surrounding it. It is an
amazing, awe inspiring structure which well deserves its National Heritage
listing.

Overall there is something intangible about this building which stirs
something deep in my soul. It is a good place. No, it is the best of places. A
safe haven at all times for those seeking divine inspiration at a time when
they feel weak of spirit or mind. However, as I walk with old Joe towards
the uncertainty of the darkened steps ahead, I feel only trepidation that
something isn't right. The darkness has eroded some of the sanctity of this
holy place. Fear has drifted in like a mist to shroud and devour the air
originally filled with hope.

What was that?

A small flame burns brilliant orange and gold in amongst the shadows
behind St. Paul's Cathedral. The glow flickers, for a brief moment, before
disappearing back into the darkness. My uncertainty about this place has
heightened my senses. There can be no doubt that someone is smoking,
hidden in the shadows. I suspect he is watching us without desiring to be
easily identified. I feel my order in the food chain has already been

determined before I even set foot in here. He is the hunter and we are the prey stepping brightly into his lair.

As we edge closer I can vaguely distinguish the silhouette of a figure, possibly a man, standing in the darkness on the steps. I am aware that something large is moving behind him though, in this light, its form is impossible to identify.

Is that a second man lurking in the shadows?

"Steve, are you there?" Joe calls out as he tries to peer into the darkness with his diminished eyesight. We can hear a regular, dull, tapping sound coming from the darkness to the left of the stairs. From where I am positioned I can see this side clearly. There is a large brick wall, standing well over two metres high, which obscures what is stowed here. Access to this area is barred by the large, solid, wooden gate which is padlocked securely. There are no portals or windows which can be used to determine what is creating the tapping noise. However it seems to be coming from behind the wooden door.

As we draw nearer, I can now see the two figures in the shadows on the stairs. The smoker drops his cigarette to the ground, stepping onto it as he swivels his foot to ground out its flame forever. He moves forward, out of the shadows, to the light where we are standing. He moves quickly, with his arm out stretched towards Joe, as he greets him like a long lost friend. His compatriot remains shrouded in darkness, his features hidden, save for his massive size.

Steve says jovially, shaking Joe's hand vigorously, "Joe! G'day mate, you didn't waste your time getting here I see."

"Got here as quick as we could. Don't think we have a moment to waste. I'd like you to meet my new friend. This is Julie; she's raspberry jam," Joe says as he motions in my direction.

The man turns his attention to me as the tapping sound continues unabated to the left of the stairs. He looks directly into my eyes as fear grips my entire body. I am mesmerized by his disfigured cheek. The scar, now a permanent fixture, dominates his face. It is a reminder of his past, dangerous life. It is hard for me to get past this scar. It portrays him as dark and sinister, no matter how bad the light is.

His eyes are fixed on my face, looking at every line, every freckle with a piercing gaze. I try to show no fear. I must be strong. He speaks in a slow, quizzical voice, "Hi, I'm Steve. Tell me my lovely, have our paths crossed before? You seem somehow familiar to me."

He must recognize me! How can he not?

I consider my response carefully, for this is my worst nightmare come to fruition. The white knight, which Joe is so desperate for me to meet and befriend, just happens to be the vile, despicable creature I encountered in the shadows that night in Enterprise Park. I can't believe it is Steve 'Mad Dog' Maddock, the evil bastard who threatened the pregnant prostitute with murderous intent, while brandishing a razor sharp knife, who is standing before me. He is not a man to be messed with; not a man to be trusted. The dilemma is that he is probably the only person I have access to who has the contacts I need in the underworld. Can I trust such an evil man? Still, I need his help to find and rescue the kidnapped little girl. I can't let her die just because I despise this worthless excuse for a man. I remain nervous and conflicted.

Don't forget, he has a knife!

I say confidently, hopefully appearing honest, "I don't think so. I never forget a face."

Steve laughs with delight as he turns slightly, showing off his disfigured face like it is a trophy for excellence in evil deeds, "Yeah, my face is so pretty, I doubt you would ever forget it."

Steve watches me intently, the whole time he speaks. His eyes paw over my skin lecherously, without any respect. It is as if he is searching for a reaction. His cold, emotionless stare unsettles me greatly. I try my best not to flinch. I am desperate to conceal both my fear and recognition of his identity. I wonder what he is thinking behind those evil eyes. Has he recognized me and is planning his revenge or is he uncertain, trying to remember if our paths have crossed before? I just don't know. All I can do is hope that he hasn't identified me and pray that he remains ignorant while I am obligated to deal with him. After all, it was very dark when we last met, maybe he didn't get that good a look at me. I must hold onto that vain hope.

"We need your help Steve, a little girl's life is in jeopardy," Joe says simply.

The figure lurking behind Steve moves forward rapidly, snorting in an excited manner. He moves to the edge of the shadows, coming up behind Steve. His face remains obscured by darkness, though his large size is self-evident. Cherubs, with golden wings, cling to the skull handled dagger carved into his arm.

Bloody Hell! It's Chris Hagatie.

I feel nauseous as I recall my time strapped to a bed in the medium security, mental health wing of the South Morang Regional Hospital. I remember Chris leering menacingly over me in my prone state. I remember him spitting the sleeping tablet into my face as he shared with me his sleazy thoughts. I remember his saliva sliding down my cheek and onto my chest. I remember most of all how Serenity saved me while I was drugged into a stupor, unable to defend myself in any way from Chris's evil advances. Oh, how I wish Serenity was here now. Joe and Oscar don't provide the same sense of security.

In an instant, my opinion changes as Oscar spits and hunches his back into attack mode. His hair stands upright as a warning to come no further. Steve places an arm outwards, preventing Chris from moving forward. I notice he uses his right arm, choosing to keep his damaged left arm by his side. I smile, hoping he is still in great pain from the damage I caused him that night.

"Whoa, big guy! Nothing for you here," Steve says soothingly, with a smarmy grin for our benefit.

"Buttercup? There's a precious little buttercup?" the big man says excitedly in a deep, raspy voice. Oscar spits once more at Chris, trying to discourage his unwanted advance.

"There's no little girl here," Steve whispers, trying unsuccessfully to conceal his voice from us. "Chris, why don't you go and deal with that noisy rat out the back there. You make him silent, just like you always wanted."

Chris turns and looks at me. He studies me up and down, "Too old. No little Buttercup here, just an old withered rose. Chris be good. He go and kill the bloody rat. That damn noisy rat. I kill him dead, so he be silent. I do good job, you see. Chris very good. Tell the mistress, Chris be very good. Then Chris get reward. Chris want reward. Chris want to play with a precious little Buttercup."

Chris speaks to me directly though, thankfully, he appears to have no recognition of me whatsoever. I think his mind is deranged to the point where he only has a short term memory at best. No doubt this helps him to avoid any guilt for the hideous crimes he commits against innocent children. Anyway, he shouldn't remember me. I am not that memorable in his eyes. I am not his type.

His white teeth shimmer in the darkness as he thinks carefully about what he is saying. He unnerves me; that is undeniable. He is obviously mentally impaired and more than a touch violent, as all his victims can attest. I am relieved to see him walk away, up the stairs and jump over the wall into the confines of the alcove. The tapping in the alcove suddenly ceases as a large cracking sound reverberates through the alley way.

Oscar backs down, curling into a ball at Joe's feet. All his energy is spent for the moment. I guess at his age, Oscar's only defense is to bluff.

A sickening feeling surfaces in my stomach as I consider that the rat, as they have called it, was exceptionally large, particularly with the size and regularity of the tapping resounding from the alcove. My crime writer mind goes into overdrive as I suspect that Chris has silenced a person, held captive, probably by breaking their neck. That would explain the 'crack' sound which echoed from the alcove before it was engulfed in silence once more.

Concentrate! Don't imagine what you don't know. Concentrate on the danger you can see in front of you. I must ensure that Chris gets nowhere near that little girl.

The presence of Chris Hagatie is a worry. If Steve is truly reformed then there is no way he would be associating with such a slimy villain as Chris. I am uncomfortable with the compromises I have to make; however, I know they are for the greater good. I need Steve's help. I can alert the police to the whereabouts of Chris once I have secured the safety of the little girl. I just need to make sure I am careful around Chris. If I become distracted, things could become deadly very quickly. He looks old but I am well aware of his strength and capabilities.

"So tell me," Steve says casually to his old friend. "What information have you been able to gleam from your dreams, Joe? What do I need to know about this mongrel who has taken the little girl?"

Joe points at me, "I didn't have the dream; Julie did."

"Really," Steve says as he turns towards me with a disturbing grin forming on his face as his interest is aroused. "Tell me Darling, do you have dreams too? I hope they are pleasant ones."

I look at Steve, wondering what venomous thoughts are coursing through his despicable mind. He obviously finds something amusing, yet I fail to fathom what that could be. Maybe it is just his arrogant manner, his way of getting under my skin till I itch uncontrollably. Maybe he thinks he has me at a disadvantage, in some way, because I have these premonitions. I just don't know.

I am not a violent person. However, I experience some satisfaction as I look at his broken arm partially exposed as his jacket sleeve rides up. As he makes an effort to pull the sleeve back into place I can see it is plastered in a haphazard fashion, like it was a homemade job rather than hospital quality. I know that Steve is cunning. I also know he doesn't always get his own way. I know, when push comes to shove, I can beat him. I derive strength from this fact. I am not stupid, I remain rightly cautious of him. It would be incorrect to say I fear him, though.

I smile as I reply confidently, "Yes I do."

"Good," Steve seems suitably impressed. "Okay, give it all to me. I need names, dates, places, Melway references, the works."

"I.... I....," I stammer, taken off guard. I wonder why he wants such detail. From Joe's outline, I expected to provide Steve with the broad outline of what I have seen. Steve would then surely use his network of contacts to fill in the gaps and find the girl. Surely that is how it works.

"Sorry Steve. She's new to this caper. I haven't had a chance to refine her natural abilities as yet," Joe explains.

"So, are you telling me that she don't have the details, just some vague impression? Very few clues, maybe?"

Joe nods, "To use your words, yes 'she don't have the details'. I'm hoping she will have another dream soon so that I can help her walk through it, gathering more crucial information."

"So do we have a name at least?" Steve asks turning his attention to me.

I shake my head in the negative, "I have not seen her. I have mainly heard her singing 'Mary had a little lamb' or asking for help."

"That narrows it down," Steve says sarcastically. "There can't be too many kids in this town that know that nursery rhyme!"

"Like I said, Steve," Joe takes up my defense. "She has not mastered the visions at this time. The next time she has the vision we will gather more useful information. I can promise you that."

Steve looks dumbfounded, "Well I should hope so. I'm not a miracle worker, you know. I need something to go on, something I can run through my associates. In my line of business, information is everything."

"And what is your line of business, Steve?" I ask, just a little too boldly. I want to see if I can shake his nerve a little. Rattle his cage, so to speak.

Steve smiles, calm under fire, "Little Darling, I don't want to bore you with the day to day necessities of my business. Suffice to say, I am a human resources manager, of sorts."

"So you're good with trouble solving, dealing with issues that arise with your employees?" I prod cheekily, hinting vaguely about our dalliance in Enterprise Park that night.

"Yes, you could say that. I tend to get the most out of the people I deal with."

I'm sure you do, you bastard!

I smile back, not wanting to appear nervous in front of such a cool and calculating criminal. I choose to be safe, not to be drawn into a long drawn out conversation with Steve; a conversation which may reveal our past connection. That would prove disastrous. He now knows I am clever, that is good. Maybe he will be a little wary of me from now on. At least I can hope.

"I just wanted you to meet Julie and see if there is anything generally on the grapevine about a kidnapped little girl," Joe explains.

"Of course, I understand. I'll check that for you, old friend," Steve says as he grasps Joe by the arm, holding him firmly. "But, I still need two things from you in order to finish this successfully."

I can see a little fear in Joe's eyes as he replies, "Sure, anything. What do you want?"

Steve hisses softly into Joe's ear, tightening his grip on his arm, "Just the usual, mate. I need more detailed information on the deed and the crims involved."

"Got it," Joe says quickly, as he gives me a sideways smile to try to reassure me. It doesn't work.

"And of course, there's the matter of our standard arrangement. You are obligated to keep to our arrangement, even if it is her dream, not yours. Do you understand that?"

Joe nods vigorously, under considerable distress, "Of course, no problem at all. I will do that."

"Good, good," Steve says as he releases his grip on Joe's arm. He brushes the creases soothingly out of Joe's crumpled sleeve, as a token act of apology. "It is always such a pleasure doing business with you, Joe. I'm sure our future will be interesting too, Miss Julie."

Steve swings his focus towards me, his unblinking gaze cuts through me. I know I have to hold it together. I must not flinch. Confidently, I reply, "I'm sure the future will be very interesting."

"By the way," Steve suggests as a bit of an afterthought. "I need a telephone number from you Julie. I would prefer a mobile. It's just in case I find something out, you know. Then I can contact you and Joe immediately."

Don't give it to him. Don't give it to him.

There is something in the way that Steve asks for this number that makes me hesitate. The voice in the back of my mind is screaming out, "Don't give it to him". We are in the middle of a game of high stakes poker here, winner take all. Cunning will only get me so far. If the cards are marked and Steve decides to cheat, I am doomed to fail. I wonder what he has hidden up his sleeve. Alternative options appear to be absent. I need his help whether I like it or not. Unfortunately, I need to take a chance. My hands are tied in this situation. I have no choice. I must save the little girl at any cost.

Reluctantly, I give him my mobile number.

Steve smiles, I know he is considering that I may have provided him with a wrong number. It won't be long before he tests it, I suspect. He swaggers, "Got it. I'm very good with remembering information; as easy as remembering faces, really. I'll see you both around, I'm sure. Bye."

"Goodbye," both Joe and I say in unison as we turn to leave. We take a few steps forward before I casually turn around to see where Steve might be lurking. He has disappeared completely into the night. His specialty, I guess.

We walk silently towards Flinders Street, back into the real world, Oscar hobbling slowly by Joe's side as we move back to a world of light, color and plenty of people. After a few minutes, I decide we are far enough away from Steve's camp to ask two questions with safety. They are questions which have been playing on my mind since our clandestine meeting with Steve.

"Joe," I begin cautiously.

"Yes, Sweetheart," he says, seemingly woken from a trance of deep contemplation.

"What is the nature of the arrangement you have with Steve?" I ask bluntly, nervous about what his answer could be.

Joe seems a little flustered, "Um... it's just a private arrangement. It's nothing that concerns you. It's just something between Steve and me. I know you probably have concerns about Steve. However, you must remember this one fact, he is a walking contradiction. Though his history would suggest that he is a colorful character, he is also a man of honor and as such he will help us if he can."

Why are you lying? I know what he is like. I have seen his true nature first hand when we fought in Enterprise Park. He is NOT reformed.

"That's fine," I lie in reply. I feel no comfort from Joe's words. There is too much left unspoken, hiding in the shadows behind them. This is too dangerous a situation to be moving into with either false or no information. Unfortunately, I am desperate to save this little girl. I don't want her death on my conscience. I don't want her spirit following me for the rest of my days looking at me with dark resentful eyes. I know I will have to trust Joe's judgment that there are things I shouldn't know. Joe seems like an honorable person. He must have good reasons for what he is doing.

"One more question, Joe," I ask. "You mentioned I was 'raspberry jam' when we first met Steve. What does that mean?"

I wait, holding my breath in anticipation of his reply. Fearing I have asked something that I shouldn't know the answer to. Some sort of code that is privy to just Steve and Joe.

Joe stops walking, turns to face me and smiles, "My dear, you don't know what 'raspberry jam' is?"

I shake my head.

"Well, I must say! Little missy, you have lived a very underprivileged life! Raspberry jam has to be the sweetest and most inoffensive thing known to man. I would highly recommend it to you," he offers before continuing on his way, Oscar close behind, as always.

We continue to walk towards the car as a smile grows steadily on my face. I think of how stupid I must appear to Joe. What a thoughtless question to ask of such a sweet old man.

Maybe Joe's not so bad after all. He might be just a tad eccentric. Like his cat!

'Overcast'

A frail old hand,
A bold new apprentice,
A dream most vivid,
But visions clouded, I sense.

Pictures frozen clear,
Words uttered as a defense,
Future situations lived,
Though visions still clouded, I sense.

Chapter 12

Tuesday, February 28th, 2006.

Morning.

Kinglake, Victoria, Australia.

"So, tell me again, just so I am clear on this. You have no problem with this 'Cat Weasel' like character coming into our home, even though you've only just met him and barely know anything about him?" Peter asks with sarcasm, arms folded, watching the little old man scurry into the house, dragging a heavy suitcase in his wake. I must admit, in his soft blue, long sleeved, crumpled shirt and drab, tan cotton trousers; he does look like someone I have picked up out the front of St. Vinnies.

Peter is right, to a certain extent. I do not know a great deal about Joe. I can only make a decision on the character of the man based on what I have seen so far. Joe has sent me a huge collection of journals and diaries with the sole purpose of aiding my education and interpretation of the visions. He has spoken about helping people and seems to be genuine in his resolve to aid people in times of trouble.

His willingness to travel back to Melbourne, when he obviously detests the larger cities, must also count in his favor. His act of pulling a gun on me, I can understand, somewhat. It was purely a misunderstanding. Self-preservation if you like. Eventually it dawned on him that I was not an F.B.I. agent or someone with intent to do him harm. He has been nothing other than a gentleman since this time. Finally, he seems eager to find this little girl and rescue her. It is an action that appears genuinely heartfelt.

Even with his good character on display, I remain somewhat cautious because of the company Joe keeps. Steve is not a man to be trusted. I have plenty of reasons to think he is far from reformed. Pure evil cannot be molded into anything other than pure evil.

His offsider, Chris Hagatie, is the definition of 'ill repute'. From news reports and my stint in the psychiatric ward, I am aware that he is a convicted child molester, murderer and total nut case. I must ensure he never has an opportunity to get near that poor little girl. She has been through enough drama, during her short life. Ensuring the police get their hands on this bastard is also a goal, though it will have to wait. I must find the girl first.

On the way back to Kinglake, I have thought long and hard about the reasons why Joe would choose to keep such company. I guess, in the end, they are the same as my reasons for continuing to deal with Joe, Steve and, if I am forced to, Chris. If I am to successfully combat evil, I will need the assistance of people that are evil or have connections to the Melbourne underworld. This is the only way I can create a level playing field. I know in my heart, I will not find this girl in time without their vital help. Unfortunately, this means working with Steve whether I like it or not.

My curiosity remains aroused in regards to the nature of the 'arrangement' between Joe and Steve. I know Steve is apparently after something from me and has coerced a guarantee from Joe that I will deliver. I wish I knew what that is all about. I think, with Steve's background, it is unlikely to be something good. Something I will readily comply with. However, at the moment, I have more pressing business to attend to; finding the little girl.

I watch as Joe carries in his last little bag of toiletries, waving it around for us to see. He asks so politely, "Excuse me Julie, where might the bathroom be located?"

I point him in the right direction, down the hall, "Second on the right."

"Right you are," Joe says as he shuffles contentedly down the hall and out of sight. To me he seems like a pig in mud. Compared to his current abode, my house must feel like staying at Buckingham Palace.

I hear the sound of unidentified items crashing to the floor as he enters the bathroom. A little concerned, I am poised to race to Joe's aid as he calls out sheepishly, "Not much damage."

I turn and place my arms around Peter's neck as I look upwards, with my most irresistible puppy dog eyes and smile. I share a lingering kiss with him, hopefully encouraging a little tolerance and understanding. I pull away slowly as I whisper in his ear, "He's harmless, really. Maybe he's a little clumsy, though harmless none the less."

Peter gives me a friendly pat on my backside which catches me by surprise. With a smile he breaks free of my grip and moves away saying softly, "Be it on your head, Sweetheart. Don't say I didn't warn you."

"It'll be fine Peter," I say watching him walk through the doorway and into the lounge room. As he disappears from view, a sharp, stabbing pain erupts in my chest. A little girl walks nervously into view. Her crystal clear blue eyes stare at me, framed by her freckled face, as she peaks around the corner of the doorway. I scream out in agony, "Oh Hell!"

Both Peter and Joe come running, Peter arrives first.

"Sweetheart, are you okay?" he asks, eyes fearful as he reaches out to me, grasping both my hands. "Are you having another vision?"

"Get away from her young man," Joe barks as he strides into the room, leaning heavily on his walking cane. "She has vital work to perform and needs all her senses. She can't afford to lose her concentration, not even for a second."

"What?" Peter asks dumbfounded as he releases my hands and backs away a little. He looks to me for some guidance, though I know I can ill afford to be distracted.

Joe urges softly, "Get out of her line of sight. She needs to establish what is real and what is not. She has to focus on discovering clues and can't be distracted by the real. She has to live her dream."

"What are you talking about?" Peter asks, more vigorously. He is obviously a little frustrated at being ordered around by a guest in his own home.

Joe gives Peter a deathly stare as he says earnestly, "For God's sake, keep out of this. There is a girl's life at stake, here."

"I can see her," I say in agony, seeking assistance as to what I should do next. Joe's concerns about my concentration are unfounded; I am fully focused on the vision in front of me. This is my chance to make a difference and I intend to take it. "I can see her. What should I do now?"

Joe continues in a soft, patient voice like a tutor trying to teach someone to read for the very first time, "Take note of everything, every detail about her and anything around her that seems to be part of the vision. If you are unsure whether something you are looking at is real or not, tell us what you see and we can confirm whether it is an element of your vision."

"Can I freeze the vision, stop it from disappearing?" I ask harking back to my experience at the Crown Towers.

Joe considers this notion for a second and then suggests, "Yes, hold onto something in your vision, something prominent."

I am mesmerized by the little girl in front of me. She is the only thing I can readily distinguish in the room that is part of my vision. I smile and move forward, holding out my welcoming hand. The little girl moves backwards as she tries to hide around the corner. She seems scared witless.

"Wait," I instinctively whisper. The little girl inches her head around the corner, blinking her eyes nervously as she checks me out. "She can hear me."

Joe smiles, "Good, you are starting to understand a few more tricks with the visions. She doesn't just hear you; she can also see you, converse with you and feel your touch. To Peter and I she doesn't exist, though to you she is real in every way. Ask her some questions. See how you go. You never know, she may be a little chatterbox once you get her started."

My mind is fully open to Joe's suggestions, no matter how incredulous. A few weeks ago I would have thought the concept of conversing with a person in my dreams was completely insane. However, after the past few weeks and what I have experienced, I know anything is possible. I just have to be receptive to these abstract concepts.

"Why don't you take my hand, Honey?" I ask softly.

The little girl shakes her head obstinately, "Not allowed to talk to strangers!"

"Well then, let me introduce myself, I'm Julie."

The little girl continues to stand her distance. Hands on hips, shaking her head, she begins to cry, "No, the bad man told me his name too and he took me away. Took me and Toto, he did. Mummy told me not to talk to strangers. That is what I must do."

I continue nudging her gently, "But Honey, that's why we are here. We want to help you. We want to get you away from the bad man. We want to take you back to your mummy. She is waiting for us to bring you back to her right now."

The little girl considers this idea, halting her tears in a series of hiccups. Eventually she asks, her face and body language relaxing a little, "And Toto? Will you help me find Toto? I can't see him. It's so dark here. We must find Toto. I miss him more than anything."

"Of course Honey, though tell me, who is Toto? Is he a dolly or teddy bear? Perhaps he is a little brother?"

The little girl strikes an indignant pose, hands placed firmly on hips once more as she corrects my ignorance, "No! Toto is my dog. He's been gone for so long now, I'm scared. I'm scared the bad man has done something to him."

I try to sooth her anxious mind, "Hey Honey, it's alright. I'm sure he's fine. I'm sure they have him somewhere close to you. In fact, they have probably fed him so much that he is peacefully sleeping it off. That is why you can't hear him."

I hope I am right. Maybe he is permanently asleep, less hassle to kidnappers that way. Particularly when you consider that the poor little fellow would have no value to the kidnappers whatsoever. The fact that he has been absent from all my visions does not inspire me with hope.

Her eyes brighten, "Do you really think so?"

I nod and lie effectively, "Yes, I do. Now please, Honey, just take my hand and we'll work it all out. We can find and save both of you. Please, won't you hold my hand?"

I watch as the little girl walks out from behind the edge of the doorway, out into clear view. She is dressed in a pink full length, ruffled cotton dress complete with open toed sandals. She looks very pretty, though her face shows the unmistakable tracks of the numerous tears that have flowed recently. Her body twitches as she chokes back her tears, forcing them to become little gulps of air, coughed intermittently out of her mouth.

Slowly she walks towards me, still hesitant to trust an adult after all that has been done to her. Little by little she moves towards me. I let her come to me. I don't want to scare her away. I realize suddenly that I am treating this experience as real, just like she is actually in the room with me. I think that was what Joe was trying to encourage me to do. If I can live the dream, I will remember and gather more details. More details equate to a better chance of finding her before it is too late.

Finally she places her little hand in mine. I can feel her smooth skin; how cold it is to touch. Her body shivers uncontrollably with fear. I can even feel her blood pulsing through her veins. It is a most bizarre sensation, considering that I know she is not real.

"See, I didn't hurt you," I say looking over at Joe who has taken a seat in the corner. He smiles; an action that makes me feel relaxed, reassurance that I am doing something right. "What's your name, Sweetheart?"

"Who's Julie talking to? There's no one here, for God's sake!" Peter screams as his agitation bubbles to the surface.

"Hush, be silent, my young man. There IS someone here. It is a vision of the little girl, the one who is missing. Julie is the only one able to see and hear her. Don't distract her or the vision may cease prematurely with catastrophic consequences."

Peter begins to speak again, though pauses momentarily as I look at him and shake my head. He remains silent as he oversees the proceedings. I ask again, "Please, Sweetheart; what is your name?"

"I'm Cassandra," she says after pausing to take a deep breath.

"Do you know where you are, Cassandra?" I ask softly, hoping the dam wall has been breached and a torrent of words and clues are about to flow freely from her lips.

"No," Cassandra says, simply.

I try my best to fish for clues, "Can you describe anything in the room?"

Cassandra shakes her head, glumly, "No, it's so dark in here."

I continue my marshmallow interrogation, "Can you tell me anything about where you are? What is the house like where you are staying? Is there something you have seen, something you have smelt, something you have heard, maybe?"

Cassandra shakes her head once more before pausing. Considering the question a little more, she nods, "Yes, there are some things I know."

I smile as I endeavor to contain my exhilaration until I have heard something more concrete, some clue that can be of use in our investigation, "What do you know?"

"I know the bad lady has a picture of a flower on her leg. She smells like red roses, I like roses."

A bad lady! Where did she come from?

"Is the picture like a rose flower?" I ask, continuing to pick at the barren ground, in search for some scarce, vital detail.

Cassandra says defiantly as she frowns, "Oh no, it's not a rose. I know what they look like. This is different. The flower has sharp teeth."

A distinctive tattoo, that is good.

"The bad lady has a tattoo on her leg, of a flower with teeth," I say looking over at Joe who, I can see, is jotting down a note of this fact. "Did this lady hurt you?"

"Oh no, she doesn't even come near me. I don't think she likes children very much. She lets the other man come to check on me. They feed me sandwiches sometimes."

"Do you know their names?"

"I know the man's name; he told me when he first took me for a ride in his car."

Knowing this could be the breakthrough we so desperately need, I ask excitedly, "What is the man's name, Sweetheart?"

Cassandra lowers her head despondently as she begins to cry, "I don't know, I forgot it."

I release her hand as I place my arms around her, giving her a comforting hug, "Hey, hey. It's alright. You're doing great. We are going to get you out of there. Don't worry. Don't fret, little one."

"But, you don't know where I am," she snuffles with a logic that defies her tender years.

"We'll work that out Honey, just stay with me."

A dull thud can be heard clearly from across the other side of the room. "What is that?" Cassandra calls out startled, stretching her neck to see what has created the noise. I am surprised that my vision of Cassandra can apparently distinguish unrelated things occurring in my own vision. This is something new I hadn't considered possible. The visions are becoming somewhat of a stroll on the wild side into a bizarre parallel universe.

I shield her eyes so she can't see the small object that has come to a halt by the far wall. I know exactly what it is, without even sneaking a peak in its direction. I have no intention of letting this little girl see a severed finger. She must be protected from harm at all costs. I try to change the subject and fish for more clues, "So, Honey, what else do you know?"

"I know there are strange sounding animals here at night, maybe they come to drink from the water. I get real scared sometimes, particularly when it is dark."

"So, there's strange sounding animals and water," I repeat for Joe's benefit. "Is it like a pond or a dam maybe?"

Cassandra shakes her head, "Don't be silly, it's a river of course!"

We both turn suddenly, distracted as we hear the sound of a squeaky door open. I am aware of the delicate perfume of roses in full bloom as it suddenly wafts through the room. A slow clicking sound is getting louder by the second. It is a sound I know all too well. The sound of woman's high heels, clicking on the wooden floor boards as she draws nearer.

Cassandra turns towards me, desperately seeking help, her face terrified. With her high pitched whispers, she pleads, "Please, that's her. She never comes here. She's going to hurt me, I'm sure. Please help me."

I sooth, "It's alright, Honey. Nobody's going to hurt you."

Cassandra jumps to her feet, breaking my grasp. She searches around her, assessing her options as she whispers, "No, I need to hide."

"Wait," I say to no avail. Cassandra runs away from me, to the left. Her image fades with each step she takes until she is gone. The sound of footsteps and the scent of roses disappear too. As the pain in my chest dissipates completely, I notice the Roman numeral 'XV' fade and disappear from down low on a side wall.

I look at Joe in disbelief. He stands up, leaning heavily on his stick. Walking a few steps closer he places a reassuring hand on my shoulder, "You did good, girl. You got a lot more details."

"It's not enough. How can we save her with that lot? It's not enough," I utter in distress. Peter moves next to me, crouching on the floor, embracing my quivering body in a bear hug.

"Please Julie; I need to check I have all the facts, so I can let Steve know precisely what we are looking for."

I nod as I compose myself and speak clearly, in a steady voice, "Two people, a man and a woman. The woman has a tattoo of a flower with teeth on her leg. She wears perfume which smells like roses. The girl can hear strange animals and there is a river nearby."

"Excellent. Is there anything else?" Joe asks, madly jotting down the additional details.

I nod and gulp, trying to clear the knot in my throat, "It's dark, it's cold and Cassandra is scared out of her mind."

"So her name's Cassandra?" Joe asks.

I nod, exhausted, as I slump into Peter's arms. Serenity smooches up to my leg as he purrs.

"That's enough for now, let her be," Peter commands Joe.

"Of course, it's been a long day. I'll give Steve a buzz and let him know what we've got. I'm sure he can help now," Joe says as he diplomatically scurries from the room to use my land line.

I lay there exhausted, relishing being in Peter's arms. I catch my reflection in the mirror on the side wall. To my horror I see my hair has suddenly changed color. I now have a narrow streak of grey to the right hand side, prominent amongst my jet black. For a moment I am shocked. I calm myself quickly as I realize I have much bigger problems to deal with. I must find Cassandra before its too late.

God I hope Steve can help us!

'Tick, Tick, Tock'

Tick, tick, tock,

Time marches on,

As the hour draws nearer,

Under the gaze of the moon,

Full and all knowing,

Time marches on,

Tick, tick, tock.

Chapter 13

April 9th 1692.

Salem, Massachusetts.

The thin, wispy fog was insufficient to mask the fact that there had been a full moon watching benevolently over Salem last night. Mary, however, was oblivious to this situation. She was unaware of the extra moonlight streaming through the tiny window of her cell. If she had been observant, she would have paid it no heed anyway. She neither watched for, nor cared, about such superstitious things as full moons. She regarded them as little more than natural occurrences, somewhat romantic in a poetic way. The notion that witches place so much value in the power and magical qualities of the moon during this phase of the lunar month she regards as nothing more than scurrilous poppycock. Her lack of interest on the topic of the full moon could be explained simply by the fact that she wasn't a witch. Though, at the present time in Salem, many would dispute the truthfulness of this claim.

Mary has never been superstitious, not even as a child. This is a curiously surprising trait considering her unswaying faith in the validity of her visions; premonitions that only she has the gift to see. She has never been unsettled by broken mirrors. She will casually stroll under a ladder without a care in the world. Throwing a pinch of salt over her shoulder she considers a sinful waste of a precious condiment. Most of all, Mary is not troubled in the least by black cats crossing her path. In fact, she loves their company. In her belongings she possesses no lucky rabbit's foot, nor any token that could be considered to be a lucky charm. She believes in God and for her, that is more than enough. She is the exception to the rule in Salem, a situation she ponders constantly now she has so much time on her hands.

The presence of the full moon over Salem last night was certainly noticed by Harold. In fact he had spent half the night watching it, the other half pacing to and fro worrying about its significance. His thoughts, last night, dwelled on the two executions, now only hours away. At times he sat mesmerized, watching the candle flickering in the darkness on the table in front of him searching, hoping for salvation. No matter what he tried, on this restless night, he couldn't reconcile his fears. He became weary as the night progressed. Yet, as he drifted towards sleep, the nightmares would begin. They brought to the fore all his inner demons and suspicions, waking him with a frightful start. Harold enjoyed not a second's sleep last night. Through bloodshot eyes he now looks out the window at the fiery red dawn with his fears multiplied and growing in his heart.

One of Mary's gifts is her ability to assess and understand how people feel, just at a glance. She can judge their emotions whether sad, happy, angry or troubled. She also has the ability to instantly see changes occurring around her and understand any threat they may pose to her or her family. These traits have served her well in the past, allowing her to manipulate people to better serve her own needs. They also keep her from walking head long into danger. Even now, she is confident those traits will serve her well in her current predicament.

Mary watches, curious, as Harold arrives at the cells much earlier than most days. She knows what an early arrival means, though the intended recipient is unclear. Mary has seen this process before. She is well aware that a lot of preparation is required prior to a hanging. A casual, yet distinctly worried glance in Mary's direction, confirms her worst fears. Today is to be the day of reckoning for her and Sarah.

The hanging of two people is far more daunting and labor intensive for an executioner like Harold, particularly when it involves witch sisters. Add to this the fact that one of the sisters has partaken in a most hideous murder, one which has shocked all of Salem, and you can imagine how overpowering the pressure for justice and retribution is growing in the community. The story of Jane's murder has made the papers in four territories so far and idle gossip continues to help it spread further. The community expectations are immense. Everything has to run smoothly, down to the very last detail. For if something should go wrong, it will be Harold's job on the line. God forbid if someone was to escape; it will be Harold's neck that feels the roughness of the noose biting ruthlessly into his scaly skin.

Harold goes about his work at a feverish pace. He is a picture of concentration as he checks and double checks everything in preparation for the big event. First he examines the ropes, running his hands over every inch of their rough plaited strands. He searches for frays or imperfections which could cause them to snap when placed under the stress of carrying the weight of a person. Harold has a rule regarding ropes, a rule he would never entertain the thought of breaking. The same rope must never be used twice. The successful rope always remains imbedded in the victim's neck, buried in perpetuity with the criminal, just outside the Christian graveyard in a pauper's grave. It is bad luck to test fate by changing the habits of a lifetime's labor. Harold has no plans for changing his routine, not today.

Harold ties and re-ties the noose until he is sure it is perfect. It must slide down the rope so that it can be positioned firmly around the victim's neck. The knot must be positioned in such a manner that it bites into the skin once body weight is added. There has to be no possibility that the person will slip out of the rope. Under Salem law, a criminal can only be hung once for a crime. A faulty knot could result in a criminal's freedom at the expense of the community's safety. However, if the knot is tied correctly it will hold firm around the criminal's neck, cutting off vital oxygen. If the executioner is lucky, there is an excellent chance the criminal's neck will snap the moment the wagon is moved away. This is what the crowd will no doubt come to see. This is Harold's ultimate goal; to please the masses and keep his own neck out of the noose.

Now that the ropes are ready, Harold leaves the cells, walking out to the town center in a direct line towards the infamous hanging tree. He checks the main horizontal branch which is some two feet in diameter, ensuring it remains sturdy and strong. The same branch has been used for three score plus two hangings over four years with its perfect record intact. However, Harold is a perfectionist, unwilling to allow a new infestation of termites or recent storm damage to undermine his work. Everything must be checked. Harold stands back with his hands on his hips. He smiles broadly as he nods his approval.

Harold walks to the stables and, after a few minutes, returns hauling the wagon across the dusty thoroughfare. He is a big man and has no problem with the weight of the wagon. With a quick fluid movement and his muscles bulging, he positions the wagon directly under the tree. Using it as a platform, he begins to tie the two ropes onto the branch, ensuring they are tied at the correct height, ready for the execution this afternoon. It is important to hang the ropes early in the morning as they become an advertisement to the good people of Salem that an execution is to take place on this day. Once they see the ropes and word is passed, people come from far and wide to see the show. Word spreads fast; crowds gather and at the usual time of 2 P.M. sharp, the event takes place accompanied by the jubilant roar of the gathered crowd.

Once the ropes are in place, Harold walks back towards the cells. Mary hears his unmistakable plodding footsteps drawing nearer though she is somewhat confused. The sound of his footsteps is merged with the steps of another. He is accompanied by someone else, but who? Mary listens intently to the sound of the steps growing closer, searching for clues as to who the second person may be. Suddenly it dawns upon her. Her eyes widen as she shakes her head in disbelief. The other footsteps are familiar to her; she has heard them so many times in her nightmares. John's footsteps are imprinted indelibly on her soul.

John struts proudly across the room until he reaches the front of Mary's cell. A broad smile extends across his face as, hands on hips, he stands, gloating at Mary. He remains silent, simply smiling incessantly in a most deranged manner. The infected scar weeping freely on his cheek adds to the image of someone who is completely unhinged. Mary holds her ground, continuing to lean casually onto the bars at the front of her cell. She is but a few inches away from John's face. Close enough to smell his putrid breath as it is carried on a subtle breeze to her nostrils. She dares not flinch for fear she will appear weak in the face of the evil that stands before her.

"What business hath thou here?" she asks, curious as to what John could possibly want with her at this stage of the proceedings. After all, in just a few hours he will receive what his heart yearns for, justice and retribution.

"Nothing, thy debt to me shall be paid in full on this day," John says, his eyes and face still beaming with delight. All John desires is to see Mary's eyes, to see her fear growing as the time of her execution draws nigh. He has imagined how she will be; hoping with all his soul that she will be overcome with the same fear his wife had experienced when Mary had stood over her, holding the carving knife in her hand, ready to plunge it deep into her stomach on that infamous day. As John looks into Mary's eyes, his smile begins to falter. He tilts his head as he tries to work out what she is feeling. To John, Mary appears remarkably calm, too calm for his liking. Something is amiss.

Mary shakes her head as she speaks, "I hath had visions. I see the future with clarity. One of us shall hang but it shan't be me. It shall not come to pass on this day."

John laughs a little nervously. He is fearful of Mary's witchcraft. His intuition tells him that the execution may not have the result he so desperately yearns for. He tries to hide his concern as he continues, "Thou be so sure, even in the face of certain death. Thou doth not know as much as thou thinketh."

"I know what I see," Mary says plainly.

"And what, pray tell, doth thou see?" John asks intrigued by Mary's confidence. He begins to wonder if he can gleam some useful information from Mary's words. Useful information which can be used against her to ensure her demise goes to plan.

Mary pauses while she considers her words. She doesn't fear John in the slightest. She knows he can do her no harm. It is this precise reason why she feels she can speak openly to him without any danger of reprisal. She offers boldly, "I dream constantly while awake."

John raises an eyebrow, a little taken aback by this revelation, "Thou doth not hath a special vision, just a soul of pure evil."

Disgusted by this, Mary retorts, "Only the guilty shall hang."

John smiles as he mocks Mary, "And so they shall."

Mary's temper begins to boil to the surface. Her face is ruddy and hot as her hands try, without success, to rip the bars away from their moorings. With contempt in her eyes she says slowly, "I doth not lie. I see many things. I doth see a lady in a blue dress bearing a yellow ribbon. She be known to thee. She be known to thee for a long time, though unbeknown to thy wife."

John's face darkens. He knows instantly whom Mary speaks of. A chill runs down his spine as he begins to wonder if Mary's witchcraft is so powerful that it can escape the restrictions of these prison walls and extend out to do harm to the one true love of his life, "Lucinda. How doth thou know of Lucinda?"

Mary smiles as she senses John's apprehension, "I see what shall come to pass. I see an unsavory man of impertinence fly into a fit of rage. I see two coffins; one filled by an act of fury, one by a decision of law."

"I will not hang!" John screams, interpreting Mary's words as a threat to both his mistress and himself.

"I hath seen the future and it will be so. Unless....."

John swallows the bile rising up from his stomach. He moves closer to the cell, seeking some divine guidance, "Yes?"

"Unless thou cease your visitation of this lady and leave this town forever."

Filled with rage, John bites into his lower lip. He turns on his heel and begins to pace around the room. After a moment he turns and moves decisively back towards Mary, "I shall not. My love for her be pure."

"It be God's will. If thou stays, she dies in an angry rage and thou shall hang. Of that I am certain," Mary calmly states, shrugging her shoulders.

John shakes his head. His emotions mix and blur. He has always had a temper though, to his mind, he has only ever used it responsibly. In his eyes, the only times he has hit Jane or Lucinda was when they had deserved it. Shaking his head, he refuses to contemplate the notion that Lucinda would someday die at his hand. It must be trickery designed to unsettle him. His brain runs from confusion to fear, then back to confusion again. In the end, all he feels is rage and hatred for Mary and her tall stories, "It all be lies! Nothing shall happen. Thou art pure evil. Thou can nay seduce me to do thy evil bidding."

Mary smiles, "Maybe it takes a pure heart to see true evil in the eyes of one such as thee."

John roars incoherently as he turns and charges towards the stairs. At the base of the stairs he pauses, just long enough to issue Mary with a parting threat. "No, thou doth speaketh lies. I shall ensure thy falsehoods stop on this day. There be no doubt that I shall watch thee die today, freeing my soul of thy devilish torment."

John runs up the stairs, two at a time. He leaves a void of absolute silence in his wake.

Mary turns her focus towards Harold who has been watching this tirade of words in its entirety, frozen with fear. Mary smiles at him, "Why doth thou fear me so?"

Panic courses through his body as Harold tries desperately to avert his gaze as he lies, "I fear naught."

Mary is eager to pursue the topic further, delighted by the prospect that her jailer is scared of her. She finds it comforting and possibly, just possibly, very useful to her slowly formulating plan for escape. Mary continues to push Harold in a provocative and somewhat playful manner, "Thou art fearful. There can be no denial. I can smell the fear in the air. Thou knoweth my words be the truth. Thou art fearful of my powers. Does one not wish to be a warty toad?"

Harold repeats himself more sternly, trying to give Mary the impression that he is in full control of his emotions, "I fear naught!" As he speaks Harold's whole body shakes uncontrollably, sweat pours down his forehead and he tentatively glances in Mary's direction as if terrified of her casting some form of hideous spell on him.

Mary laughs as she notices a subtle movement in amongst the shadows at the base of the far wall. Her plan is beginning to take shape and come to life as crucial elements steadily fall into place. She smiles as she says, "We'll see. Let there be no doubt, she is mine and she'll not do thy bidding."

A chill spreads through Harold's body as he senses something has changed in the cells. Wiping the sweat from his brow, he slowly lifts his head and searches the shadowy landscape around him. Eyes bulging, he begins to shake uncontrollably as he sees a small creature skulking in the shadows. His heart races as his brain tries to fathom what unholy creature Mary has summoned from the bowels of Hell to torment him. As the creature walks into the daylight, directly towards Harold, he can clearly see it is the worst of Satan's minions. It is the culmination of all his fears and nightmares. Jezebel moves forward before positioning herself right at Harold's feet. She sits and looks straight at Harold with her one good eye, purring incessantly, blinking occasionally.

"There still be time to redeem thy self."

Gripped by fear Harold places his head in his hands and repeats over and over again, "It be a sign. It be a sign. I be doomed, I tell thee. It be a sign."

Harold's face turns pale as all the blood steadily drains to his lower limbs. Nausea engulfs his brain as he sees the objects before him become airborne and start spinning around his head with ever increasing velocity.

His heart pounding, he faints in an instant, falling in a awkward heap on the floor. Jezebel moves forward and affectionately nuzzles Harold's right hand, looking for a pat though there is no response. Harold is out cold.

Mary's mind turns to thoughts of her sister, silent in one of the other cells, out of sight. "Sarah?" she calls out but there is no reply. She fears for her sister's state of mind. She has been in these God forsaken cells for too long now and, even worse, she has been silent for eight days. The last time they had spoken was one night which had ended with Sarah crying herself to sleep . With faith that her sister is out there and listening, Mary tries to allay her fears, "Sarah! Please listen to me. I hath seen our salvation in my divine visions. We shall not die this day. Only murderers shall die this day. We shall live beyond this day. I see what shall be. Be strong. Be strong, my Darling. Just for a little while longer."

As Mary falls silent, listening to her own words echo through the adjacent cells, tears begin to form in her eyes. Mary wishes for nothing more than to be with Sarah, to hug her tight, to brush her hair out of her eyes and sing her lullabies until she falls into a peaceful slumber. Reality hits hard as a pain starts to throb in her chest. She is resigned to the fact that it is not meant to be. Not yet at least.

'Hope'

A curious sensation,
Inexplicable in its existence.
It is part of the human complexion,
A part of our conscious reason.

It is the reason we strive,
In harsh winters we will cope.
For when the odds are nil in favor,
Don't give up, there's always hope.

Chapter 14

Tuesday, February 28ᵗʰ, 2006.

Evening.

Kinglake, Victoria, Australia.

It is eight o'clock in the evening. I made up my mind some time ago, to come out onto the porch and watch the stars for a bit. It is an isolated spot where I can find a little tranquility and peaceful solitude; a place where I don't have to think too hard, at least for a while. Somewhere my tense muscles can relax, away from my strange new world and all its problems which encircle me. The sky is clear tonight, no hint of fog at all, such a rare occasion in Kinglake. It is something to be cherished. Something I relish with unashamed abandon.

The misshapen wooden step is exceeding my expectations. Mixed with the cool summer breeze, I find it soothing, allowing much needed time for private contemplation. So much has happened in the last few weeks. It has been a roller coaster ride of conflicting emotions. Becoming comfortable experiencing lucid premonitions has taken time. It has also taken a toll on my body and soul. Even now I struggle with the graphic confrontation as strange and horrible apparitions mix with everyday items in my life.

I certainly feel uncomfortable with the direction the premonitions are leading me. The danger of trying to 'save the day' is of immense concern. My fear of failure is only matched by my fear of walking meekly into harm's way. Added to this, the people I am beginning to rely heavily upon for assistance, are definitely a worry. How could I not be worried about Steve and his sinister sidekick Chris? Harm's way might be closer than I think. I need to be wary. I need to find a better way though, at this point in time, one is not readily self-evident.

"A penny for your thoughts," Joe says, smiling at me as he staggers out through the swinging wire door.

"Hey," I say. "You should go inside, you know. It's getting cold out here."

"Not a chance, little lady. You look like there's a weight on your mind and I think you would do well to share it. If there's one thing I'm good at in this world, it's that I'm an excellent listener. So Sweetheart, spill the beans. What troubles your pretty head on this beautiful night?"

I smile. I am growing rather fond of Joe and his quirky slant on the world. It is comforting to have the support of another person who has had first-hand experience of the visions. Peter is trying his best, yet he can never possibly comprehend what I am going through. How it feels and the draining effect it has on me emotionally are things he can only guess at. He could only know these things if, for a brief moment, he could somehow change places with me and have a premonition himself. Unfortunately, that is impossible. Anyway, I would never wish these visions on another, particularly not Peter. I don't think he is strong enough to survive the mayhem they bring as baggage.

"Well," I relent with a sigh. "It's a little hard to explain exactly. I'm just feeling a little overwhelmed at the moment. Life is moving so fast, I'm struggling to find time to breathe. I'm being pulled in so many new and unusual directions all at once that I feel like I am being slowly ripped apart. It's a lot to deal with all at once; particularly when I neither sought nor desired these premonitions."

"So, I guess this is the point where I need to say to you, 'there, there. It's alright. With time it will get easier for you'," Joe says as he awkwardly holds the porch rail, slides down to the step and sits next to me, patting my leg as he lands safely on the woodwork.

"So it does get easier to handle?" I ask with an air of excitement, hoping for some much needed good news.

"If that's what you want to believe my girl, you go ahead and believe it," Joe says absent mindedly, staring out into the bush hidden by darkness in front of us. "Though honestly, you need to realize that's just not the case. It's all downhill from here. At least that has been my experience of this God damn curse."

I smile and stare into the distance too, "I had a feeling you were going to tell me that."

Joe smiles ruefully as he considers his words, "For we know in part and we prophesy in part, but when perfection comes the imperfect disappears."

I smile, surprised by Joe's eloquence, "That's so beautiful. Did you write that?"

Joe scoffs, "Don't be silly. It's just a thing I heard once in church at a friend's funeral. I think it was from Paul's first letter to the Corinthians or some shit like that. I don't remember the rest but that bit stuck with me because it aptly summed up what I was going through; what I am still going through."

"Do you believe in God then?" I ask intrigued.

"Hell no!" Joe says defiantly. "And I don't think SHE believes in me either."

I smile as I consider his contradictory statement, "Yet you quote passages from the bible?"

Joe nods his head, "It's just one sentence I took a liking to by accident. It was something that struck a chord. It gave me a little comfort. I mean, we can only ever know so much beforehand, even with premonitions. It is only when the situation plays out to its eventual finale that our imperfect view of what will be has disappeared. Then, and only then, do we catch a glimpse of what clarity looks like. Do you understand what I am getting at?"

I nod as I consider his well thought out words, "I guess I do. I just wish I had more information beforehand. It is not much use to me after the event. Hindsight is extremely frustrating to me at this particular moment."

Joe pats me reassuringly on the knee as he continues, "Don't get me wrong, the future's not all bad. You'll get better and better at interpreting the premonitions; that will certainly help you. The more you understand of what your vision is foretelling, the greater your chance for success. However, you have to realize that you are only receiving an opportunity to help people. There is no guarantee of success. You must be strong and prepare for the times when you fail. If you are not strong, failure will eat away at your very soul until you are nothing but a hollow shell. You do not want to let yourself ever get to that dark place where you feel only hollow and worthless."

I look out towards Emma's house with the police tape now in shreds. Mother nature is already clearing the crime scene, bringing a normality back to the little hamlet of Kinglake. Looking through my eyes I know I will never see normality here again. Even now, as I gaze towards Emma's house, I can see her clearly as she watches me through the front window with sorrowful eyes. There is no need for her to speak in order to relay her pain or accusations. I hear every unspoken word clearly, "I've already learned that one. You can't save everyone. However, letting someone down in this manner leaves a bitter aftertaste in your mouth."

Joe shakes his head, "That's not exactly what I'm trying to explain to you about these premonitions."

I turn and look at Joe. He has a quizzical expression on his face which is hard to read. "What is it, Joe?" I ask.

"It's..... it's just that I've done a lot of research into our family tree; our bloodline and the lives of our fellow ancestors and cousins you could say. It's quite interesting research once you get into it, though it is open to a lot of speculation."

I find myself becoming intrigued by the way Joe seems to be dancing around what sounds like an interesting story. Maybe he has garnered some insight into how our visions have some genetic connection, going back in generations past. I ask eagerly, "Did you find conclusively other family members that had premonitions during their lifetimes?"

Joe nods, "Oh, I think there have been a great number of our fellow cousins who have had a similar experience to us."

"A great number; are you talking ten, one hundred, one thousand?"

"I couldn't speculate on the exact number because I have not been able to trace all the descendants of Mary Murphy. However, I would think the number would be several hundred at least."

I am shocked by this revelation. Before I met Joe, I was hoping that there might be someone else in the world that could help me understand what I am going through. To find out there could be several hundred is just mind boggling. The more I think about it, the more I can't get my head around this notion, "So many! Are any of them still alive today?"

Joe pats me reassuringly on the knee once, more, "Sweetheart, I'm sure we are not alone. It's just a matter of whether or not anyone else wishes to risk the ridicule associated with admitting that they have premonitions too. I'm sure most are either in hiding or in denial."

"Yes," I say thinking back to my own experience. The visions are something that makes you question your own sanity. Others are quick to declare you insane without as much as a second thought. I think of my mother and her reaction to my visions. She had no hesitation having me admitted to the psychiatric ward. I fully understanding what Joe is talking about. "It does feel like we are living in a Brother's Grimm fairytale."

"No," Joe disagrees. "People are more likely to think you are just insane and leave it at that. It is easier for their feeble minds to cope with. It is human nature to expect the worst from other people. That way, they are not usually disappointed."

I think back to my stint in the psychiatric hospital, being assessed for my sanity. Without Peter's help I would still be there, rotting away, drugged to the gills in a perpetual stupor. I can see how the premonitions can provoke fear in the hearts and minds of the ignorant. They produce a potentially hostile and maybe even deadly situation for those cursed; even in these most enlightened of times, superstition can provoke powerful feelings.

"Have some of the others 'visionaries' suffered at the hands of strangers simply for having premonitions?" I ask with a heavy heart. With the years of research and effort Joe has put into studying our shared family tree, I am sure he has come across some horror stories. As I look to him now, I wonder if he is brave enough to share some with me.

Joe stares off into the distance as if he is captivated by a stage play, lacking the will or desire to avert his gaze, "Yes, I'm sure they have. Mary Murphy was tried as a witch back in the sixteen hundreds. Since that time, others have been locked away in psychiatric hospitals around the world. You and I can only imagine the extreme treatment regimes that were inflicted, such as electrotherapy, in an attempt to cure them. Many would have been betrayed by others in order to be certified as insane. Sometimes they were betrayed by family members who lacked the capacity to understand and who were overcome by fear. There seems to be a lot of documentation relating to various 'cousins' being admitted to psychiatric hospitals."

"I guess some of these people were locked away with just cause."

Joe smiles, "I'm most surprised that I'm not one of them. After seventy years, or so, of these God damn apparitions, it's a miracle I haven't been diagnosed as insane too."

"You're okay," I reassure. "You seem to have your act together."

"Some days, I'm not so sure," Joe says solemnly. "I just try to make it from one day to the next. That seems to have worked for me thus far. That is the reason why I am here now. You, Julie, have to find your own path. One you can walk with your head held high as you share your life with these premonitions. It's most important."

"Why?" I ask, curious as to why Joe's mood has slid towards morose. *What are you too scared to tell me?*

Reluctantly, Joe continues as he decides finally, to my relief, to just go straight to the point, "Well, our bloodline seems to have a large proportion of suicides and accidental deaths, many of which may well be suicides too. Some could be murders committed by their closest friends and family."

"Great!" I say, forcing a wry grin.

Joe turns, looking sharply at me, with much concern, "I didn't mean to upset you; I just want you to be fully aware of what your predicament is all about. You'll have these premonitions for the rest of your life, you know. You cannot escape your preordained destiny. Lord knows, I have tried and failed on that front. They will not let me rest for an instant. Eventually, you will find that they won't allow you any peace too."

"I know. It's something I will have to learn to live with."

Joe speaks slowly, "I want you to remember something I once heard, some positive words of great importance. They fit well with our situation without being filled with all that God damn religious mumbo jumbo that abounds today. It's just a phrase that I think of whenever I get into a scrap that seems impossible. Something that I think the Greek philosopher Aristotle once voiced. I think he was a very smart man, in any era. Well, he was smarter than me, anyway."

"What did he say?" I ask as my curiosity is aroused.

"Hope is a waking dream," Joe says plainly. "They are only five words yet somehow they are the most important ever spoken. You would do well to hold onto them, keep them close to your heart."

I smile, "When the sky is dark and foreboding, never give up. There's always hope."

"Nice words. Who wrote that?" Joe asks.

I continue to grin, "They are my words, something I've always felt, ever since I was a child. I don't know. They are just words I have always felt are important to me for some reason."

"You've got a good soul, Sweetheart. It is your beautiful soul that will help you deal with all this," Joe states. "I once had a soul like that too. Unfortunately, mine steadily eroded away till I had nothing but a handful of dust and a hollow cavity in my chest. I think it may be different for you. That is my hope at least."

"Don't be like that. You've done so much with your life. You must have helped so many people over the years. You, more than anyone else, must have reason to believe in hope."

"I guess," Joe shrugs his shoulders in a non-committal fashion as he struggles to stop the tears forming in his eyes. "It's just that when I was young, I had such grand plans that didn't eventuate. They were all my hopes and dreams, if you prefer. I was going to find someone special, someone with raven hair and Spanish blue eyes that sparkle in the moonlight. I was going to spend the rest of my life making damn sure she knew exactly how I felt about her. I had foolish dreams of being a father someday too but none of it was to be. Sometimes hope is not enough. Fate has other plans for our lives. Now, the well is dry. I am all out of hope."

Oscar quietly wanders across the porch, curling up behind Joe as he purrs contentedly. Joe reaches behind and pats his old friend. I can see they are great mates. It is strange how animals can sense when their owners are feeling low or sick. They always seem to be there, to offer comfort, when times are tough.

"I'm sorry Joe. I had no idea."

"Don't you dare shed any tears for an old fool like me, lamenting what might have been. My life is what it is and I should be thankful for that. Anyway, if I had found someone special, she would have needed to be a saint to put up with the likes of me," Joe laughs awkwardly as my mobile phone begins to ring.

"Hello?" I say hesitantly as I take the call from the unfamiliar number. "Oh, hi Steve. Yes he's here. I'll pass you over."

"Oh, excuse me for a second. Hello," Joe says taking the phone from me. He stands up arthritically and walks to the other end of the porch. I watch as he talks earnestly to Steve. It is hard to tell from his face whether the news is good or bad. He glances over at me, placing a hand over the phone to block the sound of his voice, "Excuse me Julie, do you know a place called 'Wilhelmina Falls'?"

I nod, "Yes, it's not far from here, between Toolangi and Yea roughly."

"Thanks," Joe says, rushing back to his phone conversation. He continues to wander along the porch, speaking softly into the phone.

Eventually he stops, flicks the phone shut and turns to look at me. To my relief, he is smiling broadly, "He thinks he's onto something. There are a few loose ends he needs to check out, though he thinks he's close to finding the girl."

"You're kidding?" I question, disbelieving my ears. Joe has been exuberant in assuring me that Steve is good at gathering information and helping to solve the premonitions. However, I am surprised that, with the limited information at his disposal, he has still succeeded in coming up with something tangible, so quickly.

"Yes, it's great news. He wants us to meet him about nine tomorrow morning, at Wilhelmina Falls," Joe says barely containing his obvious enthusiasm.

"Wilhelmina Falls, why there?" I ask, surprised that these isolated falls have something to do with my premonition. However, the more I think about it, the more I wonder if the 'running water' that Cassandra mentioned in the last premonition is related to this new lead.

Cassssannndraaaa! Are the Wilhelmina Falls close to where you are being kept?

"I don't know exactly. Steve must have his reasons, he always does. The falls may have something to do with this massive jigsaw puzzle. I guess we'll find out tomorrow."

I guess we will.

A feeling of dread creeps slowly into my mind. It leaves me cold and uncertain. It is just a thought which is beginning to worry me. A thought I can't displace about Steve, even though he appears to be helping. Knowing his background as a criminal and all round thug is something which I struggle to overlook. He is still a nasty piece of work. I know that from the night I met him in Enterprise Park. It is hard to merge this lasting first impression of Steve with Joe's glowing recommendations.

Can I trust him?

What is the deal he wants delivered if he helps to successfully find Cassandra?

Can I afford not to trust him?

No, I've got to try and save little Cassandra. I can't let her down. I have no choice other than to trust Steve.

I sit on the porch staring out into the darkened distance. My heart is pounding and my mind is racing sifting through numerous conflicting thoughts. I already know one thing for certain. It is going to be a very long, sleepless night. There is nothing I can do to change that.

I sit there calmly, trying to slow my heart rate. I feel we are so close now. However, as the mosquitos begin to bite, I remain just a little apprehensive about what tomorrow might bring.

'Slither'

Whispers slither harmlessly by.
Truth lies yet to be found.
Rumors are shared,
As deception abounds.

Beware the bold.
Don't think, just hear.
Stay clear and calm,
Be sure to control your fear.

Chapter 15

Wednesday, March 1st, 2006.

Morning.

Kinglake, Victoria, Australia.

Peter is greatly unimpressed when he discovers that Joe and I are going to Wilhelmina Falls this morning, chasing kidnappers. I can see by the tension in his shoulders that he is still uncomfortable with Joe. I feel his reservations about Joe stem from his fear of my premonitions and the danger they place me squarely amongst. He tries to hide his anxiety, yet it is still crystal clear from where I am standing. At least I know he is on my side as he tries to protect me from danger at all times.

The prospect of wandering about naively to a secluded location chasing an unknown number of dangerous kidnappers, all of whom wield an assortment of weapons, is doing Peter's head in. I can tell. He is struggling to understand my reasoning as to why I would plan to walk calmly into such a hostile situation. His pouting lips tell me more than words that he is not willing to let me travel with newly found friends of dubious background on such a fool's errand. After a short, vigorous discussion, Peter informs me that I am not going there without him. He storms out of the room in order to phone and cancel all his appointments for the day, slamming the kitchen door as he goes. I am not angry with him, not even in the slightest. Far from it, I feel reassured and very much in love with this marvelous man.

To our surprise, we end up with a car full of passengers. Peter, Joe and I all enter the car at once. As soon as we open the car doors, Serenity bounds into the car like a sprightly kitten. As we stand gob smacked, looking at each other, Oscar steadily plods along until he too, with some effort, paws flailing, clambers into the car. Both cats curl up together in the corner of the back seat. A little stunned, we decide not to try to evict them. These curious creatures seem to know their own minds and will never be persuaded otherwise.

It takes us about an hour to reach the gravel road leading into the picnic area at the base of the Wilhelmina Falls. A dirt track winds its way up the steep slope for approximately one kilometre, concluding at the very top of the falls. At this spot the view is incredible. You have a completely unobstructed view overlooking the rolling hills of Kinglake, Glenburn and Yea. The falls are also breathtaking if you choose to turn around.

I know these falls well. About a year ago I helped the local tourist association photograph regional landmarks. The Wilhelmina Falls were one of the major attractions they wanted to use on brochures and posters in order to promote the Kinglake -Yea region to a largely ignorant Melbourne tourist market. The local tourist association, at this time, was extremely active, attending in excess of twenty festivals and events each year to promote their wares. I was pleased to pick up a little 'tax free' pocket money for my assistance. I was also extremely chuffed that my amateur photographs were now being seen by thousands of people each year.

As Peter pulls into the car park, I catch my first glimpse of Steve. He is completely exposed for all to see, glimmering in the early morning sunlight. Cigarette held loosely in his right hand. His broken left arm, still in plaster, is hanging limply by his side. He appears skinny, though I suspect he is all muscle, no fat on his body at all. He seemed highly fit and agile moving amongst the shadows on the night I met him in Enterprise Park.

Steve is dressed in tight fitting denim jeans and a white t-shirt which exposes the top of his dark hairy chest. Over the t-shirt he has donned a black leather jacket with brown patches on the shoulders and elbows. His short black hair is slicked back with some sort of dark oily gel. He looks for all the world like the quintessential American biker, stepping straight out of the sixties.

As we come to a halt, I get a good look at his face. It is lined and creased making him look much older than the forty or so years he actually is. The left side of his face is shockingly disfigured, standing stark in the early light of day. It reveals an undeniable violent history, in any language. His past life has left him with a deep cut from the side of his mouth, up his cheek and finishes somewhere just below and behind the ear. It is a cut that must have taken at least fifty stitches or more to fix. By its appearance, he wasn't treated by plastic surgeons at any reputable hospital. It simply looks like someone has sewn it up brutally in order to prevent further blood loss. The physician gave scant regard for how it was going to look in the future. Maybe he likes it that way. It certainly makes him look a fearsome sight.

"Jesus!" Peter says softly as he exits the car. He turns his gaze from Steve towards me as he stares disapprovingly.

"Shh! He's had a hard life."

"I can see that!" Peter says sarcastically as we walk slowly towards Steve.

"Don't cause trouble, Peter," I warn as I try to keep my voice soft. "We need Steve's help. He's the only one with contacts to the underworld who would ever consider helping us."

"Yes and what does a man like that want in return?" Peter ask skeptically. "He is surely not doing this out of the goodness of his heart."

Through gritted teeth I say softly, nearly believing each word I utter, "He doesn't want anything. I think he just wants to find redemption for past indiscretions."

Peter sighs as we continue to edge closer to Steve. He whispers, almost inaudibly, as we progress to be within just a few feet of Steve, "Watch him always."

Don't worry. I will.

Steve throws his cigarette down on the ground, grinding it into the dust with a swivel of his hiking boot. He turns and faces us. Walking briskly, with a sickly grin on his face, he moves quickly over the small, intervening distance. Arm outstretched, he greets Peter, "Hi, I'm Steve. I don't think we've had the pleasure."

Peter appears under whelmed, as he shakes his hand. "I'm Peter, Julie's fiancée," he says, emphasizing the word 'fiancée'.

Eye brows raised, I stare at Peter with disbelieving eyes. He obstinately refuses to look at me, at all. He just continues to stare at the leather clad man he is meeting for the first time. I guess he is trying to assess him; to gauge whether or not he is a risk to us. Maybe he is trying to protect me. After all, Peter has never even hinted at asking me to marry him. Yet now I am his 'fiancée'. Is he showing a jealous streak or just acting overprotective? I know him well yet even I can't tell.

We will talk about this later mate! I want to know what your game is.

"Great, glad to have you on board. We will need extra people. Great to see you Joe, Julie," Steve says, unperturbed by Peter's attitude. He turns to face me, staring intently as if he is trying to assert his dominance.

Are you trying to play some sort of mind game? Do you know? Have you realized? Maybe, maybe not. The light wasn't that good at Enterprise Park. Maybe you don't know I'm the one that caused your broken arm. Or do you? I wonder.

"Hi Steve," I say confidently without an inkling of hesitation. I don't want him to sense any sign of weakness. I decide my only course of action is to keep my poker face and call his bluff. If he is going to recognize me, he would have already done so. In my mind, that presents only two possible situations. One, he doesn't recognize me and as such I am relatively safe in his company. The second would be that he has recognized me and is forming some sort of plan for revenge which he will enact, at some point, later on. I will be cautious, just in case this is the situation. However, I feel it is worth the risk. I must save Cassandra.

Steve glares directly at me with a stupid grin on his face. He says nothing for a few seconds as his eyes probe deeply into every pore of my skin. It is like he is a wild predator, waiting for his prey to lose its nerve and flinch for an instant, revealing its true underlying fear. I have no intention of flinching. He has no idea who he is dealing with. I am mentally stronger than him.

"Well let's get to it," Steve jumps to life suddenly, rubbing his hands together vigorously. "We have a dilemma which, with Peter's help, we may be able to overcome."

"What's the problem, Steve?" Joe asks intrigued.

"Sometimes the information I gleam from my 'friends' throughout Melbourne is old. Sometimes it is in the form of unsubstantiated rumors or Chinese whispers. Sometimes it's someone who has overheard a conversation in a pub between two others. They then pass this information onto a third party who then forwards the information onto me. I then offer a small gratuity for their time and effort, a little recompense for their business expenses, you may say."

Peter looks angry, "So what you are telling us is that you dragged us out here to these bloody falls, when you have no information on this .... this....."

"Cassandra," I help.

"Yes, this Cassandra or where she might be."

"On the contrary," Steve continues, smiling a toothy grin which reveals, in gleaming brilliance, his gold capped teeth. "I know quite a lot. I'm just not completely sure of all the details. I don't think we can wait for the information to become more precise. I have a feeling we are simply running out of time and need to act now. I always trust my feelings. That's how I have survived so long."

"So what do you know, Steve?" I ask, seeking enlightenment as to the wellbeing of the little girl. I can only imagine her distress having been imprisoned for all this time.

"Thanks for asking, my Darling," Steve says as he runs his good hand down my arm in a provocative gesture that hasn't gone unnoticed by Peter. "Well I know she is being held by a group of young, petty criminals called the Stevensons. They are largely inexperienced and, as far as I can tell, have only completed a few minor crimes successfully thus bringing their presence on the crime scene to prominence. Their forte has mainly been to knock over the odd service station and bottle shop here and there. They have a reputation because they are pretty brutal, when confronted. 'Overtly indignant' was how one of my sources put it."

"So if you know who has her, why can't we just go and get her, or call the police and let them deal with this gang?" Peter asks a little aggressively. His distaste for Steve is obvious. Peter is quick to make an assessment of people he meets. It is very hard for new acquaintances to change his opinion once it is set.

"Do you want to kill the girl?" Steve asks, as his grin fades. "These guys are jumpy. The first sign of cops and they'll kill her, surely. They kidnapped her from one of Melbourne's prominent underworld families. Surprisingly, they did a good job of nabbing her. They are just not sure how they should go about collecting the ransom they are asking for."

"A ransom?" I ask.

Steve nods, "Two million bucks, from what I have heard. Though, they will be lucky to spend a cent of it, if they collect. Cassandra's father will have them hunted down and murdered within hours of any drop. They know this and are unsure of how they should proceed."

"You know these blokes better than us, what do you think they will do?" Joe asks.

Steve shrugs his shoulders, "I don't know. They've got themselves into a Hell of a mess. I think in the end, they will panic and kill the girl, hiding her in the bush so they can have a head start trying to flee the bounty hunters who will surely be after their scalps."

"So you think they will do that soon?" I ask a little nauseous, feeling that this situation is becoming worse than I had first feared.

"I think that's the only assumption we can make. We have to act swiftly and get the girl back," Steve says calmly, accentuating the urgency of the situation.

"So why are we here in a car park?" Peter questions with obvious agitation.

Steve looks at him sternly, as if he is beginning to lose patience with his lip, "We are here because we have a problem. We have two locations where she might be held hostage."

I am shocked by this revelation, "What do you mean two locations? I thought you had accurate information on the people who took Cassandra?"

Steve sighs with frustration, "I told you how this works, lady. Some of the information is good, some is sketchy. What I have is a little more accurate than your dodgy premonitions, at least."

"So how can we tell if anything you know is accurate? You could be just sending us all into unnecessary danger when the girl is not with this gang of thieves at all," Peter says, his contempt bubbling to the surface. He has not been at all comfortable with Steve from the moment he first laid eyes on him. The conversation has only added to his legitimate concerns. I am hoping Peter will hold it together and not wreck our chances of using Steve to help find Cassandra.

Steve sighs once more as he pauses, glaring straight at Peter for a few seconds. Finally he starts to speak slowly, in a calm voice; turning and addressing each of us in turn, "Whether or not you believe what I have to say is up to you. In the end we have three options. We can all go our separate ways and forget about finding the little girl. This will mean she will surely die."

"I don't think any of us want to panic and do that. We all want to save Cassandra," Joe suggests, looking at Peter who simply shrugs his shoulders in acknowledgement.

Steve continues, "Option two is we can stay here all day and debate what we should do. That will probably result in the little girl being killed too."

"Look, I don't want the girl to die, Steve. I just want to make sure that we are getting the right information about where she is, so we can help," Peter suggests.

Steve ignores Peter's words, "Option three is we split up and try to rescue the little girl from both locations. You three need to have a think about what you are doing and tell me exactly where we go from here. I await your decision with baited breath."

Steve walks a short distance away from us. He stands immobile, hands on hips, back facing us. His body language gives nothing away. I guess that is the way he wants it; leaving the decision purely in our hands and on our heads. A clever move if he is telling us the truth. I guess it is also a clever move if he is lying to us too. We just won't know unless we trust him and work with him to try to rescue Cassandra from whichever of the two places is correct.

"I know what you're going to say, Julie, and it's not on. I don't like the idea of us splitting up. It's dangerous. If he is setting us up it will make it easier for him," Peter says with fear burning in his eyes. He knows I am desperate to find Cassandra. He knows I am willing to take a chance if I have an opportunity to save the little girl.

"Peter, we don't have much choice. Steve is right. There is no fourth option. The only option, that might save the day, is for us to split up and try to raid both places at once. It simply makes sense."

Peter sighs reluctantly as he tries to come to terms with my logic, "I'm not leaving you with him."

"Peter, let's just call him back and see what he has to say. Then we can work out what's best."

Peter shrugs his shoulders, "You do that, though I'm telling you now, I love you Julie and I'm not willing to leave you with a bloke I don't trust."

I smile, liking the sound of what I hear, "Let's just wait and see what this is all about. Then we can work out what is best. Steve!"

Steve turns arrogantly to face us; his cheeky grin restored as he saunters slowly back to our huddle. "So you've made a decision. What, pray tell, is it?"

"We'll do as you recommend. We'll split up and try to raid both places at once," Joe informs him. "It is the only option that makes any sense."

"Good," Steve smiles more broadly as if he is pleased he is getting his way. "The information I have says she may be at an apartment above 'Charlie's Cakes' in Main Street, Yea. This is the base of operations which the Stevensons currently use as their hideout. From what I can gleam, from my sources, this residence has only one entrance in and out. Such a set up allows for optimal security. They can see us coming well before we get anywhere near them."

"So there is no way in?" I ask, trying to figure out what Steve has planned.

Steve ignores my question as he continues his assessment of the task at hand, "For this reason we need to go straight through the shop, up a flight of stairs out the back and knock through a fortified wooden door very, very quickly. We must hope this will allow us some semblance of an advantage through boldness. They shouldn't be expecting a frontal assault; that is just foolish. If we are lucky, we may catch the watch off guard. However, we must remain aware that there will be the real danger of several heavily armed men, lurking in the room, with the little girl."

"Sounds just peachy," Peter says sarcastically.

"The second location is a little shack hidden in the bush at the top of Wilhelmina Falls. This is a location where the Stevenson's allegedly keep their plundered goods. It is not as fortified. In fact it is designed to give the appearance of being an old, abandoned shack with no obvious value. Julie and I should be able to force our way in without much effort."

"Hey, why don't you and I take the shack on the hill?" Peter asks as he folds his arms tightly in an unconscious gesture of negative body language.

"Have you been listening to me or should I talk slower?" Steve asks abruptly. "You need to go to Yea because you are the fittest and strongest one here. Do you expect your girlfriend to knock down a fortified wooden door? Or would you leave that to a one armed man or a doddering old fool? Please listen to me carefully and follow my instructions to the letter. If you do that, you never know, we might all stay alive."

I listen patiently to the conversation and know that even though he is being aggressive in his approach, Steve is none the less right. By the way Steve has described the hideout in Yea, only Peter has a chance of forcing his way into the building. I can't go with Peter to Yea because I have major doubts as to whether Joe can make the steep, arduous climb to the top of Wilhelmina Falls. It is a forty minute trek for the young and fit. In the end, the only option left is Steve's plan.

"Peter," I say quietly.

He shakes his head as he roars, "No, Julie. Not a chance."

I cup my hands around his head and look deep into his eyes, "Yes, you know it has to be this way."

"Julie, no," he says continuing to shake his head vigorously as I hold on tight.

I speak more forcefully this time, "Yes. You and Joe have to go. It is vital that we move quickly and save Cassandra one way or another. Please, Peter. Please work with me."

I can see tears welling in his eyes as they turn a little bloodshot. I know he is struggling with the notion of leaving me with Steve. After all, he is my defender. I know his mind is searching desperately for another way, yet coming up short. He forces his words through gritted teeth, "I don't like it Julie, not one bit."

"I can look after myself. I just need you to be strong and get this done. You need to forget about me. Peter! Please listen. You need to be focused on being safe. Don't take any unnecessary risks. Got it? We need to save Cassandra. We need to save her right now! But more than that, I need you. Don't take any chances. Please, don't you dare get yourself killed," I implore.

Peter lowers his gaze to the dust at our feet as he nods his approval silently.

"Hey, hey," I say, forcing him to lift his head again. We stare into each other's eyes, sending unspoken messages to each other earnestly. I can see many things in Peter's eyes: fear, anger, resignation. I embrace him in a passionate kiss before releasing him from my grasp. Patting him on the behind, I wipe away my tears and turn back to address Steve, "C'mon, let's get this done."

Steve smiles. "Sure. Do you want this?" he asks holding out a scrap of paper with a note written on it towards Peter. I assume it is instructions of how to find the Stevenson hideout at Yea.

Peter snatches the paper from his hand, giving Steve one last burning stare in the process. He trudges off towards the car silently, Joe walking slowly behind him.

"Have fun kids, we'll see you again once our job is done," Joe calls over his shoulder as he waves.

I hope so. I bloody well hope so. Take care, Peter.

Steve indicates, with a bow and a wave of his hand, towards the mile long path which leads up to Wilhelmina Falls, "Ladies first."

I move cautiously up the rough path, wondering what is in store for us at the end. It is bothering me that I have not had any premonitions about a gang of thieves holding Cassandra hostage at Yea. Maybe it is just my inexperience interpreting these 'waking dreams'. Maybe I have overlooked some crucial details. I hope that my vague readings will not have deadly consequences for any of us. It certainly seems like we are all heading into very hostile and unpredictable situations. It is strange, for the first time, I find myself wishing for a premonition. I would gladly endure the pain in my chest in order to access some more information at this point in time.

In the background I can hear Peter's car, churning up gravel, as it speeds from the car park back onto the main road. I turn slightly as I continue to walk steadily. All I can see is a cloud of dust. I suddenly feel a little scared to be alone in this isolated area with Steve.

Don't be so stupid.

I decide to break the ice a little, to get on the right footing once more, "I'd like to apologize."

"Whatever for?" Steve asks from a few steps behind me.

"I'd like to apologize for the way Peter is behaving. He's under a lot of stress at the moment. He hasn't been himself since I started getting these dreams. He still has a lot to work through. He didn't mean to offend you with any comments which show he doesn't trust you just yet," I explain.

"Water off a duck's back, Darling. No offence taken. There are many who don't trust me in this world, some are right to do so," Steve says cheerfully. "Anyway, you know what they say. You should always trust your instincts."

Click!

I halt, shaking my head as I place my hands on my hips. I know precisely what has made the soft metallic clicking sound. I turn and look at

Steve. He is holding an four inch long flick knife in his good hand as he grins mischievously. The predator has captured its naïve prey.

"Shit!" I say involuntarily though accurately. I am surprised my response wasn't a little stronger.

"I never forget a face, Darling, particularly not one as pretty as yours. Now how about we continue our little journey up to the falls," Steve suggests. "I have a little surprise for you at the top."

I sigh, turn and look up at the long, isolated path leading to the falls. I can faintly hear rushing water. In the distance, a cow bellows with a mournful cry, echoing out of the valley. I know how it feels.

I decide I have no choice. Screaming would be futile. I suspect there is no one for miles. I am sure Steve is pretty handy with that knife too, his skills perfected through murderous practice. Slowly I begin to walk up the hill.

More surprises ahead. Great! Can't wait!

I step forward, concentrating on two things only. One; I must not trip and injure myself. I must be fully fit when the time comes and I take my chance, attacking Steve when his guard is down. Two; I must develop a plan as to how I can cause maximum damage to Steve. This is my only priority. I cannot worry about Peter or Cassandra at the moment. I cannot help either of them until I help myself. I feel so stupid and weak, yet I know I must be strong. I must be like the Phoenix, rising from the ashes of my poor decisions. I must rise if I am to live beyond this day. I must rise above my troubles if I am to help Cassandra. However, at this point in time, I feel so very much alone and vulnerable. Finding a solution to my problems seems an impossible task.

I am such a fool!

I wish Peter was still here.

'Deception'

Things are rarely,
Quite as they seem.
A conjuror uses trickery,
Mirrors reflecting lies,
And a little sleight of hand,
To complete his deception,
For a penny at a time.

Chapter 16

April 9th 1692.

Salem, Massachusetts.

The crowd arrives early, much earlier than normal for this is a special day. A once in a lifetime event, something incredible is happening today. Any day when a witch is scheduled to be hung is a great day. To hang two witch sisters at one time is unprecedented, an event which cannot be missed. The tale of this day, as seen unfolding by the children, shall be passed down through the generations to come.

The people of Salem, in recent months, have endured so much hardship and angst, some real, most imaginary. However, with every witch that is hung comes joy, a flood of euphoria and an adoption of hope that their future will be free of this evil scourge. The people consider each execution of a witch as one step closer to making this hope a reality. Today is viewed by the residents of Salem as a truly great day.

By 11A.M. a small crowd has formed, bringing blankets for seating and a picnic lunch to be shared by the whole community. The food is plentiful: freshly baked bread, scones with strawberry jam and cream as well as all manner of fruit and vegetables. Of course it wouldn't be a celebration without the essential barrels of ale. Nothing gets the party started better than a jug or three of home brewed ale.

The spectators arrive early in order to pick out the best vantage points for their families. It is vital, for the children's sake, that they get an unobstructed view of the witch hangings in order to enable the children to see them as they are overcome by death. This practice is seen as the perfect tonic for the witchcraft that abounds. Hopefully it, the act of seeing the witches die, breaks the spell that has befallen the children. Hopefully it causes the fits to cease, thus allowing the children to sleep peacefully at night once again. As the crowd grows steadily, the town center develops into a party atmosphere. Church hymns are sung with gusto as the children play hide and seek merrily around the horses attached to the wagon residing beneath the hanging tree.

This joyous mood abounds up till about 1 P.M. Somberness slowly descends upon the crowd as the parents begin to feel a little uneasy. There is no reason to feel ill at ease, yet this nervousness begins to spread like wildfire throughout those assembled in the town square. Involuntarily they start to consider all the things that may possibly go wrong. Nothing has ever gone wrong before. The executions are a fairly simple process which have been tried and tested many times before to great success. Yet, even with a perfect record, there is always the chance something may go wrong. One by one, the parents call their children back into the family fold. They snuggle up close together, hoping to bolster their flagging confidence. As they watch each successive minute click away on their fob watches, they grow more and more silent. By twenty eight past one, the entire town, save for the prisoners and executioner, have arrived and taken up position in the town square. All the shops are closed, all the houses secured. The remainder of the town is deserted. All of Salem waits in silent anticipation for the show to begin.

At 2 P.M. the priest begins to ring the church bell precisely thirteen times, as has always been the custom on the day of a hanging. A man rushes to the back of the wagon, carrying a heavy wooden crate in both hands. He drops the crate onto the muddy road. The man places both his hands on the upturned crate, testing it thoroughly to see if it is stable.

Confident it will not wobble; he turns towards the Mayor, Ewan McCormack and nods, indicating that everything is in order. The man then bows politely, rushes away and is lost in amongst the eager crowd.

Ewan is dressed resplendently in his most formal attire. His knee high leather boots, tall broad brimmed hat, and long flowing crimson cape add a touch of class to the proceedings. He strides out across the town square followed closely by a servant boy. The young boy is desperately trying to keep up, maintain his footing and ensure Ewan's cape doesn't drag along the muddy road. Ewan mounts the crate boldly, standing tall like a peacock showing off its plumage. This is one of those precious moments in life. He is proud of his role in this event, knowing how important it is to the community and also his chances for re-election in the Fall. Raising both hands to silence the murmurs from the vocal crowd, he takes a moment to collect his thoughts before speaking.

"We are gathered before God in order to carry out his bidding. An evil has been discovered in our midst. Sisters who thou thought may indeed be witches have been deemed so. They hath had a fair hearing and hath been deemed guilty by the Elders of this town. It be our solemn duty to rid our town of this evil scourge and doom these witches to burn in hell for the rest of eternity. May God have mercy on their black souls."

The silence is broken as the crowd erupts into a sea of movement and a chorus of celebratory cheers. Ewan steps down from the crate, savoring the rapture of the community around him. He moves to the side of the box, joining the crowd behind the guards who gather around the wagon. Harold and the two prisoners appear from the doorway which leads down to the cells, flanked by several other guards. Whispers quickly spread through the crowd culminating in an eruption of fierce and unrelenting abuse of the foulest nature towards both of the prisoners. As Harold pushes the prisoners onward they are pelted with rotten fruit, spat on and belted by the walking canes of people reaching over the cordon of restraining guards. The guards do little to prevent the fierce attack on the prisoners. They are only there to prevent any chance of escape.

Mary and Sarah are dressed identically. Both are covered from head to toe in thick black silk which shrouds them like a cloak of anonymity. Placed over their heads is a black hood which keeps the prisoners completely blind. They rely solely on Harold to provide direction. A visible gag prevents the prisoners from screaming out or responding to the crowd. Their legs are shackled in irons preventing them from taking large steps. They shuffle their way forward, stumbling occasionally, as they walk across the square. Their hands are bound behind their backs with rope. The ties are bound so tight that they are smeared in the blood slowly oozing from where they have bitten deep into the prisoner's wrists. No concern is given as to how much pain the prisoners are enduring. Their pain and misery will end soon enough.

Both women are reticent to move forward. However, Harold is unwilling to accept any misbehavior, particularly in front of a crowd as large and hostile as this one. The prisoners suddenly stop, shaking their heads vigorously, frantically trying to mouth something inaudible to anyone who might listen. Harold reacts swiftly, giving both of them a short sharp jab with a sturdy broom handle into their lower backs. Both women groan as they begin to move forward again. Their will to struggle sapped, the women have no choice but to continue moving slowly towards the wagon and their appointment with death.

Thomas watches the procession from about twenty feet behind the main crowd. His face is hidden in darkness from his hood pulled down so as to shadow his face. The last thing he wants to do is draw attention to his presence at this ceremony. He fears that, considering the mood of the town, his identification will only lead to swift and vicious reprisal. He has seen firsthand the way so called 'normal people' react towards family members of convicted witches. Stonings, assaults, even cold blooded murder. All covered up by the authorities of course, all in the name of God and justice. Thomas knows all too well what reception he will get if spotted. The murder of Jane is a far cry from crops failing or children claiming to have witch induced fits. Even though he is surrounded by danger, Thomas has no choice other than to come here today. He continues to pray for a miracle. At the very least he is determined to try and let Mary know, someway, somehow, that she is, and always will be, loved.

John is also present; he wouldn't miss this spectacle for all the gold in the world. He stands to the side, opposite Ewan, under a tree. Shielded from view in amongst the crowd, he intently watches the scene unfolding before him. His face is disfigured with the deep scratches on his cheek from Jezebel's attack. They are infected and weeping badly. However, he does not draw any attention from the crowd. They are all, to a man, woman and child, focused on the hanging tree.

It is a warm afternoon yet John has chosen to wear a heavy, full length, canvas overcoat draped over his shoulders. Sweat drips from his forehead; partly because of the warm day, mostly due to nervousness. His nervous sweating is mainly due to the presence of his trusty shot gun, cleaned, loaded and ready, protruding from under his coat near his ankle. One hand holds the gun close by his side ready for swift action. Every now and then he uses his spare hand to dab at his cheek with a piece of cloth in order to wipe away the mixture of blood, sweat and puss which occasionally oozes from his open facial wounds.

The prisoners reach the wagon and are forced by the guards to halt. In pairs the guards lift each of the prisoners up onto the tray which is positioned directly beneath the branch from which they will be hung. Harold uses the discarded crate to alight the wagon. Two doves land at the feet of the prisoners, both facing towards the cells, both unnoticed by the fixated crowd. Harold uses his boot, agitating the birds enough to cause them to flutter away to an open spot a short distance away.

Harold arranges the women so that they are positioned correctly, just below each of the nooses. He places the noose around the neck of the first woman, tightening it, ensuring it is fitted correctly. The noose is tight without causing any discomfort. Well, no discomfort at this point, anyway.

Harold whispers in her ear, "Be calm, my dear. It shall not hurt."

He pauses for a second as he looks out into the crowd. Harold sees Thomas standing towards the back. Even with the hood over his head, Harold can see the sadness in Thomas's eyes. Harold smiles as he strolls across the tray and places the noose around the neck of the second woman. As he begins to adjust the noose, a shadow slides slowly down the main street, engulfing all the townsfolk and the execution platform. At first everyone is oblivious; just a cloud obscuring the sun. But as the shadow lingers, darkening the square, people begin to finally look skyward.

Steadily, the townsfolk raise their eyes, searching the sky to try to determine what is causing the sun to be blocked and darkness to descend. In the distance a dark object looms large. As it moves rapidly towards the town they can see it is not a cloud. No storm cloud behaves in such a manner. They stand as one, mesmerized by what is occurring, forgetting for a moment they are here for an execution. Even Harold has released his grip on the second noose as he too looks skyward. Murmurs spread through the crowd as they try unsuccessfully to work out just what it might be that is heading towards them at such a rapid speed.

Harold regains his composure and takes swift action to tighten the noose around the second woman's neck. Instead of checking with Ewan for the go ahead to execute the two prisoners, he stares at the dark mass in the sky, sweat beginning to form on his brow.

"It cannot be," he says loudly as he watches the airborne mass moving closer, his eyes bulging wide. The object appears to be moving in many directions all at once. "It be a sign. Oh my God it be a sign. We are doomed. We are ALL doomed!"

The mysterious dark mass draws close enough for the townsfolk to see it isn't one object but many, grouped together in some sort of loose formation. There are so many objects flying together that they have produced an artificial nightfall which is sweeping steadily across town. Before their eyes can identify the objects, their ears here the fearful sound of thousands of wings, flapping in unison. As the creatures reach the town center they begin to fall out of formation, choosing to fly in a random manner at different altitudes, in different directions. This allows some sunlight to filter through, revealing that the flying beasts are simply an enormous flock of several thousand white doves, each carrying something in their beaks.

The doves fly in and out over the entire town, diving and weaving as they go. Suddenly they release their cargo, showering the whole town with color. Orchids, lilies, flowers of all different kinds rain down on the townsfolk. Many of the flowers are unknown, maybe originating from foreign lands. The shower of flowers causes much mirth and excitement amongst the children. The adults, however, are gripped with fear, running and screaming, trying to get away from the unnatural event unfolding.

As the townsfolk begin to scurry, both John and Thomas watch as a visibly shaken Harold removes the noose from around the neck of the taller of the two prisoners. Thomas's heart begins to beat fast as he realizes all hope is not lost. He knows this freed prisoner is Mary; she is the taller of the two sisters.

Thomas stands watching, smiling broadly, his heart full of hope. He moves forward, forcing his way through the surging crowd which is holding him back. Undaunted, he fights hard to break through the congestion. Nothing is going to come between Thomas and Mary now.

A shot gun blast echoes across the square, making the crowd stop and flinch before they become more agitated, running in various directions in a chaotic manner. Thomas looks across and sees gun smoke rising above John as he is busy reloading his shotgun. Thomas gazes back in horror towards the wagon. The horses attached to the wagon are spooked by the blast. He watches as they rear up and charge forward, careering over bystanders while sending Mary and Harold plummeting awkwardly to the road. Sarah's body is limp, her neck broken, as she hangs by the noose in the tree.

Thomas continues his earnest attempt to move forward against the fear ridden crowd with little effect. He watches Mary intently as she struggles to get to her feet. Eventually, after much effort, she is standing. Hands bound tightly behind her back, legs still in irons, face shrouded in cloth, she attempts the near impossible. Mary begins to shuffle, moving as fast as her restraints will allow. Thomas, seeing her determination, tries more valiantly to reach her through the crowd. Suddenly he stops as a chill runs through his body. He is overcome by a sensation of hopelessness. From his vantage point he has a clear view of the destination Mary is running towards. His heart sinks as he realizes there is nothing he can do to help.

He screams as loud as he can but is drowned out by the surrounding commotion, "Mary!"

Mary is shuffling in a straight line, directly towards John. The crowd around John has dispersed. There is only the occasional person running between John and Mary as they make a hasty exit from the town's square. Otherwise John has a completely unrestricted line of sight of Mary. What's more, with every step Mary shuffles, his target gets just a little closer and his shot becomes so much easier. Gun reloaded, John looks at Thomas, smiles, then turns back towards Mary and takes aim at his prey.

John says, in a loud gravelly voice, words which nobody else hears, "God's vengeance shall be swift and just."

Lifting the gun John takes careful aim and patiently waits. He peers through the sight, holding the gun rock steady with relaxed hands, unflinching. He doesn't react when yet another person crosses his line of sight for a moment. He is fully focused on Mary and Mary alone. He waits until Mary is no more than ten feet in front of him before he acts. Thomas faints as John pulls the trigger sending a blast from both barrels straight into Mary's chest. Immediately, Mary's lifeless body is carried backwards by the force of the blast. She slumps to the ground, falling awkwardly with her legs at a strange angle underneath her completely lifeless body.

Suddenly, all the doves begin to fly upwards and away from Salem. The sky is cleared within just a few minutes as the afternoon sunlight steadily returns to illuminate the events that have taken place. The town square remains littered with a dazzling array of colors from the flowers left by the doves. The crowd is now largely dispersed with everyone returning to the perceived safety of their homes. The square is silent save for the distant sound of doors being barred and shutters closed.

John walks over to Mary and gives a solid kick to her back. Her body rolls slightly though remains limp. Still shrouded in her hood, she is sprawled in a large, ever growing pool of blood. An insane smile spreads across John's disfigured face which does nothing to hide his abundant joy.

John turns and looks at Harold. Harold is in shock, still sitting where he fell on the road at the beginning of the turmoil. John's voice resonates across the square waking Harold from his self-indulgent stupor, "Get these witches buried in their unmarked graves. Be sure they be in un-consecrated ground outside the church grounds. Do it now!"

Harold nods, picking himself up gingerly. As he moves, he realizes that he is hurt. He fears he may have broken an arm. Reason dawns on his troubled mind that his job is not yet complete, there is still much to do. His injuries will have to wait. Harold is eager to complete the horrible job he has been bestowed. Signaling to a small group of guards to give him a hand, he begins the process of disposing of the bodies. He wants the job finished as quickly as possible so that no one will ever have the opportunity to discover the unforgivable things he has done. As the guards drag Mary's lifeless body down the road towards the church, Harold is overcome by mixed emotions. He is pleased with the outcome of the day, nearly as much as he is ashamed by what he has done.

Harold looks to the sky, "Lord, please forgive me for my sins."

George Williams spots Thomas lying on the ground motionless, the crowd around him now long gone. He rushes to the aid of his friend. Bending down on one knee he gently lifts Thomas's head, slapping his cheek mildly till he wakes. Harold is watching from a distance. Seeing Thomas begin to rouse he verbally encourages the guards to move more quickly. He is now desperate for Mary's body to be removed from the roadway as quickly as possible. The grave has already been dug in preparation. Harold just needs to get her buried before Thomas recovers enough to be a problem.

Some of the other guards cut Sarah down from the tree. The two bodies are carried down the street as Thomas regains consciousness. Sitting in the dust, he watches, completely drained of energy. He continues to breathe though his life has been stolen away from his soul. Mary is gone. As the guards, led by Harold, disappear out of sight up and over the hill, Thomas begins to cry. George embraces him in a bear hug, trying unsuccessfully to provide some sort of condolences in these, the harshest of times. Alas, Thomas doesn't need comfort. He just needs Mary.

Jezebel sits calmly by the door to the cells, gently preening her whiskers with her right paw. Satisfied that her cleaning is done to a reasonable level she stops. Ears upright and alert she begins looking around the town square as if she is searching for something. Her nose begins to twitch as she sniffs the air. Her eyes dilate as she stares down the hill towards the bush which leads to the river. Turning the opposite way, she sees the last of the guards carrying Mary and Sarah up to the graveyard. She has always been around Mary, now for the first time, she is on her own. Jezebel sits still for a moment contemplating her next move. Stretching as she takes to her feet, she ignores the road leading to the cemetery. She has no intention of staging a vigil by Mary's grave. Instead she saunters casually towards the bush leading down to the river. She is well aware that this is where she needs to go. In an instant she is gone, hidden in the undergrowth. Nobody notices as she leaves town. Why should they? She is just a stray black cat after all.

'Double Crossed'

Sinister plans are hatched,

Friends you discover are not,

Fear laughs gleefully,

As hope is forsaken,

When you find yourself double crossed.

Keep your eyes wide open,

Travel cautiously this way,

Tread lightly on shifting ground,

As you pass through the bracken,

Then you might survive this day.

Chapter 17

Wednesday, March 1ˢᵗ, 2006.

Morning.

Wilhelmina Falls, Victoria, Australia.

So bloody gullible!

I shake my head in disbelief as I trudge silently onwards and up. I can't believe I have walked into such a blatant trap. The knife Steve wields grants him unassailable power in this world where only the two of us exist. Now, I find I have no choice but to accept his authority and continue to march up this hill to the top of the falls. I'm certainly not in a hurry to find out exactly what Steve has in store for me. The only thing that keeps me going is the thought that things can change, authority can be fleeting. It all depends on whose hand holds that shimmering weapon.

I have to stay alert, keep my head and think this through. I need to use my time efficiently, to formulate a detailed plan of attack. I know this track well and realize it takes about thirty minutes to reach the very top. If I slow it down, a little, I might be able to drag it out to forty minutes or more. Not a great deal of time, though it might be all the advantage I can gleam. I have to maximize my use of these precious moments in order to discover a way to escape.

Gathering information is crucial to my cause. I have no idea if Peter and Joe have been sent on a harmless wild goose chase or are headed into a deadly ambush. I can't let my mind drift to this question; I am in no position to help them, anyway. I must trust in Peter's ability to stay out of trouble. They will be okay, of that I'm sure, of that I hope.

The more information I can gather on what fate lies ahead for me, the better. Knowledge is all powerful. It may be my only hope of overcoming this perilous situation. Ignorance, on the other hand, is nothing short of deadly.

"Don't think you'll get away with this," I scold defiantly. "Peter will come back for me as soon as he realizes he has been sent on a false errand. He will hunt you down if you do anything to harm me."

Steve sniggers behind my back as he follows up the trail, "Darling, it's certainly not a false errand. Your beloved oaf will find plenty of company at the address I have directed him towards. The Stevensons are usually home at that address, at this time of day anyhow. They are dwellers of the night, just like me. They love the anonymity of the dark. If he is lucky, he will find them either drowsy or asleep. He may have a slim chance of surviving if that is the case. However, they can be rather grumpy if they are exposed to the burning light of day by strangers with less than honorable motives, motives which do not ultimately add coin to their pockets. Yes, I think their visit could be poorly received."

I pause momentarily. Steve gives me a solid shove with his shoulder, encouraging me to keep moving onwards. I stumble a few steps before regaining my rhythm. I decide a better tack is to continue my line of questioning, "I thought they were just something you made up, you know, to get me on my own."

"Don't over value yourself, my girl. I have numerous problems to deal with at any given moment. If I can kill two birds with one stone, I will. In the end I'm just a businessman and this is an economic use of my resources. None of you are important. I can find others who have the visions if need be."

"So, is Cassandra being kept as a prisoner in Yea by the Stevensons?" I ask trying desperately to work out how much danger I have sent Peter and Joe stumbling towards.

"You are a very self-absorbed person aren't you? Everything has to be about you and your problems," Steve scoffs. "No, Cassandra is not in Yea, only the Stevensons. The Stevensons are a group that have been, how should I put this, cutting into my profits of late. However, their base has been too heavily guarded to risk the lives of any of my men. If Peter's death can bring them to the notice of the police, that will be good enough for me. Free up the market a little, I suspect. If the police don't arrest them, they will have to adopt a quieter profile for a while. Either way, it will be good for my business. You have to remember, it is not like I am losing anything important if my plan goes to Hell. As for little Cassandra, she is quite safe, at least for the moment. Time will tell how that plays out too."

"You Bastard!" I scream as I continue to trudge along slowly.

Steve chuckles, "Just taking care of business, little Darlin'. Just taking care of business."

I take a deep breath, trying to regain control over my frazzled emotions. There is no point losing my cool. It will not help me. It will not help Peter, Joe or Cassandra either. However, remaining calm in the presence of such pure evil is proving difficult.

I must stay focused. I must try.

I press for more details, "So you're saying she's up ahead; at the falls I mean?"

"You ask far too many questions, do you know that? You must send your guy spare with all this endless drivel. Look around you. There are trees, birds, the sun is shining. All these things just happen without any reason. They exist and that is all. What will be, will be. No questions are needed. You just need to accept what is occurring to you and your friends and get over it. It is nothing more, nothing less than fate."

"So......"

"No, just keep walking, Bitch. You're beginning to irritate me now. This is not what you want to do, at this juncture; I can assure you of that. Others have tried, all have failed. I don't need a doctor to medicate me for my migraines. Six feet of soil tends to cure all irritations," Steve growls in a venomous tone filled to the brim with menace.

I decide to let Steve's temper cool a little as I drift into thoughtful contemplation. The sound of running water cascading over rocks in the bush ahead grows in intensity with every step I take. My time is steadily running out and I still have to work out a feasible plan for escape. However, that is not going to be easy. I have to hope Cassandra is being held at, or near, the top of the falls so I can rescue her at the same time. Escape on my own could prove deadly for her. It may push Steve over the edge. He could easily take out his anger on poor, defenseless Cassandra. No, I must ensure that we both escape. I cannot take a chance with her life.

How am I going to pull this off? It's just impossible. I still don't even know if she is here or somewhere else. At least I know from reading between Steve's words that he knows where she is. That is a breakthrough finally.

Suddenly, I have an idea. Without missing a step, I discreetly pull my mobile phone slightly out of my pocket, just enough to hit the button and activate the screen.

No reception. Damn!

I pick up my pace; moving a little ahead of Steve. Mobile phone in hand, I discreetly scroll through the menu and open the 'messaging' section. With deft skill, I open a message sent to me by Peter and choose the option, 'reply'. Without missing a stride, looking straight ahead I expertly type a single word, "Trap."

"What are you doing?" Steve roars as he increases his pace in order to close the gap between us.

Hurriedly, I push 'send' as I throw the phone with all my strength, deep into the bush further up the hill. I smile, praying that the extra altitude will be enough to get reception and a message out to Peter. Steve belts me in the back with the full force of his shoulder, sending me sprawling onto the ground. I wince in pain as my hands and arms scrape on the rocky, clay path as I roll to a bedraggled halt in the dust.

"That was pretty stupid. I thought you were more clever than that. If you had waited till we reached the top of the mountain, your phone may have worked," Steve says, pointing to the bush all around us. "Here, in this wilderness, your phone won't work. This scrub is far too thick. It's so isolated out here that no one will hear your cries for help. Jeez, I love the great outdoors! So liberating. All my problems disappear when I come up here. You're in deep shit, girl. Of course if you try that again you'll be dead, I promise you that. No more tricks!"

I sit in the dust feeling my scarred hands with my fingertips as I catch my breath. The pain tingles to the surface of my skin as the blood slowly oozes from the deep, open furrows. Holding back my tears, I glare at Steve defiantly as I spit, "You're going to kill me anyhow. Why don't you just do it?"

Steve laughs as he intentionally grabs my injured right hand. He drives his finger nails deep into my wounds as he yanks my arm, pulling me brutally back to my feet, "Just keep moving."

"You bastard," I scream as I obediently move onwards, shaking my hand in the vain hope that the pain will dissipate. Tears begin to well in my eyes. I will not grant him the satisfaction of seeing me cry.

"You're a good judge of character, my lovely. Yes, indeed, I am a bastard. How much of a bastard I am, you can only imagine in your worst nightmares."

Sore, tired, scared and alone, I stagger along. In my heart I hope, if nothing else, I will get the opportunity to deal with Steve at some point. All I live for is to take my revenge. I remain determined to concentrate, to watch, to be patient and wait for my chance. Once my chance avails itself, I will grasp it with both hands. I will give it my best shot.

No, that is not good enough.

I will be unstoppable in my fury.

Yes, that's it.

I know I can cause maximum damage to this prick of a man if only the opportunity arises.

My time will come!

A lightning flash flickers on the distant horizon.

Onwards I march, as slowly as Steve will allow.

I pray you get my message Peter.

*   *   *

"Welcome to my office. Isn't it just divine? The decor is astounding in its natural elegance," Steve says sarcastically, on reaching the clearing.

As we reach the plateau, I find myself overcome by what I see. At the top of the path, the vegetation dwindles to reveal the rocky outcrop. These huge boulders are swamped by the cascading waters which plummet over the shear edge into the valley below. Behind us, the suntanned hills and valleys between Kinglake and Yea are displayed in all their magical glory. At any other time, the view would be breathtaking. I draw no comfort from the panorama before me. It simply reinforces the fact that I am trapped with a monster, enveloped in extreme isolation.

The black storm clouds, moving swiftly towards us, are clearly visible in the distance. A flash of lightning distracts for an instant then is gone. This contrasts dramatically with the predominantly blue summer sky above and around us. I have never seen a storm like this building. As it creeps over the hills, I know it will intensify. Maybe this will be to my advantage, even the ledger so to speak.

A second thing has come to my attention. I spy a familiar figure scurrying around the rocky outcrop near the falls. The man is tall, wearing a short sleeved shirt that exposes his landscape of tattoos. These images cover both his arms and chest in an intricate mosaic. He has a lazy eye; a startling sight as he glances my way. I knew it had been him, that night, at St. Paul's Cathedral in Melbourne. Now, seeing him clearly in the daylight, I am certain of it. He remains my worst nightmare. I wish our destinies were not seemingly intertwined.

Chris Hagatie!

I hark back to my first encounter, during my 'drug affected' stay in the South Morang Regional Hospital's Psychiatric Ward. Slimy and filthy seem insufficient to describe this grotesque monster of a man. All the negative adjectives known to humanity are not enough to describe how truly evil he is. I know I was lucky to escape his clutches back then, thanks largely to the help of Serenity. The scars from his attack still weep on the left side of his face. I have no such assistance now. He is free of the restraints of the straight jacket, though even that complicated piece of clothing was insufficient to stop him. I must fend for myself. At least I have all my faculties this time round. My restraints are gone too, save for the knife pressing in my back. Somehow I feel the odds are stacked against me this time.

Cassandra, at her tender age, is no match for Chris. I hope she is far away from here. Her predicament is stark, she is clearly this monster's 'type'. Chris has worked tirelessly to earn his reputation as Victoria's most notorious kidnapper and child sex offender. He has the lengthiest rap sheet of any sex offender in Victoria's history.

Unfortunately, he is also well represented by some of the best lawyers and barristers that money can buy. Their knowledge of the law, combined with an outstanding lack of community orientated values, has led to the courts deciding not to incarcerate Chris Hagatie in a maximum security prison under constant guard. Instead, it was deemed that he should be sent for assessment, treatment and a program of rehabilitation in the medium security psychiatric ward of the South Morang Regional Hospital. No armed guards inside the ward, just doctors and nurses going about their business. He was always going to escape from there. It was just a question of how long he would choose to stay.

Not that I need it, however, seeing Chris prancing around in the clear light of day is enough to let me know, one hundred percent for certain, that Steve is NOT rehabilitated in any way, shape or form. There is no way an evil character like Chris would ever do anything other than live the depraved life he has, since he was a teenager. He is mentally broken; completely unfixable. Steve must be aware of Chris's horrible pursuits and approve of them completely. That does not sit comfortably with Steve's image of wanting to help the innocent. Neither does holding a knife to my back of course. I just wish I had seen the logic of this earlier. Maybe I could have avoided this trap altogether. I was blinded by my exuberance to find Cassandra at any cost.

I am such a fool!

As I move forward, onto the plateau itself, I try desperately to see what Chris is up to. He has his back to me now and is working feverishly on something near a large tree, close to the falls. The roar of the water looms loud as we approach. I see a flick of a rope as he works frantically on his endeavors. The size of his hulking body blocks my view completely.

"Chris!" Steve calls out as we both start to step carefully across the dry rocks towards the falls.

Chris looks in our direction. Frowning a little at first, he shields his eyes from the sun as he tries to distinguish exactly who is calling to him. His face changes, breaking out into a broad grin, as he suddenly recognizes Steve. He turns fully as he half runs half lopes to greet us, "Master! You have come?"

"Yes Chris," Steve says patting him on the arm like a cherished pet. "And I brought you another present. Aren't I good to you?"

Chris turns his attention towards me. He studies me up and down as I stand there silently, not moving a muscle. I cannot tell whether he recognizes me from our previous encounters or not. I suspect he does not. His mind is feeble. He lives for the moment.

He encroaches into my personal space. I wince as I catch a scent of his pungent body odour as he moves close to my face, sniffing my skin just below my ear. I continue to stand frozen, not wanting to tackle two strong men in such an isolated spot. I resist the urge to move even when Chris begins to lick the sweat off my skin. His tongue travels slowly down my neck to the top of my chest. I can feel his hot breath warming my skin as he lingers here for a moment or two.

Suddenly, without warning, he stands bolt upright, taking a step backwards. Before I realize what he is doing, he spits in my face, hitting me in the right eye and cheek. I moan in disgust as I wipe my face clean vigorously.

"Too old!" he yells as he wanders casually back towards the tree.

"Yeah, I know," Steve laughs, displaying a complete lack of remorse. "He likes his woman younger; much younger in fact. Just like her."

I wipe the remnants of spittle from my face, flicking some of it onto the rocks while wiping the rest on my jeans. The nauseous feeling, causing a knot in my stomach, continues to grow as I finally get a good look at the tree. Cassandra is there, tied with ropes knotted around her wrists and ankles. She is securely pinned to the trunk of the tree by more ropes around her waist.

She is staring in my direction; silent, impassive. Her cheeks stained with the lines of thousands of tears shed alone in captivity. She has stopped crying now. I wonder if she has no more tears left. Maybe she has given up. People only cry when there is hope of being rescued. She looks scared out of her wits; sucking in great gulps of air rather than breathing in a normal, regular manner. Her distress is obvious, even from this distance.

With a rapid succession of steps, Chris reaches Cassandra once more. He runs straight up to her and, without any qualms, licks squarely up the entire length of her face.

"Ahhhh!" she squeals, clenching her facial muscles and shaking her head in disgust.

"Get away from her, you bastard!" I yell, too scared to take a step forward. Though my anger boils to the surface, I am still acutely aware of the fact that Steve holds the knife, close behind me. A weapon he is willing to use if provoked. Though I know I must act to protect her, I am powerless. There is nothing I can physically do.

Chris turns and smiles at me momentarily, though effectively unfazed. He turns his attention back towards Cassandra. This time he appears to be sniffing her. He starts at her face, moving down to her arm pits, then onto her chest and down to her groin. He lingers here, sniffing loudly like the pig he is. Standing upright, he twists his body so as to look at me again. He smiles and nods like he is sharing a secret with a new found friend.

"Just right," he drools with a lecherous grin.

I can't handle the tension any longer. I go to move forward though, at the last second, voluntarily check my action. I look sideways at Steve for conformation that he is still close at hand. I see a glint of sunlight on the shiny blade of his flick knife, held firmly in his grasp.

"Don't even think about it," Steve says as he walks away from me, towards Cassandra and Chris. His movements are thoughtful, ensuring that he is facing me the whole time, watching my every move. For some reason he has moved quite a distance away from me, allowing me my freedom; If, that is, I am willing to risk the consequences of taking flight. As I stare at Cassandra, I know my freedom would come at a huge cost. Steve is an intelligent man. He knows that a strong maternal streak is part of my makeup. He knows that while he holds Cassandra captive, I will not run.

This may be it! This might be my only chance to get away. What about poor Cassandra? What will become of her if I run to get help?

I stand my ground, moving neither closer nor further away. I implore my captors in the vain hope that they will see some reason, "Let her go. You can keep me as a hostage to negotiate, just let her go. She has done you no wrong."

Chris becomes noticeably agitated by my simple request. He glances at the girl, then back at Steve, repeatedly, in quick succession, "But, the Mistress said she is mine. She is my toy, my new toy. Mistress said she is mine if Chris is good. Chris has been very good. Chris does nothing. Chris waits for the word. Mistress said she will be mine!"

"Hey, hey," Steve whispers reassuringly, trying to sooth his unpredictable, hot tempered compatriot. "She'll still be yours, mate. Just be patient"

"Not if I have anything to do with it!" I retort loudly, hoping to cause a little dissention between my foes.

"Darling," Steve mocks. "You appear to be in no position to help any of your friends at this stage. You have no weapons to injure or kill me. You don't have a phone. You have no friends with you who can help. You aren't even aware of all the circumstances here. You are blissfully unaware that you are in danger of seeing two people you love so much, loose their lives today. Face facts Darling, I hold all the cards and there is nothing you can do about it."

"What?" I ask wondering what he means.

Two people I love?

Peter is obvious. I love him with all my heart. My awareness of the danger he is moving towards tears at my soul. Yet Steve talks of 'two people I love'. Joe and Cassandra are in danger. I care for them both, though I certainly don't love either of them. Steve is so careful with his words. I can't believe he has made such a crucial mistake. Yet his statement makes no sense, no sense at all.

Curious indeed, too curious for my liking!

I suddenly realize there is movement to the left of Cassandra, approximately twenty metres away. There appears to be something or someone standing near another tree. I shift my position, little by little, straining to get a better look. I keep an eye locked on Steve as I do this. I want no surprises.

Finally, I can see clearly. There is a second person, tied to another tree. This one seems to be a slim, adult, female, dressed in a bright blue, cotton, full length dress. Her head and upper torso are covered by a large Hessian bag which conceals her identity. As I focus on this lady, I can hear some faint sounds, incoherent mumbling perhaps. Maybe her mouth is taped or gagged under the bag. That would be sensible, prevent her from screaming.

She seems familiar, like someone I should readily recognize. The blue cotton dress provokes a sense of de ja vu, something I feel I know well, yet can't quite place. I am ill at ease with this unknown person, held captive, in front of me. My ears ring repeatedly with Steve's words as I try to work out who she is.

Two people I love?

Steve marches briskly over to his victim, grinning from ear to ear. His gold teeth sparkle in the sunshine as the sound of thunder roars ominously on the distant horizon. He asks smugly, "Well, aren't you even going to say hello? She's come all this way just to see you."

Who is she? Did I miss something in my visions? Oh God, no. Who is she?

"What have you done?" I ask softly as fear begins to course through my veins.

"Nothing as yet," Steve taunts. "I just thought you needed a real life premonition to encourage you to adopt my plans for the future."

I shake my head as panic starts to set in, "No, what have you done? Who is this? Who have you captured?"

Steve smiles with perverse delight, "Can't you guess? You're meant to be the clever one, far smarter than a simple crim like me. After all, you are the interfering sod who saves people from harm by having premonitions. You are the all-knowing great sage of our time. How funny it is that you can't even guess who I have brought here. When will you open your eyes and see?"

"Who is it?" I scream as fear outweighs my better judgment.

"Maybe this will help," Steve growls, grabbing the mystery lady's exposed ring finger roughly in his hand. With one swift, slicing motion, he cuts it free of her body. She groans loudly, writhing in pain as blood drips down from her now discarded injured hand. The severed finger lies stark and motionless at her feet.

"You bastard!" I scream at the top of my lungs.

That was me. I saw the visions, I heard the screams. I know the sound I make when I scream. Unless……. No that's impossible!

"You have no idea," Steve says calmly as he bends down, picks up the finger and casually tosses it towards me. The finger lobs at my feet before rolling, collecting a thick layer of dust on its bloody surface.

I stare down at the finger before me. I shake my head, wanting, needing to disbelieve what I see. Unfortunately the finger only provides me with irrefutable proof as to what I already suspect, "No, no. It can't be."

"You should always trust your instincts, my Darling," Steve laughs. He seems to thrive on the pain and suffering he can inflict on others. I guess it makes him feel superior, like a God. He thinks he is untouchable. I know he is only a man. He too can bleed. If I get my chance, I will prove that.

I look up at the victim still writhing in pain as my eyes fill with tears. My strength fades as I begin to shake uncontrollably. I focus hard on my breathing. I cannot afford to have an asthma attack now.

My mind refuses to acknowledge what I know to be true. I just can't believe it. It is simply impossible. How did he find her? The diamond ring on the severed finger is something I am sure of, confirmation of Steve's despicable act. The ring is so distinctive with its three diamonds set in intertwining strands of white and yellow gold. I was standing next to her on the day that her husband placed it lovingly on her finger, promising a lifetime of happiness. That seems an eternity ago now. Even in its dusty and bloody state it is easily recognizable. I know I cannot be mistaken.

My venomous gaze moves to confront Steve. Without blinking my bleary eyes, I spit, "No, it's not her."

Steve grasps the Hessian bag and pulls hard, revealing his latest victim in one swift movement. He says simply, "It's amazing what you can discover if you have a name and a mobile phone number of a particular person. If you have contacts in various government departments you can track down any piece of potentially valuable information, like who you phone regularly. This sort of information allows me to find where your soft tissue lies. It makes it easier for me to stick my knife deep into your heart, even from a distance as great as this."

Her hair is messy and tangled, covered in fibers from the bag. She is coughing uncontrollably as a result of inhaling the loose fibers from the bag. Her makeup has run from her eyes down her cheeks, making her look like a sorrowful clown. All this makes her nearly unrecognizable from the girl I know and love. However, there is no mistaking who she is.

"Gina?" I call meekly, as this simple word becomes caught in my throat as I gaze in disbelief at my sister.

She looks back at me with piecing, glazed eyes. A gaze that fails to hide the pure hatred she feels towards me now. How can Gina ever forgive me for getting her involved in such an awful situation as this? She is unable to say a word because of the grey electrical tape, wound tightly around her head, completely covering her mouth. However, her eyes tell me everything I need to know.

Finally, I force myself to pull my attention away from Gina. Restraining my hatred, I ask Steve slowly, "What the Hell do you want from me?"

Steve grins like a winner, "So you're ready to talk turkey about a deal, are you my lovely?"

I am disgusted at the mere notion of this suggestion. How on earth can I possibly contemplate making a deal of some sort which will benefit this abhorrent monster, particularly after he has deliberately mutilated my own flesh and blood?

"What do you have in mind?" I ask through clenched teeth, forcing every word out of my mouth with a great deal of difficulty.

Steve rubs his hands together with glee, "My deal is quite simple. It is a marvelous opportunity for us both, in fact."

"Just spit it out, you bastard!" I drawl, tiring of Steve's inane banter.

"Now my little Darling. Don't be like that. I'm just being a business man, nothing more. This is all about business and how to make a profit. None of it is personal."

You threaten me and Peter while also hurting my sister and you don't think it's personal! You must be completely out of your mind!!!

"How on earth can I help you to make a profit?" I ask, trying to act like I am interested. I am at a complete loss as to what Steve has in mind for me. My premonitions have nothing to do with profit.

He paces to and fro between the two hostages, flicking the knife open then closed again in a nonchalant fashion, "You underestimate your abilities greatly. Open your eyes to the possibilities. They are truly incredible. At present, with your cloistered view of the world, you are a great distance away from reaching your full potential. That is so sad."

"Steve, why don't you just tell me what you want, for God's sake," I scold, letting my agitation boil to the surface.

"Okay, I'll tell you clearly what I want. I simply want you to look through any premonition you experience closely. I want you to take careful note of any information which could be valuable to me and my mates."

I remain confused, "I already do that. I can't see how any of these visions could be profitable for you. What sort of information are you seeking exactly?"

Steve paces some more as he makes a mental list, "Well let's see. Racing or sporting results on a dated newspaper lying on a table, a news bulletin outlining different events that will occur. Tattslotto results would be excellent."

I can see where Steve is coming from now and I am completely disgusted. I don't know why I get the waking dreams though I do know one thing for certain. The visions appear to have the primary purpose of providing an opportunity to save or protect innocent victims from injury or harm. This is their double edged sword, their benefit and their curse. However, this criminal before me only wants information that will benefit his bank account. He has no compassion for the victims at all or the fact that their lives are in jeopardy. He is simply an evil, greedy, vile excuse for a human being.

"Why on earth would I make such a deal with a devil like you?"

Steve looks oddly pleased to have been called a 'devil'. I guess it is a great compliment for one in his line of profession, "I think, Darling, you have no choice."

"You're wrong," I say defiantly. "I will not provide you with the information you seek. You can go to Hell!"

Steve stops pacing and stares at me with unflinching, hateful eyes, "Listen Darling, if you help me, you all get to live. It's that simple. That means you get to have your lovely little dreams and live happily ever after with Doofus in a pleasant little house with a white picket fence. I and my associates will assist you in helping to save many, many lives which is another positive you can take away. All I ask for is to be properly compensated for my time and effort. What do you think? It's a great deal, if ever I heard one. Surely it is a deal too good to resist."

"How do you know that I won't lie to you? I might offer my services to you then go straight to the police once we leave here."

Steve smiles, "That would be foolish, my Darling. The police won't believe you. I own the police. I also know where you and your family live. I don't think you are stupid enough to be contemplating playing games. The stakes are too high."

I consider Steve's words and feel he is speaking the truth. For Steve to have found out about my sister and where she lives, he must have a number of police on his payroll. Having the police squared away on his side would also help to prevent him from being captured. This greatly weakens my position. I can see Steve watching me like I am injured prey, prone and ready to be pounced upon and slaughtered.

"You have my promise that, for as long as you work for me, no further harm will come to you and your family."

"How do I know I can trust you?"

Steve rubs his chin as he considers what to do. Turning on his heel and marching back towards Cassandra his says calmly, "Tell you what I will do as a mark of good faith. If you provide me with a promise to work with me and give me some useful information right now, I will release the little girl into your custody."

"Nooooo!," says Chris, his head raised sharply on hearing that Cassandra might be released. "The Mistress promised Chris. Chris has been good, Chris get girl. Chris have fun."

Steve completely ignores Chris's protestations as he flicks open the knife which glints brightly as a lightning strike flares in the dimming light. He continues, "Of course you've seen how ruthless I can be. If you choose not to help me I'll kill the girl right here, right now, before your very eyes. Her death will not bother me. Her father gave me this beautiful face and took away my little Angel. A child's life for a child's life sounds fair. However, for you it will be different. Her death will haunt you for all your waking days."

"No!" Chris yells as his anger violently rises to the surface. He lurches awkwardly towards Steve with menacing swiftness. His hands stretch out searching for Steve's throat. With a single, quick movement, Steve steps sideways, out of his path. He stabs Chris in the stomach, lifting the knife in order to create maximum damage as he hurtles by.

"Ahhhhhh!" Chris screams as he tumbles down the rocks and over the precipice of the falls, disappearing from sight. For a few brief second the sound of breaking branches echoes out of the valley below. This sound fades as the roar of the water begins to dominate once more. All that remain of Chris is a splash of blood on the rocks at the edge of the cliff. Even this is rapidly disappearing, washed away by the turbulent waters that pound the rocks.

Steve is left kneeling on the ground as he struggles to regain his balance. The knife has been knocked from his hand, landing several feet in front of him. I make a move to race across the rocks and get the knife.

However, my efforts are in vain. Steve is too quick. He arrives at the weapon first, grasping the knife and pointing it at me in a threatening manner.

"Don't even think about it," he says as I halt in my tracks. "You have to be realistic, Julie. You must accept my offer. It is the only chance for you and your friends to survive and flourish in the future. There is no hope of escape. I have made certain of that."

Standing before Steve, with the bloody knife pointed in my direction, I begin to look from one side then the other. I can see Cassandra, her eyes fluttering like she is about to faint. Her body seems to be going into some sort of nervous convulsions. She doesn't look like she can last much longer. Stress and malnutrition are beginning to take their toll.

On the other side I can see Gina, limp and apparently unconscious. Blood continues to drip unchecked from her badly disfigured hand into a large pool at her feet. She is in desperate need of medical attention. My head droops as I am overcome by a sense of futility.

Several low voices merge together as their message is carried by a gust of wind to my ears, "Hope is a waking dream."

I shake my head as I fear I have no options. I whisper to myself, "No, there is no hope."

"There is always hope," heralds a gravelly voice from back near the top of the pathway.

I turn, startled to see old Joe standing at the plateau, leaning on his walking cane, breathing heavily. He is flanked by Serenity and Oscar. He gives me a wink and a smile as he walks towards us slowly.

"See," Steve says as he points at Joe. "He knows how good such a deal can be. Just ask him about our deal."

Shocked, I look at Joe in disbelief. Can it be true that he has made a deal with Steve? He must have, he has been using Steve to help save innocents for years. I just can't believe Joe would sell out like this. Joe has been effectively funding widespread criminal activity through Steve's wallet. It doesn't make sense. It can't be true. This is not what the visions are about.

I shake my head, watching Joe intently as I ask, "Is it true?"

Joe ignores me and looks directly at Steve as he states firmly, "We have no deal."

'Lost?'

Lost.

Lost.

Watching.

Lost.

Lost.

Lost.

Waiting.

Lost?

Chapter 18

Wednesday, March 1st, 2006.

Morning.

Wilhelmina Falls, Victoria, Australia.

Dark clouds move briskly above us, devouring all that is bright blue as they continue in their quest for total dominance of the sky. The wind howls, causing the limbs of surrounding trees to bend and creak as their fibers stretch under extreme stress. Lightning flashes occur every few seconds now; some distant, some feel like they are only a few hundred feet away. The air is electrified, announcing the arrival of the powerful storm. I flinch as another lightning bolt crashes into the earth with a thunderous ruckus close by, somewhere to my left. I stand upright in defiance of the power of the storm. I am not scared of lightning. Even on top of an exposed mountain, I pay it no heed. I am not scared of anything, anymore.

As the rain begins to drizzle down, I watch Joe as he walks past me towards a group of boulders, just in front of Cassandra. The cats guard him on either side. Hunched down, they stalk across the rocks, alert to danger. It is clear Joe is distressed, sweating and panting vigorously. He appears to be in a great deal of pain following his arduous journey up the path. I am astonished that he has been able to make it this far. It is a hard trek for someone of my age who is relatively physically fit. For Joe, who can barely amble on flat ground, the effort it has taken to make it all the way to the top of this mountain in such a swift time is quite extraordinary.

As he rests on the rocks, I can see his ruddy face. He gasps heavily for breath, trying to replenish his weary lungs. He is a picture of complete exhaustion. He doesn't fit the bill as my salvation, my dashing white knight.

Steve smiles at me smugly, feeling pleased with himself that he still has the upper hand. He speaks calmly and confidently, "So, Julie. You have a fairly simple question to ask yourself. Is it better to do nothing to save the innocents in your dreams or should you save them from harm by reimbursing me handsomely for my help? Basically, you have to work out if, like Joe here, you want to make a deal with a devil like me."

I look towards the old man sitting hunched over on the rocks, leaning on his cane for support, "Is it true? Did you make a deal with Steve?"

Joe looks up, his eyes tearful. To me, he is completely transparent. I know every word he is going to say before he utters them. I am disappointed with the expression on his face. The wind blows his lengthy grey hair across his eyes as he explains clearly, "Yes, but you have to understand. I only provided information which couldn't be used to hurt other innocent people."

"Joe's shared information has made me and my partners rich beyond our wildest dreams!" Steve says cheerfully.

"If that is the case, why do you need information from me?" I yell.

Steve smiles, "You can never be too rich, my Darling."

I shake my head and turn to face Joe again. I ask simply, "Why?"

Joe stares straight into my eyes, "I've witnessed too many deaths in my visions. My mind in clouded with hundreds, maybe thousands of victims who I have been unable to save. The lost 'innocents' continue to haunt me. They come to me every second of every day. They pursue me, they ask me why I didn't save them. They pester me to save others. I am living in my own personal purgatory. I can only do so much on my own. My body has failed me. I needed Steve's help to ensure no one else is hurt by my inaction. I had to make a deal. I had no choice."

"There's always a choice," I state categorically though I feel a little hypocritical that I chose to accept Steve's help knowing he wanted something from me. Hindsight is a wonderful thing. If we could take it back we could all make better choices second time around.

"You have to be realistic, Julie. You're only hope is to work with me. You need to make a deal with me. It will be good for both of us, I promise you."

"There is no hope," I say softly, though clearly over the rumbling of the incoming storm and the rain which is beginning to fall more heavily now.

Joe retorts calmly, "There is always hope!"

Angrily, I turn on Joe, looking him right in the eye. The rain drips down my face, merging indiscernibly with my tears which are flowing without restraint.

"Hope is an illusion. There is NO hope!" I yell.

Joe smiles at me. He is wet and bedraggled though all of his being exudes an air of confidence that seems out of place. He repeats calmly, "There is always hope, Sweetheart. You forget I have premonitions too. I know what the future can be, if we don't lose our heads."

Steve laughs heartily, "You foolish old man. You really feel that Julie has another option other than to work with me. Look around you. There is no help. There are no other options. You need to work with me or people will get hurt. Julie is right. There is no hope. There never was any hope!"

You're wrong.

I consider what Joe has stated. He knows something about our future, that much I am certain. Maybe he has experienced a premonition about this very situation that we are playing out. I don't know. However, my intuition tells me I should take a chance that he knows something, something crucial which will help. I wish I knew what his plan was. I guess I will just have to trust him implicitly. Trust him with the future of all our lives. It is a tough call yet, at this stage, I have nothing else. I have no idea how I can get myself and everyone out of this situation safely. Peter is constantly on my mind, distracting my thoughts. I am wondering where he is and if he remains safe.

I decide to provide Joe with a sign that I am following his lead. A sign that I have forgiven him for anything that he has done in order to survive the visions and save many people. I do this, hopefully, without unnecessarily alerting the suspicions of Steve. I wink, "I'm Raspberry jam."

Joe winks back and smiles, "I was rather hoping you would be more like French Mustard."

I don't have a clue what he means by that. I guess he wants me to be anything other than 'sweet and largely inoffensive', when the time comes. I know when my moment comes, I must move quickly and decisively. I must be strong. Neither hesitation nor mercy must be shown. Steve would never show me that courtesy, neither should I to him. I will have to be ruthless. I will have to be someone other than myself. I think of the fierce heroine in all the crime novels I have written.

Be Jemima Jones. Be Jemima Jones!

"Just do something, for fucks sake! Stop all the sniveling and do something," a woman's voice screams out from the bush. As I search the landscape, I see no evidence of someone hiding in the shrubbery.

Thud, thud, thud.

To my surprise, I stand aghast as I watch a beach ball bounce unexpectedly across the puddles on the rocks before disappearing over the edge of the falls. I turn to my right to see where the ball has come from. I am astounded to see a young boy, standing on the rocks, waving vigorously. He is wearing blue and white striped T-shirt, white shorts, which seem too long for him, and a pair of thongs. Curiously, he remains completely dry in amongst the drenching rain.

He looks strangely familiar. My mind struggles to deal with finding an explanation as to why he is here. It is an odd place for a child to be wandering about all on his own. It dawns on me that neither Joe nor Steve have reacted to the bouncing ball. Maybe only I can see this child. Strangely, I know I am not having a premonition; there is no corresponding pain in my chest. It is curious indeed. If he is not real and not a premonition, what is he? Suddenly, I realize who the little boy is. I know exactly who he is. Though, I haven't seen him in twenty years or more.

"Bobby?" I say cautiously.

The little boy seems pleased that I have recognized him. He strikes a highly theatrical bow then skips over to the rocks where Joe is and sits next to him. I haven't seen Bobby since my childhood. We used to be such great mates. We would play at each other's house on alternating weekends. They were great times. He tried to encourage me to swim in their new in-ground swimming pool but water terrified me at that age. I even had nightmares about drowning in that pool.

Oh my God!

It suddenly dawns on me that I have the sequence of events wrong. I started having the nightmares before I knew Bobby's family was getting the swimming pool. Maybe I had a premonition of his death. Maybe it wasn't me drowning in his pool. Maybe it was Bobby. For that's what occurred less than a month after his parents installed the pool. That has to be it. Bobby was the first person I had a premonition about, though I was too young and foolish to realize it back then. This must be what Joe meant by the 'lost innocents continue to haunt him

Joe confronts Steve, "You know this little girl has nothing to do with her father's actions. She had nothing to do with your daughter's kidnapping and murder. That was your fault alone. It was caused by your own personal 'God complex', your belief that you can do whatever you want to whoever you want and it will never come back to haunt you. She died as a result of your vanity and pride."

Why is he raising the death of Steve's daughter?

Steve's mood changes instantly, "Her father should live in my shoes, feel my pain. This is only about savoring revenge, nothing more. I don't care about anything else."

"Hey," I interject, as the rain continues to pelt down. "You promised if I helped you, the girl would be set free."

Steve looks at me, a crazed, glazed look in his eyes. He appears completely insane, his mind being torn apart by a tug of war between greed and revenge, his body tense with anger, "I control this game, girly and I choose the rules. The game has changed. If you help me I will release your sister. However, the little girl stays with me."

No deal!

I want to scream this out to the universe. However, I restrain my emotions for the greater good, keeping this opinion locked away in a distant corner of my mind. Thinking about the speed and ease with which Steve severed my sister's finger, I temper my actions. I don't want to accelerate our situation down the wrong path. Being honest is a pathway that would only lead to the death of Cassandra.

"I will help," I lie.

I glance at Joe. He has a worried expression on his face. This changes gradually as he becomes aware of my hand by my side. I discretely signal him with a 'thumbs up'. He nods slightly to acknowledge my gesture, "I guess you're right, Julie."

Bobby is trying to raise my attention, waving his arms vigorously. As I watch, he points to something lying in the mud at Joe's feet. Something shiny, even in the dim light we now have at our disposal. It is indistinct from this distance, though I can tell it is metallic. Bobby is adamant that my attention should be drawn to this item.

Why are you so anxious?

I focus my attention on the mystery item, trying not to alert Steve to its presence. It is half submerged in a pool of water, camouflaged by the steady fall of rain. However, I begin to smile as I successfully identify the item. Its curves, its shape is familiar to me though I have never held one in my hand. It must have fallen out of Chris's pocket when he attacked Steve. That is the only possible explanation for its existence in the mud by the falls. I hope it still works. When the moment comes and I get my hands on it, there is a fifty-fifty chance it just won't work. After all, the pistol is drowned in a puddle of water. I have no way of telling if it is loaded too. I guess it doesn't need to be working or loaded. It simply needs to be in my hands, pointed at Steve, in order to change the balance of power.

I face Steve and smile, a broad, happy smile. He looks back intrigued, curious as to what has caused the change in my demeanor. There is no doubt he is wondering what is going on. Even under his investigative gaze, I refuse to abandon my smile. This must be what Joe has seen in his vision. It just has to be. Maybe this is how we are going to extricate ourselves from this situation. I don't know how I am going to get that gun in my hands. However, I am glad a tiny bit of hope is lying on the ground before Joe's feet.

I must get that gun!

My pulse races as I contemplate how I am going to move to reach the gun without alerting Steve. I don't know if Joe can be of assistance. For all I know, he may be unaware of the piece of luck which lies in front of him. I can't rely on his help. My only hope is to distract Steve just long enough for me to reach the gun. I draw a deep breath as I pray my acting skills are sufficient. I hope my fake premonition has enough sincerity to deceive.

"Ahhhh!" I scream as I hunch over, placing my hands on my chest as if I am writhing in severe pain. Watching discreetly, I can see I have Steve's full attention. He has taken the bait, moving a few steps forward as he is drawn into my deception.

Good.

"Julie, what do you see?" Steve implores softly. He approaches me as if I am under his control in some form of hypnotic trance. He kneels before me, watching intently.

"You don't want to know what I see," I tease, hoping he will concentrate less on determining my authenticity if he is angry. Being in control is what he is all about. Anger is his Achilles' heel.

"Of course I want to know!" he screams. "Tell me what you see or the girl dies."

"Be it on your head," I speak, doing my best impersonation of a Disney inspired, fortune telling witch. It is the only voice I can think of to use in order to act the part. My plan relies solely on appearing authentic, "You may not be happy with what I see."

"You WILL tell me what you see," Steve says flicking open the knife once more for dramatic effect. One thing Steve doesn't do well is beg. It is not in his nature. "Or I will kill the girl right now. Do you want her blood on your hands?"

"So be it," I say standing upright and staring straight at Steve. I am not scared of his bravado. While I have his attention, I am in control. "Don't say I didn't warn you. I see a girl held in a dark place. She is crying. She tells me things."

"What does she tell you?" Steve asks as his voice softens a little. He is fully focused on my words, oblivious now as to what is happening around him. All he wants is to profit, in some way, from my vision. I will not be throwing dollars at his feet today.

I continue, hoping Joe will notice the gun and retrieve it soon, "She tells me she was kidnapped a long time ago. She doesn't know how long ago, she doesn't know her age."

"What the hell does she know then?" Steve says as his frustration boils to the surface. It is plainly obvious that he can't see any way my story can be of a financial benefit to him. It is not my intention to offer him gold bullion. I intend to offer him a carrot that is worth more. It will hurt more when I take it away. Though Steve may be a greedy, immoral, son of a bitch, I still suspect he has a heart which beats under his tough exterior. I intend to reach into his chest with my bare hand and rip it out.

"She knows her name."

"And what, pray tell, is her name, as if I care?" Steve asks a little frustrated by Julie's manner.

I sigh and say clearly, "Melinda."

Steve falls silent, in stunned exasperation. He is caught completely off guard. He takes a moment or two, trying to discern the ramifications of the one word I have said, "Melinda? My angel? Are you saying she's still alive? That's not possible. After all this time, that's simply not possible. She's long dead."

I shake my head as I press home my advantage, "The visions don't lie. She is very much alive and being held against her will."

Steve is noticeably upset by this unexpected revelation. He falls to his knees in a puddle on the rocks, drenched by the pelting rain, completely drained of spirit. The knife lays limp in the palm of his hand as he addresses Joe, "That's just not possible. She was taken four years ago for God's sake! You told me she was dead. Why would you lie to me? Why didn't you tell me the truth?"

Joe shakes his head as he stands up, leaning heavily on his stick for support, "I didn't tell you for the simple reason I never experienced a premonition like this. The premonitions aren't always a hundred per cent accurate. Different people will see different things. This is Julie's premonition now. Maybe she sees something I could not. Maybe she is the only one who sees what is coming."

With a nonchalant flick of his walking stick Joe extricates the pistol up and out of the puddle. I watch as everything seems to occur in slow motion. My heart pounds as I watch the gun rotate as it sails through the air, a little to my left. I reach out desperately as it pops up out of my grasp. In the next instant I take a fumbled catch as the pistol discharges, sending a bullet harmlessly into the bush to our right. Taking a better grip on the gun I turn and face Steve, pointing it at him from a distance of about fifteen feet.

Steve remains kneeling on the rocks as he shakes his head. Lifting his head so as I can see deeply into his eyes, he exudes a smugness which is disturbing. His ego is telling him he has nothing to worry about. He has been pinned in worse corners than this. He says calmly, "I know you Julie.

I read you well. You have a good soul. You don't have what it takes to kill me. You are not ruthless scum like me. That's why your type employs my services to do all your dirty work. You just don't have the stomach for the messy stuff. I bet you become squeamish at the sight of your own blood. That's the honest truth isn't it? I've hit the nail on the head. You can't shoot and harm a fellow human being no matter how evil that person may be."

"Don't you believe it," I say nervously as I begin to shake. Self-doubts enter my head. I know I can fire the gun. However, to point it at someone in anger and shoot is a whole different ball game. Steve has placed a mental image in my head of his body covered in blood. It disgusts me to the core. I struggle to shake this image from my head. I think Steve might be right. Maybe I don't have the stomach for the messy stuff.

Steve chuckles as he stretches to his full height and takes a step forward, "You won't shoot me. You're too much of a goody two shoes, chicken shit."

"Stay where you are," I yell, tempted to step backwards. I resist the urge trying to engender a sense of confidence. I feel Steve is not fooled by my body language in the slightest. He knows I am trying to act a role which is completely foreign to me.

Steve puts his hands forward in an apologetic gesture as he continues, "You won't shoot me for one simple reason, Julie."

"And what might that be?" I ask, aiming the gun as best I can with my trembling fingers at his head.

"You might hate me but you are not about to let my innocent daughter die. You need my help to save her. It's that maternal thing which you can't shake."

"You are forgetting a few things," I smile.

"And what might they be?" Steve says as he steps slowly forward.

I hold my ground as I say hesitantly, "Well, you kidnapped and hurt Cassandra. I abhor anyone who would conceive hurting a child in such a manner."

"That is not enough," Steve says taking another step and holding out his hand. "Give me the gun like a good girl. You wouldn't want to hurt me accidentally. You will never forgive yourself if you accidentally slip and pull the trigger. Give me the gun and this will all be over."

I fear I am losing control as anger fills my heart. My tears begin to flow. I cannot detach my emotions from this situation, though I need to desperately, "You hurt my sister, you chopped her finger clean off. That was such a depraved and unnecessary act."

"You are not vengeful. I know you Julie. You will forgive me with time. Even your sister will learn to live without that finger. She has plenty more. You're not vengeful. You will not shoot me. Now give me the gun."

I shake my head as I use both hands to try to steady the gun. It has little effect as I seem to be shaking more now, "You don't know me. You don't know I lied."

Steve smiles as he takes another step forward, "Miss Perfect is not so perfect after all. So, I'll bite. What on earth did you lie about my Darling?"

I take a deep breath and look Steve in the eyes as I say in a loud clear voice, "Your daughter died years ago. I've am not having premonitions about her."

"What?" Steve says as his eyes bulge. With uncontrollable rage he makes a move to come forward and snatch the gun from my grasp. He only takes two steps as a bullet scorches out of the barrel, hitting him in the shoulder. He flinches backwards before regaining his footing once more. A look of bewilderment spreads across his face.

My aim was for his head, however I feel strangely satisfied that I missed my intended target. Steve places his fingers in his shirt. As he retracts them, the blood is clearly visible on their tips. I struggle to come to terms with the fact that I did that to him. As the rain rapidly washes his hands clean, he states, "See, you are just as evil as me. You have no qualms about doing the wrong thing. The division between good and evil is a thin grey line."

Four white doves flitter down onto the ground in front of me. One is facing Gina, one towards Joe, yet another is facing Cassandra. The final dove is at my feet, staring up at me. They seem unbothered by the rain and the people around them. Standing passively, they quietly coo. I know they are a sign. I know I have unfinished business. I know I have not removed the danger from our lives. I have simply provoked it.

"I think what I am doing is right, the best thing for humanity. If I am mistaken, if what I am doing is wrong," I respond calmly. "Then Steve, I guess I'll see you in Hell someday."

Steve smiles unnervingly as if he pays my words no heed. A lightning flash reflects off his gold tooth.

One thought rages through my mind.

This will take the smile from your face.

I discharge the pistol repeatedly sending numerous bullets wildly in Steve's general direction. At least two more hit Steve as he reels backwards and falls over the edge of the cliff. As the cartridge empties, I stop firing and walk to the edge of the precipice. From my vantage point I cannot see where Steve has landed. The scrub below the falls is thick. Just the odd bush with broken limbs gives any clue that someone has fallen over the edge.

The birds remain standing, completely calm, while the shooting transpires. As soon as Steve falls over the cliff, they take to the air, heading north into the distance. I watch as one of the birds suddenly falters and falls from the sky, landing awkwardly amongst the bushes. I look to see if it is alright but it is hidden in amongst the dense shrubbery. I can hear its faint squawks of anguish as it tries to extricate itself. Its squawks diminish steadily until there is silence once more. I make a note to myself that I will have to ask Joe to explain the significance of the doves to me after we have made it back down off the mountain.

There is so much I need to learn.

Oscar howls out in pain behind me as I wipe the tears from my face. Breathing deeply, I turn to see what the commotion is all about, "It's okay. He's gone......."

In the pelting rain I can see Joe hunched awkwardly on the rocks. His face is pale, his eyes open and sightless. The angle in which he is contorted seems uncomfortable and unnatural. I begin to cry once more.

I walk over to Joe and kneel by his side in the mud. Holding his wrist I check for a pulse. There is nothing. I release his wrist so that it can lay down by his side. Gently I close his eyes and sigh, "I guess the hike up the hill was too much for you, old man. You knew this was when and how you were going to pass but you climbed the hill anyhow. You could have cheated death, you chose not to. I remember you spoke that you wanted your last act to be remembered by someone as 'doing a good deed to help others'. I will remember this forever. I will make sure others know of it too. You saved us today and didn't have to do any dodgy deals. You did right. I'll miss you mate."

I step away from Joe as ghostly apparitions begin to land around his lifeless body. At first just a few, though, as the seconds pass, their numbers grow drastically. Oscar falls silent as he too seems to notice the ghostly figures coming forward and gathering around Joe. They look at Joe, then at each other as they consider that which has occurred. Eventually they decide on their course of action.

One by one they begin to fly up into the sky. Suddenly, from within their huddle, an apparition of Joe appears, carried skywards by two young men. One of these men seems to fit the description of his brother. As they disappear, up and out of sight, they are rapidly followed by all the other apparitions. Within seconds, they are gone. Oscar begins to howl once more, in obvious distress, by his deceased master's side. He places a paw lovingly on Joe's leg seeking some sort of affectionate interaction. None is forthcoming. If cats could cry, Oscar would be drowning in a sea of tears.

I linger for a moment mesmerized by the strange occurrence. Finally I realize I still have work to do. I begin to move towards Cassandra as my senses register something unusual.

Roses! I smell roses.

I recall my earlier premonition of Cassandra. I study the bush around me, searching for the mystery woman who smells of roses. In the thick scrub I see nothing, though I suspect she must be close at hand. I scream at the top of my lungs, "Who are you? Show yourself. What do you want?"

Echoing out of the bush, seemingly from all directions at once, is the sound of a female voice laughing in a maniacal manner. Her voice resonates for an instant before being swept away by the rain once more. I shake my head as my focus returns. I still have the 'living' to attend to. With increased urgency I begin to untie Cassandra.

I must get Gina and Cassandra off this bloody hill!

'Nothing'

Crops wither,
In the arid dust,
Nothing thrives in this barren place.

Lightning strikes,
Lives are lost,
Nothing thrives in this barren place.

Friends are scarce,
Suspicion abounds,
Nothing thrives in this barren place.

Chapter 19

April 11th 1692.

Salem, Massachusetts.

For the last two days Thomas has simply gone through the motions without any enthusiasm for life. If not for the love of his two girls, he would be nothing more than an empty shell of a man. He has been trying, pointlessly, to remove the horrific memories of Mary's final seconds of life from his mind. The images play constantly in slow motion. He sees every last gruesome detail vividly through all his waking hours. He is woken instantly by nightmares, any time he manages to fall asleep.

From beginning to end, the execution plays out. When he sees Mary being carried off towards the graveyard, it all begins again with Mary being marched out to the town square. The only thing that changes each time is John. He is becoming more demonic each time the image replays. Thomas bears scratches across his eyelids where he has torn at his eyes trying to remove the images that curse his brain. Alas, this has not provided any freedom from torment for his soul.

Emma Williams has heeded the call of her husband George and come to the aid of Thomas in his time of crisis though she is nervous of the repercussions. She has brewed a tea made from the leaves of the Bearberries which flourish on the hillsides around Salem. It has miraculous healing qualities, particularly for those troubled in their minds. Once administered, a soothing quality pervades over the patient's ailments, curing that which bedevils them. In fact, it usually has such a soothing effect that the recipient ends up sleeping for a week, just by taking a few sips of this incredibly powerful elixir.

In Thomas's case the medicine merely calms him into a duped normality. He has been unable to sleep for very long at all over the last two days; existing rather than functioning normally. Tolerance has been absent from his emotions. However, with some gentle encouragement, he has begun to listen to what his brother in law Edward is telling him. During their conversations, Thomas has offered few words though he listens intently to the news from Salem. His heart grows heavier with each word that Edward speaks.

Edward relays a detailed account of the thoughts and opinions he has heard from various people in town. Adding to this, he includes the rumors and whispers which grow closer to fact each day. All in all, they both fear that the mood in Salem appears to have darkened, turning against their family. Thomas knows his family's stay in Salem is fast drawing to an end.

Usually the execution of a witch has a calming effect on the fears of the people of Salem. Normality, free of superstitious thoughts, should, by rights, engulf the town as the people begin to recover and go about their everyday tasks. Usually peace and tranquility reign for weeks, if not months. Unfortunately, the execution of Mary and Sarah did not have the same desired effect. The paranoid farmers believe the plague of witches is purely responsible for the failed barley crops this year. Their mood, fuelled by jugs of ale, is to seek retribution against all known witch families. The residents of Salem also want to ensure the children of witches have no opportunity to take up the craft of their parents. They feel the apple doesn't fall far from the tree.

This last revelation worries Thomas immensely and is the major reason for his lack of sleep. Edward politely waits to hear what Thomas feels on the matter. Thomas stands and walks slowly to the window. Leaning against the wall he looks out beyond their home. His chest heaves as he sighs, absorbing the view in front of him. He is mesmerized by the living watercolor before his eyes. In his opinion, there is no finer sight in the world than his two beautiful girls playing with their rag dolls under a peppercorn tree. They are completely oblivious to the evils of the world and the execution of their mother. If Thomas was to name this living portrait, he would call it 'Heaven'. Everything he has that is worth anything in this world is wrapped up in those two little girls now. He knows he must do everything in his power to protect them and nurture their growth to womanhood.

Tears well in his eyes as he thinks of their tiny lifeless bodies hanging from a tree with their faces shrouded in black cloth. Thomas is overwhelmed with determination to ensure they have a good and long life. He cannot let his precious angels end their lives like this. He cannot let history repeat itself. He cannot let his girls endure the same fate as their mother. Mary would want him to act, and act decisively, to protect them. It would be Mary's solemn wish; of that much he is certain.

Turning slightly, Thomas briefly looks George in the eye as if he is about to say something. Though he has many thoughts and feelings, no words pass his lips. Thomas lowers his head as he nods his approval. He shields his eyes from his friends as the tears begin to flow uncontrollably. He wanders slowly back to his bed where he collapses in amongst the disheveled sheets. He is comforted knowing that all the necessary packing will be done by Edward, George and Emma; they are great friends. No, they are the best of friends. All Thomas needs at the moment is some time on his own. He wants to cry, he needs to flush some of the pain he feels out of his body.

George and Emma work at a frantic pace, gathering and loading all the essentials for a life in a new town. By late afternoon the two wagons are loaded and securely tied down. Thomas's own wagon is filled with most of his possessions as well as enough fresh water, food and preserves to last them for a week. After all, in this current climate, they need to get as far away from Salem as they can in as short a time as possible. The plan is for both wagons to only stop for brief periods of time, just long enough to rest and water the horses. They must try to move swiftly away from here.

Edward has his own wagon loaded ready to go. His wagon has a supply of food and water though precious little else. He doesn't want to take with him anything that will remind him of the place that murdered his wife. The entire contents of the second wagon consist of one bag containing all of Violet's clothes, rations for a week and an antique silver locket. The locket is on a long chain, an heirloom from Violet's grandmother on Mary's side. When you open the locket it has two faded sepia photos; one of Thomas and one of Mary. It is a parting gift from Thomas that he hopes will remind her of better times when she finds it in amongst her clothes. Mary would want her to have it. She would want Violet to remember them. She would want Violet to never feel unloved.

Thomas walks to the front porch rubbing the remnants of tears from his eyes. He surveys the scene before him, satisfied the preparations are nearly complete. George is tightening the last of the cables, securing the load on the wagon Thomas will be taking. George smiles as he sees Thomas walking down from the steps and heading towards him. Thomas strolls over to George and pats him on the shoulder. It is a simple gesture of good will and thanks, though it is much appreciated by George. Thomas is fragile though able to hold his emotions together at the moment. Words are a different matter, they don't come easily.

"Meoowww"

Thomas looks down in disbelief at the black cat rubbing affectionately against his leg. It has been two days since Mary's execution and Jezebel has been missing that whole time. Jezebel has always had little to do with Thomas. It could be said that their relationship consisted of tolerance rather than love and affection. Thomas has paid Jezebel's absence little heed. With Mary gone, Jezebel no longer has any reason to stay around. He is surprised the cat has suddenly reappeared.

Mary has always had Jezebel since she was a young girl. It is a peculiarity Thomas doesn't understand. It is something he doesn't care to ponder nor want to understand. He just knows that most of the townsfolk are aware that Mary had a black cat living with her, just like witches do. A 'familiar' is the term they use.

Thomas stands staring at Jezebel, smooching up against his leg. Its head tilting as it rubs against him as if to indicate how wonderful it feels to be back with Thomas and his family. Thomas, however, is wondering why the cat has chosen to come around now. Why wasn't she around when Mary needed her? As he watches the cat weave in and out of his legs, his calm demeanor begins to steadily evaporate. Every cell in his body starts to tense and he becomes overpowered with rage. A burning hatred stirs somewhere deep in his soul, bubbling its way to the surface. He tries his best to contain this powerful feeling, to quell the fires billowing in his heart, though he is unable. The force of hatred he feels for Jezebel and other black cats like her is overwhelming. This feeling stems from just one thought going through his tortured mind.

Thou doth made Mary appear a witch. Thou doth killed my wife!

In a brutally swift movement Thomas grabs the cat by the hind legs and storms into the house carrying it upside down. In pain, Jezebel protests fiercely all the way. Shrieking, hissing, wriggling and spitting; though unable to free herself and escape his clutches. On hearing the commotion, George rushes towards the house. He is just in time to see Thomas return with a Hessian sack, tied at the top by a thin rope. The cat, apparently, inside fighting for all it's worth to escape. There appears to be something heavy at the bottom of the sack. Something making the veins in Thomas's arm bulge as he holds it off the ground.

"Thomas," George pleads feebly as he stares into the wild eyes of his friend.

Thomas shakes his head, determined that no one is going to stop him from his task, "No, this needs to be done. It be my right. I doth need to do this or I shall be cursed by regret."

"But Thomas, what shall Violet and Rose think of thee?" George continues to plead as Thomas passes him, heading down the hill towards the bush and the river.

"Nay, this doth need be done now! My girls doth not need to knoweth"

Thomas walks briskly towards the river, the squirming bag held high in his right hand. His hand turns white where he holds the bag tightly. He walks like a man possessed. George decides not to intervene. Thomas has been through so much with the horrific death of Mary and now the forced evacuation of his family. His life has been torn apart. George knows Thomas is not behaving in a rational manner. Maybe rational is something he will never be again. However, seeing him in a rage like this, he knows he can neither talk him out of his proposed actions nor prevent him from carrying out the drowning of Jezebel. He knows he has to let what will be occur, no matter whether he thinks it is right or wrong.

Emma rushes to George, her eyes bulging and tearful, seeking assistance from her husband to stop Thomas from doing his planned barbaric act. George places his hands on her shoulders then pulls her close in a loving embrace. Emma doesn't say a word, though George knows exactly how she is feeling, what she is asking him to do. As he tries to comfort her he shakes his head.

"Nay, let him be," he says as he hugs her tight. George watches Thomas over Emma's shoulder as he walks down the track leading into the bush which sweeps down to the river. Thomas takes just a few steps down the track before he is hidden amongst the undergrowth. "It be in God's hands now."

Jezebel puts up a commendable fight for the whole journey down to the river though, in the end, with little success. Her claws regularly get caught in the Hessian bag as she lashes out, frustrating and tiring the cat. By the time they reach the river, Jezebel is barely moving in the bag. Thomas stands on the edge of the river bed before stepping out onto one of the larger dry rocks in amongst the rapids. Water cascades down the steep rocky slope before tapering out to a larger, deeper pool of calm waters. These waters are deep enough to swim or fish for trout. The boulder Thomas stands on is overlooking this great pool of water. In the eyes of Thomas, this is the perfect spot.

"Meooww," Jezzie cries out in a soft, pitiful, exhausted manner.

Thomas places the bag on the rock as he sits down, his head in his hands. He begins to break down and cry as he thinks about Mary and how much she loved this damn cat. After all, the cat spent more time with her than he did. Thomas knows if Mary was here she would want Jezebel to be safe and well. That is the problem; Mary is not here anymore. Jezebel played her part in securing Mary's plight.

Wiping the tears from his eyes Thomas stands up. Looking out into the bushes on the other side of the river, he contemplates his options carefully.

He is conflicted with the question of what to do with Jezebel. Thomas considers himself to be a good and just man, one that would not unnecessarily harm another living creature. However, the fact that Mary possessed a black cat was one of the major reasons why the Elders found her guilty of being a witch. Jezebel, through no fault of her own, is thus implicated in Mary's death.

Thomas picks up the Hessian bag, purring can be heard emanating from inside. Jezebel has never purred for Thomas before. This act of affection catches him off guard. His hand pauses for a second on the rope tie that holds the bag shut. He considers opening the bag for a moment. He loosens the tie a little, creating a small opening.

"Let God be thy judge," he offers loudly as a tear is shed from his eye.

Suddenly he raises the bag, swinging it hard over his shoulder before releasing his grip and hurling it through the air until it plummets into the swirling waters of the pool below. Jezebel squirms wildly as the Hessian bag floats initially on the water. Steadily water seeps into the bag. With a flurry of bubbles the bag sinks to the bottom of the river. Thomas watches till the bag is submerged then turns and begins his slow walk back up the track to the homestead.

It takes just half an hour for Thomas to slowly trudge his way back up the hill towards the homestead. His feet weigh heavy with the burden of what he has done. Sending Jezebel to a watery grave is what he felt he had to do; to purify his household of personal demons that destroyed his and his family's lives. It is simply one more thing which he had to do in order to protect his girls. The critical thought had been that his girls may be accused of being familiar with the devil's pets if Jezebel remained in their care.

As Thomas nears the homestead, his eyes are fixed firmly on the ground in front of his next slow, deliberate step. His mind is racing, running through the different combinations of words in his head, completely lost in thought. He is desperately trying to work out how he is going to explain his actions to his two girls. He doesn't want to keep the truth from them. He doesn't want to lie either. He just doesn't know how to word the truth so that they won't look at him like he is some sort of hideous monster.

Night is beginning to fall as he sees his youngest daughter Rose rushing towards him with excitement beaming over her entire, freckled face. Thomas lowers his gaze to his ragged shoes, unable to look her in the eye. He is overcome by a deep feeling of remorse for the terrible crime he has committed. Rose tugs at his trouser leg, trying to gain his attention.

"Pa, thou doth need to come quick. Come see," Rose screeches excitedly. Grasping her father's hand, she tries to drag him up the hill with no success. His feet are firmly planted on the grass beneath him. Eventually she lets go, choosing instead to run back towards the reason for all her excitement.

Slowly, Thomas looks up. He can see his two beautiful girls playing in the grass some thirty yards in front of him. He cannot remember the last time he saw them this happy. It was certainly before Mary was taken away so cruelly from all their lives. He is pleased something has brought them happiness, though curious as to what it might be. From this distance he cannot work out what the source of their Joy might be. He moves closer until he is able to see two tiny creatures bouncing around playfully in the grass.

What art you?

Abruptly he stops, frozen with horror. His eyes bulge as he finally identifies the creatures before him, the creatures playing with his daughters, the creatures that are making them so happy. Two little black kittens, one for each of his daughters, have appeared out of nowhere, just like Jezebel did all those years ago for Mary; all those years ago when her visions first started. The appearance of Jezebel was the dawn of Mary's living nightmare.

Thomas falls to his knees, hunched over, trying to grasp the ramifications of the situation. He knows in his heart this situation is dire. It changes his girl's lives forever. Nothing is ruled by chance. Everything is preordained. They are just pawns in God's cruel game of chess.

He repeats the same words, over and over again, softly under his breath, "Thou art thy ma's girls. It be unsafe for thee here. Thou art thy ma's girls."

Thomas continues repeating these words as George and Emma begin to help him to his feet.

*　　　　*　　　　*

Darkness falls completely, covering the hills like a blanket as the two wagons set off. Thomas and Rose are in one, heading south to parts as yet undetermined. Thomas knows his options are many once he reaches the Port of Boston. Their final destination will largely be determined by fate, he is comfortable with that. It will depend on where the ships are heading and who will accept their passage. Edward and his niece Violet are in the other wagon heading west to see his first cousin Floyd. It will be a tough journey, for New York is two states away. However, with a little luck, that will be enough distance from Salem to provide her with a safe life. Thomas hopes Floyd will be receptive, providing a safe haven for Violet without asking too many questions. In each wagon, a black kitten sits, sleeping peacefully on some clothes. They have already made themselves at home.

There is not a sound on the hills tonight, though they are teeming with wildlife. The only sound that can be heard is the sound of Violet's painful cries for her father and sister. Though she is the elder of the two girls she has always been the more emotional. Thomas hopes her cries will end soon as the distance between them becomes greater. In a short space of time she has lost all her family. That is an impossible situation for a child to have to bear. He wishes he could be with her right now, to comfort her, to let her know how much she is loved. Closing his eyes he tries to ignore her pleas knowing in his heart, he is doing the right thing. The girls have more chance of a future separated.

As Thomas reaches the apex of the hill, he pauses looking back at the homestead he built with his own hands. He thinks of all the hopes and dreams he and Mary molded into that home along with their blood and sweat. All those hopes and dreams are now gone, long gone. Thomas glances at his youngest child, Rose, lying curled up asleep next to her kitten. She looks so peaceful. She has always been a contented soul, no matter what dramas have come to pass. He smiles stiffly.

Maybe we can dream in a new land. Maybe hope lies sleeping there. Maybe it shall flourish somewhere else. That is my hope, at least.

Thomas turns back and watches his homestead for a while longer. Just long enough to see the first light of hundreds of torches heading up the road leading to their now deserted home. He knows what the mob wants to do. He knows there is no way he can stop them or convince them to desist. Tears build in his eyes as he looks to the path in front of them. He flicks the reins, encouraging the horses onwards.

"Hope doth not dwell here anymore!" he mutters through gritted teeth.

'Haze'

Whispers haunt,
Rumors abound,
Resources are stretched,
But not everyone is found.

Watch people closely,
Take care what they say,
For everyone is someone,
But they are not today.

Chapter 20

Wednesday, March 1st, 2006.

Afternoon.

Wilhelmina Falls, Victoria, Australia.

The rain has eased to a gentle drizzle by the time Cassandra and I reach the car park. We have walked, hand in hand, for the last half hour, completely silent. Cassandra has clung onto my hand from the moment I first released her from her bonds. We glance at each other as we walk briskly down the track, though, after all that has occurred, we are both lost for words. I guess I will have the opportunity to talk to her later. Maybe she won't want to talk about her ordeal at all. I just hope she is not scarred too deeply by all that has occurred.

I have reluctantly left Gina at the top of the falls. She is simply too weak for the long journey down the slope. For some curious reason, Serenity has chosen to stay by her side, curled up, taking a cat nap. I am comforted that he has stayed to watch over her while I go seek help. He has indeed, a most strange disposition for a cat. He seems highly intelligent, almost human-like at times. With the 'rose perfumed lady' still lurking somewhere in the bush I know no further harm will come to Gina while Serenity stands guard.

To our surprise the car park is swarming with emergency services personal as we arrive. A group of heavily armed policeman come running to our assistance. I baulk, remembering how Steve had spoken about how he had paid off many in the police force. I hold Cassandra's hand tight as I wonder whether these men are friend or foe.

Two policemen snatch Cassandra from my grasp, lifting her up and carrying her away from me. She screams, reaching out unsuccessfully, trying to re-grasp my outstretched hand. They carry her straight down to a waiting ambulance. I am exhausted. I can do little, other than watch, as they abscond with her. I pray their intentions are honorable.

"Hi, I'm Senior Sergeant Colin MacPherson. I need you to remain calm. Please, you must remain calm. I have a few important questions for you. How many more people are up at the top of falls? Do you know what condition they are in? Are there any perpetrators with weapons?"

"What?" I say distracted, looking down towards Cassandra who, I can see, has two paramedics examining her, checking her vital signs as well as tending to her scratches and cuts. Everything seems to be above board as far as I can tell.

"How many more are up at the top of the falls and what condition are they in?"

This time the question registers in my frazzled brain. Slowly I begin to answer, "Yes, um, Joe is dead on top of the falls, my sister Gina is badly hurt. She couldn't walk down unaided. She needs medical help; she's lost a lot of blood. That bastard chopped off a finger."

"Is that everyone?" the Senior Sergeant asks.

"Yes. No. I mean no. Chris is stabbed and Steve is shot. I think they are both dead. They both fell over the cliff."

"Strewth!" the Senior Sergeant exclaims as he swings into action. "It sounds like it's a bloodbath up there men. We're going to need four stretchers, several paramedics and all police up here to implement a coordinated search and rescue plan pronto. Thanks miss. We'll go and retrieve your sister and the others. Please don't fret, she'll be fine, we'll look after her."

I nod as I continue down the path, unaided. My frazzled mind is more content now that I know the police are here to help. Two paramedics run towards me and take me by the arms, down to the ambulance where Cassandra has been receiving treatment a moment ago. I ask, as the ground before me begins to spin, Where is she?"

"It's okay," the female paramedic says as she takes my pulse. "She's resting on a stretcher in the ambulance. She is a little dehydrated and suffering from shock but I think she will make a pretty quick recovery. Kids are resilient like that."

I nod feebly, as exhaustion mixed with relief floods my body. My eyelids flutter as I become light headed. As I faint, I hear the paramedics call out, "Hey, I need some help here, stat!"

*　　　　　*　　　　　*

"Hello sleeping beauty," I hear a familiar voice say as I begin to open my eyes. Standing before me is the grinning face of Peter.

"You're alive," I say croakily as I try unsuccessfully to sit up.

Peter's mouth continues to move though his words are silent, lacking any discernable tone or inflection. I become mesmerized by the scene playing out behind Peter. I can see everything clearly though my brain refuses to believe the images before me.

Slowly yet purposefully Chris and Steve are walking towards Peter from behind. They are clearly badly injured though somehow able to force themselves onwards towards one final, despicable act.

I am silent, unable to speak or signal Peter of the danger as he stands before me, speaking his unvoiced words. Only my eyes move, going from side to side as I switch my view from predator to prey and back again.

Everything moves in slow motion as the two monsters move within ten feet of Peter now. Their arms outstretched their eyes bloodshot and unflinching. Chris's stomach is cut wide open, bleeding profusely and exposing the pulsing red tissue inside. Steve is pale, his shirt bloody and scorched where my bullets have dug deep into his torso. I can't believe they are alive, let alone so agile.

To my horror they reach out and take Peter from me by the shoulders and arms dragging him backwards as they begin to punch him………

*   *   *

"Hello sleeping beauty," I hear a familiar voice say as I begin to open my eyes. Standing before me is the welcome, grinning face of Peter.

"You're……you're alive!" I say croakily as I try unsuccessfully to sit up. I nervously search for Chris and Steve however, this time, they are not to be found. My aching brain slowly registers the fact that their attack on Peter was nothing more than a horrible nightmare.

"Whoa baby," he says, placing a hand on my shoulder, preventing my forward movement and forcing me to lie back down. "Of course I'm alive."

"But it was a trap," I say.

Peter smiles casually, "I know that. I knew that the moment we spoke to Steve. His yarn just didn't ring true. I needed to get to a spot where I could get some phone reception. It took a while to find a location however, once I did, I was able to get all the troops gathered together. I wasn't sure what we needed so I ordered the lot. I'm glad I did."

"Have they brought the others out yet?"

"Yes, Gina has gone off to hospital. She's lost a fair bit of blood, though the paramedics reckon she'll recover just fine. I grabbed Serenity, he's in the car. Put up a helluva fight though. Wouldn't let the paramedics near Gina, then when I snatched him he did this to me," Peter says as he shows off the deep scratch marks on both his arm. Those two never see eye to eye. Suddenly his face grows more somber as he searches for the right words. Eventually he just decides to be direct. "Um, Joe's dead though."

"Yes, I know. The hill climb was simply too much for him. We wouldn't be alive without him though. He knew he had to help us or we would all die at Steve's hand. However, he knew he would die if he made that climb, he had seen that in his visions. His efforts were a purely selfless act. He's the hero of this whole drama. "

"Oh, I wasn't sure you knew. I guess he wasn't such a bad old codger after all. Anyway, they've brought him off the hill now. If you thought Serenity was angry, no one could get near that damn cranky old cat of his. It refused to leave his side, travelling on the stretcher the whole journey to the waiting ambulance. Anyway, they brought out another body too."

A chill runs down my spine as I ask, "Who was that? Is it Steve?"

"No, no it's not Steve. It's a large, old guy with strange tattoos on his arms."

"That's Chris. What about Steve? Did they find him? He fell down the cliff too."

"No sign as yet. They've been searching for an hour or so and haven't found anything yet. All they've found is a blood trail which leads into the thick scrub. They've called for sniffer dogs because of the terrain. They will find him, dead or alive; there is no place for him to go."

"He fell over a cliff, he had severe injuries. I shot him several times. There must be a trail to follow. Surely he can't be hard to find!"

"Don't stress, Julie," Peter reassures, taking my hand. "I'm sure they will track him down. It's just that the scrub is so hard to search through. It is pretty rough terrain."

I relax back on the stretcher as the paramedic jumps into the back with me. "I'm sorry sir, we have to go now."

"Righto," says Peter as he kisses me on the lips. "I'll see you at the hospital, when you get there."

The doors close and almost immediately, we set off down the road.

"It's you!" calls the tiny voice beside me.

Twisting a little, I look at the other stretcher. Cassandra's freckled face glows with excitement as she smiles at me. I answer, "Yes, I'm the one who rescued you."

"No," Cassandra says, a little indignantly. "That's not it."

My curiosity aroused, I ask, "What are you talking about, Honey?"

"You're the lady I saw on the footpath when the bad man took me."

"I think you are mistaken, Sweetheart. I only just met you today."

"Yes, you were, I saw you. You were there with your cat with the droopy ear. You were watching," Cassandra pouts.

I slump back into the stretcher, completely exhausted, my mind racing rapidly. I know I wasn't there when Cassandra was kidnapped. I would have remembered that. I would have tried to stop that from occurring. That only leaves one possible option, as far as I can tell. Is it possible that Cassandra had a premonition like me? If this is the case then she must have been having a premonition about herself and our meeting at Wilhelmina Falls.

Is that possible? I don't know. Maybe. Maybe it was just a dream she had. Maybe it was something else. I don't know.

"Did your chest hurt, Honey?" I ask softly.

"Yep, it hurt something rotten though I didn't cry"

"You'll get used to the pain after a while," I smile as I drift off to sleep.

"You spoke to me too," Cassandra chimes sweetly.

"What did I say, Honey?" I say, not bothering to open my heavy eyelids. My energy levels are dwindling rapidly.

"You said 'hope is a.....a.....a.....'"

".......waking dream. It certainly is, my Sweet," I say smiling, finally falling into a peaceful sleep. "It certainly is."

'Ghosts'

In a darker time,
When superstition runs rife,
Witchcraft is common,
Just an everyday part of life.

One thing is known,
About what occurs after light,
Ghosts haunt the woods,
So beware of the night.

Chapter 21

April 14th 1692.
Salem, Massachusetts.

Sam Williams is beginning to feel a little frustrated as he wanders cautiously through the burnt out remains of the Murphy homestead. Using a stick, he looks under yet another smoldering log with no success. A scowl forms on his sooty face as he continues to search for anything he can salvage as 'treasure'. He is disappointed with what he has found thus far. His haul consists of nothing more than two bent nails and a broken clay pitcher. Everything within the mud brick shell of the house is burnt beyond recognition. All that remains is smoldering black charcoal which is steadily attaching itself to Sam's, shirt, trousers and boots.

His gaze wanders out through the doorway into the grassy paddocks. Hunched over, he spies something glinting in the sunlight, just beneath the Peppercorn tree. In an instant he moves, scrambling over the sooty boards in a reckless manner as he clambers to leave the derelict house. Once his feet reach the surety of the grass, he travels rapidly to the tree. In a matter of seconds he finds himself standing over the object, looking down, wide eyed at the discovery of his treasure.

"Wow!" he says as he picks up the rag doll with silver button eyes.

A dirty, scarred hand reaches over his shoulder, taking the doll from his grasp. Surprised, Sam turns and faces his visitor as he takes several nervous steps backwards. He looks at the bedraggled figure holding the doll, handling it like it is a precious baby, gently caressing its hair. The visitor is a woman. Her dark hair, though dirty and tangled in knots, shimmers in the daylight, highlighting her patch of grey. Her clothes are torn and dirty. She looks just like the beggars in town, the ones his parents warn him regularly to be wary of. Her face is pale and distraught. Her eyes are open but lifeless; unblinking with an insane gaze. Her appearance gives rise to the notion that she is someone who has lived a hard life, a very hard life indeed.

The woman seats herself down cross-legged in the grass under the tree as she cradles the doll. Sam can see from his vantage point a second woman begin to walk towards the Peppercorn tree from the bush leading up from the river. Suddenly this second woman is passed by a mangy black cat who hobbles swiftly in a straight line towards the woman with Sam. The cat nudges the woman for attention. The lady begins to shake as she struggles with her emotions. Sam suspects she is on the verge of crying as she speaks.

"Violet! Rose! Where art thou? Oh Jezebel, where be my girls?" she asks as she begins to pat the cat under its chin.

Jezebel winks with its one good eye while it purrs softly. Her blind eye doesn't close any more. There is a deep scar just above this eye from where her head was cut as she scrambled amongst the rocks at the bottom of the river during her escape from the Hessian bag. It was, however, these same sharp rocks that had been her salvation. They caused the rope tie to tear creating a wider opening in the bag. It was enough of a gap that Jezebel was able to squeeze through and swim to the surface.

"Art thou ghosts?" Sam asks completely unperturbed by the strange visitors in his midst. He is five years old, a purely innocent age, far too young to be afraid of anything. He is simply curious, excited by the prospect that this might be his first bona fide encounter with ghosts. In fact, it is better than that. If the rumors are true, then these would be witch ghosts, something truly incredible.

The woman slowly turns to look at the boy with the beaming smile. Disorientated momentarily, her brain struggles to comprehend what Sam is asking her. Eventually the words register in her mind and clarity begins to seep slowly into her thoughts. Her face lightens somewhat as if she is waking from a deep, peaceful sleep. She reaches out, taking his hand in hers as she looks into his eyes. Smiling, with tears smudging her dirty face, she says calmly, "Nay, I be Mary. I live here. Though I be dead inside, I be no ghost."

The boy considers these words for a second then laughs, startling Mary. She is unaware she has said anything funny. Sam explains the situation to her clearly, "Nay, nobody lives here. The townsfolk burnt it to the ground so it be rid of foul demons. Thou must be a ghost. Art thou a ghost?"

Mary shakes her head, saying softly under her breath, "Nay, I be alive."

Mary releases her grip on Sam as she stands and turns to face the ruins of her house. As she walks towards the homestead, clutching the rag doll in her hand, she is stunned by the complete devastation caused by the fire. Everything is gone. Every remnant of her life has been swept from the face of the earth, save for the old rag doll. Fear fills her heart as she begins to wonder if her husband and daughters were here at the time it was torched. Mary stops breathing as she wonders if maybe, just maybe, they were all trapped and devoured by the flames which so ravenously devoured their house. She reaches for her chest as a sharp, stabbing pain shoots through her.

Breathlessly she seeks resolution to her torment from Sam, "Where be my children, the family that once lived here?"

"They left before the fire," Sam says as he wanders around, casually looking for more items in amongst the rubble.

"Where did they go, I beg you to tell me?" Mary implores, placing a hand on the Sam's shoulder preventing him from moving farther away.

"A girl and her Pa went south, the elder one west with her Uncle," Sam says as he stares into Mary's eyes. Their sea blue color bulges from within the scratches and dirt which hides the rest of her features. He is a little fearful of her now. She appears to him like a wild creature, one that is strange and dangerous.

"What? Where?" she asks more strongly though incoherently.

"I know not," Sam says as he starts to squirm, trying to free himself from Mary's grip on his shoulder, a hold which grows tighter by the second. He is worried by Mary's agitation.

"Where?" Mary yells, grabbing both his shoulders and shaking Sam's body violently.

"I know not. Please let me be," Sam yells back trying desperately to wriggle out of Mary's grasp.

Sarah wanders over to Mary and places a comforting hand on her shoulder, "Let the boy be. He knows not where thy family art."

Mary suddenly realizes what she is doing. In horror she releases her grip. "I'm sorry," she says as Sam takes his opportunity and runs, screaming from the ruins. He heads swiftly back across the paddocks towards his house without looking over his shoulder once. Mary outstretches her hand towards him in a futile gesture of good will as he disappears over the rise and out of view. She begins to weep again, more vigorously than before.

She falls to her knees amongst the black soot as the reality of her situation begins to sink in. Mary's list of tragedies is mounting, weighing heavily on her heart. Her home is gone, burnt to the ground beyond recognition. Thomas and her two angels are gone to destinations unknown. Her family has been split, with Violet travelling in a different location. This will make it harder to track their journeys and bring them all back together once more. To make a bad situation worse, Thomas thinks she is dead. This means they won't be slowing their pace nor leaving any clues for her to find. Thomas won't be expecting to see her again. All in all, Mary is living the life of a dead person. She is a lost soul. Forsaken, it seems, by even God himself.

It has been five days since Harold, the executioner, was overcome with superstitious fears and doubts. Harold has seen witches tried before that he has considered may be innocent. With Mary it was a different story; he was convinced she was a witch of the highest order, there could be no doubt. She even had her devilish familiar stalking him. He feared being cursed. His young family had their lives ahead of them. If he was to kill a witch with such powers, he would surely be cursed with her final words tainted by her filthy, venomous breath. He could not take the chance. He did what he had to do.

There were plenty of prisoners to choose from; they were nearly all guilty of something. Harold chose two who looked the same height and shape as Mary and Sarah. After binding and shackling the prisoners, he placed a bag over each of his victim's heads. Gagging them prior to escorting them out into the main street, thus ensuring there was no chance of them raising the alarm or calling for help. He was completely confident no one would become aware of his deception. It was a perfect plan, considering he would be doing the burials afterwards.

Very early on the morning of the executions, he released Mary and Sarah, pointing them in the general direction of the river. He was comforted by Mary's smile. He could see the relief on her face and the hope burning brightly in her eyes that, once again, she would be reunited with her family. He took it as a sign he was in her favor, a sign that he would be safe. Neither he nor his family would be cursed.

Mary now kneels in the soot considering all the effort she has made to get here, wondering to herself, 'what is the point of it all? Why was she released only to be condemned to a life of torture and misery?'

Ripping the crucifix from around her neck, she stares towards the heavens. Holding it in the palm of her hand from her arm outstretched, she reaches out to God, "Why doth thou torture me so? I do thy bidding. I do thy work to save thy unfortunate souls. Why doth thou curse me so?"

Mary waits for a moment, waiting for a reply that doesn't come. She stands shaking her head, letting the crucifix slide through her trembling fingers and land in amongst the blackened soot. She begins to walk from the house, staring out into the distance. Sarah retrieves the crucifix, holding it firmly in her hand, before catching up and walking by her sister's side.

Mary looks towards the south first, then turns and gazes to the west. In both directions there is nothing save trees and scrub. Taking a deep breath, she screams as loudly as he dry raspy throat will allow, "Violet, Rose. Please hear my call. We are of the same blood; we are of the same line. Feel this tortured heart of mine, for it beats in your chest as it does in mine. Feel its pain so brutal and know that I love thee. I am not whole without thee. I will never rest till we be together once more. My heart be broken......."

Her words taper off as the pain in her chest stings like she is cut by a thousand swords. Her words spoken to the hills, in full view of the God she has trusted implicitly all her life. This is the God that, in her eyes, has failed her terribly. She walks slowly and silently back down towards the river.

Waiting in a beam of sunlight at the edge of the bush is Jezebel. Mary picks up the disheveled cat, with all her scars and wounds. She pats the cat for a second as an aimless thought enters her mind. What if Jezebel is a sign? Maybe she is a sign that no matter what life throws at you there is always hope. A sign that you can battle your way through whatever crisis and achieve what you want to achieve. After all, Jezebel has survived many dramas and found her way back to her every time. With hope still flickering faintly in her heart, Mary sets out to find Thomas and her girls.

She gives Jezebel one last pat before placing her on the ground. The cat falls in behind her, limping as it marches happily along the track. One by one, Mary, Sarah and Jezebel disappear silently back into the bush, never to be seen in Salem again.

Some legends say Mary died in the forest, never leaving the place where she tried to build a life for her family. After all, this is the place where her heart remained. After her family left, there was nothing more for her in this life.

Others say she travelled on. After much consternation she chose a direction and went to find her family, or at least part of it. They say she kept looking for her family till she died of a broken heart.

A few believe that after much searching she found part of her family and in so doing eased the agony she felt in her heart and replenished her soul; rekindling her faith in God.

If the truth be known, most of the townsfolk didn't believe Sam William's tale about meeting Mary. Some thought he was a liar, others thought he may have seen a ghost. Interest in Sam's story waned rapidly; no search of the river banks was ever done. No one even spoke to Harold to find out if it was possible that Mary could be alive. For the townsfolk had witnessed it with their own eyes; the attempted hanging and subsequent shooting of Mary Murphy. There was no doubt in their minds, she was dead.

Little did they know….

Epilogue

Five Months Later.
Saturday, August 5ᵗʰ, 2006.
Noon.
Kinglake, Victoria, Australia.

"Something blokey, somebody you would invite over for a few beers. Someone you would have as a mate. Jack, or Charlie perhaps. Thomas, no Tom or Tommy," Peter says as he leans on the door jam. He is quite a sight in his multicolored, thigh length shorts, Hawaiian style T-shirt and a beer in one hand. I guess it is the weekend after all, a time to kick back and relax.

He has taken my attention away from the delicious view outside my window. I smile as I lean on the window ledge, admiring Peter's tenacity and dedication to the task at hand. "No," I say simply as I shake my head and take another bite of my toast smothered in raspberry jam. I have become addicted to this stuff in recent times. My cravings for the spread have dogged me all day. It is a simple, acceptable indulgence for one in my position. It brings back pleasant memories as it reminds me of Old Joe. Two reasons good enough to explain why I am devouring my fourth slice this hour.

"Ahhhh!" he screams as he storms off into the kitchen. Peter is clearly becoming frustrated by my thinly veiled indifference to his suggestions. I know this feeling is tempered by the overriding sensation of absolute elation of the prospect that he will soon be a father.

My elation is tempered with the great sadness associated with Gina and my mother both moving to secret addresses, with silent phone numbers, as a result of the fracas with Steve. It is like a self-imposed, witness relocation program. Even I don't know their new names and addresses. They have chosen to have nothing more to do with me and my premonitions. As I look out my window, into my new home in Ferny Creek, I understand how they must feel to be forced to change their identities overnight. I just wish we were still on speaking terms.

Gina has suffered huge emotional problems which have been compounded by insomnia at night. Her nightmares have been frequent and horrific. Under doctor's orders, she has left Melbourne for an undisclosed location. Hopefully this will provide her with a little peace and she can rid herself of her fears that Steve is coming back for her.

"What about something more toffy? Maybe Jamie, Alistair, Graham?" Peter says as he sticks his head around the doorway with hope shining brightly in his eyes. This soon fades as I simply shake my head and bite down hard on the crispy toast. He looks so disappointed as he slinks away again, dragging his tail between his legs.

I miss my family, though I know their exile is for the best. I am fully in favor of my family hiding out; it is better to make sure we are all safe. I just hope Gina and my mother will forgive me one day for the evil I have brought into their lives. My only wish is to see them again sometime, hopefully in the next few months, once the baby is born. I will have to wait and see with that. Honestly, it could be years before I see them again, if ever. I must be patient; you never know what might happen. That is the lesson I have learned as a result of the events I have lived through over the last few months.

Their fear of Steve is real. Though I have not had any clear premonitions involving him, I fear he is out there, somewhere, biding his time and preparing his revenge. The police were unable to find him in their extensive search of the Wilhelmina Falls over a two week period. I feel in my heart that he is not dead or lost somewhere deep in the scrub. After all, cockroaches are hard to kill. Instead, I think he has somehow found his way to safety, maybe with the aid of the mysterious rose perfumed lady, and is currently recuperating from his ordeal. Until the day he is tracked down and captured, I know he remains a serious threat to my life and the lives of my family. Armed with this knowledge, I am more vigilant than ever before.

I wish that I still had access to Joe's valuable assistance. There is so much I need to learn about these premonitions. His help has proven invaluable by pointing me down the right path towards enlightenment. However, I am under no illusions. The journey I am undertaking will be long, arduous and, at times, dangerous. I now feel the visions are more of an honor than an inconvenience at this stage. Maybe that will fluctuate with time. I might not be so composed on a particularly bad day.

I glance towards the open trunk, over near the wall. I smile as I realize my mistake.

Old Joe is still here.

I slide off the window ledge and waddle over to the floor in front of the trunk. With some effort, I sit down on the carpet awkwardly.

"What about Xavier or Hugh, you love that Hugh Jackman don't you?" asks Peter with pleading eyes.

I shake my head and look at him sternly, "No, and anyhow I have already picked out a name."

Peter looks surprised, "Okay, little miss smarty-pants. What is your name for our son? Oh, I know. No, I get it. Ahhhhhh, of course; it has to be. A little Peter Jnr."

I look at him with my doe eyes, that I know he can't resist, as I correct him, "Our daughter's name will be Jessica."

Peter laughs, "Listen to you. How do you know that we are having a daughter? That is just silly. I'm certain we're having a boy."

I watch as Peter leaves the room. I look down and gently caress my stomach. I smile as I feel Jessica kick from inside. I talk quietly to her, "Your Daddy's the silly one. I know it is you Jessica because I experience premonitions."

Opening the trunk I begin to shuffle through the journals, cassette tapes, videos and scrap books. I have no idea where I should start on this great, disorganized, repository of knowledge. I guess there is no other way than to start from the top and work down. I will have to sift through all the information in both these trunks before too long. I wonder what secrets they will unveil.

A glint of something shiny catches my eye. I reach in to the left side of the trunk and pull out a strangely curled tool. It appears to be manufactured out of stainless steel, crafted with an octagonal end which seems to be designed to fit into something, maybe a lock. The other end is fashioned as a curved handle. Possibly some sort of winch which could be used to open something. That is the burning question, what does it open?

Attached to the tool is a large, brown, cardboard label, attached with a piece of string. As I turn the label over, I can see writing of immaculate quality. I read the message silently:

For Julie,

Keep this key in your possession on the 7th November, 2007. I had it fashioned especially, just to help you in your crusade. Best of luck.

Joe.

How odd. I wonder what he has seen, something that I am yet to discover?

I search the contents of the trunk for anything else that appears out of the ordinary. I spy a paper bag protruding from under one of the journals. With a slight tug I am able to extract it. Its contents feel soft. I wonder if they will enlighten me as to what this strange tool is meant to be used for.

I open the bag and smile. It is nothing to do with the tool at all. I reach in and pull out a pair of pink knitted booties. Another note is in the bag:

For Jessica,

I know they have that God damn political correctness thing these days but I don't care. A baby girl should be dressed in pink! I wish I was there to see the little one but I am so glad I was able to help save her. Maybe you will remember me to her when she is old enough to understand. It's just a small gift. I am sure they will fit.

All the best for you and the little one,

Joe.

I shake my head.

So Joe had a premonition in relation to me being pregnant and being in danger by Steve's hand. That would explain a lot.

"Julie, you've got to come and see this, you won't believe it," Peter says as he storms briefly into the room before scurrying back towards the open front door.

I stand up awkwardly, without his assistance, cursing at how difficult I am finding everyday tasks now that I am seven months pregnant. My stomach has ballooned considerably over the past month. It isn't so much the extra weight being the problem, more so my size and shape preventing mobility.

"Quick, come quick," Peter calls. "He's acting very strangely."

Having regained my footing, I wander slowly towards the front door, "I don't know if you've noticed but I'm seven months pregnant. I can only move so quickly."

"Sorry, Angel," Peter says as he runs back to assist me, grasping my arm to help support me towards the front door. "I just thought you had to see this for yourself."

"See what?" I say as I finally reach the doorway and peer through. At this precise instant, a pain in my chest grows sharply. I wince and lean more heavily onto Peter for support.

"Hey, are you alright?"

I nod as I try to ignore the pain and open my eyes to look around. I can see exactly what Peter has called me to view. Serenity is sitting on our front lawn. Gathered in front of him in a small, perfect semi-circle are four other black cats and one tiny pure white kitten with haunting black eyes. They are all different shapes and sizes. It looks for all the world that Serenity is chairing a meeting of some kind. I laugh. That is too fanciful to even contemplate. Though, by the manner in which the cats are arranged, that seems to fit the bill.

The cats, as one, look towards our doorway before slowly slinking away. Serenity casually walks past us into the house without so much as a murmur. The smell of smoke fills my nostrils as I see dark billowing clouds hovering over Melbourne. A man dressed in army fatigues stands next to a woman at the edge of the garden. The woman's eyes glow red as she licks his neck with a slender, lizard like tongue.

"That's odd," I say absentmindedly.

"What's that, Angel?" Peter asks.

"Can you see that smoke over Melbourne?" I ask Peter as I decide it is not worth sharing the lady with the lizard tongue with Peter. He would surely think I am losing the plot.

"No, just a bit of a smog haze"

I choose to fall silent as fear engulfs my heart. I can clearly see a huge billowing black cloud emanating from the heart of Melbourne. It is so large it gives the impression that the whole CBD may be on fire. The smell is overpowering; like a mountain of burning tires, yet even more toxic. It is a smell I can't place; I have no point of reference. I know if Peter can't see or smell what I am experiencing, then it must all be part of the premonition; a fairly devastating one, to be sure.

I sigh deeply as the pain subsides and the smoke and fumes disappear. I brace myself for an uncertain future. I have an overwhelming feeling that darkness will descend over Melbourne, sometime over the next few months. An evil force is at work here, the likes of which we have never experienced before.

What the hell is going on?

I am comforted by one thing only. It is just a little thing which no one else could possibly understand. There is not a white dove to be seen anywhere in my immediate proximity. I sigh. Nothing bad will come to pass this day.

I still have some time to work this out.

I watch the last of the black cats walk steadily towards the bushes. Suddenly it flinches as a Raven swoops down, trying to grasp it with its talons. I gasp in horror as the cat scurries into the safety of the shrubbery.

That was close.

As I turn and walk inside, I wonder to myself if that might be a sign. I shake my head and dismiss the notion out of hand. I am not obsessed in any way with superstitions or signs. At least I think I'm not.

A voice whispers on the breeze, "Always trust your instincts. Hope is a waking dream."

I whisper to myself, "Yes, I must hold on tight to hope. I fear troubled times loom ahead."

"Did you say something, Angel?"

"No, nothing Babe," I lie. "It's all good"

A sense of unease floods over me....

Grave Misgivings

Book 3

Hope

By C. E. Sundstrom

"Hope Is A Foolish Notion"

By ?????????

Prologue

Thursday, August 9th, 2006.

Morning.

Ferny Creek, Victoria, Australia.

Do you ever sense the storm coming before a single drop of rain has fallen onto your bare, pure skin? Does your nose tingle? Do the hairs on your arms stand up like soldiers? Do your bones ache? Or do you just have a feeling that something is coming?

I do. It is mainly my heightened intuition that warns me, an intuition I am growing to trust more with each passing day. I am somewhat of a human barometer on these matters. I know when a storm is coming. I just know. One is on its way now. Perhaps it is a big one. Maybe I can stop its rage. I will know soon enough when it comes. It is not the first tempest I have dealt with and, while I still draw breath, it will surely not be the last. My storms come to me in the form of premonitions of the future. They are vivid premonitions of future tragedy which I can neither escape nor hide. They are strange dreams which come to me while I am awake.

Before you decide to shun or ask the obvious question, I will gladly answer it for you. No, I am not insane. Though others fail to understand what I am going through, I myself have come to the conclusion, after much soul searching, that I am indeed sane. Ha! Life would be much simpler if I was indeed bonkers. No, I simply see the world in a different way. I see more than others realize exists. I am more attuned to unexplainable things which are invisible to the naked eye.

The problem is not mine. The problem is a plague which causes selective blindness in all the other people of the world. What you know as real is only a small fraction of what exists. No one else can possibly understand that. No one else can handle that concept. It is far less scary to go through life just acknowledging only what you can see, touch and smell.

I am the enlightened one.

I seem to be the only one.

It has only been six months since all this drama enveloped my life. Before that time I was living a normal life as a crime fiction writer. I simply didn't twig that I was seeing images of the future from time to time. I guess I convinced myself that what I saw on occasion was either nonsense, a simple daydream or just a foolish nightmare. Anyway, I paid the visions no heed. Unfortunately, people around me paid for my ignorance with their lives. Bobby, a young neighbor during my childhood, drowned after I experienced numerous nightmares about his future death. Recently as an adult, I saw the murder of Dr. Khan, a resident doctor working in the Psychiatric ward where I was briefly detained. Though the images of his murder were clear enough, I still failed to lift a finger to help prevent his untimely death. My mind failed to believe the images my eyes saw.

I also experienced visions of my new neighbor Emma. I discovered that her fate was to be brutally murdered by her husband Malcolm. I tried to help her though my efforts were too insignificant to make a difference. I should have tried harder. They visit me from time to time now, along with others. They are the ghosts that will torment me for my failures for the rest of time.

On the other hand, there have been some people along the way that I have managed to help. I saved a lady from a hit run accident, a pregnant prostitute from a callous stabbing, my sister Gina from a slow painful death and a little girl called Cassandra who was abducted as revenge for the murder of Steve "Mad Dog" Maddock's daughter during a gangland war in Melbourne. I gain some comfort from the fact that I can change the future for the better, I just have to be more open, more observant, more careful and, most of all, more pro-active.

During my period of 'Awakening', I discovered that I was not the first in my family to experience visions. Four hundred years ago a lady called Mary Murphy supposedly discovered she had a 'gift" for seeing the future. Unfortunately, in those unenlightened times in Salem, America she was deemed a witch and, though the history of her demise is a little vague, she was tried unjustly and hung till breathless. According to detailed family history charts given to me, I am meant to be a descendant of this woman. The extensive charts show many others who are suspected of having experienced visions of the future. Many of these 'cousins' have died as a result of murder, suspicious accidents or suicide. Some have even been committed to mental institutions for the natural term of their life. These visionaries have a commonality of being betrayed by those closest and dearest to them.

I only know of two people in the present day who have the waking dreams. Joe Hawkins became a friend recently and aided with my rapid education. He experienced the dreams for around seventy years prior to his death from a heart attack at the top of the steep Wilhelmina Falls. His journey to the top of these falls was a selfless act that saved three lives at the expense of his own. He did not let his advanced age hinder him. At a crucial moment, he was in the right place at the right time. He was able to flick a discarded pistol out of a pool of water with his walking stick, straight into my quivering hands. I was then able to defend and rescue Gina and Cassandra. More importantly I was able to shoot Steve, our tormentor. Joe's tutelage lives on with the huge repository of tapes and journals he has bequeathed to me. They cover every aspect of the waking dreams. With Joe's ghostly guidance I will continue to learn as much as possible about this strange phenomena. Perhaps, with diligence, I can avoid some of the mistakes that he made.

The second person I am certain has experienced the visions is little Cassandra. As we were leaving the Wilhelmina Falls in an ambulance she mentioned to me that she had seen me previously, when she was first abducted. She spoke about the sharp pain in her chest which I know accompanies the visions. At least I think she told me all of this. I may have just been dreaming. I fell back to sleep after our brief conversation and, as fate would have it, I haven't seen her since. My questions will have to wait a little longer. Maybe my mind just needed someone else to be having these weird visions of the future. I don't know. I am conflicted. I don't want to be the only person alive who is experiencing this. However, I don't want anyone else to be suffering as a result of being burdened by this gift.

Today my chest aches with the now familiar stabbing pain of a thousand swords being pressed deep into my skin at every perceivable angle. I do not care, nor raise a quizzical eyebrow. This is the all too familiar prelude to the waking dreams. Remaining calm, I simply shuffle over to my comfortable armchair, plonk myself down and slide comfortably back, ready to enjoy the ride.

I do not worry about the pain anymore. Though I don't know exactly why I am afflicted, I know two things for certain. The first is that the pain is more symptomatic than life threatening. It is my alarm signal to let me know that some objects I see around me may not be real. It alerts me to the fact that the visions are coming and that I need to take careful note of anything that has changed. These changes can initially appear insignificant. In the long run they can prove vital in solving the pending mystery and crucial in saving the life of someone in danger.

The second thing I know is that the visions cannot hurt me. They are not real. They are merely jumbled up glimpses of one or several events which are yet to take place at some point in the future. I can reach out, touch and feel the people in these waking dreams, even converse with them at length. However, when they try to do me harm, it is all a visual illusion. They cannot hurt me. I have no fear of what I see anymore.

I search the room for anything that has changed. I expect to find something which is out of place or foreign to my living room. Strangely there is nothing. Nothing, that is except for the putrid smell of industrial smoke which burns inside my nostrils. I have experienced this part of the premonition many times over the last few months. So much so I have become complacent, considering the smell a normal part of my every day.

Suddenly I notice something else.......

Everything is still.

Everything is silent.

I feel cold.

It is far too calm.....

Here comes the storm!

BOOM!

I remain undaunted as the room around me explodes into tiny glowing particles that race towards and through me. I experience no pain as the world I know and love is obliterated before my very eyes. I am conscious it is only a premonition, a magical illusion that I am witnessing. Though it can do me no harm, I still find my 'change of reality' confronting. I repeat to myself over and over again in my mind a simple yet complex phrase.

It is only a waking dream. It is only a waking dream.

I watch as the blinding fireworks fade and I become able to distinguish objects in my immediate vicinity once more. It is a strange scene laid bare for my consideration. My home is in ruins, just the odd piece of framework left standing, defying the cataclysm. Everything is on fire, save that is, for the items that are real, not premonition. The free standing lamp, the awful poster of "Dogs Playing Cards" and the box television remain in pristine condition. The armchair I rest in is also left unscathed.

Serenity walks from within the dark swirling smoke in front of me and lithely leaps onto my lap before settling quickly. I hear the familiar sound of his ferocious purring. I guess nothing is amiss in his world.

I am startled as I turn my attention forwards. I see a skinny young girl with raven colored hair standing impassively in front of me as the flames lick around her without scarring her skin. I guess her age would be around fifteen or sixteen years of age. It is hard to tell these days; kids seem to mature far more quickly than in previous generations. She reminds me a lot of myself though her face is more freckled than mine. Even so, I feel a familiarity with this girl. I am instantly drawn to her and her sparkling blue eyes. She raises a hand seeking the embrace of mine. She remains silent, eyes sorrowful and scared.

I look down and touch my swollen belly as I wonder as to the identity of this mysterious girl, "Jessica?"

Glancing back at the girl I see her surroundings have gone. There is no fire, no smoke, no remnant buildings. The world has become divided into two, with teenage Jessica acting as the dividing line between the two realms.

Jessica's right side is lost in a pitch black darkness that engulfs everything. All I can hear is the slivering movement of some large, as yet un-envisaged creature moving along the floor intermittently. All I can see is her right eye reflecting a strangely luminous red glow in the pitch black. I am not one who is easily scared in the dark however this darkness seems unnatural in its blackness. I am scared of the secrets that it hides within its depths.

To Jessica's left there is a brilliant glow which silhouettes her outline. Again the entire landscape is shrouded from curious gaze by the burning light. However I feel a warmth which I find comforting in some sort of strange fashion. I cannot explain this other than it is just my weird first impression. I hear footsteps, though as yet no one has emerged into clear sight.

Suddenly I hear indistinct murmurs coming from both the dark and light worlds. It is as if the creatures or people who inhabit these voids are engaged in a furious dispute. I cannot discern the nature of the discussion; their words are whispered and incoherent to my ears. One thing is certain; the discussion is frantic in nature. I can see that Jessica is aware of the discussion too as she becomes distracted, searching for the right direction to move towards.

"Sweetheart," I scream. "Come to me. Please come to me!"

Jessica fails to heed my words delivered to her on the wings of fear. Instead she decides to turn slightly, enough of an angle to allow her to stare deeply into the black, limitless nothing. I jump as I think I see a huge lizard like tail slide through the shifting fog and across her feet before disappearing without trace back into the black void. Jessica doesn't react at all. I question the validity of what my eyes have seen. Maybe my mind is making things up? My deep seated fears for Jessica's wellbeing erupt to the surface.

A hand suddenly appears, sparkling like a luminous star from out of the bright light. Jessica has seen it and, to my relief, takes a step towards it.

I don't know what is in the light but it has got to be better than that creature lurking in the dark!

"Hope is a waking dream," I hear uttered by a man's voice seemingly emanating from within the glorious light. I am calmed by these simple words. I myself have heard these words many times by unseen voices carried on the breeze to my accepting ears during times of need. These words hold no fear for me. They seem to indicate some sort of unseen force which is strangely watching over my every movement. Maybe these 'benevolent spirits' are watching over Jessica too.

Jessica briefly looks back towards the dark then turns her back, ready to walk towards the waiting sparkling hand and the world of light. I would prefer that she was walking towards me. However this option will be sufficient for now.

A foul stench drifts out of the darkness. Chilling laughter echoes all around us as sinister words are spoken by a craggy voice.

"Hope is a foolish notion," informs the unknown female speaker.

Before Jessica has an opportunity to react she is grasped by a lizard-like claw and drawn roughly into the dreaded depths of the endless darkness. The sparkling hand explodes into tiny glittering stars which fall and are lost at my feet. Dark smoky clouds billow out of the darkness, merging with the luminous light. The overpowering light disappears without trace. All is darkness, deep, endless darkness.

Jessica's screams and protestations are shrill though taper quickly. They decline in volume until silence abounds once more. I listen closely for any clue as to which direction she has been taken. I hear nothing. I fail to see anything, the darkness devours all. I take a moment, draw in a deep cleansing breath of precious air and blink three times.

"Nooooooo!" I scream as I realize my worst nightmare has come true. She is gone.

I feel someone's breath on the back of my neck before they begin to laugh in my ear. Alarmed I jump from my chair, sending Serenity flying. I swivel on my heel to confront the creature that has come for me. I see nothing in the pitch black. My heart rate races as I brace for the attack. No attack is forthcoming.

The smell of perfumed roses replaces the pungent smoke and fills the room as an invisible woman whispers in my ear, "So pretty, such a waste."

I search for the owner of the voice. I see no one. Looking down at my stomach I see a growing pool of blood soaking through my shirt. My body temperature drops rapidly. I search for a cut on my stomach, an injury of some description. I find none. I feel faint as I hear the distinct, though faint sound of a baby's mournful cry.

In that instant all returns to normal. The premonition has gone, so has the pain in my chest. My shirt is once again untainted. My house is intact in all its humble glory. Reality has resumed its rightful place. The only thing which has changed is that I am covered in sweat, heart pounding at a million miles per minute.

"What the ………?" I ask Serenity, expecting and receiving no answer. I look down at my swollen belly and speak to Jessica, "I don't know what that all means but rest assured, I will find out. I will never let anything bad happen to you. I promise you that."

I remain seated shaking my head, mind spinning, not knowing where to start. There are too many premonitions jumbled together for me to decipher what they mean.

I am alert and worried. Involuntarily I say a single word softly, "Hope……."